FOREVER AN EATON

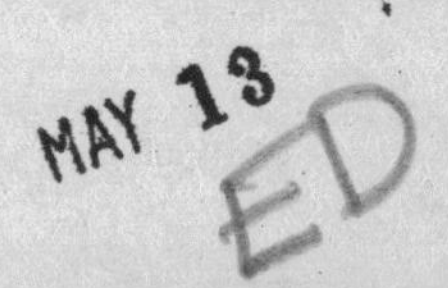

ROCHELLE ALERS

FOREVER AN EATON

An Eaton Novel

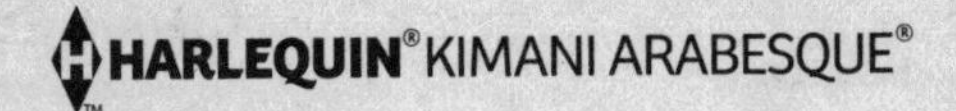

FOREVER AN EATON

ISBN-13: 978-0-373-09126-3

Recycling programs for this product may not exist in your area.

This edition published May 2013

For questions and comments about the quality of this book, please contact us at CustomerService@Harlequin.com.

HARLEQUIN®
www.Harlequin.com

Printed in U.S.A.

CONTENTS

Dear Reader,

Welcome to the Eaton family miniseries. This collection will take you back to where it all began with two incredibly *sweet* stories about a second chance at love.

In *Bittersweet Love,* Philadelphia high-school history teacher Belinda Eaton has made it a practice to avoid Griffin Rice. Now she finds her future inexorably entwined with his when they share custody of their goddaughters following a family tragedy. In this story, Belinda encounters a very different Griffin when the high-profile sports attorney romances her, and proves he can be a loving father *and* husband.

In the second installment of the Eaton family miniseries, Zabrina Cooper's wish is granted when she reunites with Myles Eaton at his sister's wedding. But will the secrets she has coveted for more than a decade bring them closer—or destroy a future that promises forever? Myles only has the summer to uncover why—Zabrina broke their engagement weeks before their wedding—to marry an influential Philadelphia politician. As you read *Sweet Deception,* please keep in mind what Zabrina has had to sacrifice in order to protect her family.

Yours in romance,

Rochelle Alers

To Michele Robinson…

A true Philadelphia princess.

Hear, O children, a father's instruction,

be attentive, that you may gain understanding!

BITTERSWEET LOVE

Prologue

No one sitting in Grant and Donna Rice's family room had even noticed Belinda Eaton's brittle smile, clipped replies or that her delicate chin was set at a stubborn angle. They had come together to celebrate the birthday of twelve-year-old fraternal twins Sabrina and Layla Rice.

The two girls took turns opening envelopes, reading birthday cards, unwrapping gifts and hugging and kissing their parents as well as both sets of grandparents and their aunt and uncle.

Belinda, the twins' aunt, hadn't realized she was grinding her teeth until she felt the pain in her gums. It was either clench her jaw or spew expletives that were poised precipitously on the tip of her tongue. Her eyes narrowed when the object of her fury flashed his Cheshire cat grin.

That's it! she raged inwardly. *It ends tonight.* Bracing her hands on the arms of the club chair, she rose to her feet and made her way to where Griffin Rice stood with his arm around his mother's shoulders. The expressive eyebrows that framed his olive-brown face arched with her approach.

"Excuse me, Mrs. Rice, but I'd like to speak to your son." Belinda deliberately neglected to acknowledge Griffin by name.

Griffin Rice's large, deep-set dark brown eyes widened appreciably. Whenever he saw his brother's sister-in-law, which wasn't often enough, she looked different. Belinda had a wealth of thick dark hair that she'd styled in a ponytail. The soft glow from the recessed lighting in the room flattered her flawless sable face. A light dusting of makeup accentuated her exotic slanted eyes, high cheekbones, short nose and generously curved lips.

A hint of a smile lifted the corners of his lips as he stared boldly at the fullness of her breasts under a burnt-orange cashmere pullover, which she'd paired with black wool slacks and suede slip-ons. He'd always found her alluring, but Belinda gave off a vibe that made her seem snobbish and aloof. She'd been that way at nineteen, and now at thirty-two she was even more standoffish. Her request to speak to him was somewhat shocking yet a pleasant surprise.

"Where would you like to talk?"

"Outside."

The response came across as a direct order and Griffin curbed the urge to salute her. He pressed a kiss to Gloria Rice's forehead. "I'll be right back, mother." Grabbing Belinda's arm, he steered her toward the rear of the house.

"The front porch," Belinda ordered again. The back porch was too close to the kitchen and she didn't want anyone to overhear what she had to say to him.

Reversing course, Griffin led her through the dining and living rooms and out to the front porch of the modest Dutch Colonial–style house. He held the front door open, waiting for Belinda to precede him, then stepped out onto the porch and closed the door behind them.

Leaning against a thick column on the porch, he slipped his hands into the pockets of his slacks and crossed his feet at the ankles. The seconds ticked off as Belinda sat on a cushioned love seat. Twin porch lanterns flanking the door provided enough light for him to make out her features. Griffin glanced away to look at the large autumnal wreath hanging on the door.

"What do you want to talk about?"

Belinda sat up, her spine ramrod straight. "What the hell do you think you're doing buying the girls a PlayStation when I told you that I planned to give it to them for Christmas?"

Nothing moved on Griffin, not even his eyes as he glared at the woman who was godmother and aunt to his nieces. "You told me nothing of the sort."

"When I spoke to Donna and asked what the girls wanted for their birthday she told me to give them gift cards for their favorite stores and to save the electronics for Christmas. I also remember her saying that she was going to tell you the same thing." She'd given her nieces gift cards to several popular clothing stores.

"Your sister didn't say anything to me, so take it up with her."

"No, Griffin, I'm taking it up with you. Every year you do this. We talk beforehand about what we're going to give the twins for Christmas and their birthdays, and invariably you do the complete opposite." She stood up and closed the distance between them. "This is the last time I'm going to let you play Big Willie to my nieces."

"*Your* nieces, Lindy?" he said mockingly. "How did you come to that conclusion when they're *my* brother and your sister's daughters?" He held up a hand when she opened her mouth to come back at him. "Unlike you, I don't have the time or the inclination to hang out in the mall. Layla and Sabrina said they wanted an Xbox, Wii or PlayStation, and I gave them the PlayStation."

Belinda closed her eyes rather than stare at Griffin Rice's gorgeous face. As an attorney for some of sports' biggest superstars, Griffin had become a celebrity in his own right. Paparazzi snapped pictures of him with his famous clients, glamorous models, beautiful actresses and recording stars. His masculine features, cleft chin and exquisitely tailored wardrobe afforded him a spot on the cover of *GQ*. He not only looked good, but he smelled delicious. His cologne was the perfect complement to his natural scent.

"Next time speak to me before you decide to give them what they want."

"Are you asking or telling me, Belinda?"

Her chest rose and fell, bringing his gaze to linger on her breasts. "I'm asking you, Griffin," she said in a softer tone.

Straightening, Griffin stared down at his sister-in-law, wondering if she was aware of how sexy she was. If he'd had a teacher who looked like Belinda Eaton he would've failed, just to have to repeat her class.

He dipped his head and brushed a kiss over her ear.

"I'll think about it." Turning on his heels, Griffin went back into the house, leaving Belinda staring at his back as he walked away.

Her fingers curled into fists. She'd called him out for nothing. He had no intention of checking with her. It was as if they were warring parents competing to see who could win over their children with bigger and more expensive gifts.

She folded her arms under her breasts and shook her head. There was no doubt Griffin would continue to undermine her when it came to their nieces, but there was one thing she admired about the man: since he wasn't a father himself, he'd spared some woman a lifetime of grief.

Belinda waited on the porch a few minutes longer until the dropping temperature forced her indoors. Affecting a bright smile, she walked into the dining room in time to sing happy birthday before Sabrina and Layla blew out the candles and cut their cake.

Chapter 1

The soft-spoken attorney shook hands with Belinda Eaton and then repeated the gesture with Griffin Rice. "Congratulations, Mom, Dad. If you need a duplicate copy of the guardianship agreement I recommend you call this office rather than go to the Bureau of Records. I've heard that they always have a two-to-three-month backlog."

Belinda still could not believe she was to share parenting of her twin nieces with her sister's brother-in-law. Less than a year after she became an aunt, her sister had asked Belinda to raise her daughters if anything should happen to her and her husband. At that time she'd wondered, *why would a happily married, twenty-two-year-old woman with two beautiful children think about dying?* Apparently, her older sister, Donna, was more prophetic than she knew. Just weeks after the twins' twelfth birthday, their mother and father had been killed instantly when a drunk driver lost control of his pickup, crossed the median and collided head-on with their smaller sedan.

Belinda forced a smile. The meeting with the attorney and signing the documents that made her legal guardian of her twelve-year-old nieces had reopened a wound that was just beginning to heal. Her sister and brother-in-law had died days after Thanksgiving and it'd taken four months for their will to be probated.

"Thank you for everything, Mr. Connelly."

Impeccably dressed in a tailored suit, Jonathan Connelly stared at the young schoolteacher whose life was about to dramatically change. Her nieces were moving from the two-bedroom condo where they were temporarily living with their maternal grandparents into her modest house in a Philadelphia suburb. Although the children had been well cared for by their grandparents, Jonathan, the executor of her sister and brother-in-law's estate, felt that the emotional and social interests of the twin girls would be best served living with their aunt.

His shimmering green eyes lingered briefly on her rich nut-brown attractive face with its high cheekbones, slanting dark brown eyes and hair she wore in a flattering curly style. With her wool gabardine suit with a peplum jacket, pumps and the pearl studs that matched the single strand gracing her slender neck, Belinda appeared more like a young executive than a high school history teacher.

"If you need legal advice on anything, please don't hesitate to call me," Jonathan said, smiling.

A slight frown began to creep across Griffin Rice's good looks. "I believe I can help her with any legal problem," he said curtly. Griffin intended to make sure that he was available for Belinda if she needed legal counsel.

He had spent the better part of an hour watching Jonathan Connelly subtly flirt with his sister-in-law. He and Belinda shared guardianship of their nieces, but he'd be damned if he'd allow the smooth-talking, toothpaste-ad-smiling, little-too-slick-for-Griffin's-taste attorney take advantage of her.

Although they were related through marriage, Griffin and Belinda hadn't spent much time together and when they did, they usually butted heads. Most of the time, he was involved in contract negotiations for his pro-athlete clients or taking a much-needed vacation. And whenever he invited her to his home for an informal get-together, she always declined. The last time they had been together was when the two families were making funeral arrangements for Grant and Donna.

Reaching out, he cupped Belinda's elbow. "I think it's time we leave."

Belinda forced herself not to pull away from the pressure of Griffin's hand on her arm. She didn't like him, had never really liked him, but now they were thrown together because they shared custody of their nieces. She didn't know what her sister was thinking when she and Grant decided on Griffin as the girls' guardian. The high-profile, skirt-hopping sports attorney lacked the essentials for fatherhood.

She gave Jonathan a dazzling smile that curved her full, sensuous mouth. "If I need your assistance, I won't hesitate to call you."

Belinda sensed her brother-in-law's annoyance at her rebuff of his offer of legal help when his fingers tightened around her elbow. At five-six and one hundred thirty pounds she knew she was physically no match for Griffin's six-two, one hundred ninety pound vise-like grip. Glancing over her shoulder, she glared at him.

"I'm ready."

Griffin led Belinda out of the lawyers' offices and waited until she was seated in his late-model Lexus hybrid and he was beside her before he allowed himself to draw a normal breath.

"Did I not say that I would take care of your legal concerns?"

Belinda shifted on the leather seat, glaring at the cleft in the chin of an otherwise incredibly handsome man who'd landed unceremoniously in her life. She'd lost count of the number of times women colleagues had asked her whether Griffin was available.

"Watch your tone, Griffin. I'm not one of your dim-witted girlfriends who is honored just to be in your presence." Belinda knew she'd struck a nerve when she saw his flushed face.

"In case you didn't notice, the man wasn't looking to offer legal advice."

She frowned. "Then please tell me what he was offering."

"His bed."

Griffin's comment caught her off guard for several seconds. "How would you know that?" Belinda said when she recovered her composure.

A subtle smile parted Griffin's lips as his gaze slipped from Belinda's face to her breasts and back to her stunned expression. "I'm a man, Belinda. And as such, I recognized all the signals Jonathan was sending your way."

Heat pricked little pinpoints across Belinda's skin as

she struggled not to look away from the large dark eyes that were sending sensuous flames through her body. She couldn't move or blink. "Not every man who looks at me wants me in *that* way, Griffin."

Griffin's smile widened. "With your face and your body, you look nothing like the spinster schoolmarm."

"Wrong century and definitely wrong woman," she countered. "I'm not a schoolmarm but an educator. And whether I'm thirty-two or sixty-two I'll never think of myself as a spinster."

"The fact remains that Jonathan wants you. So I suggest that you not lead him on *if* or *when* you need legal advice. And, the offer still holds. If you need a lawyer, then I'm always available to you."

She shook her head. "Why would I need you when my brother is a lawyer?" Her older brother, Myles, had recently resigned as partner at a leading Philadelphia law firm to teach at Duquesne, a private university law school in Pittsburgh.

Griffin inserted the keyless fob in the ignition slot and pushed a button, starting up the SUV. "Just make certain you use *him*."

As Griffin maneuvered out of the parking lot, Belinda wondered if he was as brusque with the women he dated or slept with. Other than his looks and his money, she didn't know why any of them would put up with his attitude.

They'd agreed that the girls would stay with her during the week and with Griffin on the weekends. But she doubted, with his busy social life, that there would be many weekends that the twins would stay with Griffin. That suited Belinda just fine, because what they needed more than anything was stability.

Sabrina and Layla Rice had lost both parents and since then had been living with their grandparents for the past four months. Now they would be moving again when they came to live with her. The fallout after the funeral and burial was difficult when grandparents and relatives began arguing about who would raise the twins. As an investment banker, Grant Rice and his family had been financially sound. And the prospect of the girls' inheritance drew relatives Griffin hadn't known or seen in decades like hungry sharks to the smell of blood.

The speculation as to the extent of Grant's wealth ended when Griffin announced that he and Belinda were the legal guardians, and that Belinda was the beneficiary of Grant and Donna's multimillion-dollar insurance policy. He had inherited vacant parcels of land that developers were interested in. The only thing he and Belinda had agreed upon was that all the proceeds and profits would be put aside for their nieces' education and financial future.

Belinda had used the few months that the girls were living with their grandparents to decorate her house to accommodate the growing twins. She wanted the transition to be smooth and stress-free for everyone involved. She'd had more than ten years of teaching young adults, but this was to be the first time Belinda would become a parent in every sense of the word.

The drive from downtown Philadelphia to a nearby suburb was accomplished in complete silence. When Griffin turned off into the subdivision and parked in the driveway where her parents had purchased the town house after selling the large house where they'd raised their four children, Belinda was out of the car before Griffin could shut off the engine. She didn't see his scowl, but registered the slam of the driver's-side door when he closed it.

Ringing the bell, she waited for her mother to come to the door. *It's not going to work,* she thought over and over as the heat from Griffin's body seeped into hers when he moved behind her. How was she going to pretend to play house with the girls' surrogate father when she could barely tolerate being in the same room with him?

The door opened and Roberta Eaton stood on the other side, her eyes red and swollen. Belinda knew her mother hadn't wanted her granddaughters to leave, but the law was the law and she'd abide by her late daughter's request and the court's decision to have Sabrina and Layla live with Belinda.

"Hi, Mama." Stepping into the entryway, she leaned over and kissed her cheek. "How are the girls?"

Roberta pressed a wrinkled tissue to her nose. "They're much better than I am. But then, you know how adaptable young folks are. I've spent most of the day crying, while they came home going on about an upcoming class trip." Roberta glanced over her daughter's shoulder to find Griffin Rice's broad shoulders filling out the doorway. "Please come in, Griffin."

Griffin moved inside the house with expansive windows and ceilings rising upward to twelve feet. The elder Eatons had downsized, selling their sprawling six-bedroom farmhouse for a two-bedroom town house condo in a newly constructed retirement village. Unlike his parents, who divorced when he was in high school,

Dr. Dwight and Roberta Eaton had recently celebrated their forty-second wedding anniversary.

He hadn't remembered a day when his parents did not argue, which had shaped his views about marriage. His mother said her marriage was a daily struggle, one in which she was always the loser. His father remarried twice and after his last divorce he dated a woman for several years, but ended the relationship when she wanted a more permanent commitment.

When his brother had contacted him with the news that he was getting married, Griffin had at first thought he was joking, because they'd made a vow never to marry. But within three months of meeting Donna Eaton, Grant had tied the knot. At first he had thought his brother wanted a hasty wedding because Donna was pregnant. But his suspicions had been unfounded when the twins were born a year later. When he'd asked Grant about breaking his promise to never marry, his brother had said promises were meant to be broken when you meet the "right" woman.

Griffin dated a lot of women, had had several long-term relationships, yet at thirty-seven he still hadn't found the "right woman."

"Aunt Lindy, Uncle Griff!" Sabrina, older than her sister by two minutes, came bounding down the staircase. "Sorry, Gram," she mumbled when she saw her grandmother's frown.

Her grandmother had lectured her and Layla about acting like young ladies—and that meant walking and not running down the stairs and talking quietly rather than screaming at the top of their lungs.

Belinda held out her arms, and she wasn't disappointed when Sabrina came into her embrace. Easing back, she stared at her niece, always amazed that Sabrina was a younger version of herself. She used to kid Donna by saying that her fraternal twin daughters' genes had been a compromise. Sabrina resembled the Eatons, while Layla was undeniably a Rice.

"How's my favorite girl?"

Sabrina rolled her eyes at the same time she sucked her teeth. "How can I be your favorite when you tell Layla that she's also your favorite?"

Belinda kissed her forehead. "Can't I have two favorite girls?"

Sabrina angled her head, and her expression made her look much older. Not only was she older than Layla, but she was more mature than her twin. She preferred wearing her relaxed shoulder-length hair either loose, or up in a ponytail. It was Layla who'd opted not to cut her hair and fashioned it in a single braid with colorful bands on the end to match her funky, bohemian wardrobe. Both girls had braces to correct an overbite.

"Of course you can," Sabrina said. Pulling away, she went over to Griffin. Standing on tiptoe, she kissed his cheek. "I like your suit."

The charcoal-gray, single-breasted, styled suit in a lightweight wool blend was Griffin's favorite. He tugged her ponytail. "Thank you."

Sabrina gave her uncle a beguiling smile. "You promised that Layla and I could meet Keith Ennis. The Phillies will be in town for four days. Please, please, please, Uncle Griff, can you arrange for us to meet him?"

It was Griffin's turn to roll his eyes. Keith Ennis had become Major League Baseball's latest heartthrob. Groupies greeted him in every city and his official fan club boasted more than a million members online.

He'd considered himself blessed when the batting phenom had approached him to represent him in negotiating his contract when he'd been called up from the minors. The Philadelphia Phillies signed him to a three-year, multimillion-dollar deal that made the rookie one of the highest-paid players in the majors, and in his first year he was named Rookie of the Year, earned a Gold Glove and had hit more than forty home runs with one hundred and ten runs batted in.

"I'm having a gathering at my house next Saturday following an afternoon game. You and your sister can come by early to meet him, but then you have to leave."

"How long can we stay, Uncle Griff?" asked Layla, who'd come down the staircase in time to overhear her uncle.

Belinda shot Griffin an *I don't believe you* look. Had he lost his mind, telling twelve-year-olds that they could come to an adult gathering where there was certain to be not only alcohol, but half-naked hoochies?

"Your uncle and I will have to talk about this before we agree whether an *adult* party is appropriate for twelve-year-olds." She'd deliberately stressed the word *adult*.

Layla pouted as dots of color mottled her clear complexion. "But Uncle Griff said we could go."

"Your uncle doesn't have the final say on where you can go, or what you can do."

"Who does have the final say?" Sabrina asked.

Belinda felt as if she were being set up. Unknowingly, Griffin had made her the bad guy—yet again. "We both will have the final say. Now, please say goodbye to your grandmother. I'd like to get you settled in because tomorrow is a school day."

Most of the girls' clothes and personal belongings had been moved to her house earlier that week. Belinda had hung their clothes in closets but left boxes of stuffed animals and souvenirs for her nieces to unpack and put away.

"We'll see you for Sunday dinner, Gram," Layla promised as she hugged and kissed Roberta.

Roberta gave the girls bear hugs accompanied by grunting sound effects. "I want you to listen to your aunt and uncle, or you'll hear it from me."

"We will, Gram," the two chorused.

Belinda lingered behind as Layla and Sabrina followed Griffin outside. "Why didn't you say something when Griffin mentioned letting the girls hang out at a party with grown folks?"

Roberta crossed her arms under her full bosom and angled her soft, stylishly coiffed salt-and-pepper head. She wanted to tell her middle daughter that becoming a mother was challenging enough, but assuming the responsibility of raising teenage girls, who were still grieving the loss of their parents, and had just started their menses and were subject to mood swings as erratic as the weather, would make her question her sanity.

"I wouldn't permit anyone to interfere with me raising my children, so I'm not going to get into it with you and Griffin about how you want to deal with Layla and Sabrina. Not only are you their aunt but you are also their mother. What you're going to have to do is establish the rules with Griffin before you tell the girls what's expected of them."

Frustration swept over Belinda. Her mother wasn't going to take her side. "I can't understand what made him tell—"

"There's not much to understand, Belinda," Roberta retorted, interrupting her. "He's a man, not a father. What he's going to have to do is begin thinking like a father."

"That's not going to be as easy as it sounds. Layla and Sabrina will spend more time with me than with Griffin. Although he's agreed to take them on the weekends that doesn't mean he'll have them every weekend."

"Griffin Rice is no different than your father. As a family doctor with a private practice he was always on call. If it wasn't a sprained wrist or ankle, then it was the hospital asking him to cover in the E.R. Dwight missed so many Sunday dinners that I stopped setting a place for him at the dinner table."

"Daddy was working, and there is a big difference between working and socializing."

"You can't worry about Griffin, Lindy. Either he will step up to the plate or he won't. At this point in their lives, Sabrina and Layla need a mother not a father. Once the boys start hanging around them, I'm certain he'll change. Your father did."

Belinda wanted to tell her mother that Griffin Rice was nothing like Dwight Eaton. With Griffin it was like sending the fox to guard the henhouse. And, if Griffin didn't take an active role in protecting his nieces now, then she would be forced to be mother *and* father.

"Let's hope you're right." She hugged and kissed her mother. "We'll see you Sunday."

Roberta nodded. "Take care of my girls."

"You know I will, Mama."

Belinda walked out of the house to find Griffin waiting for her. He'd removed his suit jacket, his custom-made shirt and tailored slacks displaying his physique to its best advantage. Sabrina and Layla were seated in the back of the car, bouncing to music blaring from the SUV's speakers. Belinda fixed her gaze on a spot over Griffin's shoulder rather than meet his intense gaze.

There was something about the way he was staring at her that made Belinda slightly uncomfortable. Perhaps it was his earlier reference to her face and body that added to her uneasiness. The first time she was introduced to Griffin Rice she was stunned by his gorgeous face and perfect body, but after interacting with him she'd thought him arrogant and egotistical when he boasted that he'd graduated number one in his law school class.

Subsequent encounters did little to change her opinion of him. Every time the Eatons and Rices got together Griffin flaunted a different woman. After a while, she stopped speaking to him. Even when they came together as godmother and godfather to celebrate their godchildren's birthdays, she never exchanged more than a few words with him.

"We have to talk about the girls, Griffin."

His thick eyebrows arched. "What do you want to talk about?"

"We need to establish some rules concerning parenting."

"I'll go along with whatever you want."

"What I don't want is for you to promise the girls that they can attend an adult party," added Belinda.

"I didn't tell them they could attend the party. I said—"

"I heard what you said, Griffin Rice," Belinda interrupted angrily. "The girls will not go to your house to meet anyone."

Griffin's eyes darkened as he struggled to control his temper. He didn't know what it was about Belinda Eaton, but she was the only woman who managed to annoy him. He'd stopped speaking to her because she had such a sharp tongue. And rather than argue, he ignored her. But it was impossible to ignore her now because he would have to put up with her for the next eleven years. Once Sabrina and Layla celebrated their twenty-third birthdays he and Belinda could go their separate ways. Having his nieces stay at his house on weekends would put a crimp in his social life, but he was totally committed to his role as their guardian.

Griffin knew what meeting Keith Ennis and getting his autograph meant to the girls. His dilemma was finding a way to get around Belinda's demands. "Are you willing to compromise?"

"Compromise how?"

"You act as my hostess for the party. Let me finish," he warned when she started to open her mouth in protest. "You and the girls can spend the weekend with me. You can be my hostess, and I'll ask Keith to come early so that Sabrina and Layla can meet him. As soon as the others arrive they can go to their rooms while you and I—"

"Will meet and greet your guests," Belinda said facetiously, finishing his statement.

Grinning and displaying a mouth filled with straight, white teeth, Griffin winked at Belinda. "Now, doesn't that solve everything? The girls get to meet their idol, I get to interact with my friends and clients and you will be there to monitor Sabrina and Layla."

I don't think the girls need as much monitoring as you do, Belinda mused. "I hope when the girls stay over that you won't expose them to situations they don't need to see at their age."

It took a full minute for Griffin to discern what Belinda was implying. "Do you really believe I'm so depraved that I would sleep with a woman when my nieces are in the same house?"

"I don't know what to believe, Griffin." Belinda's voice was pregnant with sarcasm. "What you're going to have to do is prove to me that you're capable of looking after two pre-teen girls."

"I don't have to prove anything to you, Belinda. The fact that my brother thought me worthy enough to care for and protect his daughters is enough. And, regardless of what you may think—legally I have as much right to see my nieces as you do. I agreed to let them stay with you during the week because their school is in the same district where you live. It would be detrimental to their stability to pull them out midterm to go to a school close to where I live."

He took a step, bringing him within inches of his sister-in-law, his gaze lingering on the delicate features that made for an arresting face. What he hadn't wanted to acknowledge the first time he was introduced to Belinda Eaton was that she was stunningly beautiful. She had it all: looks and brains. Also, what he refused to think about was her lithe, curvy body. The one time he saw her in a bikini he'd found himself transfixed by what had been concealed by her conservative attire. It took weeks before the image of her long, shapely legs and the soft excess of flesh rising above her bikini top faded completely. That had been the first and only time that Griffin Rice was consciously aware that he wanted to make love to Belinda Eaton.

"Okay, Griffin. I'll compromise just this one time. But only because I don't want to disappoint Layla and Sabrina."

Griffin smiled, the expression softening his face and making him even more attractive. "Why, thank you, Belinda."

Belinda also smiled. "You're quite welcome, Griffin."

Chapter 2

"Aren't you coming in with us, Uncle Griff?" Sabrina asked as Griffin stood on the porch of Belinda's two-story white house framed with dark blue molding and matching shutters.

Cupping the back of her head, Griffin pressed a kiss to her forehead. "I can't. I have a prior engagement."

Sabrina blinked once. "You're engaged?"

Throwing back his head, Griffin laughed. "No. I should've said that I have a dinner appointment."

"Why didn't you say that instead of saying you were engaged?" Sabrina countered, not seeing the humor in her uncle's statement.

Griffin sobered quickly when he realized she wasn't amused. Everyone remarked how Sabrina had an old spirit, that she was wise beyond her years, while Layla the free spirit saw goodness in everything and everyone.

"It looks as if I'm going to have to be very careful about what I say to you."

Sabrina winked at him. "That's all right, Uncle Griff. I'll let you know when I don't understand something."

Belinda listened to the exchange between Griffin and his niece. It was apparent he'd met his match. "If you're not coming in, then I'll say good night."

Watching him drive away, she was grateful that Griffin had elected not to come inside because she wanted time alone with her nieces, to see firsthand their reaction to the rooms she'd organized and decorated in what she felt was each girl's personal style.

Belinda glanced at her watch. "Girls, please go upstairs, do your homework and then get ready for bed. I'm going to have to get you up earlier than usual because I'm going to drive you to school. I also have to fill out another transportation application changing your bus route." The sisters headed for the staircase, racing each other to the second floor.

Their bus route had changed when they'd gone to live with their grandparents, and it would change again now that they lived with her. It'd taken Belinda two months for the contractor to make the necessary renovations to her house when she realized the twins would have to live with her. She hadn't known that when she'd moved out of her Philadelphia co-op and into the three-bedroom house. She'd originally bought the house because she'd been looking to live in a less noisy neighborhood with a slower pace. Now she would end up sharing the house with her nieces.

The house's former owners, a childless couple who taught in the same high school as Belinda, had covered the clapboard with vinyl siding, updated the plumbing and electricity and had landscaped the entire property as they awaited the adoption of a child from Eastern Europe. The adoption fell through and the wife opted for artificial insemination. After several failed tries, she found herself pregnant with not one, but four babies. They began looking for a larger house at the same time Belinda put her co-op on the market. She made the couple an offer, and three months later she closed on what had become her little dream house.

Ear-piercing screams floated down from the second story. Glancing up, she saw Layla hanging over the banister. "Are you okay?" she asked with a smile, knowing the reason for the screaming.

Layla gestured wildly. "Aunt Lindy, I love, love, *love* it!" she shrieked incoherently before running back to her bedroom.

Minutes later Belinda stood in the room, her arms encircling her nieces' waists. The contractor had removed the door leading into the master bedroom and installed doors to adjoining bedrooms that led directly into the space she'd set up as a combined office, study and entertainment area. The furnishings included two desks with chairs that faced each other and built-in bookcases along three of the four walls.

The remaining wall held a large flat-screen television. A low table held electronics for a home-theater system. Empty racks for CDs and DVDs were nestled in a corner, along with a worktable with a streamlined desktop and laptop computers and printer. Although the television was equipped with cable, Belinda had programmed parental controls on both the television and internet. French doors had replaced a trio of windows that led to a balcony overlooking the back of the property.

"I know which bedroom is mine," Sabrina crooned.

"Mine is the one with the bright colors," Layla said, her voice rising in excitement.

Sabrina pressed closer to her aunt. "This is the first time we're not going to have to share a bedroom."

Belinda gave her a warm smile. She recognized them as individuals and sought to relate to them as such. "I have a few house rules that I expect to be followed. You must keep your bedrooms and bathroom clean. I don't want to find dirty clothes on the floor or under the beds. The first time I find food or drink upstairs there will be consequences."

Layla shot her a questioning glance. "What kind of consequences?"

"There will be no television or internet for a week. The only exception is to do homework. You'll also have to give up your iPods and relinquish your cell phones—"

"But we don't have cell phones," Sabrina interrupted, sharing a look with her sister.

A mysterious smile tipped the corners of Belinda's mouth. "If you look in the drawer of your bedside tables you'll find a cell phone. The phones are a gift from your uncle Griffin. He's programmed the numbers where you can reach him or me in an emergency. You'll share a thousand minutes each month, plus unlimited texting. You..."

Her words trailed off when the girls raced out of the room, leaving her staring at the spots where they'd been.

She'd turned the master bedroom into a sanctuary for her nieces, decorated Sabrina's room with a queen-size, off-white sleigh bed, with matching dresser, nightstands and lingerie chest. Waning daylight filtered through sheer curtains casting shadows on the white comforter dotted with embroidered yellow-and-green butterflies. Layla's room reflected her offbeat style and personality with orange-red furniture and earth-toned accessories.

Belinda had moved her own bedroom to the first floor in what had been the enclosed back porch. It faced southeast, which meant the rising sun rather than an alarm clock woke her each morning. Layla and Sabrina returned, clutching Sidekick cell phones while doing the "happy dance."

"Girls, I want you in bed by nine."

"Yes, Aunt Lindy," they said in unison.

She walked out of the study and made her way down the carpeted hallway to the staircase. Giving her nieces the run of the second floor would serve two purposes: it would give them a measure of independence and make them responsible for keeping their living space clean.

Griffin couldn't remember the last time a woman had bored him to the point of walking out on a date. However, he'd promised Renata Crosby that he would have dinner with her the next time she came to Philadelphia on business. The screenwriter was pretty, but that's where her appeal started and ended. From the time she sat down at the table in one of his favorite restaurants, Renata had talked nonstop about how much money she'd lost because of the writer's strike in Hollywood. He wanted to tell her that everyone affected by the strike lost money.

"Griffin, darling, you haven't heard a word I've been saying," Renata admonished softly.

Griffin forced his attention back to the woman with eyes the color of lapis lazuli. Their deep blue color was the perfect foil for her olive complexion and straight raven-black, chin-length hair.

"I'm sorry," he mumbled apologetically, "but my mind is elsewhere."

Renata blinked, a fringe of lashes touching the ridge of high cheekbones. She'd spent the better part of an hour trying to seduce Griffin Rice, but it was apparent her scheme to get him to sleep with her wasn't working. She'd met the highly successful and charismatic sports attorney at an L.A. hot spot, and knew within seconds that she had to have a piece of him.

At the time, he was scheduled to fly out of LAX for the East Coast. So she had followed him to the parking lot where a driver waited for him and got him to exchange business cards with her. She and Griffin had played phone tag for more than a month until one day he answered his phone. She told him that she was meeting a client in Philadelphia, and wanted to have dinner with him before flying back to California. Of course, there was no client and it appeared as if she'd flown three thousand miles for nothing.

"You do seem rather distracted," she crooned, deliberately lowering her voice.

Griffin stared at his fingers splayed over the pristine, white tablecloth. "That's because it isn't every day that a man becomes the father of twin girls."

An audible gasp escaped Renata. "You're a father?"

Griffin angled his head and smiled. "Awesome, isn't it?"

Pressing her lips together, Renata swallowed hard. When she'd inquired about Griffin Rice's marital status she was told that he wasn't married. Had her source lied, or had Griffin perfected the art of keeping his private life *very* private?

"I'd say it's downright shocking. You didn't know your wife was having twins?"

"I'm not married."

"If you're not married, then you're a baby daddy. Or should I say a *babies'* daddy."

Griffin registered the contempt in Renata's voice. Although he wasn't remotely interested in her, he was still perturbed by her reaction. After all, he'd only agreed to have dinner with her to be polite. Raising his hand, he signaled for the check.

"I'm going to forget you said that."

Renata concealed her embarrassment behind a too-bright smile. "I'm sorry it came out that way. Please, let me make it up to you by sending you something for your girls," she said in an attempt to salvage what was left of her pride.

"Apology accepted, but no, thank you." He signed the check, pushed back his chair to come around the table and help Renata. When she came to her feet, he offered, "Can I drop you anywhere?"

Renata was nearly eye to eye with Griffin in her heels. She knew they would've made a striking couple if some other woman hadn't gotten her hooks into him. She'd met more Griffin Rices than she could count on both hands. Most were good-looking, high-profile men who were willing to be seen with women like her, but when all was said and done they married women who wouldn't cheat on them, or whom other men wouldn't give a second glance. As soon as she returned to her hotel room she planned to call an entertainment reporter and give him the lowdown about Griffin Rice having fathered twins.

"No, thanks. I have a rental outside."

He took her arm. "I'll walk you to your car."

Griffin gave Renata the obligatory kiss on the cheek, waited until she maneuvered out of the restaurant's parking lot and then made his way to where he'd parked his car. He wasn't as annoyed with Renata's inane conversation as he was with himself for wasting three precious hours he could've spent with his nieces. Glancing at the watch strapped to his wrist, he noted the time. It was eight thirty-five, and he wanted to talk to Sabrina and Layla before they went to bed for the night.

He exceeded the speed limit to make it to Belinda's house in record time. She'd bought a house a mile from where Grant and Donna had lived, the perfect neighborhood for upwardly mobile young couples with children. Grant had tried to convince him to purchase one of the newer homes of the McMansion variety, but Griffin preferred the charm of the nineteenth-century homes along the Main Line. Though less exclusive than it once was, the suburb west of the city was still identified with the crème de la crème of Philadelphia society.

Whenever he closed the door to his three-story colonial on a half-acre lot along the tree-lined street in Paoli, he was no longer the hard-nosed negotiator trying to make the best deal for his client. Sitting on his patio overlooking a picturesque landscape of massive century-old trees and a carpet of wildflowers had become his ultimate pleasure. He opened his home on average about three times a year to entertain family, friends and clients. Living in Paoli suited his temperament. After growing up in a crowded, bustling Philadelphia neighborhood he'd come to appreciate the quietness of the suburb of fifty-four hundred residents.

Griffin maneuvered into Belinda's wide driveway and shut off the engine. His dark mood lifted when he saw soft light coming through the first-floor windows. It was apparent Belinda hadn't gone to bed. He rang the bell, waited and raised his hand to ring it again when the door opened and he came face-to-face with Belinda as she dabbed her face with a hand towel. Judging from her expression it was apparent that she was as shocked to see him as he to see her in a pair of shorts and a revealing tank top. And, with her freshly scrubbed face and headband that pulled her hair off her face, she appeared no older than the high school students to whom she taught American history.

"What are you doing here?" Belinda asked, her voice a breathless whisper.

Leaning against the doorframe, Griffin stared at the rise and fall of her breasts under the cotton fabric. He swallowed a groan when a part of his body reacted involuntarily to the wanton display of skin.

"I came to see if the…my daughters are okay."

Belinda was surprised to hear Griffin refer to his nieces as his daughters. It was apparent he intended to take surrogate parenting seriously. "Of course they're okay, Griffin. If you hadn't run off you would've known that."

Griffin straightened. "I had a prior engagement."

She rolled her eyes at him. "Call it what it is."

"And that is?"

"You had a date, Griffin."

A slow, sexy smile found its way over Griffin's face. "Do I detect a modicum of jealousy, Eaton?"

"Surely you jest, Rice. Let me assure you I'm not attracted to you, and there's nothing about you that I find even remotely appealing."

Griffin brushed past her, walking into the entryway. "Sheath your claws, Belinda. What you should do is channel your frustration in an anger management seminar because we're going to have to deal with each other until the girls celebrate their twenty-third birthday. You don't like me and I have to admit that you're certainly not at the top of the list for what I want in a woman."

Belinda affected a brittle smile. "At least we can agree on one thing."

"And that is?" he asked, lifting his expressive eyebrows.

"We won't interfere in each other's love lives."

"You're seeing someone?"

"Does that surprise you, Griffin?" she asked, answering his question with one of her own.

Belinda's revelation that she was involved with a man came as a shock to Griffin. He never saw her with a man, so he'd assumed that she spent her nights at home—alone. "I hope you're not going to schedule sleep-overs with *your* man now that the girls are living with you. It wouldn't set a good example—"

"He'll only come when the girls stay at your place," she interrupted.

Griffin didn't know where he'd gotten the notion that Belinda wasn't seeing anyone. Although he would never admit to her that he was attracted to her in *that way,* it didn't mean that other men weren't. Earlier, he'd sat watching Jonathan Connelly unable to take his eyes off her. And Griffin didn't blame the man because Belinda Eaton was stunning.

If she hadn't been so unapproachable he would've considered asking her out. Even when they'd come together as best man and maid of honor for the wedding of their respective siblings, he'd thought her shy and reticent. But then he hadn't expected more from a nineteen-year-old college student who'd lived on campus her first semester, then without warning moved back home, driving more than thirty miles each day to attend classes. When asked why she'd opted not to stay on campus, her response was as enigmatic as the woman she'd become.

Griffin remembered why he'd come to Belinda's house. "May I see the girls?"

"I'm sorry. They've already gone to bed."

He glanced at the clock on the table filled with potted plants. "It's only nine-fifteen. Isn't that a little early?"

"No, it isn't, Griffin. My mother had a problem with getting them up on school days, so I've instituted a nine o'clock curfew Sunday through Thursday and eleven on Fridays and Saturdays."

"That sounds a little strict, Belinda."

"Children need structure."

"Structure is one thing and being on lockdown is another."

Belinda walked around Griffin and opened the door wider. "I don't want to be rude, but you really need to go home, Griffin. I'm going to be up late grading papers, and hopefully I'll be able to get a few hours of sleep before I have to get up earlier than usual to drive the girls to school. I need to stop in the school office to update their emergency contact numbers and bus route."

After seeing that Layla and Sabrina had completed their homework, she'd eaten leftovers, applied a facial masque and sat in a tub of warm water waiting for it to set. By the time she'd emerged from the bathroom the girls had come to kiss her good-night. They'd gone to bed, while she would probably be up well past midnight.

Griffin heard something in Belinda's voice that he'd never recognized before: defeat. Although they shared custody of their nieces, it was Belinda who'd assumed most of the responsibility for caring for them five of the seven days a week. And for the weeks when he had to travel on business, it would be the entire week.

"What time do your classes begin?"

"Eight. But I have a sub filling in for me."

Griffin knew he had to help Belinda or she would find herself in over her head. It was one thing to raise a child from infancy and another thing completely when you found yourself having to deal with not one but two teenagers with very strong personalities.

"Let me help you out."

Belinda stared at the man standing in her entryway as if he were a stranger. "*You* want to help *me*."

Slipping his hands into the pockets of his suit trousers, Griffin angled his head. "Yes. I'll take the girls to school and take care of the paperwork. That way you don't have to have to miss your classes."

"It's too late to cancel the substitute."

Attractive lines fanned out around his eyes when he gave her a warm smile. "Use the extra time to sleep in late."

His smile was contagious as Belinda returned it with one of her own. "It sounds good, but I still have to get up and prepare breakfast."

"Can't they get breakfast at school?"

"Donna wouldn't let them eat school breakfast because they weren't eating enough fiber."

"I'll fix breakfast for them," Griffin volunteered.

"It can't be fast food."

He winked at her. "I didn't know you were a comedian. Why would I give them a fast-food breakfast when it has a higher caloric content and more preservatives than some cafeteria food? I'll cook breakfast for them."

Belinda hesitated, processing what she'd just heard. "You're going to come here from Paoli tomorrow morning in time to make breakfast and take the girls to school?" The ongoing family joke was that Griffin Rice would be late for his own funeral.

"Yes."

Belinda waved a hand. "Forget it, Griffin. I'll get up and make breakfast *and* take them to school."

"You doubt whether I'll be here on time?"

She leaned closer. "I know you won't make it."

The warmth and the subtle scent of lavender on Belinda's bared flesh wafted in Griffin's nostrils, making him more than aware of her blatant femininity. For years he'd told himself that he didn't like his sister-in-law because she was a snob—that her attitude was that she was too good for him because she came from a more prestigious family.

But in the past four months he saw another side of Belinda Eaton that hadn't been apparent in the dozen years since they first met. Not only was she generous, but also selfless in her attempt to become a surrogate mother for her sister's children. She had reconfigured the design of her house to accommodate the teenage girls. He hadn't known she had a man in her life, and apparently that relationship would also change now that Layla and Sabrina were living with her.

"I'll make it if I stay over."

"You can't stay here," Belinda said quickly. "Have you forgotten that I no longer have an extra bedroom?"

She'd turned the master bedroom into the office/ entertainment retreat for the twins and added half baths to the two remaining bedrooms. There was still a full bathroom on the second floor and a half bath off the kitchen, but with three females living under one roof everyone needed a bathroom to call their own.

Griffin affected a Cheshire cat grin. "I can always sleep with you."

Belinda stared at him as if he'd lost his mind. "You're crazy as hell if you think I'm going to let you sleep in my bed with me."

"And why not?" he asked quietly. "Aren't we family, Aunt Lindy?"

"First of all I'm not your aunt. And secondly, you and I don't share blood, therefore we're not family. If you want to stay over then you're going to have to sleep in the living room on the sofa. It converts to a queen-size bed and the mattress is very comfortable."

"How would you know it's comfortable?"

"I slept on it before my bedroom was completed." Although she'd moved her bedroom from the second to the first floor she liked her new space because it was larger, airy and filled with an abundance of light during daytime hours.

Griffin nodded. "I'll take your word that it's comfortable, but if I wake up with a bad back then I'm going to hold you responsible for my medical expenses."

"You won't need a chiropractor after I walk on your

back," Belinda countered confidently. "My feet and toes are magical."

He glanced down at her slender pedicured feet in a pair of thong slippers. Her feet were like the rest of her body—perfect. Belinda Eaton was physically perfect, yet so untouchable. He wondered about the man who'd managed to get next to her. There was no doubt he was nothing less than Mister Perfect himself.

"We'll see," he replied noncommittally. "I'm going to head out to Paoli, get a few things. Are you sure you'll be up when I get back?"

"I have an extra set of keys you can use."

"What about your alarm?"

"I won't set it."

"Set it," Griffin ordered. "I'd feel better knowing you and the girls are protected by a silent alarm before I get back. Now, give me the password. Please," he added when Belinda glared at him. He repeated it a couple of times aloud, then to himself. "I'll bring back a set of keys to my place for you, and I'll give you my password."

Belinda turned and walked in the direction of the kitchen where she retrieved a set of keys to her house from a utility drawer. She returned to find Griffin standing in the middle of her living room staring at photographs on tables and lining the fireplace mantel. His gaze was fixed on one of himself, Grant and Donna together at an Eaton-Rice family picnic. It'd taken her weeks to come to grips that her sister and brother-in-law were gone and that she would never hear their laughter again. She'd put away all of their photographs, then caught herself when she realized that if she wanted to remember them, it would be best to see them smiling and happy.

"Griffin."

Griffin turned when Belinda called his name, his expression mirroring the sadness and pain that returned when he least expected it. There had only been he and Grant, the two of them inseparable. Grant was two years older, but he never seemed to mind that he had to take his younger brother everywhere he went.

They were always there for each other throughout their triumphs and failures. Grant was gone, but his spirit for life lived on in the daughters he had called his "princesses." Grant had asked him whether he'd take care of his "princesses" if anything ever happened to him and Griffin hadn't hesitated when he said *of course,* unaware that a decade later he would be called upon to do just that. Grant had also revealed that Belinda Eaton had agreed to share guardianship of his children with him. He'd always thought Donna's younger sister was shy and very pretty, but that had been the extent of his awareness of the young woman who'd been Donna's maid of honor at his brother's wedding.

Now standing several feet away wasn't a shy, pretty girl but a very confident, beautiful woman who always seemed confrontational, something he'd never accept from other women. But he had to remember that Belinda Eaton wasn't just any woman. She was now the mother and he the father to their twin nieces.

"Yes?"

Belinda held out her hand. "Here are your keys." He took the keys suspended from a colorful Lucite souvenir from Hershey Park. "I'll make up the sofa and leave a light on for you."

Griffin nodded. "Thank you. I'll lock the door and set the alarm on my way out."

Belinda was still standing in the middle of the living room when she heard the soft beep that signaled that the alarm was being armed. In another forty-five seconds it would be activated.

Today she'd spent more time with Griffin Rice than she had since planning and rehearsing for her sister's wedding. Her opinion of him hadn't changed over the years. She still found him outspoken, brash and a skirt-chaser. What had changed was that she saw for the first time that he truly loved his nieces. His reference to Sabrina and Layla as his daughters really shocked her, and his volunteering to take them to school was a blessing. He'd stepped up to the plate much sooner than she'd expected he would.

Perhaps, she thought as she made her way upstairs to the linen closet, Griffin did have some redeeming qualities after all. What she didn't want to linger on was how good he looked and smelled. He'd removed his tie and jacket and when she opened the door to find him standing there in just a shirt and trousers she discovered that her pulse beat a little too quickly for her to be unaffected by his presence, and at that moment she knew she was no different than the thousands of other women who lusted after the sports attorney who'd become a celebrity in his own right.

What Belinda had to do was be careful—be very, very careful not to fall victim to his looks and potent charm.

Chapter 3

Belinda woke as daylight filtered through layers of silk panels covering the French doors. Every piece of furniture and all the accessories in her bedroom were in varying shades of white. The absence of color in the bedroom was offset by the calming blue shades in an adjoining sitting/dressing room. Blue-and-white striped cushions on a white chaise, where she spent hours reading and grading papers, and a blue-and-white checked tablecloth on a small table with two pull-up chairs were where she usually enjoyed a late-night cup of coffee and took her breakfast on weekend mornings.

Stretching her arms above her head, she smiled when the sounds of birds singing and chirping to one another shattered the early-morning solitude. It was spring, the clocks were on daylight saving time and she'd spent the winter waiting for longer days and warmer weather after a brutally cold and snowy winter season. Rolling over on her side, she peered at the clock on the bedside table. It was six-thirty—the same time she woke every morning.

She'd just gotten into bed when she heard Griffin come in around midnight. She didn't know why, but the notion of whether he slept nude, in pajamas or in his underwear made her laugh until she pulled a pillow over her head to muffle the sound. That was her last thought before she fell into a deep, dreamless slumber.

Sitting up, she swung her legs over the side of the bed and reached for the wrap on the nearby chair. Today was Thursday and she had a standing appointment with her hairdresser. Wednesdays were set aside for a manicure and pedicure and she planned to ask her nieces if they wanted to accompany her.

The house was quiet as she took the back staircase to the full bathroom on the second floor. Belinda hadn't wanted to walk past the living room where Griffin slept. Her feet were muffled by the hallway runner as she made her way past the closed doors to Sabrina's and Layla's bedrooms. She'd told the girls to set their alarms, because she wasn't going to be responsible for waking them up. Like Griffin, they also liked to sleep in late. It had to be a Rice trait.

Belinda didn't linger. Having completed her morning routine, she left the bathroom the way she'd come, encountering the smell of brewing coffee. A knowing smile parted her lips. Griffin was up.

By the time she'd made up her bed, slipped into a pair of faded jeans, T-shirt and brushed her hair, securing it into a ponytail, the sound of footsteps echoed over her head. It was apparent her nieces had gotten up without her assistance. Donna had made it a practice to wake them up and the habit continued with Roberta.

When she and Donna were that age, Roberta had insisted that they set their alarm clocks in order to get up in plenty of time to ready themselves for school. Griffin had accused her of being rigid, while she thought of it as preparation for the future. No one would be coming to their homes to wake them up so they could make it to work on time.

Belinda walked into the kitchen to find Griffin transferring buckwheat pancakes from the stovetop grill onto a platter. The white T-shirt and jeans riding low on his slim hips made her breath catch in her throat. Her gaze was drawn to the muscles in his biceps that flexed with every motion. She regarded Griffin as a skirt-chaser, but after seeing him moving around her kitchen as if he'd done it countless times she realized he would be a good catch for some woman—provided he would be faithful to her.

"Good morning."

Griffin glanced up, smiling. "Well, good morning to you, too."

Belinda walked into the kitchen and sat on a high stool at the cooking island. "I didn't know you could cook."

He winked at her. "That's because you don't know me."

She decided not to respond to his declaration. "How's your back?" Belinda asked instead.

"Good. Remember when you banish your man to the couch that it's not going to be much of a punishment."

"When I have to put a man out of my bed he won't

end up on the couch but on the *sidewalk.*" She'd stressed the last word.

Griffin grimaced. "Ouch!"

Belinda slipped off the stool. "Do you want me to help you with anything?"

"I stopped at a twenty-four-hour green grocer and bought some fruit. I put it in the refrigerator, but if you prepare it for me I'd really appreciate it."

Working side by side, Belinda washed and cut melon, strawberries and pineapple into small pieces for a fresh fruit salad while Griffin finished making pancakes. When Sabrina and Layla came downstairs, dressed in their school uniforms—white blouse, gray pleated skirt and gray blazer and knee socks—the kitchen was redolent with different flavors of fruit, freshly squeezed orange juice, pancakes and coffee for Belinda and Griffin. There was only the sound of a newscaster's voice coming from the radio on a countertop as the four ate breakfast.

"I have an appointment for my hair this afternoon," Belinda said, breaking the comfortable silence. She looked at Sabrina, then Layla. "Who would like to go with me?"

"I do," Sabrina said.

"Me, too," Layla chimed in.

"I'll pick you up from school, and we'll go directly from there to the salon. Make certain you bring your books so you can do your homework while under the dryer. Thursday is girls' night out, so let me know where you'd like to eat."

Belinda's last class would end at two and the twins weren't dismissed until three. The half-hour drive would afford her more than enough time to pick them up. However, if she ran into traffic, then she could call her mother to have her meet them. Layla peered over her glass at her uncle. "Even though it's for girls, can Uncle Griff eat with us?"

Belinda stared at Griffin, silently admiring his close-cropped hair and the smoothness of his clean-shaven jaw. Mixed feelings surged through her as she tried to read the man sitting in her kitchen who continued to show her that there was more to Griffin Rice than photo ops with pro athletes, A-list actors and entertainment celebrities. His success in negotiating multimillion-dollar contracts for athletes was noteworthy, while his reputation for dating supermodels and actresses was legendary. A tabloid ran a story documenting the names of the women and a time line of his numerous relationships—most of which averaged six to nine months.

"I can't answer for him, Layla."

She smiled at her uncle. "Can you eat with us, Uncle Griff?"

Dropping an arm over Layla's shoulders, Griffin kissed her mussed hair. "I can't, baby girl. I'm going to see my folks before they leave on vacation."

In their shared grief over losing their firstborn, his parents had become at sixty what they hadn't been in their twenties—friends. Now they were embarking on a month-long European cruise they'd always planned to take for their fortieth wedding anniversary. Lucas and Gloria Rice's marriage hadn't survived two decades. However, both were older, wiser and sensible enough to know they couldn't change the past, so were willing to make the best of the present.

"When are Grandma and Grandpa coming back?" Sabrina asked.

"They won't be back until the beginning of May." Griffin stared at the clock on the microwave.

Layla wiped her mouth with a napkin. "Are you going to fix breakfast for us tomorrow, Uncle Griff?"

"Your aunt and I agreed you would spend the weekends with me, and that means I'll make breakfast for you Saturday and Sunday mornings."

"I hope you don't expect me to make pancakes every day, but I'll definitely make certain your breakfasts will be healthy," Belinda said when the two girls gave her long, penetrating stares. "As soon as you're finished here I want you to comb your hair. Your uncle will drive you to school this morning."

A frown formed between Layla's eyes. She appeared as if she'd been in a wrestling match, with tufts of hair standing out all over her head. "I thought the bus was picking us up."

Belinda stood up and began clearing the table. "Griffin will fill out the paperwork today changing your official address to this house. As soon as it's approved, you'll be put on the bus route."

"Layla's boyfriend rides the bus," Sabrina crooned in a singsong tone.

A rush of color darkened Layla's face, concealing the sprinkle of freckles dotting her pert nose. "No, he doesn't!" she screamed as Griffin and Belinda exchanged shocked glances. "Breena is a liar!"

Resting his elbows on the table, Griffin supported his chin on a closed fist. "Do you have a boyfriend, Layla?" His voice, though soft, held a thread of steel.

Layla's eyes filled with tears. "Stop them, Aunt Lindy."

Belinda felt her heart turn over. Her sensitive, free-spirited niece was hurting and she knew what Layla was going through, because she'd experienced her first serious crush on a boy in her class the year she turned twelve. She'd confided her feelings to her best friend and before the end of the day everyone in the entire school, including Daniel Campbell, knew she liked him.

"If Layla likes a boy, then that's her business, not ours."

Griffin sat up straighter. "She's too young to have a boyfriend."

"But I don't have a boyfriend," Layla sobbed, as tears trickled down her cheeks.

Belinda rounded on Griffin. "Griffin, you're upsetting the child. She says she doesn't have a boyfriend." She held up a hand when he opened his mouth. "We'll talk about this later. Sabrina and Layla, I want you to finish your breakfast then please go and comb your hair. And don't forget what I said yesterday about leaving clothes on the floor."

Layla sprang up from the table, leaving her twin staring at her back. Sabrina closed her eyes. "I didn't mean to make her cry."

Belinda shook her head. "If you didn't mean it then you shouldn't have said what you said. Remember, Sabrina, that your words *and* actions have consequences."

Nodding, Sabrina pushed back her chair. "I'll tell her I'm sorry."

Belinda closed her eyes for several seconds and when she opened them she found Griffin glaring at her. "What?"

"The girls can't date until they're eighteen."

"Are you asking me or telling me, Griffin?"

He stared, not blinking. "I'm only making a suggestion."

"I believe seventeen would be more appropriate."

"Why?"

"By that time they'll be in their last year of high school and that will give them a year to deal with the ups and downs of what they'll believe is love. Then once they're in college they'll be used to the lies and tricks dogs masquerading as men perpetuate so well."

Griffin's expressive eyebrows shot up. "You think all men are dogs?"

Belinda rinsed and stacked dishes in the dishwasher. "If the shoe fits, then wear it, Griffin Rice. If a woman dated as many men as you do women, people would call her a whore."

"I don't date that many women."

"Why, then, didn't you sue that tabloid that documented your many trysts?"

"I don't have the time, nor the inclination to keep up with gossip."

Resting a hip against the counter, Belinda gave him a long, penetrating stare. "Are you saying what they printed wasn't true?"

There came a lengthy pause before Griffin said, "Yes."

"What about the photographs of you and different women?"

"They were photo ops."

"They were photo ops for whose benefit?"

"Most times for the lady."

"So, all that dishing about you being a womanizer is bogus."

Leaning on his elbow, Griffin cradled his chin in his

hand. "If I'd slept with as many women as the tabloids claim I have I doubt whether I'd be able to stand up."

Belinda turned her head to conceal her smile. "Real or imaginary, you're going to have to clean up your image now that you're a father."

Now that you're a father.

Belinda's words were branded into Griffin's consciousness as he got up to take the rest of the dishes off the table. He, who hadn't wanted to marry and become a father because he didn't want his children to go through what he'd experienced with his warring parents, now at thirty-seven, found himself playing daddy to his adolescent nieces.

When Jonathan Connolly had called to tell him that he had received the documents legalizing the girls' adoption, Griffin felt his heart stop before it started up again. He'd feared his life would change so dramatically, that he would have to hire a nanny to take care of his nieces and that he wouldn't be able to recognize who he was or what he'd become until he remembered Belinda telling him she would have the girls live with her, and if he chose he could have them on weekends.

Belinda's suggestion had come as a shock to him. He'd thought of her as the consummate career woman. She taught high school history, spent her winter vacations in the Caribbean or Florida and traveled abroad during the summer months.

He had vacillated between indifference and newfound respect for Belinda when she'd decided to renovate her house to address the needs and interests of the two children she'd thought of as her own within days of them losing their parents.

Belinda Eaton had sacrificed her day-to-day existence for "her children" while he hadn't given up anything. When he'd come to her house the night before he said he'd come to see his children. They weren't only his children or Belinda's children. Sabrina and Layla Rice were now legally the children of both Belinda Eaton and Griffin Rice.

"I'll try, Belinda."

She gave him a level look. "Don't try, Griffin. Just do it."

He nodded in a gesture of acquiescence. "I'm going to change my clothes. I want to get to the school early enough so I don't have to wait to be seen."

Belinda turned back to finish cleaning up the kitchen. She didn't have to be at the high school until eleven, which left her time to dust and vacuum. As the only person living in the house her house was always spotless. But she knew that was going to change because Donna hadn't taught her daughters to pick up after themselves.

As a stay-at-home mother and housewife Donna didn't mind picking up after her husband and children. Roberta Eaton had picked up after her four children, and Donna continued the practice. However, that would end with Belinda. As a certifiable neat-freak, the girls would either conform to her standards or they would forfeit their privileges.

She'd loaded the dishwasher and had begun sweeping the kitchen when Sabrina and Layla walked in with backpacks slung over their shoulders. Both had combed and neatly braided their hair into single plaits. The fuzzy hair around their hairline was evidence that it was time for their roots to be touched up.

"Before you ask, Aunt Lindy, we brushed our teeth," Sabrina announced with a teasing smile.

Resting her hands on her denim-covered hips, Belinda looked at her from under lowered lids. "I wasn't going to ask, Miss Prissy."

"Who's prissy?" asked a deep voice. Griffin stood at the entrance to the kitchen dressed in a lightweight navy blue suit, stark white shirt, striped silk tie and black leather slip-ons.

Belinda couldn't contain the soft gasp escaping her parted lips as she stared at Griffin like a star-struck teen seeing her idol in person for the first time. Now she knew why women came on to Griffin Rice. He radiated masculinity like radioactive particles transmitting deadly rays. Her knees buckled slightly as she held on to the broom handle to keep her balance.

A nervous smile trembled over her lips. "Your daughter."

Smiling, Griffin strolled into the kitchen. "Which one?"

"Sabrina," Belinda and Layla said in unison, before touching fists.

Looping his arm around Sabrina's neck, Griffin lowered his head and kissed her forehead. "Are you being prissy, Miss Rice?"

Tilting her chin, she smiled up at her uncle. "I don't even know what prissy means."

He ran a finger down the length of her short nose. "Look it up in the dictionary."

Sabrina snapped her fingers. "How did I know you were going to say that?"

"That's because you're smart."

Belinda propped the broom against the back of a chair. "Come give me a kiss before you leave."

She hugged and kissed Sabrina, then Layla. "Remember we have hair appointments this afternoon."

"Yes!" they said in unison.

Griffin shook his head. He didn't know what it was about women getting their hair and nails done that elicited so much excitement. He got his hair cut every two weeks, but he didn't feel any different after he left the hair salon than when he entered.

"Girls, please wait outside for me. I'll be right out after I talk to your aunt."

Belinda didn't, couldn't move as Griffin approached her. The sensual scent of his aftershave washed over her, and she was lost, lost in a spell of the sexy man who made her feel things she didn't want to feel and made her want him even when she'd openly confessed that she hadn't found him appealing.

She'd lied.

She'd lied to Griffin.

And she'd lied to herself.

"What do you want, Griffin?" Her query had come out in a breathless whisper, as if she were winded from running.

He took another step, bringing them only inches apart. "I just wanted to say goodbye and hope you have a wonderful day."

She blinked. "You didn't have to send the girls out to tell me that."

"But I couldn't do this in front of them," he said cryptically.

"Do what?"

"Do this." Griffin's arm wrapped around her waist,

pulling her flush against his body at the same time his mouth covered hers.

Belinda didn't have time to respond to the feel of his masculine mouth on hers as she attempted to push him away. Then the kiss changed as his lips became persuasive, coaxing and gentle. Her arms moved up of their own volition and curled around his neck, and she found herself matching him kiss for kiss. Then it ended as quickly as it had begun.

Reaching up, Griffin eased her arms from around his neck, his gaze narrowing when he stared at her swollen mouth. Passion had darkened her eyes until no light could penetrate them. Belinda had called Sabrina prissy, when it was she who was prissy. And underneath her prissy schoolteacher exterior was a very passionate woman, and he wondered if her boyfriend knew what he had.

"Thank you for the kiss. You've just made my day." Turning on his heels, he walked across the kitchen, a grin spreading across his face.

"I didn't kiss you, Griffin," Belinda threw at his broad back. "Remember, you kissed me."

He stopped but didn't turn around. "But you kissed me back."

"No, I didn't."

"Yeah, you did. And I liked it, Miss Eaton."

Belinda wanted to tell Griffin that she liked him kissing her. But how was she going to admit that to him when supposedly he didn't appeal to her? The truth was she did like him—a little too much despite her protests.

"Have a good day, Griffin," she said instead.

"Trust me, I will," he called out.

Looking around for something she could throw at his

arrogant head, Belinda realized she'd been had. Griffin hadn't kissed her because he wanted to but because he wanted to prove a point—that she was no more immune to him than the other women who chased him.

Well, he was about to get the shock of his life. She'd go along with his little game of playing house until she either tired or lost interest. And in every game there were winners and losers and Belinda Eaton didn't plan to lose.

Belinda stabbed absentmindedly at the salad with a plastic fork as she concentrated on the article in the latest issue of *Vanity Fair.* She glanced up when she felt the press of a body next to hers.

"What's up, Miss Ritchie?" she asked.

"That's what I should be asking you, Miss Eaton," said Valerie Ritchie as she slid into the chair beside Belinda. "You didn't come in yesterday, and when I saw a sub cover your classes this morning I was going to call you later on tonight."

Closing the magazine, Belinda smiled at the woman whom she'd met in graduate school. Valerie was one of only a few teachers she befriended at one of Philadelphia's most challenging inner-city high schools. Much of the faculty, including the administration, remained at the school only because they were unable to find a similar position in a better neighborhood. But she and Valerie stayed because of the students.

"The guardianship for my sister's children was finalized yesterday," she said softly.

"That was fast."

"The lawyer and judge are members of the same country club."

Valerie shook her head. "Why is it always not what you know, but who you know?"

"That's the way of the world."

Belinda stared at Valerie, a world history and economics teacher. Recently divorced, Valerie had rebuffed the advances of every male teacher who'd asked her out, claiming she wanted to wait a year before jumping back into the dating game. The petite, curvy natural beauty had caught the attention of the grandson of a prominent black Philadelphia politician who pursued her until she married him, much to the consternation of his family, his father in particular. Tired of the interference from her in-laws, Valerie filed for divorce and netted a sizeable settlement for her emotional pain and anguish.

"I don't envy you, Belinda."

"Why do you say that?"

"It's very noble of you to want to raise your sister's kids, especially when you have to do it alone."

A math teacher walked into the lounge and sat down on a worn leather love seat in a corner far enough away so they wouldn't be overheard. Belinda had made it a practice to keep her private and professional lives separate.

"I'm not going to raise them by myself."

Valerie gave Belinda a narrow stare. "Have you been holding out on me?"

"What are you going on about, Valerie?"

"Are you and Raymond getting married?"

Belinda shook her head. She and Dr. Raymond Miller had what she referred to as an I-95 relationship when he accepted a position as head of cardiology at an Orlando, Florida, geriatric facility. They alternated visiting each other—she visited during school recesses and

Raymond whenever he could manage to take a break from the hospital.

"No."

"Why not?"

"We're just friends, Valerie."

"Do you think you'll ever stop being friends and become lovers?"

"I doubt it."

Valerie's clear brown eyes set in a flawless olive-brown face narrowed. "Are you in love with someone else?"

Belinda shook her head again. "No. Griffin and I share custody of our nieces."

"Griffin Rice," Valerie repeated loud enough for those in the room to turn and look in their direction.

Belinda angled her head closer to Valerie's. She'd just finished telling her about the arrangement she'd established with her brother-in-law when the bell rang, signaling the end of lunch. Papers, magazines and the remnants of lunch were put away as teachers left the lounge for their classrooms.

Chapter 4

"How is she getting along, Dad?" Griffin asked his father when he joined him at the picture window in the living room of the spacious apartment in Spring Garden, a neighborhood that had been completely transformed by gentrification. The nighttime view from the high-rise was spectacular.

He knew exactly what he'd look like in twenty years. An inch shy of the six-foot mark, sixty-two-year-old Lucas Rice claimed a ramrod-straight back, slender physique and a full head of shimmering silver hair. Balanced features, a cleft chin and a sensual smile drew women of all ages to him like sunflowers facing the sun. His looks and charisma posed a problem for his wives because women loved Lucas, and he in turn loved them back.

Nevertheless, Grant's death had humbled Lucas,

making him aware of his own mortality. In his shared grief with Gloria and his surviving son, he'd confessed his many transgressions. It hadn't made it any easier for Griffin to hear about the number of women his father had slept with while still married to his mother, but he realized how much strength it took for Lucas to confess.

The confession signaled a turning point for everyone—especially Gloria. Surprisingly, she forgave her ex-husband, saying they'd married much too young and for the wrong reason. They'd met in college where Gloria was a library science major and Lucas was pre-med. Gloria discovered halfway through her sophomore year that she was pregnant. And instead of going to medical school, Lucas married his pregnant girlfriend and switched his major to pharmacology. Most of their marital strife was the result of Lucas not fulfilling his dream of becoming a doctor.

Lucas stole a glance at his son's profile. "She's pretty good during the day, but I found that she's a wreck at night."

Shifting slightly, Griffin turned to give Lucas an incredible stare. "What are you talking about?"

"I've been checking up on her since we…we lost Grant. We talk every day, and several nights each week we have dinner—either here, at my place, or at a restaurant. I always call her to say good-night, but that's when I lose it, son."

A slight frown furrowed Griffin's smooth forehead. "Why, Dad?"

Lucas closed his eyes, his chest rising and falling heavily. "The sound of her crying rips my heart out. I know she used to cry whenever we had an argument, but this time it's different."

"She's still grieving. We're all still grieving."

"Not like your mother, Griffin. That's why I suggested taking the cruise. I know I can't go back forty years and right all the wrongs, but I promised myself that I would spend what's left of my life making your mother happy."

"Do you love her, Dad?"

A sad smile crinkled the skin around Lucas's eyes. "I've always loved her and I will always love her."

"What about your other women?"

"There are no other women, and there hasn't been one in a long time."

Griffin chose his words carefully. "Is it because you're trying to insinuate yourself back into my mother's life?"

Lucas shook his head. "Don't worry, son. I won't hurt her."

"I'm not worried, Dad. *You* will be sorry if you hurt her again."

Lucas met Griffin's withering gaze, knowing he wasn't issuing an idle threat. He hadn't stayed to see Griffin grow to adulthood, but he was proud of how he'd turned out nevertheless. He was proud of both of his sons, and had never hesitated to give Gloria all the credit for their successes.

"Glo has been hurt enough. I'd rather walk away than cause her more pain."

Griffin smiled. It'd been a long time since he'd heard his father shorten his mother's name. Reaching into the pocket of his slacks, he took out a small envelope, slipping it into Lucas's shirt pocket. "There's enough on that gift card to buy something nice in Florence or Rome for your cabin mate."

Lucas took the envelope, staring numbly at the value of the gift card. It was half of what he'd paid for two first-class tickets for the month-long European cruise. "I can't take this, Griffin."

"You can and you will, otherwise I'll give it to Mom, and you know she'll buy gifts for everyone but herself."

A smile flashed across the older man's face. "You're right about that. I want to bring something back for the twins. Do you have an idea of what they'd like?"

Griffin pondered his father's question for several minutes. "I believe Layla would love a Venetian *Carnevale* mask, the kind revelers wear. Sabrina likes fashion, so anything from Rome or Paris will make her very happy."

"What about Belinda?"

"What about her, Dad?"

"What do you think she'd like?"

Lucas mentioning Belinda's name quickened Griffin's pulse, as images of the kiss they'd shared came back with the force and fury of rushing rapids. He'd kissed her to see if she was actually a prude even after she'd disclosed that she was seeing someone. He hadn't believed her. He'd discovered there was indeed fire under her staid exterior. The revelation had not only shocked him, but also made him jealous of the man who was on the receiving end of Belinda Eaton's passion.

"Perfume." He'd said the first thing that came to mind because he loved the way she smelled.

"What fragrance does she wear?"

"I don't know."

"What don't you know?" asked Gloria Rice as she walked into the living room carrying a tray with dessert plates of tiny butter cookies and petits fours.

Griffin walked over and took the tray from his mother. She looked better than she had in months, and he attributed that to the anticipation of going away for a month with the man who'd been and apparently still was the only one she'd ever loved.

In preparation for her trip, she'd had her hair cut into a close-cropped natural that showed off her delicate features and flawless chestnut-brown skin. Her dark almond-shaped eyes made her look as if she were perpetually smiling.

When she'd been informed of her son and daughter-in-law's death Gloria had stopped eating. It was only after Griffin threatened to have her force-fed that she had begun eating again, and then only small portions but enough to keep up her strength.

Now that Lucas had come back into her life, she'd managed to regain some of the weight she'd lost. When he'd asked his mother whether she was sleeping with her ex-husband, Gloria had come out with an unequivocal "no." She claimed all Lucas was good for was companionship.

"Do you know what perfume Belinda wears?"

"Yes. It's Dior's J'adore. Why do you want to know?"

"Dad's putting together a list of souvenirs he wants to bring back."

"I'm done with my list." She smiled at Lucas. "Please bring in the coffee. It should be finished brewing."

Reaching for Gloria's hand, Griffin seated her on her favorite chair. He sat on the matching ottoman, cradling her feet in his lap. "If you come back from Europe carrying my little sister or brother," he teased quietly, "I'm going to give Dad a serious beat down."

Throwing back her head, Gloria laughed until tears rolled down her face. "You don't have worry about beating up your father because it's not going to happen." Gloria sobered. "Speaking of children, Griffin."

"What about them, Mom?"

"I know you've adopted Grant's children, but do you see yourself having children of your own?"

There came a long silence as he pondered her question. "If I were to be completely honest I'd say I don't know. Playing daddy is still too new for me to make a decision. But I must admit I'm enjoying what little I've experienced."

"How are you getting along with Belinda?"

"We're doing okay. It's obvious she's going to be the stricter parent, while I'll probably let the girls do whatever they want—except when it comes to boys. If it were up to me they wouldn't have a boyfriend until they graduate from high school."

Gloria shook her head. "That's unrealistic. Your father was my first boyfriend and you see how that ended. My granddaughters should have boys as friends so they learn to differentiate between the good guys and the ones who only want to sleep with them." She paused, seemingly deep in thought. "I believe if I'd had a daughter, Lucas wouldn't have been such a philanderer."

Griffin wanted to tell Gloria that she was wrong. Lucas would've cheated on her if they'd had a dozen daughters. Unfortunately, it'd taken a catastrophic incident to bring Lucas Rice to the realization that he'd misused and mistreated the best woman he'd ever had and would ever hope to have. Perhaps, he mused, it wasn't too late for his parents to start over.

* * *

Layla and Sabrina were waiting on the front porch for Griffin when he maneuvered his SUV into the driveway and parked behind their aunt's Volvo. They were bundled in down-filled jackets, bracing against the rapid twenty-point decline in the temperature. The past week the weather had challenged the late-March season, and won.

He smiled as he got out of his car. Maybe it was the profusion of hair flowing down and around their shoulders that made them appear older, as if they'd become young adults virtually overnight.

He wasn't disappointed when they raced off the porch to launch themselves at him. The spontaneity reminded Griffin they were still young, and as they'd done when they were children, they wanted him to catch them in midair.

"Whoa!" he cried out when he collapsed to the floor of the porch under their weight.

The front door opened and he looked up to find Belinda smiling down at him as Sabrina and Layla held him down while pinning him with what they thought were wrestling holds. Lamps flanking the door flattered her slender body in a pair of fitted jeans she'd paired with a chunky pullover. She'd also changed her hairstyle. Instead of the usual curly look it was smooth, the feathered ends curving under her chin and down around the nape of her neck.

"Do you give up?" Layla shouted, tightening her headlock.

"Yes!"

"Count him out, Aunt Lindy!" Sabrina said excitedly.

Playing along with her nieces, Belinda went to her

knees and slapped the porch close to Griffin's head. "One, two, three. You're out!" The girls released Griffin, falling back and gasping in surprise when he reached for their aunt, pinning her under his body.

Burying his face against the column of her scented neck, he pressed his mouth to the silken flesh. "Come with us this weekend," he whispered near her ear.

Belinda swallowed a moan. There was no way she could ignore the hard body molded to hers, the solid pressure of bulging muscle between Griffin's thighs. She closed her eyes when a gush of moisture bathed the area between her legs.

"I… I can't." She could hardly get the words out.

"If you give her a headlock she'll give up, Uncle Griff," Layla suggested.

Griffin eased his arm under Belinda's neck. "Give up, baby," he crooned for her ears only. "Are you coming with us?" he asked loud enough for his nieces to overhear his entreaty.

"No-o-o-o!"

Sabrina went to her knees. "Please, Aunt Lindy. Please come with us. Uncle Griff said we were going to have a movie night."

"Pul-eeese," Layla moaned melodramatically.

Belinda closed her eyes. *Oh no!* a silent voice shouted when Griffin ground his groin against hers. She couldn't believe what he was doing to her—in front of their nieces no less. If she didn't stop him, then she was going to embarrass herself. Her long-celibate body indicated that she was on the brink of climaxing.

"Okay. I'll go."

"Pinky swear?" Griffin asked, grinning triumphantly.

She nodded. "Yes. Pinky swear."

Layla and Sabrina exchanged high fives as they turned to go back into the house to retrieve their overnight bags. They'd spent most of the afternoon exchanging text messages with their uncle to enlist his help in getting their aunt to join them for the weekend after she revealed she hadn't planned to do anything but read and watch DVDs.

As soon as the door banged behind them, Belinda said between clenched teeth, "Get the hell off me!"

Griffin eased up, but not enough for Belinda to escape. He didn't want to stand up until his erection went down. He hadn't expected his body to betray him, nor had he expected Belinda's response.

"Watch your language, baby. You don't want *our* children to grow up using foul language."

"They've heard worse," she said flippantly, "and no doubt from their classmates."

"I know you hear it at the high school, but I'd prefer that Sabrina and Layla not hear it at home."

Belinda affected a facetious smile. "Please let me up, Griffin."

He smiled. "That's better, darling."

Waiting until Griffin moved off her and helped her to her feet, Belinda caught the front of his sweatshirt. Standing on tiptoe, she thrust her face close to his. "If you ever hump me in front of the girls again I'll hurt you, Griffin Rice."

Griffin winked at her. "Would you prefer that I hump you in private? I know I don't appeal to you, but your body is saying something else."

Her fist tightened. "What exactly is my body saying?"

"That regardless of how we may feel about each other, our bodies are in agreement." He leaned in closer. "I could smell sex coming from your pores."

Belinda let her hand fall at the same time her jaw dropped. "How dare you! Your arrogance just supplanted whatever common sense—"

"Cut the act, Belinda!" Griffin said angrily, cutting off her tirade. "It's only a normal reaction between a man and woman, so don't confuse sex and desire with love. I'm not in love with you, and I doubt whether you'll ever be in love with me. Circumstances beyond our control have forced us into a situation we never would've or could've imagined. I didn't ask to be a father but I intend to make the best of it, and if that means making sacrifices to keep my vow to my dead brother then I will."

"Pray tell, Griffin, just what are you sacrificing?"

The seconds ticked off as he stared at the woman who intrigued him more than he wanted. The sexy godmother who made him want her when everything said that she was so wrong for him.

"Having a normal relationship with a woman."

"Don't you mean sleeping with other women?"

"That, too."

"My heart bleeds for you, Griffin. If you think I'm going to become a replacement for your *other* women, then think again, mister. I don't play house."

His eyebrows flickered. "Do you play at all?"

"Yes," she retorted. "What I do play is for keeps."

"If you play for keeps, then where is your so-called boyfriend?"

Oh, you're trying to be slick and get into my business,

Belinda mused. "You'll get to meet Raymond when he comes up from Florida this summer."

"Why do I have to wait for the summer?"

"That's when he'll be able to get away."

"Don't you mean that's when he'll be paroled?"

"Oh, no you didn't!"

"Yes, I did, Belinda. Is your Raymond in a Florida jail? I'm asking because I don't want that type of element around my daughters."

"Why are they always *your* daughters, Griffin?" Belinda shot back, the timbre of her voice escalating along with her temper. "Aren't they also my children?"

"I thought we now belong to both of you."

Belinda and Griffin spun around. They hadn't heard Sabrina when she'd come out of the house. They were so busy going at each other that they hadn't realized they weren't alone.

Belinda went over to hug her. "Of course you belong to both of us. You and Layla are my daughters."

"What about Uncle Griff?"

"You're his daughter, too."

"If that's true, then why were you fighting?"

"We weren't fighting, sweetheart."

"It sounded to me as if you were fighting."

Belinda met Griffin's knowing gaze over Sabrina's head. As new parents they'd made an unforgivable faux pas—argue in front of their children. "There're times when adults don't agree with something, so it may sound as if we're arguing. Your uncle and I love you and your sister. We made a promise to take care of you and make certain you're safe. I'm going to ask you and Layla to be patient with us because we're newbies playing mom and dad."

Sabrina smiled. "You already sound like a mom even though Uncle Griff needs more practice at being a daddy."

"Well, excuse me," Griffin drawled. "What do I have to do to sound like a daddy?"

"First of all you have to learn to say *'that's enough, young lady.'*"

Griffin forced back a smile. He'd lost count of the number of times Grant had issued his favorite warning. "What else?"

Sabrina narrowed her gaze. "There's *'did you do what your mother told you to do?'*"

Belinda pressed her palms together. "I like that one."

"You would," Griffin mumbled under his breath.

Layla, carrying a large quilted tote, joined them on the porch, frowning. "Aunt Lindy, I thought you were coming with us."

"I am. I just have to put a few things in a bag. Don't leave without me."

"We won't" came three voices.

Chapter 5

Proper attire for movie night in Paoli was pajamas and fuzzy slippers. Belinda, her head supported on a mound of overstuffed pillows, lay on the carpeted floor beside Griffin, while Layla and Sabrina were huddled together, sharing a large throw pillow. They were watching *Akeelah and the Bee* for the umpteenth time. The film had become a favorite of the twins, along with most of the feature-length animated films from Disney/Pixar. Sabrina, who'd demonstrated promise as a budding artist, had expressed interest in becoming an animator.

It was only Belinda's second trip to Griffin's house, and there were a few changes since her last visit more than five years before. He'd added an in-ground pool, expanded the outdoor patio to include a kitchen and added another room at the rear of the house that served as a home office. File folders bulging with contracts, strewn over a workstation, were a testament to a less-than-efficient filing system.

Griffin made a big production of preparing for movie night when he taught the girls how to build a fire in the fireplace. Refreshments included popcorn, s'mores, bonbons and cherry Twizzlers.

"Who wins the bee?" Griffin whispered to Belinda.

Layla sat up. "Don't tell him, Aunt Lindy!"

Belinda tickled Griffin's ribs through his T-shirt. "I'm not telling."

Griffin caught her fingers. "Don't do that."

"Are you ticklish?"

Not releasing her hand, he stared at Belinda for a full minute before lacing their fingers together. "Yes."

Smiling, she winked at him. "Do you have any other weaknesses I should know about?"

Griffin closed his eyes rather than let Belinda see how much she affected him, how much she'd changed him and his life in less than a few weeks. How could he tell her that he liked her because she was different from the other women he'd been involved with, that he wanted what she gave Raymond—her Sunshine State lover—and like Belinda, if he had to play then he wanted it to be for keeps? Spending a Friday night at home watching movies with Belinda and the girls was the highlight of his week—and something he could very easily get used to.

"That's it," he lied smoothly, redirecting his attention to the large plasma screen mounted on the wall. Griffin pretended interest in the movie when it was the woman pressed to his side that he found so intriguing.

* * *

Belinda had just dozed off when she heard the soft knock on the door. Sitting up, she turned on the bed-side lamp. "Who is it?"

"It's Count Dracula, and I've come to suck your blood" a deep voice crooned in a perfect Romanian dialect.

Belinda smiled. "Sorry, count, but I'm all out of blood."

"Curses!" he snarled, this time sounding like a pirate.

"Come in, Griffin." The door opened and Griffin walked in, wearing a pair of black pajama pants and matching T-shirt.

Friday night at the movies had not only been enjoy-able but also enlightening. She had seen another side to Griffin's personality, the opposite of the aggressive and competitive attorney who'd become notorious for holding out until he got the best deal for his clients. He had a really wicked sense of humor, telling jokes and deliberately flubbing the punch lines. Sabrina and Layla had adored the attention he lavished on them and they, in turn, reciprocated in kind.

"Is movie night over?" She'd found herself dozing off and on until she decided it was time to go to bed, leaving before the end of the film.

Griffin nodded. "When I told the girls they had to brush their teeth before turning in, they said I sounded like Aunt Lindy."

"Is that a good thing?" she teased, smiling.

"I'd say it is."

"What are you doing?" she shrieked when he ran and jumped onto the bed, flopping down on the mattress and pressing his back to the headboard.

Crossing his bare feet at the ankles, Griffin gave Belinda a sidelong glance. "I came to talk." Before settling down to watch the movie, he'd watched as she brushed and pinned Layla's and Sabrina's freshly relaxed hair, covering theirs with bandannas before doing her own. Her smooth transition from aunt to surrogate mother was nothing short of amazing.

"What's so urgent that you can't wait until tomorrow?"

"What do you think about getting the girls a dog?"

Belinda went completely still. "What kind of dog, Griffin?"

"Don't worry, Belinda, it won't be a pit bull or Rottweiler."

"What kind of dog?" she asked again.

"A Yorkshire terrier. One of my neighbors has a purebred bitch that whelped a litter of pups about three months ago. She's sold off all but two, and I told her that I would have to talk to you before offering to buy one."

"A puppy," she whispered. "You want me to take care of a puppy?"

"Sabrina and Layla will take care of it."

"I don't think so, Griffin. You're fooling yourself if you believe girls their age are going to take care of a dog. I'll wind up feeding, bathing and walking it. And what's going to happen when it gnaws on my rugs and furniture?"

Griffin dropped an arm over Belinda's shoulders, bringing her cheek to his chest. "You've got it all wrong."

"No, I don't."

"Please don't say no until you see them. They're adorable."

"I'm certain they're adorable but—"

"Baby, please," he crooned softly. "Grant promised the girls they could have a dog."

Tilting her head, Belinda stared at Griffin looking down at her. The soft glow from the lamp flattered the contours of his lean face. "Donna didn't say anything to me about getting a dog."

"Grant wanted to surprise them. I'll buy the cage, wee-wee pads, food and chew toys. I'll also commit to covering the vet and grooming expenses, and of course the pooch will need one of those designer puppy carriers that cost an arm and two legs."

She smiled. "Why does it sound as if you're running a con on me?"

He returned her smile. "I didn't mean for it—"

"It's okay," she said, cutting him off. "When are we going to look at the puppies?"

Griffin kissed her forehead. "Tomorrow after breakfast."

"I must have *sucker* written on my forehead."

He laughed softly, the warm sound rumbling in his chest. "Why should you be any different from me?"

"Are we really soft, Griffin?"

"No. We're just two people who want the best for the children we've been entrusted to love and protect."

"You're right," Belinda said after a pregnant pause. "I always believed I'd grow up to fall in love, marry and have children of my own. Never in my wildest dreams would I have thought that I'd be raising my sister's children. What makes it so challenging is that they're not little kids, but pre-teens who're beginning to assert their independence. I try and do the best I can, but what frightens me is what will I do or say if, or when, they come out with *'you can't tell me what to do because you're not my mother.'*"

"Let's hope it never happens, but if it does then I'll step in."

Belinda tried to sit up, but was thwarted when Griffin held her fast. "You're not going to hit them."

He frowned at her. "I'd never hit a child. What I can assure you is that my bark is a great deal louder than yours."

"I'll not have you yelling at them."

"What's it going to be, Belinda? You can't have it both ways. There's going to come a time when they're going to challenge you, because all kids do it. But the dilemma for us will be how do we deal with it as parents. And if I have to raise my voice to get them off your back, then I will. Remember, they're twins, so they're apt to tag-team you."

Belinda remembered when Donna broke curfew and Roberta was sitting in the living room waiting up for her. Donna said something flippant and all Belinda remembered was Roberta telling Donna that she'd brought her into the world and she could also take her out. Her mother's tirade woke up the entire household and it took all of Dwight Eaton's gentle persuasion to defuse the situation.

It was after the volatile confrontation that Belinda made a promise to herself: if and when she had children she would never scream at them, because not only was punishment more effective, but also the results lasted longer.

"If you're going to raise your voice, then I don't want to be anywhere around," she told Griffin.

"Dammit, Belinda, you act like I'm going to verbally

abuse them. When it comes to discipline we are going to have to be on the same page, or else they're going to play one off the other."

"I know," she whispered, burying her face between his neck and shoulder.

"What do you do when your students act out?"

"I put them out of my class, and then write them up."

"Do you have problems with the boys?"

"What kind of problems?"

"Do they try and come on to you?"

"A few have tried, but when I give them a 'screw face' then they usually back off."

"Show me a 'screw face.'" Easing out of Griffin's comforting embrace, Belinda sat up and glared at him. There *was* something in Belinda's gaze that was frightening. "How do you do that?" he asked.

She smiled. "Practice, practice, practice. I have more problems with my female students than the males. Some of them outweigh me, so they believe they can take me out with very little effort. In not so many words, I tell them I can roll with the best of them."

"You're not talking about fighting a student?"

"Of course not. But what they don't know is that I have a black belt in tae kwon do, with distinction in sparring and power breaking. Myles studied karate for years, earned his black belt, but didn't like competing. I, on the other hand, loved competitions."

"Do you still compete?"

"No. It's been a long time since my last competition. A lot of teachers refuse to teach in rough neighborhoods, but the confidence I gained from a decade of martial arts training and the fact that these kids need dedicated teachers is why I stay."

"So you can kick my butt."

Belinda smiled. "With one arm tied behind my back," she said, teasingly.

"Ouch!" he kidded, pressing her back to the mattress. "When I first met you I thought you were cute and I wanted to ask you out, but you were Miss Attitude personified."

"I was nineteen and you had already graduated law school, so I thought you were too old for me."

"I'm only five years older than you. I graduated high school at sixteen, college at twenty and law school at twenty-three. That made me an accelerated student, not an older man."

"You seemed so much older then."

"What about now?"

"When I saw you rolling around on the porch with Layla and Sabrina I had serious doubts as to your maturity."

"They love it when I wrestle with them," Griffin drawled. "Fast-forward thirteen years, and I'm going to ask you something I should've asked when you were nineteen. Belinda Eaton, will you go out with me?"

"You're kidding, aren't you?"

"Why do you think I'm kidding?"

"Not only are we aunt, uncle and godparents but our nieces' legal guardians. We sleep in each other's homes, you have a key to mine and I to yours, but right now we're in bed together. Dating would be ludicrous given our situation."

"You're right about us sharing a situation."

"Is there something wrong with that, Griffin?"

"There's nothing wrong with it, but I would prefer having a relationship with you aside from what we share with Sabrina and Layla. That way I could get to know you better."

Belinda was strangely flattered by Griffin's interest in her. She experienced a gamut of emotions that didn't let her think clearly. Circumstances beyond their control had brought them together and the man whom she'd come to believe couldn't be faithful to one woman wanted a relationship with her.

"I'll have to think about it."

His expressive eyebrows lifted. "What's there to think about?"

Belinda gave him a long, penetrating stare. "I have to decide whether I'm willing to see you exclusively."

"Does that mean you'll give up Sunshine?"

"Who's Sunshine?"

"Your pen-pal chump living off the taxpayers in a Sunshine State prison."

"Raymond is not a chump," she said in defense of the kindest man whom she had the pleasure of knowing.

"He's in Florida and you're in Pennsylvania, which means you live at least a thousand miles apart. How often do you see him, Belinda? Or better yet—how many times a year, if he's not incarcerated, does he make love to you? How do you know if he's being faithful to you?"

Her temper flared as she sat up. "How do I know you'll be faithful to me?"

"You don't. All you'll have is my word."

Belinda wanted to tell Griffin that she was beginning to like him, in fact, like him a little too much to be indifferent to his sexual magnetism. When he'd held her down on the porch she'd been on the verge of climaxing and that just looking at him made her body hot and throb with a need long denied. Griffin was right about Raymond. She didn't know whether he was sleeping with another woman but that wasn't her concern because he was her friend. She'd fallen in love only once in her life, and it ended with her moving off campus to come back home. It took years before she trusted a man enough to sleep with him.

"If I can't have Sunshine, then it definitely has to be no skanks, 'chicken heads' or hoochies for you."

Throwing back his head, Griffin laughed. "You drive a hard bargain, Lindy Eaton."

"It has to be all or nothing."

Griffin ran a forefinger down the length of her nose. "If you ever have to negotiate a deal always remember to give your competitor an out."

"Is that how you see me, Griffin? Am I a competitor or an opponent?"

"Neither."

"Then what am I?"

"I'm someone who's concerned about you. You'd fallen asleep less than half an hour into the movie. I know you're exhausted. You no longer cook, clean, wash and iron for one, but three. Layla told me you spent more than an hour folding laundry."

A scowl settled into Belinda's features. "You have the girls spying on me?"

"No, Belinda. I only asked them how their week went and both were only too willing to tell me. The reason I want to take you out is to give you a break. It can be one night a week. We can leave Layla and Sabrina at your parents' or with my mother when she comes back. You can let me know in advance what you want to do or where you'd like to eat and I'll make it happen."

Belinda's expression brightened. "If all you want to do is to take me out to dinner, then that means that I don't have to give up Raymond."

"It doesn't matter because I get to see his woman a lot more than he does."

The slow, sexy smile that never failed to make women sit up and take notice of Griffin Rice spread over his face as he moved over Belinda, supporting his weight on his elbows.

Belinda's breasts felt heavy, her nipples swelling as she leaned into the solid wall of his chest. For years she'd watched Griffin with other women, wondering why, other than his gorgeous face, they chased him and now she knew. He was inherently masculine *and* sexy, and it didn't matter that she was another in a long line of women who would get to sample what the celebrity lawyer was offering. She opened her mouth to his kiss, drowning in the sexual heat, succumbing to the sensual spell that made her feel as if she and the man holding her to his heart were the last two people on earth.

Griffin's heart slammed against his ribs when he showered kisses around Belinda's lips and along her jaw. Lowering his head, he fastened his mouth along the column of her velvety, scented neck, nipping, suckling, licking her as if she were a frothy confection.

"You taste and smell so good," he mumbled over and over.

Baring her throat, Belinda closed her eyes. She wanted to tell Griffin that he felt and smelled good, too, but the words were locked in her throat when a longing she'd never known seized her mind and body, refusing to let her go.

Without warning the spell shattered when his hands

moved under her pajama top and cupped her breasts. "Griffin, no! We can't!"

"I know, baby," he gasped near her ear. He couldn't make love to Belinda while the girls were in the house, and not when he couldn't protect her against an unplanned pregnancy.

Her breathing coming in uneven pants, Belinda moaned softly. "Go to bed, Griffin."

He smiled. "I'm already in bed."

"*Your* bed," she ordered softly. "Good night, Griffin."

Burying his face between Belinda's breasts, Griffin closed his eyes. He didn't want to let her go, but he had to. Reluctantly, he moved off the bed. "Good night, Belinda."

It took a long time after Griffin left her bedroom for Belinda to fall asleep. The thrumming in the lower part of her body had become a reminder of what she'd missed and needed.

Chapter 6

"I'll take both of them."

Belinda turned on her heel, walking out of the room to wait on the Sandersons' back porch. She had to get away from Griffin or say something she would regret for the rest of her life.

Griffin had called his neighbor and set up an appointment to see the puppies. He'd told his nieces that they were going shopping after eating out at a local diner. But they were totally unaware that *going shopping* meant looking for a dog.

The remaining three-month-old Yorkies, both males, were spirited, friendly *and* adorable. The only question was which one Sabrina and Layla would choose. Belinda realized the quandary when each girl picked up a puppy, cradled it to her chest and then refused to relinquish them when Griffin told them to pick one. He'd become a victim of his own negotiating skills when each girl pleaded her case as to why they didn't want to share one dog.

"I think your wife is a little upset," Nicole Sanderson said in a quiet voice to Griffin. "Why don't you go and see what's wrong."

Nicole was pleasantly surprised when Griffin Rice followed through on his promise to set up an appointment to look at the puppies. She, however, was more than surprised when he revealed that he was also coming with his wife and daughters. Paoli was a small town, with a population of fifty-four hundred, and it was inevitable that most residents' paths would occasionally cross in the friendly, close-knit community. When Griffin Rice purchased a home in Paoli nearly eight years before, the town's grapevine hummed with the news that they had a celebrity living among them.

"I'll be right back," Griffin said to the woman who was looking forward to selling her last two purebred Yorkshire terriers. Opening the door, he saw Belinda with her back to him.

"Lindy, baby."

"Don't you *dare* say a mumbling word to me, Griffin Rice!" With wide eyes, she rounded on him. "Don't call me Lindy, and I'm not your *baby.*"

Griffin didn't understand what'd set her off. She'd agreed to their nieces having a dog, so what could be so wrong with them having one more? "What's wrong?"

"What's wrong?" Belinda repeated, approaching him. When she closed her eyes the tips of her lashes touched her cheekbones, and when they opened again the dark orbs were awash with moisture. "Marriages fail because couples don't communicate. They argue about money, child rearing and lack of affection but not necessarily in that order. We are *not* communicating, Griffin, and we aren't even married. I agreed to one puppy. How on earth did it become two?"

Griffin resisted the urge to pull Belinda in his arms. "Didn't you hear what Layla and Sabrina said? They said this is the first time in their lives they're not treated as if they're joined at the hip. You're the only one who doesn't refer to them as *the twins,* or who bought them matching outfits. They had to wait twelve years to get their own rooms, where they won't grow up as copies of each other. You relate to them as freethinkers, individuals, and that's what they've become. Sabrina doesn't want to share her puppy with Layla and vice versa."

"Two puppies translate into twice the mess."

Taking a step, Griffin rested a hand on the nape of Belinda's neck. "A mess you won't have to deal with. Each girl will be responsible for her own puppy. Not having to share will eliminate arguments as to whose week it is to clean the crate."

Belinda tried ignoring the subtle, seductive fragrance of Griffin's aftershave—but failed. "Why do you insist on complicating my life?"

"How am I doing that?"

"Instead of looking after one puppy when *our daughters* are away on their class trip, I'll have to look after two."

Griffin brushed a light kiss over her parted lips. "Remember, Lindy, you're not in this alone. I'll help you."

"When? Don't you have a company to run?"

He nodded. "A business I'm currently downsizing from six to two. I've already begun moving files from the Philly office to Paoli. I'm putting my marketing manager on retainer, and I expect to hire a retired paralegal who wants to come on board part-time, which fits perfectly into my business strategy. She'll be responsible for typing contracts and filing court documents."

"You're moving your office." The question was a statement.

"Yes. That's why I built the addition onto the house. To be honest, I should've done it years ago. The money I've spent renting a suite of offices in downtown Philly could've fed every child in a small African country for at least a year."

"Where are you going to conduct your meetings?"

"In whatever city the team owners' call home. If it's local, then I'll reserve a room at a restaurant with good food and service, or a hotel suite."

The seconds ticked off as Belinda and Griffin stared at each other. He hadn't shaved, and the stubble on his lean jaw enhanced rather than detracted from his classic good looks. Dressed in an olive-green barn jacket, jeans, black crewneck sweater and matching low-heeled leather boots he reminded her of a Ralph Lauren ad.

"When did you decide all this?" she asked, breaking the silence.

"It was the day I went to clean out Grant's office—something I'd avoided doing for weeks—because I didn't want to admit to myself that my brother had been right when he said that the price of success is grossly overrated.

"As I stood in his twentieth-floor corner office overlooking downtown Philadelphia I could hear a voice in my head. At first I thought it was my imagination, but it wasn't because I was reliving the one time I saw my brother drunk. He'd just gotten a promotion and a coveted corner office. I'll never forget his face when he stared at me, then said, *'Success don't mean shit when you look at what you have to sacrifice in order to achieve it.'* At first I thought he was just being maudlin until he talked about how he was able to remember everything about his clients' stock portfolios but he couldn't remember his wife's birthday or their wedding anniversary. He talked about the meetings and business trips that took him away from home where invariably he'd miss a recital or his daughters' school plays. For Grant, making it had become all-consuming. I suppose it had something to do with proving to your parents that Donna hadn't made a mistake when she agreed to marry him."

"My parents were never against your brother marrying my sister," Belinda said, defensively.

"I didn't understand how Grant felt until I met your family for the first time. My first impression was that the Eatons were snobs. You come from generations of teachers, doctors and lawyers, while my mother and father were the first in their family to graduate from college. Grant had less than a month before he would get his degree and he still hadn't heard from any of his prospective employers when your father took him aside and said that if he ever needed money to take care of his daughter or grandchildren then he shouldn't hesitate to come to him. His offer cut Grant to the quick, but he smiled at Dr. Eaton and said that he wouldn't have married his daughter if he hadn't been able to support her.

"So, the day Grant got his seven-figure salary and all the perks that went along with his position, he warned me about putting success before family. I never wanted children because I didn't want them growing up with parents who fought more than they made love. And since life doesn't always play out the way we want it to, I'm committed to making the best of the hand I've been dealt. I promised my brother I would take care of his children in the event anything happened to him, and that means being available for parent-teacher conferences, school concerts, supervising sleep-overs and chauffeuring them when it's time for college tours."

Belinda tried to hide her confusion. She'd believed that Grant worked long hours so that Donna could be a stay-at-home mother and the envy of the other women in their social circle who were jealous because they were working mothers.

"I didn't know," she said softly when she recovered her voice.

"I doubt if Donna knew how Grant felt. He wasn't one for opening up about himself—not even to his wife. In that way he's a lot like my dad. It has taken my father more than forty years to tell my mother that he'd been carrying around a world of resentment because she got pregnant and he had to drop out of medical school to take care of her and their child."

Belinda couldn't stop the frown forming between her eyes. "He should've accepted half the blame. After all, she couldn't get pregnant by herself, Griffin."

"You're preaching to the choir, beautiful. People always blame others when something goes wrong in their life because it's easier than accepting responsibility that perhaps they, too, were wrong."

Belinda lowered her gaze, staring at Griffin's strong, brown throat. "I should apologize to you."

"For what?"

"I retract what I said about you not having any redeeming qualities."

"You said no such thing." Belinda's head came up, her exotic-looking eyes filling with confusion. "You said, and I quote, *'I'm not attracted to you, and there's nothing about you that I find even remotely appealing.'*" He placed his free hand over his heart. "You have no idea of how much you hurt me when you said that."

Belinda was hard-pressed not to laugh at his affected theatrics. "Suck it up, Rice. What I said pales in comparison to when you said I wasn't at the top of your list for what you'd want in a woman."

Griffin angled his head and smiled. "Guess what?"

"What?"

"I lied."

Her smile matched his. "I suppose since we're into true confessions, then I'll admit that I lied, too." She wanted to tell Griffin that she was attracted to him and found him *very* appealing.

Griffin brushed a light kiss over her parted lips. "Let's go back inside and close this deal. I'm certain Sabrina and Layla are anxious to take their puppies home."

Belinda caught the sleeve of Griffin's jacket. "Before we go in I just want to remind you that the girls are leaving to go on a class trip to D.C. two days before I'm out for spring break. We're going to have to make arrangements to board the puppies for those days."

"They won't have to go to a kennel."

"They're too young to be left alone."

"Don't worry so much, Lindy. I'll stay at your place until you come home."

"What if you have to leave town on business?"

"Whatever it is can wait," he said softly. "Remember, family comes first, even if it's of the four-legged furry persuasion."

Roberta Eaton smiled at her granddaughters, each holding a tiny puppy with dark fur and tan markings. "What do we have here?"

"Grams, this is Cecil Rice," Sabrina announced in a loud, dramatic voice. "He's a Yorkshire terrier."

"And this is Nigel Rice," Layla said, introducing her puppy. "We gave them British names because Aunt Lindy told us that Yorkshire is in England."

Roberta Eaton pressed her palms together. "They're so tiny. How much do they weigh?"

"Nigel is two pounds and three ounces and Cecil two pounds and six ounces," Sabrina answered, bragging like a proud mother.

Roberta shook her head in amazement. "Together they don't even weigh five pounds." She leaned over, kissing her granddaughters who were now as tall as she was. "Go show your Gramps the puppies, then put them away because it's time to eat."

Belinda hugged and kissed her mother before heading toward the kitchen. She hadn't missed sharing a Sunday dinner with her parents since Donna passed away because she knew what it meant to her mother to have at least one of her children with her for what throughout past generations had become a family day.

Myles, who lived and worked in Pittsburgh, wasn't expected to return until the end of the school year, and her younger sister, Chandra, was now a Peace Corps worker assigned to teaching young children in Bahia.

Roberta gestured to the tall, casually dressed man standing behind her daughter, clutching the handle of a crate. "Griffin, please find some place to put that doggy prison, and then come eat."

Griffin complied, putting the wire crate in a corner of the spacious entryway. "I have to go back to the car and bring in dessert."

"You didn't have to bring anything. I made a coconut cake."

Smiling and sharing a knowing look with Belinda, Griffin said, "I guess ours will keep."

"No doubt," Belinda crooned, playing along with him.

Roberta caught the surreptitious exchange between her daughter and Griffin. "What did you bring?"

"Carrot cake."

"From where, Griffin?"

"Ms. Tootsie's Soul Food Cafe."

"Bertie, stop playing," Dwight Eaton called out with his approach. "You know you love Ms. Tootsie's carrot cake. But then again, any dessert from Ms. Tootsie's isn't as good as yours," he added quickly, always the diplomat.

Belinda gave her father a wide grin. He always said the right thing. Dr. Dwight Eaton was only a couple of inches taller than his wife, but what he lacked in height he compensated for with wit and personality. His patients loved him as much for his medical expertise as his gentle bedside manner. His dark brown face was smooth, except for a few lines around his equally dark eyes behind a pair of rimless glasses.

"How are you, Lindy?"

"Wonderful, Daddy."

Dwight smiled at Griffin. “Are you taking good care of my girls?”

“I’m doing the best I can, sir.”

The older man waved a hand. “Please, Griffin, none of that ‘sir’ business. Don’t forget you’re family.”

Voices raised in excitement preceded a streak of dark fur running across the living room. Roberta caught a puppy—Belinda still couldn’t distinguish whether he was Nigel or Cecil because their markings were identical—and Griffin put the runaway puppy into the crate, while she went to retrieve the cake from his SUV.

A quarter of an hour later, everyone sat down at the dining room table to enjoy a traditional Southern dinner of macaroni and cheese, smothered pork chops, collard greens, buttery corn bread and sweet tea.

Sabrina and Layla talked nonstop about school, the students who rode the bus with them on their new route and the research they’d gathered from the internet on Yorkies. It was the first Sunday dinner since the death of their parents that the sisters were animated and their mood ebullient. Both decided to forego dessert to play with the whining, yipping puppies that were anxious to be released from their confinement.

Griffin, at Belinda’s urging, said their goodbyes at six to return home and prepare for the upcoming week. When Belinda retired for bed later that night her thoughts were of Griffin—how she’d come to look forward to seeing him, sharing meals and the responsibility of raising their nieces.

Belinda stared at her reflection in the mirror, not recognizing the image. It wasn’t so much that her face had changed but the woman to whom the face belonged—*she* had changed.

She never would've imagined four months ago, or even four weeks ago that she would've accepted Griffin Rice's request to step into the role as his hostess. She'd rehearsed for the part by making his house appear lived in. With the exception of his home office, every room in the large colonial was picture perfect, as if each piece of furniture and objet d'art had been selected and positioned for a magazine layout.

Griffin admitted to hiring a design firm to decorate his house in a style reminiscent of grand Caribbean plantation homes erected during the British colonial period. Dark, heavy mahogany four-poster beds with posts engraved with decorative pineapples, leaves and vines, tables with curving legs, highboys, armoires, secretaries, settees, wall mirrors and chests of drawers transported you back to an era of ruling-class elegance whose enormous wealth was derived from slaves, sugar and rum.

It'd taken her less than a day to transform the house into a home with large green plants in glazed hand-painted vases, fresh flowers and dozens of pillars, votives and tea lights in decorative holders. The gathering was small, with a confirmed guest list of fourteen. A caterer and bartender arrived an hour before the first guests were scheduled to arrive.

For the first time in a week, anticipation at meeting their sports idol shifted Layla's and Sabrina's attention from their pets to the party. Much to Belinda's surprise, the girls kept their promise to take care of the puppies. They set their clocks to rise earlier than usual to clean the cage and put out food and clean water for Cecil and

Nigel before readying themselves for school. Playing with the puppies had become a priority. As soon as they came home after school the cage was opened and each puppy bounded out to pounce on its respective owner.

She'd continued to call the Yorkies by the wrong name until Griffin pointed out that Nigel had a tiny tan spot on the tip of his tail. The dilemma of transporting the puppies and their supplies between households was eliminated when Griffin bought a cage large enough to accommodate both pups and purchased an ample supply of wee-wee pads, food, treats and chew toys to have on hand in Paoli.

Peering closer in the mirror, she checked her makeup for the last time, pleased with the results. Eye shadow, which she rarely wore, and vibrant vermilion lipstick highlighted her eyes and lips. And, because the get-together was casual, Belinda had chosen a pair of black stretch cuffed capris, a long-sleeved, off-the-shoulder fitted top and added an additional three inches to her five-six height with peep-toe pumps.

She left the bedroom and walked down the hallway to the staircase, shiny curls bouncing around her head and face with each step. After a week of painstakingly brushing her hair each night to keep the strands smooth, she'd gone back to her curly hairstyle.

Her steps slowed as she looked down to find Griffin waiting for her at the bottom of the staircase. Belinda smiled. She and Griffin were dressed alike. He was wearing a black pullover, slacks and slip-ons. The recessed light glinted off his close-cropped black hair.

Griffin extended his hand, helping Belinda as she stepped off the last step. His gaze lingered on the curls framing her round face, then moved lower to her full mouth outlined in a shimmering, sexy red shade. However, it was her eyes, the lids darkened, lashes spiked and lengthened by mascara that held him enthralled. Expertly applied makeup had served to highlight and accentuate Belinda Eaton's natural beauty.

He hadn't lied to Belinda when he told her that he'd dated his share of women, although he was very discriminating with whom he slept. But none of them could match her natural beauty.

"You look so incredibly beautiful." The sincerity in his compliment was evident.

Lowering her gaze, Belinda glanced up at him through her lashes. "Thank you."

He angled his head and pressed a kiss to her ear. "You're welcome." He didn't think he would ever get used to her smell. It was an aphrodisiac he was helpless to resist.

It'd taken Griffin only two weeks to come to the realization that he *did* like his nieces' surrogate mother, that he'd changed his opinion of her and he wanted to get closer to the intelligent, intriguing woman who unknowingly made him forget all the others.

Increasing his protective hold, he tucked her hand into the bend of his elbow and led her across the living room. Recorded music floated from concealed speakers throughout the first floor. An outdoor fireplace provided additional warmth for those who wanted to dine or sit outdoors.

"I asked Keith to get here earlier than the others. That way Sabrina and Layla can talk to him one on one."

Belinda smiled. "I'm willing to bet they'll do more gawking than talking."

"You're probably right." Reaching into a pocket of

his slacks, he took out an ultra-thin digital camera. "Evidence," he drawled, grinning. "I'm certain they're going to want to prove to their friends that they *do* know Keith Ennis."

"I hope it doesn't backfire on them."

Griffin's expression mirrored confusion. "Why would you say that?"

"If they tell everyone their uncle's on a first-name basis with a major league ballplayer, some students can get jealous. I've seen it happen enough at my school with a few situations escalating into bullying and fighting."

"I've seen that happen, too, but thankfully most are good kids."

"Speaking of good—you know the girls adore you, Griffin."

He lifted his eyebrows. "They don't adore me any more than they love you, Belinda. I'm sure they see me as Santa or a magic genie that grants their wishes. It's you who must deal with them twenty-four-seven, but instead of withering they've bloomed. I know they miss their mom and dad, but you've saved them."

Belinda didn't know why, but she felt as if she was holding her breath and waiting for the time when one or both of the twins would experience a meltdown. "You have to remember that they were in therapy only days after we buried Donna and Grant," she reminded Griffin. "I don't want to think of what would've happened to them if they hadn't had professional help."

Griffin shook his head. "Therapy aside, it's you and how you relate to them that makes the difference. I overheard them talking about how much they love manipedies—whatever that is—and getting their hair done every week."

"A mani-pedi is a manicure and pedicure. I go every week, so I just take them along with me."

"Stop trying to minimize your importance in their lives, Belinda," Griffin chided softly. "You're not Donna, but she knew what she was doing when she asked you to take care of her children. In other words, Belinda Eaton, you are an incredible mother, and I hope Mr. Sunshine knows how lucky he is to have someone like you."

Belinda was caught off guard by the warmth in Griffin's voice and wanted to tell him that he didn't have to concern himself with Raymond Miller. "I need to tell you—" The chiming of the doorbell preempted what she was going to tell Griffin about the man who was her friend and not her lover.

Griffin pressed his face to Belinda's soft, sweet-smelling hair. "I'll be right back."

She stood in the middle of the living room staring at the massive floral arrangement on an antique English pedestal table until delicious wafting aromas coming from the kitchen propelled her into action, and she turned and made her way toward the rear of the house.

The night before, Sabrina had admitted that she liked staying over in her uncle's house because it made her feel as if she'd stepped back in time. What the teenager liked in particular was that although Griffin had enclosed the back porch, it was still accessible through the French doors. When the doors were open the space was perfect for dining al fresco. Belinda viewed it as the perfect place for having tea or simply enjoying the landscape while rocking on the porch.

She stopped at the entrance to the kitchen. A toque-wearing chef, wielding a whisk with a vengeance in a large sauté pan, ordered a waiter to bring him a platter. "Today, please!" he drawled impatiently.

Leaving as quickly and quietly as she'd entered, Belinda reversed course, passing the dining room where the bartender was setting up. Griffin had decided on buffet-style service because it was more in keeping with the casualness of the gathering. His invitations stressed casual attire, and anyone wearing a tie or suit would be ushered out the door.

Grant and Donna had been frequent guests at the social gatherings Griffin hosted at his house, but Belinda always had responded by politely declining. At first the invitations slowed in frequency then they stopped entirely. Donna always called to tell her who she'd met, or brag about the quality of the food, then ended the conversation with *"You don't know what you were missing."* Belinda's rejoinder was always, *"What I don't know, I don't miss."*

Avoiding her brother-in-law had strained their relationship. She'd spent years believing what she read in the tabloids, and never bothered to ask Griffin if the stories about him were true. She'd fallen victim to a very human fault—believing what you read.

A deep voice, on an even lower register than Griffin's, reached her as she walked into the living room. Keith Ennis appeared taller, larger than the images she'd seen on television. She'd suggested Sabrina and Layla remain in their rooms until the ballplayer's arrival.

Griffin approached Belinda, beckoning. "Come, darling. I want to introduce you to a client who's also a good friend. Keith, this is Belinda Eaton. Belinda, Keith Ennis."

Belinda was too starstruck to register Griffin's endearment as she smiled at the larger-than-life superstar ballplayer. His sparkling raven-black eyes, shaved head, mahogany-hued smooth skin and trimmed silky mustache and goatee were mesmerizing.

She offered him her hand. "It's a pleasure to meet you."

Keith raised the delicate hand that he had swallowed up in his much larger one. "I can't believe Rice has been holding out on me," he crooned, winking, his baritone voice lowering seductively. "Where has he been hiding you?" he asked Belinda.

A rush of heat stung her cheeks. "I've been around."

Griffin looped a proprietary arm around Belinda's waist. "Sorry, man, but she's not available."

"If the lovely lady is unavailable, then why isn't there a ring on her finger, Rice?"

Belinda grimaced when she felt the bite of Griffin's fingers as they tightened on her waist. She flashed Keith a tight smile. "Please excuse me. I'm going upstairs to get Sabrina and Layla so they can meet you before the others arrive."

Belinda mentioning his meeting Griffin's nieces reminded Keith why he'd come to his attorney's home. His team had played a Saturday afternoon game, and he'd planned to unwind at his condo with the woman who usually kept him occupied during home games. However, Griffin got him to change his mind and his plans when he gave him a generous check as a donation to his alma mater.

Keith's gaze lingered briefly on Belinda Eaton before

coming back to rest on Griffin's scowling face. "Look, man, I know I was out of line."

"You were." The two words were cold, exacting.

Keith recoiled as if he'd been struck. "Will you accept my apology?"

The seconds ticked off, the silence swelling and growing more uncomfortable with each tick. Griffin's face was a glowering mask of controlled fury. His client had stepped over the line. He'd taken Keith Ennis, a naturally talented athlete from a disadvantaged Baltimore neighborhood to instant superstar status with a five-year multimillion-dollar contract, along with high-profile product endorsements.

Griffin was normally laid-back, quick to smile, slow to anger and willing to give anyone three strikes. Unfortunately, Keith Ennis had just used up one of his three. He angled his head. "That's something I'm going to have to think about. Can I get you something to drink?" he asked in the same breath.

Keith flashed a tremulous grin. "Sure."

Layla and Sabrina stared at their sport idol, tongue-tied as Griffin snapped pictures of them shaking hands with Keith, flanking him when they posed as a group picture and when he autographed their brag books. The ballplayer, seeking redemption for his misstep, signed autographs for their teachers and fellow students. Clutching their treasured memorabilia to their chests, the sisters raced upstairs to text their friends.

Griffin and Belinda became the consummate host and hostess as they greeted guests with exotic cocktails and hors d'oeuvres. The Moroccan-style meatballs, deviled eggs with capers, mini crab cakes and beluga caviar on toast points were the highlight of the cocktail hour.

It didn't take Belinda long to understand why her sister liked socializing at Griffin's house. Excellent food, top-shelf liquor, friendly, outgoing guests and an attentive host made for certain success.

The thirtysomething crowd included college classmates, frat brothers and three newlywed couples. She knew a few of the guests were surprised to see her as hostess, but they soon got used to it. The music, which included old-school and new-school jams, had several couples up and dancing when everyone filed out of the dining room to the back porch.

It was ten o'clock when Keith bid his farewell, saying he had to get up early for batting practice. Others followed suit over the next hour. Griffin paid and tipped the bartender, the chef and waitstaff, then led Belinda out to the patio, seating her on a cushioned chaise. The outdoor fireplace emitted enough heat to warm the mid-forty-degree temperature. Dozens of candles lining a long wooden table flickered, competing with millions of stars in the clear night sky.

Belinda slipped off her heels. "I'm going to need a throw or a blanket," she said, as Griffin joined her on the chaise.

Griffin nuzzled her neck. "I'll warm you up." Without warning, he effortlessly lifted her so that she sat between his outstretched legs. "Lean back against me."

Fatigue swept over her, and she closed her eyes. "It was a nice little get-together."

"It was nice," Griffin said in agreement, as he, too, closed his eyes.

She opened her eyes and peered up at him over her

shoulder. "Some of your friends were somewhat surprised when you introduced me as your hostess. Were they perhaps expecting to see you with some other woman?"

Griffin opened his eyes. "I don't know what they expected, Belinda, because I've never concerned myself with how other folks see me. If I did, then I'd stop being who I am. And I deliberately didn't introduce you as my brother's sister-in-law because I felt it was none of their business."

"Did you tell Keith that I'm the girls' aunt?"

"Nope."

"Do you plan on telling him?"

"Nope."

"Why are you so monosyllabic?"

Using a minimum of effort and movement, Griffin changed positions until Belinda lay under him. "I don't feel very much like talking, Miss Eaton, because I'd rather do this."

She knew Griffin was going to kiss her, but was helpless to stop him. The truth was she didn't want to stop him. She'd lost count of the number of times she'd replayed him kissing her over and over—in and out of bed. Griffin had ignited a spark that grew hotter and more intense each time she saw him. A part of her wanted him to stay away—the sensible Belinda. Then there was the other Belinda—the sexually frustrated woman who hadn't slept with a man in three years.

Blood-pounding desire rushed through her veins. Her lips parted, she swallowed Griffin's warm, moist breath as his mouth covered hers in a hungry joining that left them tearing at each other's clothes. Belinda grasped the back of his sweater, pulling it up from his waist and baring flesh in her journey to get to know every part of Griffin Rice. She'd become addicted to him, his scent and the hard contours of his toned, slender body.

Griffin kissed Belinda with an outward calm that belied his hunger to take her—on the chaise and without protection. One hand slipped under her blouse, while the other slid up her inner thighs. The heat coming from between her legs was an inferno. Belinda was on fire, the flames spreading and racing out of control. He fastened his mouth over a breast, the nipple hardening when he suckled her through the cup of her lace bra.

"You are exquisite," he whispered, pressing his groin to hers so she could feel how much he wanted and needed her.

Looping her arms under Griffin's shoulders, Belinda held on to him as if he were her lifeline while waves of ecstasy rocked her like a ship in a storm. He suckled one breast, then the other before trailing moist kisses down her belly. She was hot, then cold as Griffin released the zipper on her slacks, pushing them down her thighs; his head replaced his hands as he pressed his face to the apex of her legs.

Griffin inhaled the womanly essence through the scrap of silk. His longing to be inside Belinda bordered on insanity, but sanity won out when he moved up the length of her quivering body, his heart pounding in his chest like a jackhammer. He sat up, swinging his legs over the side of the chaise.

"One of these days we're going to finish this," he promised.

Belinda nodded rather than speak. She was afraid, afraid that she would beg Griffin to make love to her on the chaise and out in the open where Sabrina or

Layla could possibly discover them. Raising her hips, she eased up and zipped her slacks and adjusted her top. An owl hooted in the distance as she reached for her shoes.

She stood up and stared at the outline of broad shoulders in the muted darkness. Griffin was so still he could've been a statue. "Good night, Griffin, and don't forget to put out the candles."

Getting up from the chaise, Griffin smiled at the woman who'd wound herself into his life and his heart. "Good night, Lindy."

Chapter 7

"Miss Ferguson, please take your seat. Mr. Evans, you know the rules. No hats or do-rags." The high school administration had banned cell phones and do-rags for male students while classes were in session. Students had to wear picture IDs, and they'd installed metal detectors because of an incident in which one student stabbed and killed another with a knife he'd concealed under his cap. Their attempt to ban gang colors was voted down by the school board, and the result was a proliferation of red, blue and gold bandannas and jackets.

Belinda knew her students were restless and looking forward to spring break, and she was no exception. She would use the week to sleep in late, weed her flower garden, clean out her closets and hopefully catch up on her reading.

Sabrina and Layla, who attended a private school, had begun their spring break two days before their public school counterpart. They were on a week-long class trip that would take them from Washington, D.C., to Williamsburg, Virginia, and finally the Gettysburg National Military Park before returning. With the girls away and Griffin in Chicago on business, if it hadn't been for Cecil and Nigel's barking the house would've been as silent as a tomb. The past two mornings she'd gotten up early to take care of the puppies, and she knew she couldn't linger after classes because she needed to get home to see after them.

"Miss Eaton, tell Brent to get out of my seat."

Belinda let out an audible sigh. "Mr. Wiley, please find your own seat."

Brent Wiley took his time sliding off the chair to sit on another in the next row, all the while glaring at the petite, dark-haired female student with whom he had a love-hate, on-again, off-again relationship since the school year began. Their enmity escalated when it was rumored that Petra Rutherford was dating a rival gang member.

He pointed a finger at her. "I'm gonna fix you, ho!"

Petra Rutherford jumped up. "Your momma's a ho, bitch!"

Belinda had had enough. "Mr. Wiley, out!"

Brent Wiley knew the drill. Whenever Miss Eaton ordered a student out of her classroom it meant a visit to the dean. It also meant a call home, and that meant big trouble for him. His old man was on his back because some of his friends were in a gang, but what Brent couldn't understand was that his pops had been in a gang when he was in his teens, did a bid in prison but after he was paroled found religion. Pushing back his chair, Brent stood up. He nodded to another boy, pulled up his baggy jeans, then gathered his books and left the classroom.

Belinda waited until she had everyone's attention. She glared at Petra. "Miss Rutherford, count yourself lucky, because you also should be in the dean's office."

Petra rolled her eyes. "I ain't gonna let nobody call me a ho," she mumbled under her breath.

Leaning against the front of her desk, Belinda crossed her legs at the ankles. The girls sitting in the front row glanced down at her shoes and smiled at one another. She knew the female students in particular monitored what she wore. On several occasions they'd ask if a jacket or blouse was new because they hadn't seen it before, which led Belinda to believe they were cataloguing her wardrobe.

She felt it important to wear business attire, unlike those teachers who sometimes wore jeans and sweats. Today she wore taupe linen gabardine slacks with a white silk man-tailored shirt and waist-length tan suede jacket. Her footwear was a pair of brown leather pumps. Not only was she an educator but also a role model for her students. In order to be a professional she also had to look the part.

"Yesterday I gave out copies of three things—two newspaper cartoons and one photograph. I wanted you to analyze them and write a paragraph on what message the cartoonist and photographer are trying to express." A hand went up in the back of the room. "Yes, Mr. Sanchez."

"The photograph with the man holding a sign with Burn All Reds is expressing his hatred for communists."

"You're right, Mr. Sanchez. But couldn't he just as easily been protesting fascists, immigrants or even the police officers you see in the photograph?"

"No way, Miss Eaton. I showed my grandpa the picture and he said the woman holding the sign, Rosenberg Traitors Must Die For Their Crime, was because the Rosenbergs who were communists sold the atom bomb secrets to the Russians."

Belinda smiled. It wasn't easy to engage her students about what they considered "old news" that had nothing to do with their lives. "Did your grandfather tell you what happened to the Rosenbergs?"

Jaime Sanchez flashed a wide smile. "They lit up the commie bastards in the electric chair."

Belinda shifted so the students wouldn't see her smirk as they laughed loudly. She didn't think she would ever get used to their colorful language. She tried to keep the use of expletives in her classroom to a minimum, but knew she was fighting a losing cause.

"Yes," she said, "they were found guilty of spying for the Soviet Union and sentenced to death by execution. Does anyone else have a comment about the photograph?" No hands went up as students lounged in their seats as if in their living rooms. "I need someone to analyze the cartoon from the *Birmingham News* dated June 27, 2002. It's a picture of Uncle Sam with a copy of the Constitution, holding a pencil with the word *security* stamped on it. Uncle Sam's thinking, *So...where do I draw the line?*

"What is the central focus of this cartoon drawn after September 11, 2001? Is the cartoonist saying that the United States should abandon the Constitution, or..." Belinda's words stopped when she saw a student get up and open the window. “Sit down, Mr. Greer,” she ordered when he reached out the window.

The words were barely off her tongue when sunlight glinted on a shiny object in the student’s hand. “Everybody get down!” Belinda screamed before an explosion and flash of light changed the lives of all in the classroom.

Televised footage of past school shootings came back with vivid clarity. Belinda struggled to remember the protocol for such an incident. How was it she could remember the tragic faces of parents and students but not what she’d been told if a similar situation occurred at her school?

It was the second gunshot that jolted her into action as shards of glass and plaster rained down on those huddled under desks. She had to alert the office to initiate an immediate school lockdown. The wail of approaching sirens drowned out the sounds of students’ screams when two more shots shattered the windows. The classroom was under siege as shell casings littered the floor.

Belinda knew it was impossible to reach the wall phone installed in each classroom without exposing herself to the gunman. Crawling on her belly, she opened the lower drawer of the desk, grabbing her handbag. She found her cell and punched in three digits. Her voice was surprisingly calm when she told the 911 operator what was happening. The operator told her that someone else had called in the gunfire and first responders would be there in minutes.

She placed another call—to her mother—and then prayed.

* * *

Griffin sat at the conference room table with the senior vice president of an upscale clothing manufacturer, staring numbly at downtown Chicago through the wall-to-wall window in a towering office building.

Oakley Donovan wanted to offer GR Sports Enterprises, Limited, a lucrative seven-figure deal for a flamboyant tennis pro to model sportswear for next year's spring and summer line. He would've agreed to the deal, yet held out because he wanted Oakley Donovan to commit to all four seasons. A deal which should've been inked in one day but was now into its fourth.

Before he boarded the flight to Chicago, Griffin and Belinda saw their nieces off as they got the bus with twenty-eight other seventh graders for their class trip. She drove him to the airport, and his flight touched down at O'Hare forty minutes before his scheduled meeting. Instead of checking into a hotel he took a taxi directly to Donovan's office building where he was told that Oakley Donovan's wife had gone into labor, giving birth to a baby boy, and he regretfully had to postpone their meeting.

Griffin informed Donovan's executive assistant that he could be reached at the Palmer House in the event that the new father wanted to set up another meeting. During the two days it took for Donovan to reschedule, Griffin attended a Cubs versus Mets baseball game at Wrigley Field, sent Donovan's wife a gift basket for the newborn and sampled the much-touted Chicago hot dog and deep-dish pizza. He became a tourist, picking up souvenir caps and T-shirts for Sabrina, Layla and Belinda.

He'd planned to spend the week at Belinda's house if

he hadn't had the Chicago meeting. Having her so close whenever she slept under his roof and kissing her under the guise of a greeting had begun to test the limits of his patience, of which he had very little.

Griffin laced his fingers together and counted slowly to ten. "It's unfortunate you'll only commit to the spring and summer, because if you decide to use Keats for subsequent seasons, then the price goes up exponentially."

Oakley Donovan found it hard to concentrate. He still hadn't recovered from witnessing the birth of his first son, whom his third and much younger wife insisted on naming after him. "How much more, Rice?"

Griffin's head came up and he stared at the man, who at fifty-nine, should've been rocking his grandchildren instead of a newborn. Oakley Donovan reminded him of a shark—he was all teeth. But he wasn't taken in by the wide grin and genteel manner. Under the custom-made shirt, handmade silk tie and tailored suit beat the cold heart of a shark. Donovan sold a likeness of a model to a cigarette manufacturer without securing a release from the model. It took a decade for the model to settle for an amount, which had made him quite wealthy. He knew Oakley wanted tennis ace David Keats to model his clothing line and Griffin was prepared to hold out until Oakley met his price.

"Double, but only if I'm feeling generous."

Donovan's Adam's apple bobbed up and down like a buoy in choppy water. "And if you're not feeling generous, Rice?"

"It quadruples."

Streaks of red crept up Donovan's neck to his smooth-shaven cheeks. "You're joking, aren't you?"

Griffin shook his head slowly. "No. I'm not very

good when it comes to telling jokes." He almost felt sorry for the man who was the epitome of sophistication. It was easy to see why Oakley Donovan was able to attract women half his age.

The door to the conference opened and a woman with salt-and-pepper hair nodded to her boss. "I'm sorry to disturb you, Mr. Donovan, but I thought you'd want to know that there's been a shooting at a high school in Philadelphia. So far, the newscasters haven't identified the school."

Oakley's teenage daughters from his second marriage lived and went to school in Philadelphia. The color drained from his face at the same time Griffin stood up and pushed back his chair.

Griffin met Oakley's wild-eyed stare. "Do you have a television?" His first thought was of Belinda, who taught at one of the most notorious high schools in the city.

"Yes. In my office."

Minutes later, the two men stood in front of a wall-mounted screen, their gazes fixed on the images of uniformed police in riot gear taking up positions around the perimeter of the school. Fear, stark and vivid, seized Griffin as he read the crawl at the bottom of the screen. A police negotiator had made contact with a lone gunman who was holding his teacher and classmates hostage.

Reaching for his BlackBerry, Griffin punched in a number on speed dial. "Answer the phone, Belinda," he whispered, but the call went to voice mail. His next call was to Roberta Eaton. "Roberta, Griffin. Have you heard anything?"

"Belinda called to let me know that she's okay. She must have turned off her cell phone because it's going straight to voice mail. I've been on my knees praying ever since she called. I don't know what I'd do if I lost another child."

"You're not going to lose her, Roberta."

"I pray you're right. Where are you, Griffin?"

"Chicago."

"When are you coming back?"

"I'll be back as soon as I can book a return flight."

Oakley pulled his gaze away from the television. "Thank goodness it's not my daughters' school."

Griffin glared at the man who was responsible for taking a small apparel company from virtual obscurity to compete with Ralph Lauren and Tommy Hilfiger. "Lucky for you," he drawled facetiously. "The woman I love teaches at that school."

Oakley looked contrite. "Maybe I can help you out. I'll have my driver take you back to your hotel where you can pick up your luggage. From there he'll take you to the airport. The company jet will fly you directly into Philly." He turned to his assistant. "Call the pilot and have him fuel and ready the jet. He'll have one passenger going to Philadelphia International. Also call Leonard and have him bring the car around." He smiled at Griffin. "You better get going, Rice. Call me when things settle down."

Griffin shook the businessman's hand before sprinting out the door. It wasn't until he was seated on the leather seat in the small private jet that he realized he'd spoken his thoughts aloud.

He'd fallen in love with Belinda Eaton.

The jet landed on a private runway at Philadelphia International and Griffin rang Belinda's cell phone.

Again it went to voice mail. He stopped in a terminal long enough to watch a reporter on CNN recap the events of the school shooting and standoff that lasted less than two hours. A police spokesperson reported they had taken one suspect into custody and details of the incident would be made public at a city hall press conference later that evening. Classes were canceled for the next two days and counselors would be available for students, faculty and staff.

He called Roberta again, who told him that Belinda stopped by to prove she was okay.

"Where is she now?"

"Home. I tried to get her to stay, but she said she needed to be alone."

"That's what she doesn't need," he argued.

"I agree, Griffin. Perhaps she'll listen to you."

He smiled for the first time in hours. "I'll take care of her."

There was a noticeable pause. "I know you will."

Griffin flagged down a taxi and gave him Belinda's address. He wasn't convinced that she was all right until he saw her for himself. The driver pulled away from the curbside as if he were taking a road test.

Griffin tapped the Plexiglas partition. "Hey, my man, can't you drive any faster?"

The cabbie glanced over his shoulder. "I take it you're in a hurry?"

Griffin flashed a supercilious grin. "Yes, I am." The taxi driver maneuvered around a slow-moving van, accelerated and took the road leading out of the airport. Pressing his back against the worn seat, Griffin closed his eyes. "Thanks."

Why, he asked himself, did it have to take a life-

and-death situation for him to open his eyes? His relationship with Belinda had been rocky at first until they realized fighting each other was not healthy for their nieces.

He would never replace Grant as their father no matter how hard he tried. But, on the other hand, Belinda had slipped into her role as mother as if she were born to it. Perhaps it had something to do with her being a teacher. She understood children needed and wanted boundaries if they were to feel secure. Sabrina and Layla were given a list of chores they had to fulfill and it was on a rare occasion that a task went undone.

Griffin mentally rehearsed all the things he wanted to say to Belinda but when the taxi maneuvered into the driveway leading to her house they were forgotten when he saw her Volvo parked behind his Lexus.

He felt like a mechanical windup toy when he paid the driver and gathered his bags and mounted the porch steps. Lengthening afternoon shadows shaded a portion of the porch where Belinda liked to sit out in the evening to watch the sun set. She claimed it was her favorite time of the day—the period between dusk and sunset when the world seemed to settle down for the night. It was only when he'd joined her one night that he felt what she felt—a calming peace where poverty, hunger and disease, for a brief nanosecond, did not exist.

Reaching for a key, he inserted it into the lock and pushed open the door. A lamp on the table in the entryway emitted a soft glow as he left his bags in the corner next to a coatrack. Placing one foot in front of the other, Griffin walked through the living room and down the narrow hallway that led to Belinda's bedroom.

The clothes she'd worn that day were on a chair in the dressing room.

Retracing his steps, he headed for the staircase, then stopped when he heard barking coming from the direction of the kitchen. When they were home alone, Nigel and Cecil were given the run of their cage with food and water in an area between the kitchen and pantry.

Griffin checked on the puppies, who, when they saw him, started whining to get out. The bottle attached to the cage was filled with water, the food dishes filled and the bottom of the cage was lined with clean pads. He smiled and shook his head. Despite all that she'd encountered, Belinda had still found time to take care of the puppies. She took care of everyone, but there was no one to take care of her.

Griffin had promised his brother that he would take care of his children and he'd also promised Roberta that he would take care of Belinda—and he would. He took the back staircase to the second floor. The door to the bathroom stood open and when he peered in Griffin was stunned by the scene unfolding before him.

Belinda lay in the bathtub filled with bubbles, sipping from a wineglass. A half-empty bottle of wine rested on a low table next to the tub. Music flowed from a radio on a corner shelf. Leaning against the doorframe, he stared at the moisture dotting her face. Wisps from her upswept hairdo clung to her forehead and cheek, but she didn't seem to mind getting her hair wet.

"Would you like company?"

Belinda sat up, nearly upsetting the table with the wine when her elbow knocked into it. "What are you doing here?" she asked in a breathless whisper.

Straightening, Griffin gave her a tender smile. "I came to see if you're all right."

Placing the glass on the table, Belinda slipped lower into the water. "Of course I'm all right. Why wouldn't I be?"

A slight frown creased his forehead. Had she forgotten what had happened at her school that afternoon, or had she deliberately blocked it out of her mind? "Are you sure you're okay, Belinda?"

"Of course I am! I wish everyone would stop asking me if I'm all right. I'm alive, Griffin. Isn't that enough?"

The tears Belinda had managed to keep at bay pricked the backs of her eyelids, but she was helpless to stop them once they fell. Fat, hot tears rolled down her face and into the froth of bubbles.

Taking off his jacket and tie, Griffin dropped them on a chair and went to his knees. He reached down and lifted Belinda into his arms. "Cry and let it all out. I'm here," he repeated over and over until her sobs lessened to soft hiccuping sounds. It was then that he wrapped her naked body in a bath sheet and carried her downstairs to her bedroom.

Placing her on the bed, his body following hers down, they lay together, his chest against her back. "Feeling better, baby?"

"I think I'm drunk, Griffin. I drank more than half the bottle of wine."

He kissed the nape of her neck. "Go to sleep."

"All the kids were screaming."

"Don't, baby. Go to sleep. We'll talk about it tomorrow."

"Will you stay with me tonight?"

"Of course. I'll stay with you tonight, tomorrow night and every night after that."

"Do you know what?" Belinda's words were slurring.

"What, darling?" A silence ensued, and Griffin thought she'd fallen asleep.

"I like you, Griffin Rice."

There came another prolonged silence before he spoke again. "And I love you, Belinda Eaton." The sound of snoring answered his confession. She'd fallen asleep.

He dimmed the table lamp to the lowest setting, removed the bath sheet and pulled the sheet up over her body. He wanted to stay in bed with Belinda, but it was too much of a temptation. If and when he did make love to her he wanted her willing and not under the influence.

Griffin lost track of time as he sat on the side of the bed, watching her sleep. When he did finally get up it was to let the water out of the bathtub, cork the wine bottle, and turn off the radio and light.

He sat in the living room staring numbly at the television as the mayor, police department and school officials all took credit for quickly defusing a volatile situation without loss of life.

Reporters had interviewed students who speculated as to what had had happened but they were unable to get the true story because the students in the American history and government classroom where the shooting and standoff had occurred refused to speak to the press.

Griffin felt a sinking feeling in the pit of his stomach. He knew the student with the gun was Belinda's.

Chapter 8

Bright sunlight coming in through the windows and the fragrant smell of coffee greeted Belinda when she sat up in bed. She peered down at her naked breasts and realization dawned. Griffin had come, and he'd put her in bed. Reaching for the silk wrap at her feet, she pushed her arms into the sleeves and belted it. The sour taste on her tongue was a reminder of the wine she'd drunk the night before. Right now she needed to brush her teeth and rinse her mouth, shower and get dressed. She walked out of the bedroom and made her way to the half bath off the kitchen.

Belinda's stomach did a flip-flop when she ran into Griffin. "Good morning," she mumbled, not breaking stride.

Griffin smiled. "Good morning, beautiful." He'd gotten up early to take care of the puppies, and instead of going back to the sleeper-sofa he decided to surprise Belinda with breakfast in bed.

"I'll be out in a few minutes," she said, closing the bathroom door behind her.

He waited for Belinda to emerge from the small bathroom, handing her a mug of steaming coffee. She smelled like mint. "Take this and go back to bed. Breakfast should be ready in about ten minutes."

Belinda pressed her lips to his stubbly jaw. "I have a confession to make."

Griffin resisted the urge to kiss the full, lush lips inches from his own. If he knew it would've been a mistake to sleep with her the night before, he was more than aware this morning that if he kissed Belinda Eaton he wouldn't finish breakfast, and he would carry her into the bedroom, put her on her back and be inside her before he'd be able to stop himself.

He closed his eyes, shutting out the image of her mussed hair falling provocatively around her scrubbed face. Griffin knew what lay under the silky fabric, and if she didn't leave—now—he doubted whether he'd be able to control the lower portion of his body.

"What is it?" His question sounded angry.

Tears filled Belinda's eyes. "I lied to my mother yesterday when I told her I was all right. I wasn't, Griffin. When that kid fired that gun all I thought about were mothers having to bury their children. And if he'd killed me, then it would be the second time in less than six months for my mother."

Griffin eased the mug from her fingers and put it on the cooking island. He cradled her face in his hands. "If you want to talk about it, I'll listen. But we don't have to do it now. You're going to eat, and then pack a bag. I'm bringing you home with me."

Belinda shook her head. "I don't—"

"I don't want you to fight with me, Lindy," he interrupted. "Now, take your coffee and get into bed."

She took the mug. "Why are you trying to sound like a daddy?"

"That's because I am a daddy."

Belinda hadn't walked out of the kitchen when the doorbell rang. The sound set off a chorus of barking from the Yorkies. She glanced over at the clock on the microwave. It wasn't eight o'clock.

Griffin held up a hand. "I'll see who it is."

He didn't want her answering the door wearing next to nothing. After showering, he'd slipped into a pair of jeans and T-shirt. After his first sleep-over he left several changes of clothes, underwear and grooming products at Belinda's house.

He opened the door to find two conservatively dressed young black men standing on the porch. "Whatever you're selling we're not buying."

The taller of the two held up a hand. "Wait, mister. We're reporters and we'd like to talk to Belinda Eaton about the shooting incident in her classroom yesterday."

"Miss Eaton is not home," Griffin lied smoothly. "Now, I'd appreciate it if you'd leave."

"But isn't that her car?" the other man asked, pointing to the Volvo with her high school faculty parking sticker affixed to the rear bumper.

A muscle in Griffin's jaw tensed as he clenched his teeth. "Get off this property before I have you arrested for trespassing."

"Look, my brother, we're just trying to get a story for our college newspaper."

Griffin bit back a smile. "Oh, now I'm your brother. What college?"

"Temple," they said in unison.

"Do you have a press badge?"

"Sorry."

"I forgot mine."

"What kind of idiot do you take me for, *my brothers?*" Griffin shouted. "Any self-respecting, aspiring journalist would have a press badge. I graduated Temple even before you two were zygotes, and I remember that anyone who worked on the college paper carried identification. I'm Miss Eaton's attorney and as such I've instructed her not to speak to the press. I'm going to give you some advice for which I usually charge my clients seven hundred-fifty an hour." He glared at the two young men. "Never play the race card, because it's immature and cheesy. Good day, gentlemen."

Stepping back, Griffin closed the door, leaving them staring at the door, then each other. Someone wanted an eyewitness account of what had occurred in her classroom and they were willing to pay to get it. If Belinda wanted to talk to the media she would've done it yesterday, unless she was instructed not to say anything by school officials.

The school board had closed the high school, giving students two extra days of spring break. Griffin would use the time to help Belinda heal, and hopefully forget that she could've possibly become another school shooting statistic.

"Why are you treating me as if I were an invalid?"

Griffin tightened his hold under Belinda's legs as he

carried her to the patio. "Haven't you ever had a man spoil you?"

"No—I mean, yes."

"Which is it, Lindy?"

Belinda closed her eyes, shutting out his intense stare. She hadn't been given a choice when Griffin told her to pack a bag with enough clothes to last a week, adding that she should include a few for dining out. He put Nigel and Cecil into the crate he stored in the back of his SUV and called Roberta to let her know that he was taking her daughter to his house to get away from the hysteria. They made one stop—to the post office to fill out the form to stop the delivery of her mail. Smiling and looking quite smug, Griffin headed out in a westerly direction towards Paoli.

She opened her eyes when he lowered her to the chaise. "I don't want to be spoiled."

Leaning over her prone figure, Griffin kissed the end of her nose. "What do you want?"

"I wanted to be respected as a grown woman, Griffin, and not someone who can't think for herself."

He folded his body down beside her. "You think I don't respect you? If I didn't respect you, Belinda, I would've taken advantage of you last night. You'd had too much to drink, and even though you claim you can beat me up with one arm tied behind your back I doubt whether your martial arts training would've become a factor." He leaned closer. "Black belt notwithstanding, physically you're no match for me."

For a long moment, Belinda looked back at Griffin, mesmerized by the stubble on his jaw and chin and asking herself which Griffin Rice she liked better—the urbane attorney who wore tailored suits and Italian footwear, or the laid-back unshaven man who was visually delicious in a pair of jeans and T-shirt. Seeing him dressed down with the sunlight providing a backlight for his rich olive-hued face answered her question. She much preferred this version.

"I know. I just said that to scare you."

His eyebrows shot up. "You don't have a black belt?"

"Oh, I have the belt."

"Why, then, did you want to scare me?"

Belinda hesitated, choosing her words carefully. "I didn't want you to get too close to me."

"Why, Lindy?"

Her delicate jaw tightened. "Because the only man I ever let get that close hurt me physically and emotionally, and I swore it would never happen again."

Griffin placed a hand on the side of her face. "What did he do to you?"

Belinda formed her thoughts in some semblance of order. What she was going to tell Griffin was something she'd never revealed to anyone, including her parents. The incident was branded in her memory for eternity, changing and making her into what she'd become.

"Joel Thurman and I started dating in high school, and when it came time to go to college he switched his first choice so we could be together."

"Were you sleeping with him?"

Belinda nodded. "My first time was the night of our senior prom. We both lived on campus, and he slept in my dorm room more than he did his own. But everything changed when I joined a study group and he thought I was cheating on him with another boy. We argued constantly because he wanted me to quit the group."

"Did you?"

"No. The kids in the group were my friends, and if I'd left then it would prove I'd been cheating on him. One night he came to my room and found one of my study buddies sleeping in my bed. The boy had asked to lie down because he wasn't feeling well. Joel told me he was going to the library to pick up a book. I should've known something wasn't right when he said I'd better be alone when he got back.

"I woke Khaled and told him he had to leave. He'd come down with the flu and I had to get several guys to help get him back to his room. Joel returned, closed the door and told me that if he ever found me alone in my room with a man again he would kill me. He threw me on the bed, ripped off my panties and proceeded to rape me. I started to fight back until something told me not to move. When I went completely still, he pulled out, and all my martial arts training came back as if I were in a competition.

"What amazed me is that no one came to see what the noise was all about. I literally kicked his ass all around the room. It was the first and last time I ever felt like murdering another human being. Joel jumped out a second-story window to escape. After I came to my senses, I straightened up my room, then called Myles, asking him to come and get me. Three days later I went back to school, cleaned out my room and moved off campus."

"What happened to Joel?"

"He broke his right arm in the fall, but told everyone he'd slipped and fell headfirst down a flight of stairs."

"Did he move off campus, too?"

Belinda shook her head. "He stayed while I commuted. Every time he saw me he went in the opposite direction."

Now Griffin had the answer to why Belinda moved back home. "You didn't think about charging him with attempted rape?"

"No. If I'd told my brother that Joel tried to rape me he would've killed him. He took his role as older brother to three sisters very seriously. It's a wonder that Grant was able to get close to Donna after my brother's brutal interrogation."

"That's because Rice men don't scare easily."

Belinda lowered her gaze to stare at him from under her lashes. "Does anything frighten you?"

Cradling her face between his palms, Griffin leaned even closer. "Not having you in my life frightens the hell out of me."

Her lashes flew up, her heart beating like that of a tiny, frightened bird. "But I am in your life, Griffin. We'll be together for the next eleven years."

"A marriage of eleven years isn't that long," he teased.

"It doesn't matter because we're not married."

He nodded. "You're right."

They weren't married and Griffin wondered if he or Belinda would ever marry. In eleven years they would be forty-eight and forty-three, respectively. Not too old to marry, but in his opinion a bit old to become parents. But with the advances in modern medicine, many forty-year-olds were giving birth to healthy babies.

Realizing he'd fallen in love with Belinda Eaton was an awakening and sobering experience. It left him reeling from a sense of fulfillment that graduating college, law school, passing the bar or negotiating multimillion-dollar contracts couldn't match.

Griffin closed his eyes for several seconds. "Would you like to get married?" he asked, staring at the woman who unwittingly had captured his heart. The brilliant sunlight flattered her smooth skin, affording it the appearance of rich dark-chocolate mousse.

Belinda's eyebrows lifted. "Are you proposing or asking a question?"

Griffin would've said proposing if he was certain Belinda was in love with him. Admitting that she liked him wasn't tantamount to a marriage proposal or a commitment to spend the rest of their lives together.

"I was asking a question," he said instead.

Belinda shrugged a shoulder. "I think I would one of these days. But it can't be until the girls are legally emancipated. It would be unfair to bring a new man into their lives when they're so attached to you."

Now you're talking, he mused. That meant she wasn't going to marry Sunshine—at least not for the next eleven years. "I feel the same way about other women."

"I thought you didn't have other women."

"I *used* to see other women." He brushed a kiss over her parted lips. "Do I detect a hint of jealousy?"

She wrinkled her nose. "Maybe a little."

"Now, why is that?" Griffin asked as he placed light kisses at the corners of her mouth.

"Because I like you."

"I'm willing to wager that I like you more than you like me."

Looping her arms under his shoulders, Belinda leaned into the man who made her ache for him. While she'd lain on the floor of the classroom, waiting for death, she thought about her parents, brother, younger sister and her nieces who'd recently lost their parents and could possibly lose their aunt. Then, when she least expected it, images of Griffin Rice had swept over her. She'd recalled everything about him: his face, smile, the attractive cleft in his strong chin, his melodious baritone, the natural masculine scent of his bare skin that elicited erotic fantasies and his touch that ignited a fire only he could extinguish.

"It doesn't matter, Griffin, because I don't gamble."

He gave her a wink. "I do like you, Lindy Eaton."

She returned the wink. "Why don't you show me how much you like me."

Griffin was about to finish what they'd started and stopped so many times. He wanted Belinda so much that he couldn't remember when he didn't want her. She'd become as essential to him as breathing was to sustaining life. Reaching out, he swept her off the chaise and carried her into the house. Aside from Cecil and Nigel, who were huddled together in their cage asleep, there was just the two of them.

Belinda buried her face between the neck and shoulder of her soon-to-be lover, closing her eyes. She needed him to take away the hurt and pain that marred the good times in her life. As the third child, and the second daughter of Dwight and Roberta Eaton, she'd grown up loved and protected.

Then there was Joel Thurman, the young man to whom she'd given her most precious gift—her virginity—who'd shattered her trust in men. It took years before she felt secure enough to become involved with another man. Her second foray into the dating game started well but ended badly. She learned to never date someone with whom you work.

She was no longer a virgin and she didn't live or work with Griffin. He wasn't looking to get married and neither was she. They shared custody of their nieces, which meant they would always share a special bond that would continue beyond Sabrina and Layla's twenty-third birthdays. The bond was further strengthened because her sister had married his brother.

They were family.

Griffin concentrated on counting the number of steps that took him to his bedroom rather than think of the woman in his arms. His vow not to become involved with his nieces' godmother was shattered the first time he kissed her. He knew he'd been attracted to Belinda during their first encounter, which now seemed so long ago. Yet his ego hadn't allowed him to admit that a woman hadn't succumbed to his so-called charm. What had worked with so many women was wasted on Belinda Eaton. Most times she looked past him as if he didn't exist, or when she did meet his gaze he saw revulsion and indifference.

Annoyed because he liked her and she appeared to merely tolerate his presence, he thought she was stuck-up, a snob. What he hadn't known was that if she hadn't fought off her attacker, then she would've been a rape victim. If he'd known Joel Thurman at that time he would've sustained more serious injuries than a broken arm. Griffin would've broken his neck.

Belinda opened her eyes when she felt the firmness of the mattress under her body. She lay on a king-size bed with massive carved posts. Her gaze widened when

Griffin moved over her, supporting his weight on his elbows.

Griffin studied her intently. “Let me know if you’re ready to do this.”

Belinda framed his lean face with her hands as a mysterious smile softened her mouth. “I was ready a long time ago, but I didn’t know it.”

She’d fallen in love with Griffin Rice on sight. She’d watched her sister with Grant, praying she could have the same with Griffin.

It was not to be. While she pined for him from afar he flitted from woman to woman like a modern-day Casanova. His rakish behavior had become a sobering awakening to her yearning for what she would never have, and in the end she concluded she hadn’t been in love, but just infatuated with her brother-in-law.

Now, she wasn’t so sure.

Chapter 9

Belinda felt a rush of desire, anticipation and a physical craving for the man who made her question why she'd been celibate and why she continued to deny the very reason she'd been born female.

Griffin's hands slipped under her T-shirt, gathering fabric as he began the task of baring her body. Her breath quickened, her chest rising and falling as his fingers traced the outline of her breasts through the sheer white bra. With a minimum of effort, he released the clasp, freeing the firm mounds of flesh.

His heated gaze caressed bared flesh. "You're more perfect than I'd imagined." He'd only caught a glimpse of her naked body the night before.

Griffin had waited years for Belinda, waited while the world changed, he'd changed and she'd changed from a reticent nineteen-year-old college student into a sensual, confident woman who kept him off balance. She'd had a sexual encounter that'd left scars, and he knew he had to get her to trust him if they were going to have a fulfilling love life.

His hands traced the curve of her midriff, the indentation of her waist and the flare of her hips. Lowering his head, he brushed his mouth over hers, moist breaths mingling, tongues tasting and fusing as banked passions stirred to life. Griffin wanted to take Belinda hard and fast but forced himself to go slow.

"I won't hurt you, baby. I'll never hurt you."

Belinda didn't know whether Griffin was talking about physical or emotional hurt. She knew instinctually that if he did hurt her it would be unintentional. His hands and mouth were doing things to her she'd forgotten, and she resisted the urge to move her hips. But her body refused to follow the dictates of her brain when she arched off the mattress with the intent of getting closer to him.

Her need, the urgency to feel him inside her, communicated itself to Griffin. Sitting back on his heels, he released the waistband and zipper on her jeans and eased them down her legs, the denim fabric joining her shirt and bra on the carpet beside the bed. All that remained was her bikini panties. They, too, joined the pile of clothing, and Griffin was able to see what layers of fabric had concealed from his inquisitive gaze.

He smiled. Belinda Eaton's body matched the exquisiteness of her face. Shapely calves, slender ankles and feet, flat belly, a narrow waist and rib cage he could span with both hands and a pair of firm breasts that didn't require the support of a bra to hold them up. His hungry, heated gaze lingered briefly on her parted lips before journeying down the length of her body and then reversing itself.

Belinda closed her eyes as a slow, warming desire raced through her body. She couldn't understand why Griffin continued to stare at her rather than make love to her. He knew she was waiting for him, that she'd been ready for him for what now seemed a lifetime ago. On the Friday or Saturday nights she'd sat home alone because she didn't have a date or had turned one down, she pondered where would she have been if she hadn't rebuffed Griffin Rice's subtle overtures. Would she still be single and childless if she hadn't declined his invitations?

She'd loved him from afar, but that love was bittersweet because she had gotten him by default. Fate had intervened and offered her a chance to be with the man she loved, if only temporarily. They were given eleven years to be together before going their separate ways to lead separate lives. But Belinda was facing a dilemma. After sharing her body with Griffin would she be able to walk away unscathed? Would she become an emotional cripple and not be able to let him go? Or would she revert to the woman who with a single hostile glare was able to keep men at a distance and out of her bed?

"Are you certain you want this?" Griffin asked Belinda. "Are you willing to do this for the next eleven years without asking for more?"

Belinda was too stunned to speak. So she did the next best thing. She nodded. Why would he ask her something like that? She lay in his bed, butt-naked, her body thrumming from a desire only he could assuage, and he wanted to ask her about eleven years from now.

No one knew where they'd be the next day, so a decade was more than a stretch.

Reaching for the hem of his T-shirt, Griffin pulled it up and over his head. He felt as if he were in a hypnotic trance—that what was about to happen wasn't actually happening, that he was dreaming and when he awoke he would be in bed—alone. He'd lost count of the women with whom he bedded or dated that had become Belinda Eaton in his fantasies. It took a long time for him to rid himself of the guilt that he was lusting after his sister-in-law, because they didn't share a bloodline. His brother had fallen in love with her sister, and he, in turn, had fallen in love with her.

He smiled at Belinda. "I had to ask."

His hands were steady as he relieved himself of his jeans and boxers in one, smooth motion. He glanced down when he heard Belinda gasp and saw the direction of her gaze. He was aroused. His erection so hard it was painful—exquisite, pleasurable pain.

What Griffin had hoped for wasn't going to happen. He'd wanted making love with Belinda to be slow, but the inferno in his groin threatened to incinerate him. Leaning over, he opened the drawer to the nightstand and took out a condom. His hands shook slightly when he opened the packet and sheathed his tumescence in latex.

They shared a smile when Belinda raised her arms and opened her legs to welcome Griffin Rice not only into her life but also into her body. She'd had years to prepare for something she'd fantasized over and over. Instinctively, her body arched toward him, her arms going around his neck.

She was helpless to halt the gasps and soft moans

that slipped past her parted lips when Griffin's rapacious mouth explored the skin on her neck, shoulders, journeying down the length of her body to stake his claim between her thighs. Men had touched her *there,* but none had ever kissed her *there.*

Griffin's tongue searched and found the swollen nub shimmering with moisture, his tongue worshipping the folds between the tangled curls concealing her femininity. Belinda smelled sweet, tasted sweet. The smell of desire became an aphrodisiac that threatened to take him beyond himself. He pushed his face closer while inhaling her essence. Now he knew what men meant when they claimed they wanted to climb inside a woman.

Passion pounded, whirling the blood through Belinda's heart, head and chest. She was mindless with desire for a man she hadn't planned to love, a man whom she'd never let know she loved him.

She was on fire! Griffin's hands and mouth had started a blaze and there was only one way it could be extinguished.

Her hands came down, her fingertips biting into the muscle and sinew covering his shoulders. Her body was throbbing, between her legs was thrumming an ancient rhythm that forced her to move.

"Griffin! Please stop." Her whispered entreaty became a litany of desperation. "Don't torment me."

Griffin pressed a lingering kiss to Belinda's quivering thighs. He couldn't believe she was begging him not to torment her when that's exactly what she'd been doing for thirteen years. Well, he was going to end the torment—for both of them.

He positioned his rigid flesh at the entrance to her femininity. Like a heat-seeking missile locked on its target, he eased his sex into Belinda, registering the gasps against his ear. It was his turn to gasp when the walls of her vagina closed tightly around him, holding him captive in a sensual vise from which he didn't want to escape.

Griffin pushed gently, in and out, setting a strong thrusting rhythm Belinda followed easily.

He pushed.

She pushed back.

He rolled his hips.

She rolled her hips.

Still joined, Griffin went to his knees, slipped his hands under her hips and lifted her legs off the mattress. Together they found a tempo that bound their bodies together, making them one.

Belinda stared up at her lover, awed by the carnal expression on his face as she felt his sex swell, becoming harder and plunging deeper into her once-chaste body. She and Griffin had become man and woman, flesh against flesh. He'd become her lover and she his. The flutters began softly, growing more intense and seeking an escape.

"Griffin!"

She screamed his name in strident desperation, making the hair on the back of Griffin's neck stand up. Heat, followed by chills and another swath of heat shook him from head to toe, finally settling at the base of his spine. He affected a slow, rocking motion that escalated to powerful thrusts punctuated with groans overlapping moans of ecstasy when Belinda and Griffin succumbed to a shared passion and they surrendered all they were to each other.

Collapsing on the slender body beneath him, Griffin waited for his breathing to return to normal at the same time Belinda's breath came in long, surrendering moans. She was exquisite—in and out of bed.

Belinda pushed against Griffin's shoulder in an attempt to get him to move off her. "Darling, you're crushing me."

Rolling off her, Griffin reversed their positions, sandwiching her legs between his. He smiled up at her moist face. "Am I really your darling?"

She offered him a small, demure smile. "Yes. But that's because I'm your baby."

A soft chuckle rumbled in his broad chest. "That you are."

Belinda sobered quickly. "If we're going to sleep together, then I'm going on the Pill."

"You don't trust me to protect you?"

"It's not about trust, Griffin. It's personal. If I did become pregnant, then it becomes my responsibility."

Griffin didn't have a comeback to her decision to take responsibility for contraception. It was her body, and he had no right to tell her what to do with her body. And, he also wanted Belinda to trust him—with her life and her future.

"Are you sure?" he asked.

Belinda nodded. "I'm very sure. I want to plan for my children. If and when I decide to start a family I'd like to get pregnant in the fall and deliver as close to the summer as possible. Then, I'll have two to three months to bond with my baby before the start of the next school year."

Griffin stared at Belinda in disbelief. She was more anal that he'd originally thought. "What happens if you don't get pregnant in the fall?"

"I'll wait and try again the following year."

He wanted to tell her that her view of family planning was asinine but didn't want to say anything to jeopardize the fact that they'd taken their relationship to another level. Asinine or not, he loved Belinda, enough to agree to almost anything and everything she wanted.

Belinda moved off Griffin's body and lay beside him. Turning on her side, she settled back against him, enjoying the feel of his arm around her as she pressed her hips to his groin and they lay like two spoons. The slight ache between her legs was a reminder of certain muscles she hadn't used in a long time. She emitted a soft sigh as she closed her eyes and shifted into a more comfortable position.

"Are you all right?" Griffin's breath swept over the nape of her neck.

Belinda frowned. "I'm good. I'm really good."

"No flashbacks from yesterday?"

Griffin hadn't broached the subject of the school shooting because he wanted Belinda to open up to him on her own. But she hadn't, and he feared she'd suppressed the horrific incident. He wanted and needed her to talk about it before their charges returned home. If Belinda had a meltdown in front of the girls, he feared it would prove damaging to their continuing emotional healing.

"No. That's not to say I won't have nightmares later on."

"Do you plan to talk to a counselor?"

"I don't know. I'm praying I don't lose it when classes resume."

"I think you should consider seeing a counselor."

"I don't need one when I have you. I've revealed

things to you about my past that I've never told anyone. And I'm counting on attorney-client privilege that you won't repeat it."

Griffin laughed. "What goes on in the bedroom stays in the bedroom."

There came a prolonged silence, as Belinda mentally relived the two hours before the police negotiator was able to defuse what could've been a massacre if the student had panicked.

"I was more afraid for the kid with the gun than for myself and the other students," she said in a soft voice that Griffin had to strain to hear. "He had become a victim in a situation not of his choosing."

"Why would you say that?"

"He's what I call an outsider. He doesn't fit in with the nerds or with the jocks. He was taken in by a boy who wanted him to shoot a female student because she wanted nothing more to do with him."

"If your school has metal detectors, then how did he get the gun past the security checkpoint?"

"Someone passed it to him through the window. He must have lost his nerve because he fired shots at the ceiling and windows rather than at his intended target. After I called 911, I tried to convince him to throw the gun out the window. He started crying and fired off another round. We lay on the floor under desks until a SWAT team surrounded the school building and a police negotiator called the classroom and tried to convince him to release his hostages."

"How did it end?" Griffin asked.

"He gave up his friend who'd set up the hit, then asked to speak to his mother. I don't know what she said to him, but he removed the clip from the gun and tossed both out the window. The police stormed the classroom like marines hitting a beach, and that was more traumatizing than someone with a gun who hadn't the nerve to step on a bug. I hope wherever he winds up that he'll get some help."

Griffin splayed his fingers over her belly. "Let's hope his parents can convince a judge that he's not a criminal, but a troubled youth."

Turning over, Belinda stared at her lover. "He's a good kid, and one of my best students. His mother is a single mother with five kids who works two jobs to keep her family together. Do you think you can—"

Griffin stopped her when he put his hand over her mouth. "No, baby, I will not take on his case. I'm shaky at best when it comes to criminal law. What I'll do is call a friend who'll occasionally take pro bono cases to see if the boy has been appointed a public defender."

Belinda trailed her fingers down Griffin's smooth chest to his belly and still lower to the flaccid flesh between his muscular thighs. "Thank you, darling."

Griffin felt his sex harden quickly when Belinda caressed him in an up-and-down motion. A swath of desire left him gasping as he struggled to force air into his lungs. Her hands and fingers worked their magic, squeezing and manipulating his erection until he feared spilling his passion on the sheets.

Somewhere between the vestiges of sanity and insanity, he managed to extract her hand, slip on protection and entered Belinda in one, sure thrust of his hips. He rode her fast, hard and when they reversed positions Belinda, bracing her hands on his chest and thighs, took him to heights of passion he'd glimpsed but never experienced. It ended when they collapsed to the moist sheets, both struggling to breathe.

Belinda stared at Griffin through half-lowered lids when he slipped off the bed to discard the condoms. She went into Griffin's outstretched arms when he returned. They lay together, limbs entwined, and fell asleep.

Chapter 10

Belinda avoided watching television because she didn't want to be reminded of the incident at her high school. Her mother had called to say reporters had come by when they were informed that the teacher whose classroom was under siege was the daughter of Dr. Dwight Eaton.

Belinda, sitting on a high stool in Griffin's kitchen, rolled her eyes even though Roberta couldn't see her. "Mama, why is the media trying to turn this into a Columbine? And what the hell are they talking about when they said the school was under siege? I'm not attempting to minimize what happened but shouldn't everyone be happy that no one was killed?"

"Bullets and carnage sell newspapers and commercial airtime, not feel-good stories. You should know that, Lindy."

"I do, Mama."

"If you do, then you should know the entire country is looking at us, because most of the school shootings have been in rural areas, not a major urban city like Philly. What I'm afraid of is copycat idiots who want either their names in the paper or are looking for martyrdom. It seems as if there're more fools out here than sensible folk."

"I think you're right."

"I know I'm right, Lindy. Now, how are you getting along with Griffin?"

"We're good."

"I didn't ask about Griffin. I asked about you, Belinda Jacqueline Eaton."

Belinda took in a quick breath. It wasn't often her mother called her by her given name, and it was even rarer when she referred to her by her full name. "I'm getting along very well with him, thank you very much. In fact, we're going out to dinner tonight."

"I've always liked Griffin. It always struck me as odd why he hasn't settled down."

"Maybe you should ask him the next time you see him, Roberta Alice Stewart-Eaton."

A soft laugh came through the earpiece of Belinda's cell phone. "Of all my children you were always the most vocal one, Lindy."

"Didn't you raise your daughters to speak their minds?"

"Yes, I did. Outspoken or not, I'd like to see you married so you can give me a few more grandchildren."

"It's not going to happen, Mama, until Sabrina and Layla turn twenty-three."

"Twenty-three is not a magic number, Lindy. Things

will begin to change next year when the girls turn thirteen and become young adults. Staying home with their mom and dad playing Scrabble or Uno will no longer hold their interest. It'll be the mall, movies, the beach and sleep-overs. You'll have to make an appointment just to see them once they start driving. After that it'll be college, football games, fiancés and marriage. And where will you be? Sitting home waiting for someone to knock on the door to tell you that he's the man you've spent your life waiting for? I don't think so, Belinda."

Belinda couldn't stop the smile spreading across her face. "I get your point, Mama."

"If that's the case, then I'm going to hang up because *my man* is waiting to take me away for the weekend." Roberta had cancelled Sunday dinner because her granddaughters were away.

"Have fun, Mama, and tell Daddy if he can't be good, then he should be careful."

"I will," Roberta said, laughing. "Enjoy your night out."

"Thank you. Enjoy your weekend."

Belinda ended the call and slipped off the stool. She went still when she saw Griffin standing at the entrance to the kitchen. How long had he been there, and how much of the conversation with her mother had he overheard?

She flashed a brittle smile. "I'm ready."

Griffin approached Belinda, his dark gaze unreadable. They'd spent the past three days "playing house." They slept and took turns cooking. He'd returned to Philly to finalize the relocation of GR Sports Enterprises, Limited. All of the files were in cartons and labeled with their contents. He'd contracted with a bonded moving company, and the cartons were delivered earlier that morning. Griffin knew he had to go through every sheet of paper to ascertain what he would keep and what would be shredded.

Unlike many sports attorneys and agents his client list was limited to six. It was a number he could manage without taking on a partner, and it permitted him the option of being very selective. There were athletes who'd solicited him to represent them and he'd turned them down—some because of a history of substance abuse or run-ins with the law, or those who wanted him to become a miracle worker when they requested astronomical salaries that were out of line. His baseball-attendance clause was legendary. If a ballplayer put fans in stadium seats, then they were guaranteed a share of the profits. He'd done well for his clients, and the money he earned from negotiating their contracts and endorsements afforded him a very comfortable lifestyle.

"You look very chic."

Belinda nodded. "Thank you."

When Griffin informed her that he'd made dinner reservations at Barclay Prime, a popular steak house in Rittenhouse, the former neighborhood of Philadelphia's blue bloods, she'd decided to wear a tailored light gray wool gabardine suit with a darker gray silk blouse. Her accessories were a single strand of pearls and matching studs in her pierced lobes. Griffin was drop-dead gorgeous in a chocolate-brown suit, white shirt and checked tie.

He winked at Belinda. She wore the straighter, sleek hairstyle he favored because it made her appear more sophisticated, womanly. Whenever she affected the curly style her personality reflected her more playful side.

Reaching for her hand, Griffin brought it to his lips, kissing her fingers before he tucked it into the bend of his elbow. "We have to leave now." He'd had to work a minor miracle to secure a reservation on such short notice. He'd become a regular customer since he dined there with his clients, their friends and family members.

Leaning into him, Belinda rested her forehead against his ear. "I have something to tell you," she whispered cryptically.

Griffin froze. Was she going to tell him what he'd been waiting to hear? Each time they made love he had to bite down on his lower lip to keep from blurting out that he'd fallen in love with her.

He gave her a sidelong look. "What is it?"

A mysterious smile played at the corners of her mouth. "I could very easily get used to playing house with you."

Griffin couldn't help smiling. It wasn't what he wanted to hear, but it was close enough. "I'm very happy to know that."

Belinda blinked once. "Do we have to stay in character while in public?"

His smile faded. "What are you talking about?"

"We're going out together and how do you want me to relate to you? Am I a friend or something more?"

"We are what we are."

"And what's that, Griffin?"

He glared at her. "We are lovers," Griffin spat out, enunciating each word.

We are lovers. The three words stayed with Belinda during the drive from Paoli and into Philadelphia, while Griffin parked his sport-utility vehicle in a garage on

Chancellor Street, and it reminded her of their status when she and her *lover* were seated in the lounge waiting for a table.

Griffin caressed her hair, smoothing wayward strands clinging to her cheek. "Have you ever dined here?"

It hadn't surprised Belinda that Griffin was on first-name basis with the maître d' and waitstaff. She stared at a spot over his shoulder, refusing to look directly at him and still smarting from his brusque response to her query as to their status. It was Griffin who was the cause célèbre whom paparazzi photographed with actresses, models or recording artists.

Fortunately for her, her fifteen minutes of fame was thwarted by the school superintendent's refusal to disclose or verify the names of his teachers or students to the press, leading Belinda to believe it was a student or a parent who'd leaked her name.

"No. This is my first time."

Resting an arm on the bar, Griffin stared at Belinda's tight expression. "I'm sorry."

"For what, Griffin?" Belinda decided she wasn't going to make it easy for him. She wasn't going to establish a precedence of having him snap at her, only to apologize later when he didn't have to use the tone from the onset.

"I'm sorry for the way I spoke to you. I had no right—"

"You better believe you had no right," she countered. "I told you before I'll not be talked down to or yelled at. Why is that so difficult for you to grasp?"

"Dammit, Belinda! I said I was sorry. What do you want me to do, get on my knees?"

Pursing her mouth and appearing deep in thought, Belinda gave him a direct stare. The sooty shadow on her eyelids made her eyes look seductive and mysterious. "No, Griffin. I don't want you to crawl. It wouldn't be good for your image."

"What image?"

"Griff, darling. Is that you?"

Belinda and Griffin turned at the same time to see a woman in a stretch-knit black dress that was at least two sizes too small for her voluptuous body. Her balance was compromised by four-inch stilettos, a platinum wig circa 1760 and breast augmentation; layers of nut-brown pancake makeup failed to conceal an outbreak of adult acne.

Griffin moved off his stool, frowning. He loathed having to acknowledge a woman he wanted to forget. "Hello, Deanna. How are you?"

"It's all good, handsome." Light brown eyes framed by thick black false lashes focused on the woman with Griffin Rice. "How long has it been, Griff?"

"It has to be a couple of years."

"Try three," Deanna drawled. "You're forgetting your manners, darling. Aren't you going to introduce me to your *little date?*"

Wrapping an arm around Belinda's waist, Griffin moved behind her stool. "Belinda, this is Deanna…"

"Monique," Deanna supplied. "Remember you used to joke about me having two first names?"

Griffin's expression was impassive. "Belinda, this is Deanna Monique," he began again as if Deanna hadn't interrupted him. "Deanna, this is Belinda Eaton."

Deanna waved her left hand and light caught the fire of a large diamond solitaire on her ring finger. Belinda found it difficult to pinpoint the woman's age, so she estimated somewhere between thirty-five and forty. She thought her cute in a Kewpie doll sort of way.

"It's nice meeting you, Deanna."

Deanna waved her hand again. "Let me give you a little piece of advice where it concerns Griff Rice. If you're hoping to get married, then you're with the wrong man."

Belinda didn't like people who kiss and tell, and apparently Deanna either wanted to make her aware that she'd dated Griffin, or it was a case of sour grapes because he'd refused to marry her.

Griffin's arm tightened around Belinda's waist. "In case you're not familiar with the name, baby, Deanna Monique is a columnist who writes for a supermarket tabloid."

Peering up over her shoulder, Belinda made an attractive moue. "I never read them."

A waiter came over to Deanna. "Miss Monique, your table is ready. Will you kindly follow me." Waving to Griffin and Belinda, the reporter followed the waiter, tiptoeing as if she were walking on ice.

"She's quite a character," Belinda said after she'd disappeared from view.

Griffin signaled to the bartender. "That she is," he remarked, retaking his stool. "Eccentric but harmless. I'm going to order a martini. Would you like something?"

"I'll have an apple martini."

The bartender had just served their drinks when a waiter informed them that their table was ready. Belinda felt the way Deanna appeared, as she attempted to maintain her balance while she carried her cocktail to the table without spilling it. She placed the glass on the table and thanked Griffin when he seated her. Their waiter handed them menus, then stood a short distance away, waiting for them to select their entrées.

She glanced around the dining room. “This is very nice, Griffin.” The ground floor of a Rittenhouse Square apartment building had been transformed into a restaurant resembling a library with elegant crystal chandeliers, marble tables and walnut bookcases.

Reaching for his glass, he extended it, and he wasn’t disappointed when Belinda raised her glass and touched his. “Here’s to the woman who makes me appreciate being a man.”

Her face burned as she recalled what had passed between them earlier that morning. They’d been insatiable—making love, sleeping and waking up to make love again. “Same here. But, of course, being a woman.”

Belinda took a sip of the icy concoction, finding it delicious. The chill warmed and spread to her chest and lower, to the nether portions of her body. By the time she’d had her second sip she’d forgotten her former annoyance with Griffin and settled back in her chair to enjoy her drink and the man whom she loved with every fiber of her being.

“That is the best steak I’ve ever eaten.” Belinda had ordered the Australian Tajima Kobe filet that literally melted on her tongue.

Griffin smiled. “Eating here will turn a hard-core vegetarian into a carnivore.”

“Shame on you,” she chided softly, smiling.

“It made a believer of me.”

Her fork halted midair. "You were a vegetarian." Her query came out as a statement.

Dabbing his mouth with a napkin, Griffin angled his head. "There was one time when I flirted with the notion of becoming a vegetarian. I'd given up beef and chicken, eating only fish, veggies and fruit."

"That's sacrilegious, Griffin."

"Why is it sacrilegious?"

"It would mean giving up a Geno's Philly cheesesteak."

"That's easy. Now, if you'd said Pat's King of Steaks I'd have to agree with you."

Belinda placed a hand over her chest and pretended to swoon. The mellowing effects of martini had kicked in. "What! You prefer Pat's to Geno's?"

"It's been documented that Pat outsells Geno twelve-to-one."

"I beg to differ with you, counselor. It just appears that way because if ten people crowd into Geno's, it's packed. But twenty-five or even thirty can fit into Pat's with room to spare."

Griffin and Belinda continued the good-natured debate over who made the best Philly cheesesteak over a dinner of premium aged beef, truffle-whipped potatoes, asparagus and shared a Barclay salad for two. Both agreed that substituting pork or chicken for beef was truly a crime.

Reaching across the table, Belinda rested a hand atop Griffin's. "It's still not too late to convert to vegetarianism. I've heard there is a veggie cheesesteak."

"How can a steak not be meat? And is there such a word as *vegetarianism?*"

She managed to look insulted. "Of course there's such a word. After all, I am a teacher."

"A history teacher, Miss Eaton," Griffin reminded her.

"Oh. Are you implying that history teachers don't read, Mr. Rice?"

"They know dates and historical facts."

"We also read," she insisted, smiling.

"I'm going to give you a pop history quiz."

"Let's hear, counselor."

Griffin's eyes glittered with merriment. "Who were the candidates in the…" He hesitated. Presidential elections were always held during a leap year. "Who were the candidates in the eighteen seventy-six presidential election?"

Belinda wanted to tell her lover that he'd walked into a trap of his own choosing. She knew the details of every election from Washington to the sitting president.

"Republican Governor Rutherford B. Hayes of Ohio ran against New York Democratic Governor Samuel J. Tilden, who won a majority of the popular vote, but was one electoral vote short of a necessary majority, while Hayes was twenty votes short."

"Tilden had more votes, yet Hayes became President?"

Belinda stared at Griffin, wondering how much he knew about the centennial election. "Yes. Charges arose of irregularities concerning vote-counting procedures in three Southern states: Louisiana, South Carolina and Florida where the election boards were under the control of Reconstruction-era Republicans."

Belinda's intelligence never ceased to amaze Griffin. She was very smart and she knew it. It was why she came back at him whenever she felt he was talking down to her. "I know Hayes was sworn in as president, but how did he pull it off being down twenty votes?"

"After the election board count indicated these three states had given Hayes the majority, Democrats charged the vote in each state actually went to Tilden, which would've given Tilden the victory. The three states sent two sets of returns to Congress, one to the Democrats and one to the Republicans.

"Congress then established a fifteen-member electoral commission—the Electoral Count Act—to resolve what had become an unprecedented constitutional crisis. After a lot of rhetoric, the commission members agreed to accept the Republican returns, giving Hayes a one-vote electoral victory. The two parties decided to play nice with each other when the Democrats agreed Hayes would take office in return for withdrawing federal troops from the last two remaining states—Louisiana and South Carolina. The action officially ended military Reconstruction in the South. Most people are unaware the 2,000 election wasn't the first time questions as to voting irregularities had become a national issue."

"It looks as if our election process hasn't come that far in one hundred twenty-four years."

Belinda wrinkled her nose. "It's called *poli-tricks.*"

Griffin stared at her and then burst out laughing. "Speaking of poli-tricks, I have tickets to a fundraiser for a local politician next month, and I'd like you to come with me."

"Will it be a date?" she teased.

"Of course it is. Don't you know when you're being courted, Miss Eaton?"

A cautionary voice whispered in her head that Griffin was changing the rules of their relationship. To her, courting meant a social interaction that led to an engagement and marriage.

It was apparent he was sending mixed signals. “No, I didn’t.”

“Well, consider yourself warned.”

She stared at him with complete surprise etched on her face. The seconds ticked off, then she said, “Point taken.”

Chapter 11

Griffin peered over Belinda's shoulder as she gathered the ingredients for Sunday dinner. Not wanting to break a family tradition, she'd offered to cook rather than go out or order in.

"What are you going to do with Bruiser?" A large whole chicken rested on a cutting board.

Belinda smiled up at Griffin. "I'm going to put garlic butter under the skin, stuff the cavity with carrots, potatoes and shallots and cook it in a roasting bag."

He took a step and grasped the chicken's wings, lifting it in the air. "Hey, dude, you look as if you've pumped a little iron. Lindy, look at the thighs on this sucker."

"Griffin! Put that bird down. I just washed it."

"You think you can take me?" he asked the roaster, shaking it from side to side. "No? What are you? Are you chicken? You're not a chicken. You're a punk," Griffin said, continuing his monologue with the bird. He gave the roaster a final shake. "Tell me now. Who's ya daddy?"

Belinda couldn't help herself doubling over in laughter. The sight of Griffin Rice challenging a chicken to a fight was priceless. She was laughing so hard that tears rolled down her face.

"Stop it," she ordered, hiccuping while trying to catch her breath.

Griffin tossed the chicken on the board. "You're an embarrassment to the poultry community. I wash my hands of you." Using his elbow, he activated the long-handled faucet in one of the two stainless-steel sinks, washing and rinsing his hands.

Belinda handed him a paper towel. "You know you're a very sick man."

"Why would you say that?"

"You were talking to a chicken, Griffin. A dead chicken."

"Nigel and Cecil refuse to play with me, so Chicken Big was next."

She shook her head in amazement. Griffin was a bigger kid than his nieces. "Why won't they play with you?" He'd gotten up early to clean the cage and give the pups fresh food and clean water.

"I don't know. When I opened the cage door they just sat there looking at me. And when I reached in to take them out Nigel tried to bite me, while Cecil started growling and showing his teeth."

"You can't deal with two three-pound puppies, so you decide to take your frustration out on a chicken—or should I say our dinner."

Resting his hands on Belinda's shoulders, Griffin kissed the nape of her neck. "I'm sorry about abusing Bruiser."

"An idle mind is the devil's workshop. Perhaps I should put you to work..."

"What do you want me to do?"

She glanced up at him. "I need for you to make garlic butter."

He brushed a kiss over her lips. "Yummy."

"Sweet," Belinda crooned, deepening the kiss.

Griffin enjoyed cooking with Belinda. He wasn't a novice when it came to food. Most of his dishes were simple and palatable. However, Belinda would add the pièce de résistance with exotic seasonings and presentation.

He had to admit they worked well together—in and out of bed. They didn't agree on everything, and he still found her rigid and unrelenting when it came to some child-rearing issues. Griffin attributed that not so much to her upbringing as to her career as a teacher. Ten years of teaching young adults was challenging. Teaching young adults in one of Philadelphia's most challenging high schools was not only demanding, but difficult.

After the classroom shooting incident he'd broached the subject with Belinda of possibly transferring to another high school, one that was less violent. She'd calmly replied, "When I want or need your advice I'll ask for it." It was a not-so-subtle way of her telling him to mind his own business.

What Belinda needed to understand was that she was as much his business as Sabrina and Layla, and he was as much her business as her nieces. The four of them were inexorably linked by blood and marriage.

His bloodline and Belinda's would continue with their nieces and that meant they were family.

Griffin inserted a clove of garlic in a garlic press. The fragrant and distinctive aroma filled the kitchen. He added it to the dish of butter that had been left to soften to room temperature. "Is one clove enough?" he asked.

Belinda stopped peeling carrots. "It could use another one. Don't blend it yet. I want to add a few sprigs of fresh chopped parsley. Who taught you to cook?" she asked Griffin when he chopped parsley as if he were a professional chef.

"I had a girlfriend who was a chef," Griffin admitted reluctantly. He didn't want to talk about a woman or the women in his past. The soothing sound of music coming from a built-in radio under the kitchen cabinet punctuated the silence that ensued.

Belinda smiled as she sprinkled coarse sea salt on small redskin potatoes. "Lucky you."

His head came up as he stared numbly at her. "Why would you say that?"

"You don't have to rely on a woman to cook for you. Do you know how many men hook up with women because they're looking for someone to feed them?"

"That's a lot of bull, Lindy. They could always pay someone in the neighborhood to cook meals for them. They hook up with women because some of them are parasites. There's a guy I know who refused to commit to one woman because he said he needed variety. There was Sandra, who was always willing to cook, whenever he dropped by for breakfast, lunch or dinner. Then he had Jackie because she did everything he wanted her to do in bed. And then there was Melissa, his baby mama, who opened her door to him even if he stayed away for months because she claimed she wanted her son to have a relationship with his father."

"That's ridiculous, Griffin. A child can't bond with a parent when he or she sees them only two or three times a year."

"That's what I'd tell Jerrold, but anything I said fell on deaf ears. Although my parents lived under the same roof, my dad's cheating not only affected my mother but Grant and me."

Belinda gave Griffin a sidelong glance. His expression was one she'd never seen before. It was obvious his father's infidelity had scarred him. "I don't believe Grant ever cheated on my sister."

"That's because he couldn't cheat, not after hearing my mother argue with Dad because he'd come home with the scent of another woman still on him. Grant used to put his hands over his ears to shut out their shouting at each other."

"What did you do, Griffin?"

"I sat on the back porch until Dad left. It didn't matter how late he stayed out screwing other women, he always came home and he always went to work."

"Why didn't your mother leave him?"

Griffin's motions were slow, methodical as he folded the chopped parsley and minced garlic into the softened butter. "Her father died when she was a little girl, so she said she didn't want her children to grow up without their father."

"But your father cheated on her."

"Yes, he did. And the ultimate indignity was that he didn't try to hide it."

"Why do men cheat?"

Griffin's eyes caught and held hers. "Why do women cheat?"

"They don't cheat as much as men."

"Are you certain about that statistic? Didn't Oprah have a segment about women who admitted to cheating? That the percentage of women who cheat is a lot higher than most people believe, so let's not get into comparing genders."

"I didn't ask the question for you to answer with another question." Belinda's voice was low and soft.

The seconds ticked away as they regarded each other. "I wouldn't know, Lindy, because I've never cheated on a woman. Even if I thought about it I don't think I would cheat because I saw what it did to my mother and how it affected Grant and me. Instead of being children and enjoying the things little boys did, we were drawn into a battle that involved marital problems. Six- and nine-year-olds shouldn't have to hear words like *pussy* and *dick* thrown around like *please* and *thank you*—especially from their parents."

"Even though she didn't grow up with her father, your mother didn't have to stay, especially when you and Grant were older."

"That was something Grant and I asked her, and her response was that she loved her cheating husband. That was something I couldn't wrap my head around until Gloria Bailey-Rice told me about the man she'd fallen in love with, who was not the one he'd become."

Belinda knew she would never stay with a man who she knew was cheating on her. When she'd discovered the teacher she was dating was also dating another colleague she ended the relationship before he could open his mouth to explain.

"Why did she finally divorce your father?"

Inhaling, Griffin held his breath and then let it out slowly. "She didn't divorce him. He divorced her."

"But… But why? Why would he leave, Griffin?" Belinda stuttered. "He had the best of both worlds—a married man with a family behaving as if he were single."

"Grant and I threatened him." Griffin recognized shock and another unidentifiable emotion in Belinda's eyes when she met his gaze. "I was a junior in high school when Grant came home from college during a school break and we sat down together to discuss our parents' marriage. Nothing had changed in more than twenty years. My dad was still sleeping with other women, and my mother was still fighting about something she couldn't change or control.

"She'd become an insomniac. She stayed up half the night, hoping to witness the time he came home. I had no idea what she was going to do with that information except to use it if or when she decided to divorce him. And, even worse, she'd begun following him and confronting his women.

"I told my brother we were going to lose our mother to an emotional breakdown or she was going to confront the wrong woman and end up dead. We set up a private meeting with Dad and told him that if he didn't move out of the house we were going to kick his ass and throw him out. To this day I couldn't say for sure whether I would've actually hit my father. Thankfully I didn't have to be put to the test."

"How soon after did he leave?"

"It took him a week to get up the nerve to tell his wife he was leaving and filing for divorce."

"What was your mother's reaction?"

Griffin flashed a devastatingly sensual smile. "She went to a spa in Sedona, Arizona, for two weeks and came back with a new look and new attitude. She occasionally goes out with other men, but she vowed never to marry again."

"Don't you think it's odd that your mom and dad went away together for a month?"

"Not really," Griffin said, shaking his head. "Mom could care less who her ex-husband sleeps with, and because she'd doesn't care, Dad knows he has no power over her."

Belinda smiled. "Would you like for them to reconcile?"

"Maybe I'm selfish, but no. There's more respect between them now than there ever was when they were together."

"Your father is wonderful with his granddaughters."

"That's because he spoils them."

And, you don't, Belinda thought, giving Griffin a knowing smile.

He moved closer, trapping her body between his and the countertop. "What's that look all about?" he whispered near her ear.

"What look?" said she innocently.

Griffin pressed closer, his groin pressed to her hips. "The one that said I'm also culpable."

"Do you really think you know me so well that you can read my mind?"

Lowering his head he fastened his mouth to the nape of her neck, smiling when he felt a faint shudder go through Belinda. "I can't read your mind, but I can read your expressions. Your face is like an open book. You'd never make it as a poker player because everyone would know when you're not bluffing."

"It doesn't matter because I don't gamble."

"You've never gambled on anything in your life?" he asked, trailing a series of light kisses down the column of her long, scented neck.

Belinda smothered a gasp when she felt her knees weaken as his mouth searched the flesh bared by her tank top. "Griffin, stop or we're not going to eat tonight."

Griffin's hands were busy searching under her top. "Speak for yourself, Lindy. I plan to eat even if Bruiser never makes it into the oven."

It took a full minute before she realized Griffin wasn't talking about food. "I happen to like my meat well done."

"And I like a little pink in mine," Griffin countered.

She bit back a smile. "You are *so* nasty, Griffin Rice."

"So are you, Lindy Eaton, or you wouldn't have known what I was talking about."

Belinda managed to make Griffin take a step back when she elbowed him in the ribs. Shifting, she gave him a direct stare. "I wasn't nasty before I hooked up with you."

"Am I to take credit for unleashing the nastiness?"

She affected a moue, bringing his gaze to linger on her mouth. "Only some of it."

Griffin lifted his expressive eyebrows. "Are you saying that there's more?"

Pressing her breasts to his chest, Belinda went on tiptoe. "There's so much more, lover. You've only begun to scratch the surface."

Crushing her to his length, his lips descended slowly to meet hers, drinking in the sweetness of her kiss. Deepening the kiss and forcing her lips apart with his thrusting tongue, Griffin wanted to devour Belinda where they stood.

He wanted to take her on the kitchen floor. Now he understood animals in heat whose sole intent was to mate. And that's what he wanted to do with Belinda. He wanted to mate with her again and again to guarantee that his gene pool would continue. All he thought of was ripping her clothes from her curvy, lithe body and taking her without a pretense of foreplay, but the revelation of her near-rape stopped his traitorous musings. What he didn't want to do was trigger a flashback of the traumatic episode.

The kiss ended as quickly as it'd begun. Belinda took a step backward, her chest rising and falling as if she'd run a race. She glanced away. "I have to finish preparing dinner." Her voice was a whisper.

"I'll be in the back," Griffin said as he spun on his heels and walked out of the kitchen.

Belinda's hands were shaking uncontrollably from the build-up of sexual tension that lingered like waves of heat. She knew she'd been as close to losing control as Griffin. It seemed as if every time they came together the encounter was more passionate and explosive than the one that preceded it.

If Griffin hadn't stopped when he did she would've begged him to make love to her in the kitchen, without protection and when it was the most fertile time in her cycle. She'd called her gynecologist and asked that he call in a prescription to her local pharmacist for a supply of birth control pills that she would pick up the following day. She informed Griffin that he would have to continue to use protection until she went back on the Pill. They'd agreed to play house, but having a baby was not a part of the agreement.

Belinda sat staring at the same page in the book that lay on her lap, seeing but not reading any of the words. This was to become her last night in Paoli that she and Griffin would share a bed. The bus carrying Sabrina, Layla and their classmates from Gettysburg was scheduled to arrive at the school around three the following afternoon.

A moving company had delivered cartons of files from Griffin's Philadelphia office to the one he'd set up in his home, and the woman he'd hired as a part-time secretary/paralegal spent three full days conferring with him while she set up a filing system.

Belinda left Griffin a note, telling him that she was taking his car to go to her post office to pick up the mail they were holding for her. She also stopped at the pharmacy to pick up the three-month supply of low-dose birth control pills. She visited briefly with her mother, who'd insisted on making lunch for the two of them. Roberta hadn't asked about Griffin, which led her to believe that she knew they were sleeping together. It'd taken her a while to come to the conclusion that mothers knew more about their children than they let on. She returned to Paoli to discover Griffin had prepared a dinner of roast salmon with basil and sweet pepper sauce and a salad.

Griffin had suggested going for a walk after dinner and when strolling the quiet tree-lined streets holding hands she felt as if she'd stepped back in time when her father had given her permission to date. Most times she and her boyfriend sat on the porch, or if they left the porch it was to walk around the neighborhood under the watchful eyes of neighbors who were more than willing to report anything that appeared inappropriate to the elder Eatons.

"When are you going to turn the page?" asked a deep voice behind her.

Belinda closed the novel, stood up and turned to find Griffin standing less than three feet away; she wondered why she hadn't heard his approach. "I guess I was daydreaming."

Griffin stared at the woman who'd become an integral part of his life. It'd been raining off and on for two days and while the weather hadn't affected him because he'd been busy setting up his home office, it'd played havoc with her nerves.

She complained she wasn't used to sitting around doing nothing, which if she'd been home she'd keep busy doing housework, doing laundry or grocery shopping. It was different in Paoli because a cleaning service kept the house spotless and a landscaping company maintained the yard. Griffin shopped for groceries every other month, with the exception of perishables, at a supermarket warehouse, buying in bulk and storing it in the finished basement.

Belinda had changed in front of his eyes. Her body appeared more rounded, which she attributed to eating three meals a day. Sitting outside on the patio during daylight hours had darkened her face to a rich sable-brown. And with her scrubbed face, hair secured in an elastic band, faded jeans and oversize T-shirt she could easily pass for one of her students.

They'd played house for eight days and it would end in less than twenty-four hours when they picked up their nieces.

"Good or bad?"

Belinda smiled. "Daydreams are always good. It's the nightmares that are bad."

Griffin angled his head. "Do you ever have nightmares?"

Her eyelids fluttered wildly. "I used to."

He closed the distance between them, his hands sliding down her arms and tightening around her waist. "I'm glad they're gone."

There was something in Griffin's voice, the way he was touching her that made Belinda want to weep—not in sorrow but in joy.

She loved him.

She'd fallen in love with her sister's brother-in-law, her nieces' uncle, godfather, legal guardian and surrogate father. What had begun as a teenage crush was now full-blown passion with no beginning or end.

Burying her face against his strong, warm brown throat, she closed her eyes. "Love me, darling. Please make love to me for the last time."

"It's not going to be the last time, Lindy."

"Surely you're kidding, Rice. I'm not going to knock boots with you while the girls are in the house."

Attractive lines fanned out around his eyes when he smiled. "Are you afraid they'll hear you screaming in the throes of passion?"

Belinda gave him a soft punch in the middle of his back. "So, you got jokes. At least I don't sound like a bull. You make more noise than I do when you're—"

"Don't say it, baby," Griffin warned. He tightened

his hold on her waist. "I get the whole picture—sound and visuals." Bending slightly, he swept her up and into his arms. "Let's go make some noise."

Giggling like a little girl, Belinda tightened her hold around his neck. "How nasty do you want me to be?" she teased.

Throwing back his head, Griffin laughed loudly. "I want you to crank that nasty meter to the highest setting."

She caught his earlobe between her teeth, nipping it gently. "I hope you'll be able to handle it."

"Don't worry about me. Just serve it."

Belinda stared at the slight indentation in his strong chin before her searching gaze moved up to meet his resolute stare. "I'm going to make you scream like a bitch."

"Don't you mean a bull?"

"No-o-o," she drawled with so much attitude that Griffin bit down on his lower lip to keep from smiling.

She tucked her face into the hollow between his neck and shoulder as he left the porch. "Let's take a shower together," Belinda suggested as Griffin entered his bedroom.

Griffin did not drop his gaze as he lowered Belinda until her feet touched the sisal rug under his feet. He undressed her then stood with his arms at his sides while she undressed him, their chests rising and falling in a syncopated rhythm.

Belinda closed her eyes, her breath quickening when his fingers grazed the outline of her breasts. She opened her eyes and smiled. Resting a hand on Griffin's chest, she ran her fingertips over his clavicle, the muscles in his shoulder and lower to his breastbone.

He gasped audibly when her fingers grasped his sex, holding him fast. He hardened almost instantaneously. "Come with me." Like an obedient child, Griffin let Belinda lead him into the adjoining bathroom and shower stall, she still holding on to his erection. "Don't move, darling."

Griffin wanted to tell her he couldn't move even if his life was in the balance. He gasped when she touched a preset dial and lukewarm water flowed down on their heads. Going on tiptoe, she slipped her tongue into his mouth, while her hands worked their magic. Then, without warning, she slid down the length of his body, her mouth replacing her hand. He'd asked Belinda to crank the nasty meter up to its highest setting, demanding that she serve it and that's exactly what she'd done.

Bracing his palms against the tiles, he closed his eyes and tried thinking of something—anything but the image of Belinda on her knees, his sex moving in and out her hot mouth. Heat, chills and then more heat overlapped the iciness snaking its way up his legs and settling at the base of his spine. A groan slipped through his lips when his knees buckled and involuntary tremors had him shaking like a fragile leaf in a strong wind. The muscles in his belly contracted violently when a moan of helplessness, coming from deep within his chest, exploded. He threw back his head and opened his mouth and bellowed.

Belinda didn't make love to Griffin. She commanded him with a raw act of possession, branding him with an indelible mark. He was hers and hers alone. Griffin had taken himself out of circulation and she would make certain he would forget every woman he'd ever known. She was relentless, using her hand, tongue and teeth to bring him to the brink of release. Then without warning, she pressed the pad of her thumb against the large vein behind the shaft, manually slowing down the headlong rush of desire to climax.

Griffin's hands moved with lightning speed when he bent over, anchoring his hands under Belinda's armpits and pulling her to her feet while forcing her to release his engorged flesh. Supporting her back, he lifted her high in the air.

Belinda's small cry of shock was smothered when Griffin covered her mouth with a savage kiss that sucked the oxygen from her lungs. She barely had time to react to the rawness of his sexual onslaught when she found herself on her back and he inside her. Moaning aloud in erotic pleasure, she reveled in the sensation of bare flesh fusing. It was the first time they'd made love without the barrier of latex. Her menses, though scant, had come and gone.

The sensations of falling water, the feel of the coarse hair on his legs against her smooth ones and the unrestrained groans near her ear roused Belinda to a peak of desire bordering on hysteria. Passion radiated from her core, spreading outward to her extremities and beyond.

The turbulence of Griffin's lovemaking hurtled her into a vortex of the sweetest ecstasy. Belinda screamed when she felt him touch her womb and love flowed like heated honey, and she soared higher and higher until she climaxed, experiencing free fall, as Griffin, for the first time, succumbed to *le petit mort.* She couldn't move, didn't want to move as she lay drowning in the lingering aftermath of pure, explosive pleasure.

Griffin recovered before Belinda, coming to his feet. Walking on shaky legs, he reached over and turned off the water. A smile tipped the corners of his mouth when he shifted and saw that Belinda had curled into a fetal position. He hunkered down and eased her off the tiled floor.

Her spiked lashes fluttered when she opened her eyes. "Was I nasty enough for you?"

Shaking his head in amazement, he carried her wet body out of the bathroom and into the bedroom. "You were beyond nasty, darling."

Her lips parted in surprise. "You didn't like it?"

Griffin smiled at Belinda as if she were a child. "I loved it." He placed her on the bed and lay beside her, unmindful of the water from their bodies soaking the sheets. He loved her and making love to her. Staring down into the eyes the color of dark coffee, he knew their relationship had changed with the wanton coupling. Belinda Eaton was sexy, passionate *and* incredibly nasty—the way he liked her.

Fatigue pressed Belinda down to the mattress like a lead blanket. It took Herculean strength to keep her eyes open. She fought valiantly but Morpheus proved victorious. "Good night, darling."

"Good night, baby."

Griffin, supporting his head on folded arms, stared up at the ceiling. He lay motionless, startled by the sudden thought that flashed through his mind. How had he forgotten about the man in Florida who'd claimed Belinda first?

And he wasn't so vain or naive to believe that just because Belinda opened her legs to him it meant she would open her heart to him. After all, he'd slept with women he liked, but didn't and would never love.

He was in too deep and didn't know how to extricate himself.

Never had he missed his brother as he did now. Grant had been the levelheaded older brother, wise beyond his years, and whenever he went to Grant in a quandary he came away buoyed with confidence.

He closed his eyes when, without warning, a wave of sadness held him captive then fled as quickly as it'd come. *If she's worth it, then fight like hell for her,* said a voice in his head that sounded remarkably like Grant's.

"Thank you, brother," Griffin whispered. He had his answer.

Chapter 12

Belinda and Griffin waited in the schoolyard along with other seventh-grade parents for the bus transporting their children from Gettysburg, Pennsylvania.

She'd elected to wait in his sport-utility vehicle, reading, while Griffin was engaged in a lively conversation with several men. The topic invariably turned to sports: baseball, football and hockey.

What garnered Belinda's rapt attention was that several women had drifted over to join the small group of men. They seemed to linger on the periphery until one was bold enough to rest her hand on Griffin's shoulder.

What the... Belinda caught herself before she screamed out the open window that she could look, but not touch. She sat motionless, watching the woman become more and more brazen until Griffin reached over to remove her hand. Within minutes her hand was back, this time on his back.

Griffin felt the warmth of the hand pressed to his back, and he curbed the urge to grab her wrist and fling it off. He glared at the woman who'd insisted on crossing his personal boundaries to touch him without permission. Now he understood Belinda's insistence on it.

What annoyed him was that the others hadn't invited the petite doll-like woman with a profusion of neatly braided hair flowing down her back to join the conversation. Glancing at her left hand he noticed it was bare. He found her attractive, but whatever she was offering he didn't want or need. Cupping her elbow, he led her away from the small crowd that was speculating whether the Flyers would make the Stanley Cup finals.

Bending closer to her ear, he affected a tight smile. "See that woman sitting in the white hybrid staring at us?" The woman nodded. "She happens to be my wife. I told her to stay in the car because she didn't take her medication this morning, and whenever that happens she tends to be a little violent. So I suggest you go back and stand with your friends, because once she goes off I have a hard time trying to control her."

A pair of round eyes widened with his disclosure. "You mean she's violent?" He nodded slowly. "Thanks for the heads-up."

Instead of returning to the men he headed to his vehicle and got in beside Belinda. "Don't you dare say anything," he warned, deadpan.

Belinda averted her eyes to conceal the grin stealing its way over her face. "I would've helped you out if you didn't look as if you were enjoying her so much."

Griffin crossed his arms over his chest. "You did help me out."

Shifting, she noted his smug expression. "What?" Belinda's jaw dropped when she listened to Griffin's explanation for thwarting his admirer. "Medication, Griffin? You told her I was crazy?"

"Aw, baby, don't take it that way. I had to tell her something or she would've come home with us."

"I don't think so, love," Belinda drawled. "She would've gone home with *you,* not us."

"Four women in my life are enough, thank you."

A slight frown furrowed her brow. "Who's the fourth?"

"Gloria Rice."

Belinda nodded. How could she have forgotten her nieces' other grandmother? There came a flurry of activity as parents and their children spilled out of vehicles as the tour bus maneuvered into the schoolyard.

Griffin placed his hand on Belinda's arm. "Wait here. I'll get their luggage."

"What's the matter? You don't want anyone to see the crazy woman?"

He rolled his eyes at her. "Are you ever going to let me live this down?"

"I'll think about it," she teased.

A smile softened her features when she saw Sabrina, followed by Layla step off the bus. They appeared exhausted. Any semblance of a hairstyle was missing from both girls. Sabrina had parted her hair in the middle, but it appeared as if she couldn't decide whether to braid it or leave it loose. Layla had half a dozen braids, secured with colorful bands, shielding her face, while a thick plait hung down her back. They had two days to recover from their weeklong educational trip before returning to classes. It would become their last extended break until the end of the school term.

Shifting on her seat, Belinda smiled at her nieces when they slipped onto the second row of seats. "Welcome home."

"Hi, Aunt Lindy," they mumbled in unison.

"Are you girls hungry?"

Layla closed her eyes. "No, Aunty Lindy. I just want to take a bath and go to bed."

"Me, too," Sabrina said around the yawn she concealed behind her hand.

"We're not going to stop to eat," Belinda informed Griffin when he slipped behind the wheel. "They're exhausted."

Griffin nodded. "Home it is."

It took a full day before Sabrina and Layla reverted to their chatty selves. They climbed into bed with Belinda and talked nonstop about the buildings they'd visited in Washington, D.C., the historic preserved city of Williamsburg, Virginia, and Gettysburg National Military Park and Gettysburg National Cemetery.

They listened intently when Belinda related the events of the Battle of Gettysburg. "The battle began on July first and didn't end until the third of July, eighteen sixty-three. Not only was it one of the bloodiest battles of the Civil War, but it was significant because it marked the northernmost point reached by the Confederate army. It also marked the end of rebel supremacy on the battlefield."

Layla shifted into a more comfortable position as

she rested her head on a mound of pillows. "Why was that, Aunt Lindy?"

Belinda smiled at her nieces flanking her. "Confederate General Robert E. Lee had crossed the Mason-Dixon line into Pennsylvania for strategic and logistical reasons. The general was a student of another famous general, Napoleon Bonaparte, who had the audacity to use small forces against larger ones. Now historians differ as to why General Lee ventured into Northern territory. Some say he was foraging for shoes for his troops, while others claim Lee was overconfident because he'd defeated Union General Joseph Hooker at Chancellorsville."

"Where's Chancellorsville?" Sabrina asked.

"Virginia," Belinda said, smiling. Her nieces, who admitted to not liking history, had taken a sudden interest in it as the result of their class trip. "Whatever his reason it spelled ultimate defeat for the rebel forces."

"Why did the battle last so long?" Sabrina questioned.

"I have a book on Civil War battles you can read."

Layla made a face. "Aunt Lindy, we don't have time to read other books. Please tell us."

Just like they'd done when the girls were much younger and slept over at Belinda's house, she'd gather them in her bed and tell them stories about the lives of enslaved Africans and free men, the Underground Railroad, the Great Depression and the wars spanning the Revolutionary to Vietnam rather than the ubiquitous fairy tales. It had taken a week for the historical fairy tales to become a reality when they'd come face-to-face with the history of their country.

She told of President Lincoln's criticism of General

Meade who'd chosen not to pursue the defeated Confederates, as he had thought that immediate action would have shortened the war; although the conflict continued for another two years, the Union forces victory at Gettysburg proved to be the turning point in the war, while amassing the most devastating roster of casualties: fifty-one thousand, North and South combined.

When Belinda's voice faded and she waited for more questions that never came, she realized her nieces had fallen asleep. In the past she would carry each to their beds, but at twelve the girls were two inches shorter than her five-six height and weighed more than one hundred pounds. If Griffin had stayed she would've asked him to take them to their bedrooms.

Reaching over Layla, she turned off the lamp and then settled down to join her nieces as they slept soundly. Belinda forced herself not to dwell on sharing a bed with Griffin because whenever she recalled what they'd done to each other her body betrayed her.

A few times she'd asked herself if she'd fallen in love with Griffin after they slept together or if she had had feelings for him before. And the answer was always the same: she'd fallen in love with Griffin Rice when she was still a teenager, that she resented the women in the photographs who clung possessively to his arm because she'd wanted to be them. She'd regarded him as a skirt-chaser because it made him more unappealing.

How could she have been so wrong about a man their nieces adored? Cecil and Nigel, who had been overjoyed when they saw Sabrina and Layla, no longer growled or showed Griffin their tiny teeth. When he had sat on the floor they jumped all over him as he pretended to fight off their attack. The girls had joined the fracas and pandemonium had ensued with barking, screams from the girls and hysterical laughter from Griffin. Strange feelings always arose when she watched him interact with the puppies and his nieces. But it had been in that instant that Belinda knew he would make an incredible father.

Belinda started up her Volvo and backed it out of the driveway, always mindful of the schoolchildren making their way to bus stops. Sabrina and Layla had walked two blocks to a classmate's house to wait with her and her younger sister for the bus that stopped on their corner.

Since her nieces had come to live with her, Belinda had begun speaking to many of the mothers who lived in the neighborhood. Some had invited her to come to their homes for coffee, and her nearest neighbor had invited her and Griffin to a dinner party. And, with the warmer weather, cooking outdoors had become the norm.

Her cell phone rang and she smiled. She knew from the distinctive ring that Griffin was calling her. "Good morning, darling," she crooned, activating the Bluetooth device.

"Good morning, baby. How are you?"

Her smile faded. "I'll let you know at the end of classes." It would be her first day back since the high school shut down two days early for spring break.

There came a pause. "You don't have to play Superwoman, Lindy."

"I would've rather you said Wonder Woman. Her outfit was sexier than Superwoman's."

"I'm not joking, Belinda."

A frown furrowed her forehead. "Neither am I, Griffin. I've had more than a week to deal with what happened, and I'm good."

"I don't want to have to tell you I told you so when you have a meltdown."

"What are you so worried about, Griffin? Are you afraid that if I lose it, you'll have to raise the girls by—"

"Don't say it," Griffin warned in a dangerously soft voice. "Please don't say what I think you're going to say. This is not about the girls. This is about you, Belinda."

"I'm not a fragile hothouse flower that will wilt if you touch me. I can take care of myself. Didn't I prove that when I fought off a rapist?"

"Physical scars are not the same as emotional scars."

Belinda blew out a breath. She knew no amount of arguing would get Griffin to believe that she wasn't going to suffer lasting effects from one of her students firing a gun in her classroom.

"I thought we talked about this, Griffin, and decided it was nothing."

"You decided it was nothing, Lindy, not me. If you exhibit any behavior that proves injurious to our children's emotional well-being I'm going to have to take action. They've been through enough without…"

Touching a button, she disconnected the call. She would not put up with any man threatening her. The threat had begun and ended with Joel Thurman. Her cell phone rang again and she turned it off. She didn't want to talk or argue with Griffin, not when she wanted to use the time to fortify herself for when she met with her students again.

* * *

Belinda arrived at the high school and parked in the area designated as faculty parking. She nodded to the science teacher she'd dated, quickening her pace to avoid talking to him. Reaching into her handbag she removed her photo ID and hung it around her neck. What she found strange was the absence of noise. Students stood around in small groups, talking quietly among themselves, while teachers and staff members filed silently into the school building.

The incident had brought home the reality that, in a moment of madness, someone with a gun could've possibly taken the life of a classmate, relative, teacher or staff.

As she clocked in, Belinda was aware of the surreptitious glances directed her way. Valerie Ritchie walked in and punched her card. "Come with me," Belinda whispered as she turned on her heels and left the office.

"How are you doing?" Valerie asked when they found an empty first-floor classroom.

"I'm okay, Valerie. I am really all right," she said when Valerie gave her a look of disbelief. "What do I have to do to convince everyone that I don't need tranquilizers, or that I'm not a candidate for a straitjacket."

Valerie leaned closer. "Weren't you scared?"

Belinda stared at the teacher who was never seen with a hair out of place or her makeup less than perfect. Valerie had given an award-winning performance as a politician's wife, and although she was no longer in that role she continued to play the part.

"Of course I was frightened. But once I realized Sean Greer posed more of a threat to himself than to me or the other students in my class I stopped being afraid. You had to be there to hear him talking to the negotiator. He was nothing more than a frightened kid who just wanted to fit in—be accepted. Unfortunately, Brent Wiley got to him first."

What Belinda didn't reveal to Valerie was that she'd been afraid that Sean was thinking of shooting himself when he'd placed the gun to his head. And, when she'd asked Griffin about helping to get competent legal counsel for the troubled youth, he'd told her that his friend had agreed to defend him pro bono.

The bell rang, signaling the beginning of classes, followed by an announcement from the principal that assemblies for each grade would be held throughout the day with counselors available to answer questions or talk one-on-one to students who requested individual sessions.

Belinda and Valerie exchanged a familiar look. The fallout from the school shooting would claim another day.

Belinda returned home to find Griffin's SUV parked in her driveway. He was seated on the chaise in her sitting room, waiting for her, his impassive expression revealing nothing.

She flashed a warm smile. "Good afternoon."

"Is it?"

"Of course it is, Griffin. I survived my first day back." Spinning around on her toes, she extended her arms. "See, no bullet holes." She wasn't given a chance to get her balance when she found herself pulled against Griffin's chest.

"Don't play with me, Belinda, or I'll—"

"Or you'll what!" she screamed at him. "Or you'll

take my children from me? Is that what you were going to say? I don't think so, Griffin Rice. I don't care what kind of legal connections you think you have, but if you…"

An explosive kiss stopped her outburst. Belinda fought Griffin, but she was no match for his superior strength as his sensual assault shattered her fragile defenses. She found herself swimming through a haze of feelings she didn't want to feel and a desire so strong that it frightened her with its intensity.

His fingers eased around her wrists as he pulled her arms behind her back, holding her captive. "Don't ever hang up on me again," he warned softly.

Belinda stared up at him through her lashes. "I wouldn't have had to hang up on you if you hadn't threatened me."

Lifting her effortlessly with one arm, Griffin made his way out of the sitting room to her bed. "I didn't threaten you, Lindy."

"Yes, you did," she managed to say as her back made contact with the mattress. "I…" For the second time within minutes she found herself speechless.

Griffin's hands were busy searching under her skirt for the waistband of her panty hose. In one smooth motion, her hose and panties lay on the floor and her legs were anchored over his shoulders.

"No, Griffin! Please!"

Pleas became sobs of ecstasy as Griffin utilized his own method to defuse her anger, and the degree to which she responded to his raw, sensuous lovemaking left her shaking uncontrollably. She surrendered completely to his rapacious tongue, drowning in the passion that left her shaking and crying at the same time.

Griffin lowered her legs and moved up her body. He kissed her deeply, permitting Belinda to taste herself on his tongue. "Now, can we talk?"

Belinda pushed against his shoulder. She didn't want to talk. All she wanted to do was sleep. "Not now, Griffin."

He smiled. "When, baby?"

"Later."

Griffin's smile grew wider. Making love to Belinda was the perfect antidote for defusing her temper. She was snoring lightly when he undressed her and pulled a nightgown over her head. He retreated to the half bath, soaped a washcloth and returned to the bedroom to clean away the evidence of their lovemaking. He'd covered her with a sheet and blanket when he heard the distinctive chime indicating someone had opened a door.

He met Sabrina and Layla as they dropped their backpacks and headed toward the rear of the house to see their pets. "What do you want for dinner?"

Layla stopped, giving him a bright smile. "Aunt Lindy said she was going to make spaghetti and meatballs."

Griffin didn't tell his niece that if her aunt didn't get up in time to prepare dinner, he would. He had to make several business calls to the West Coast, but it was something he could accomplish either at his house or Belinda's.

He planned to stay the night despite the fact it wasn't the weekend. Spending eight consecutive days with Belinda had spoiled him. Not only had he fallen in love with her but missed her whenever they were apart.

How had it happened so quickly? How had he fallen so hard for a woman he'd known for years? The questions continued to plague him later that night as he lay on the sofa bed waiting for sleep to overtake him, when he didn't have to think of the woman who made him plan for a future that included her as his wife and the mother of their children.

Chapter 13

Griffin's hands drummed rhythmically on the steering wheel when he stopped for a red light, mimicking the hand clapping in "Hand Jive," the infectious song from the classic musical *Grease.*

He'd come to know most of the words from the play over the past month because Layla and Sabrina had decided to participate in their school's musical production for the first time. Layla had auditioned for a singing part in the production, while Sabrina worked behind the scenes, using her budding artistic skill on set decorations.

They stayed after classes to rehearse and as the day for the actual performance neared they'd begun full-day weekend rehearsals.

Belinda had scoured Philadelphia's thrift and vintage shops for replicas of poodle skirts and saddle shoes. In the end she had to resort to the internet to gather the names of collectors of 1950s memorabilia. Her perseverance paid off, because she'd purchased an authentic poodle skirt and a pair of black-and-white saddle shoes that were a perfect fit for Layla.

He'd made arrangements with his mother for her granddaughters to spend the night with her. Gloria and Lucas had returned from their month-long vacation cruise tanned, relaxed and looking forward to spending time with their granddaughters.

Layla leaned forward in her seat and tapped Griffin's shoulder. "Uncle Griff, please repeat that track."

Griffin pressed a button on the dashboard, tapped his finger on the steering wheel while the interior of the car was filled with the catchy tune. Layla and Sabrina shared a smile when their uncle's voice joined theirs. They'd always liked their Uncle Griff, but since he'd become their stepfather they'd come to love him as if he were their father.

They went to him to enlist his aid when they wanted something they knew their aunt would probably not approve of. His "I'll discuss it with her" usually predicted success, if not a compromise which they were always ready to accept.

Griffin took a right turn down the street that led to Gloria Rice's condo. "Make certain you finish your homework before your aunt and I pick you up tomorrow night."

"We will," the two girls chorused.

He and Belinda were scheduled to attend a political fundraiser later that evening and Saturday evening Sabrina and Layla were invited to a birthday sleep-over for a classmate who lived nearby.

Maneuvering into a space set aside for visitor parking, Griffin shut off the engine. The girls gathered their overnight bags and together they made their way to the modern doorman building. He gave his name to the uniformed man who rang Gloria's apartment to let her know that she had visitors.

"She's expecting you, Mr. Rice. The elevator to her apartment is on the right."

Sabrina, waiting until the elevator doors closed behind them said, "Why does he have to say *'she's expecting you, Mr. Rice'* when he already knows you're Grandma's son?"

Griffin gave his niece a direct stare. "That's what's known as doing one's job. He has rules or a protocol to follow, and no matter who comes into the building he has to follow the rule that all visitors must be announced."

"It sounds like a silly rule to me," Layla mumbled under her breath.

"Would it be so silly if he let someone into the building whose intent is to rob or hurt a tenant?" Griffin asked.

"No, Uncle Griff, that's different," Layla argued.

"No, it isn't, Layla. What if someone who looks exactly like me decides he wants to burglarize Grandma's apartment and the doorman just let him walk in. Legally the owner of the building would be responsible for the loss because the doormen are his employees."

The elevator came to a stop, and the doors opened smoothly. Griffin stepped out, holding the door while his nieces filed out and made their way down the carpeted hallway to where Gloria stood outside the door waiting for them. Cradling their faces between her hands, she kissed each girl on the cheek. Griffin wanted to tell his mother that her granddaughters had reached the age where they shied away from public displays of affection, but decided to hold his tongue.

Leaning over, he kissed his mother. "Hey, beautiful."

Gloria swatted at his shoulder. "Save that stuff for someone who isn't as gullible as your mother."

Griffin smiled at her. "When have you known me to lie?"

Gloria angled her head, seemingly deep in thought. "Not too often." Her expression brightened. "Can you spare a few minutes to share a cup of coffee with your mother, or do you have to run?"

"I have some time."

"Come sit in the kitchen while I brew a cup."

Slipping off his jacket, Griffin hung it on the coat tree near the door. He'd come with Gloria when she talked about purchasing a unit either in a renovated or new building going up in the gentrified Spring Garden neighborhood. He'd wanted her to purchase the one-bedroom unit, but Gloria had insisted that she needed the additional bedroom for whenever her granddaughters came for a visit. Layla and Sabrina loved visiting because it was closer to downtown Philadelphia with its theaters, museums, restaurants, department stores and specialty shops.

Gloria Rice had downsized her life and the furnishings in her apartment reflected her new lifestyle. Every piece of furniture had a purpose and the pale monochromatic color scheme reflected simplicity at its best.

Griffin followed his mother into an immaculate ultramodern stainless-steel kitchen. "What are you cooking for dinner?"

"I'm not," Gloria said as she reached for a coffee pod from a rack on the countertop. "I asked the girls what they wanted me to cook and they said they wanted to eat out."

"Have you decided where?"

Gloria's eyes sparkled when she smiled. "I told them it can be their choice."

"You're spoiling them, Mom."

"And you don't, son? I'm their grandmother and that gives me the right to spoil them rotten. You, on the other hand, don't have the same rights."

Griffin stared at his mother dressed in a stylish linen pantsuit. The reddish-orange color flattered the former librarian's dark complexion. "As a dad I do."

Reaching for a cup in an overhead cabinet, Gloria placed it under the coffee-brewing machine then pushed a button to start the process. "You enjoy being a father." The question was a statement.

Bending his tall body to fit into the chair in the dining nook, Griffin nodded. "I do. At first I kept telling myself that I couldn't do it, that I'd fail miserably, but thanks to Belinda I've been holding my own."

Resting a hip against a granite-topped countertop, Gloria met her son's direct stare. "I never thought I'd say this, but I'm going to anyway. Belinda's a better mother than her sister. Donna was totally disorganized and much too lax with her daughters. When I told her that the girls left their clothes wherever they stepped out of them her excuse was that was what she was there for—to pick up after them."

"Belinda changed that, Mom."

"I know. Layla called me when she got her cell phone to tell me about her new bedroom and study area. She also said she had to keep her room clean otherwise she and Sabrina would lose certain privileges."

Griffin nodded. "At first I thought Belinda was being a little too strict, but unlike Donna she's not a stay-at-home mother. She has enough to deal with at the high school without having to come home and pick up after teenagers."

There was only the sound of brewing coffee as mother and son regarded each other. "She's good for the girls and she's good for you," Gloria said after a comfortable pause.

"Belinda's an incredible mother, and an even more incredible woman."

"I take it you like her." Griffin closed his eyes and when he opened them they were filled with an emotion Gloria had never seen before. There was no doubt her son was taken with his nieces' godmother.

"It goes beyond liking, Mom. I'm in love with Belinda."

"Does she know it?"

Griffin shook his head. "I don't think so."

"When are you going to tell her?"

"I don't know. I suppose I'm waiting for the right time."

"There's never a right time when it comes to affairs of the heart, Griffin Rice. You wait too long and you're going to lose her."

"I'm not going to lose her."

"Why? Because you say so?"

A muscle quivered at Griffin's jaw. "No. Because it's not going to happen."

Gloria saw movement out of the corner of her eye. "What is it, Sabrina?"

"Layla wants chicken and waffles and I want a hamburger."

"Don't worry, sweets. We'll find a restaurant where Layla can get her chicken and waffles and you your burger."

"Thank you, Grandma."

"You're welcome, Sabrina. I can't believe they're growing up so quickly," Gloria remarked after Sabrina returned to the spare bedroom she shared with her sister whenever they came to visit.

"That's what frightens me, Mom. What am I going to do when the boys come knocking on the door?"

"You'll know what to do when the time comes."

"I hope you're right."

"Do you think it'd be any easier if they were boys?" Gloria asked.

"Yeah, I think so. At least I'd be able to tell them what *not* to do."

Gloria added a teaspoon of sugar and a splash of cream to the cup when the brewing cycle ended, handing it to her son. "Stop stressing yourself, Griffin. Everything will work out okay."

Gloria's "everything will work out okay" played over and over in Griffin's head during his return drive to Belinda's house. And, when he opened the door to find her standing in the middle of her bedroom in her underwear, he told himself that his mother was right. As long as he had Belinda in his life he didn't have anything to worry about.

Crossing the room, he brushed a kiss over her mouth. "I'll be ready as soon as I shave and shower."

* * *

Belinda walked into the grand ballroom of the Ritz-Carlton, her hand tucked in the bend of Griffin's elbow over the sleeve of his tuxedo jacket. The night was warm enough for her to drape just a silk shawl over the customary little black dress. The one-shoulder satin-organza with a generous front slit showed off her legs and matching Christian Louboutin four-inch pumps with each step. Her stylist had cut her hair, and it highlighted the roundness of her face when it feathered around her delicate jawline.

She'd taken special care with her makeup, applying smoky and raspberry colors to her lids, cheeks and lips. It had been a while since her last black-tie affair, and it was fun to dress up for the event.

Griffin was breathtakingly, drop-dead gorgeous, and as comfortable in formal attire as he was in casual clothes. He'd elected to wear a platinum-tone silk tie with his tuxedo rather than the usual black.

The event was to raise funds for an up-and-coming politician who'd announced his intent to challenge the controversial, but very popular incumbent mayor. It wasn't until Belinda was introduced to the charismatic mayoral candidate that she learned that he and Griffin had attended law school together. Griffin had graduated first and the candidate number two in their class.

Patrick Garson's dark blue eyes took in everything about the woman beside Griffin Rice in one sweeping glance. Reaching for her hands, he brought one hand to his mouth and kissed her fingers. "Lovely. You are simply lovely—"

"Belinda," Griffin supplied. "Her name is Belinda Eaton. Belinda, this is my good friend and hopefully the next mayor of Philadelphia, Patrick Garson."

Belinda smiled and mouthed the appropriate responses. There was something about Patrick Garson that was too perfect. Not a strand was out of place in his wavy honey-blond hair. Even his sandy-brown eyebrows were perfect, and Belinda wondered whether he had them plucked or waxed. She approved of metrosexual men, but she believed men like Patrick were apt to spend a little too much time in the mirror.

"Pat, darling. Oh, there you are," a woman drawled with a thick Southern inflection.

Belinda turned to find a statuesque blonde heading in their direction. The light from the chandeliers overhead glinted off the large solitaire on her left hand. Smiling, she looped her arm through Patrick's.

Barbie and Ken. A knowing smile touched Belinda's lips. Patrick and the woman who probably was his fiancée were the perfect prototypes for the popular dolls.

Her topaz-blue eyes lit up when she spied Griffin. "Griff, darling. How are you?"

Griffin touched his cheek to hers. "I'm good, Jessica. How are you?"

Holding out her arms, Jessica spun around on her designer stilettos. "As you can see, I'm really good. It was a bitch trying to lose the last ten pounds, but I did it."

Belinda stared at Jessica, stunned. The woman was practically skin and bones. She was at least five-eleven in her bare feet, and probably weighed less than Belinda.

Wrapping an arm around Belinda's waist, Griffin

pulled her against his length. "Belinda, I'd like to introduce you to another of my law school friends. This is Jessica Ricci, Pat's fiancée and hopefully the next first lady of Philadelphia. Jessica, Belinda Eaton."

Jessica flashed her practiced smile, exhibiting a mouth of perfect porcelain veneers. "I'm charmed to meet you, Belinda. Please call me Jessie. Jessica sounds so staid."

Belinda couldn't help but return the friendly infectious smile that crinkled the blonde's brilliant eyes. "Then Jessie it is."

"Are you a lawyer, too?" she drawled.

"No. I'm a teacher."

"Do you teach the little babies?"

Shaking her head and smiling, Belinda said, "No. I teach at the high school level."

"How do you keep the boys from coming on to you?"

Belinda felt the heat from Griffin's gaze when he stared at her. It was the same question he'd put to her, what seemed so long ago. "I don't entertain their advances."

Griffin's fingers tightened. "Belinda and I are going to get something from the bar, then we're going to circulate. I'll call you later, Pat, and we'll set up something where the four of us can get together without reporters and photographers shadowing you."

Patrick patted Griffin's shoulder. "I'll be waiting for your call."

"Thanks," Belinda whispered under her breath as Griffin led her across the ballroom to one of three bars set up around the perimeter.

"I should've warned you about Jessica. She's a little chatty, but she's perfect for Patrick."

"They remind me of Ken and Barbie dolls."

Griffin chuckled. "One time we had a Halloween party and they came dressed as Ken and Barbie."

"Does she have an eating disorder?"

"No. She had an accident several years back, and a doctor put her on cortisone, which made her put on about fifty pounds. She finally came off the medication and it took two years of diet and exercise to lose the weight."

"Are you supporting him because he's a friend, or because you feel he's the best candidate for the office?"

"Both," Griffin stated emphatically. "Patrick has one of the most brilliant minds of anyone I've met or known. He would make a very good mayor." His gaze lingered on Belinda's mouth. Patrick had called her lovely—and that she was. "Now, what can I get you to drink?"

"I'll have a white wine."

His eyebrows lifted. "Are you sure you don't want anything stronger?"

"Very sure, darling. I've appointed myself the designated driver for tonight, so I don't want to overdo it."

Griffin leaned closer. "I'm going to have to have one drink, so you don't have to worry about my being impaired."

"I'll still have the white..." Her words trailed off when she spied someone she hadn't seen in years. "Excuse me, Griffin. I'll be right back."

He stood motionless, watching Belinda as she wove her way through the throng crowding in the ballroom. He wasn't aware that he'd been holding his breath until he saw her talking to a woman who looked vaguely familiar.

* * *

Belinda tapped the shoulder of a woman with skin the color of palomino-gold. Surprise, then shock froze the features of Zabrina Cooper when she turned around.

"Belinda."

"Zabrina Mixon." There was no emotion in Belinda's voice.

"It's Cooper. I've gone back to using my maiden name."

Belinda stared at the incredibly beautiful woman who, if she'd married Myles, would've become her sister-in-law. But weeks before they were scheduled to exchange vows, Zabrina ended the engagement and married a much older man—a prominent Pennsylvania politician. And when she gave birth to a son nine months later, rumors were rampant that she'd been sleeping with Thomas Cooper while engaged to Myles Eaton.

Belinda wanted to hate the woman who'd embarrassed her family and broken her brother's heart. She'd felt personally responsible for the breakup, because she'd been the one to introduce her then-best friend to her brother.

"I'm sorry to hear about your husband."

"Don't feel sorry for me, Belinda. It's Adam who needs your sympathy. It's not easy for a ten-year-old to adjust to losing his father."

Belinda went completely still. It was apparent Zabrina wasn't going to play the grieving widow. "You never loved him, did you?"

"If you want to know the truth, Belinda, then I'm going to tell you the truth. I hated Thomas Cooper as much as I loved your brother."

Belinda recalled the images of Zabrina Cooper staring blankly at photographers when they snapped frames of her stoic face at her husband's funeral. Thomas Cooper had come from a long line of African-American politicians dating back to the 1890s, and when the confirmed bachelor announced his engagement a collective groan went up from women all over the state. And nine months later when his young wife delivered a son, rumors as to his hasty nuptials were put to rest.

"If you hated him, then why did you marry him, Brina?"

Zabrina blinked back tears. It'd been years since anyone had called her Brina, and hearing it come from her childhood friend took her back to a time when all was right and pure in her world.

"I can't tell you. I swore an oath that I'd never tell anyone."

Belinda moved closer. "You don't have to tell me if you don't want to."

"I need a friend, Belinda. When I married Thomas he made me get rid of all my friends."

Belinda felt her pain. "Do you have a piece of paper?"

"Why?"

"I want to give you my phone numbers. Maybe we can get together to have lunch or even dinner."

Opening her small evening bag, Zabrina took out her cell phone. "I'll program your numbers into my phone."

Three minutes later, the two women parted with a promise to get together to talk. They couldn't change the past, but Belinda knew Zabrina needed a friend.

"Wasn't that Thomas Cooper's widow?" Griffin asked when Belinda returned.

"Yes."

He'd heard rumors why Zabrina Mixon married a man old enough to be her father, but they'd remained just that—rumors. What he did know was that when she ended her engagement to Myles to marry Cooper she'd been vilified in the press until Thomas Cooper used his political influence to pull the articles.

Belinda accepted the glass of wine Griffin had ordered for her. "We're going to have lunch or dinner one of these days," she said after taking a sip of the cool liquid.

"Good for you."

"Oh, you approve?"

Griffin nodded. "Yes. Look at us, once we were able to clear the air about how we feel about each other."

"You're right, darling."

Griffin knew she liked him, but what he didn't know was how much she'd come to love him—enough to want to spend the rest of her life with him.

Chapter 14

Sabrina leaned closer to her sister as they sat in front of the computer monitor. "I don't like that dress."

Layla rolled her eyes. "You don't have to like it. We're just looking at different styles."

"Isn't it too soon to think of bridesmaid's dresses when Uncle Griff hasn't given her a ring?"

Layla's hand stilled on the mouse. "Wasn't it you who said you overheard him tell Grandma that he was in love with Aunt Lindy?"

"Yes, but that still doesn't mean they're going to get married."

"I just want to be ready in case they are ready. I know we'll be in the wedding, but I am not going to wear a dress I don't like."

Sabrina stared at her twin. "Maybe it's better if we

design the invitations first. Then the only thing we'll have to do is fill in the date."

"Okay," Layla conceded. "We'll do the invitations. What if we get some bridal magazines and look through them. It would be easier than trying to come up with our own designs."

"That's a good idea. Let's ask Uncle Griff if he can take us to the mall."

Layla shook her head. "I don't know if he's going to take us again. We were just there yesterday."

Sabrina pursed her mouth. "I could always tell him that we need to get a gift for Aunt Lindy's birthday."

"Let's do it," Layla said, shutting down the computer.

Belinda's cell phone rang, and she reached over to the table next to her rocker to retrieve it. She pushed the talk button without glancing at the display. "Hello."

"Hello, Belinda."

She sat up after recognizing the voice coming through the earpiece. "Raymond. Long time, no hear. Where are you?"

"I'm still in Orlando, but I'm coming up your way next week. Do you think you can find some time to see me?"

"Where are you going to be?"

"I have to attend a conference at Johns Hopkins, but I can stop in Philly for a few days either before or after."

"You're going to have to give me a date, Raymond. My nieces are living with me now, and I have very little free time."

"How do you like playing mother?"

A slight frown appeared between her eyes. "I'm not 'playing mother,' Raymond. I am a mother."

"I'm sorry about that."

She smiled. "Apology accepted. Look, Raymond, I'm not in the house right now so there's no way for me to check my planner. Can you call me tomorrow evening and I'll let you know when we can get together?"

"You've got it, doll. Good afternoon."

"Good afternoon, Raymond."

Belinda looked at Griffin staring back at her. He'd overheard her conversation with Raymond. "Raymond's coming up next week."

"I thought paroled cons weren't allowed to leave the state," Griffin said, deadpan.

"That's enough, Griffin."

Griffin left the cushioned love seat on Belinda's front porch and came over to hunker down in front of her. "Sunshine's coming up next week and what, Belinda? Are you going to ask me to take care of the girls while you open your legs for him?"

"Stop it!" Her eyes filled with tears. "You have so little respect for me that you think I'd sleep with two men at the same time?"

"What's with you and this dude?"

"He's a friend, Griffin. A friend I'm not sleeping with," she added in a softer tone.

"Of course you're not sleeping with him because you're sleeping with me. But what's going to happen when he comes up?"

Suddenly it dawned on Belinda that Griffin was jealous—jealous of a man he'd never met. "Nothing's going to happen. I told him that I have the girls living with me, so he's going to stay at a hotel."

"And what if the girls weren't living with you. Where would he stay?"

"In my guest bedroom."

Griffin blinked once. "You really mean that you're just *friends?*"

She threw up a hand. "Yes, Griffin Rice! We are *f-r-i-e-n-d-s!*" She spelled the word for him.

A smile lit up Griffin's face like the rising sun. "Well, damn, Eaton. Why didn't you say that in the first place?"

"I did, Rice," she countered. "You just chose to believe what you wanted to believe, that a woman can't be friends with a man and not sleep with him."

"I've had women as friends that I didn't sleep with."

Belinda emitted an unladylike snort. "Yeah, right."

He leaned closer. "We were friends before we started sleeping together."

She ran a finger down the length of his nose. "Wrong, Rice. We were in-laws before we started sleeping together."

"We're still in-laws."

"True," Belinda drawled.

Reaching for her wrist, Griffin eased Belinda off the rocker and onto the floor of the porch. "I've been doing some thinking about hanging out here during the week and at my place on the weekends."

"You know you're dangerous when you start thinking," she said teasingly.

"I'm serious, Belinda."

She sobered. "Talk to me."

His eyes were fathomless pools of dark brown when he focused on Belinda's mouth. "Why don't we blend households?"

"Please explain blending, because I thought that's what we've done."

"Either you live with me, or I'll live with you."

Belinda shook her head. "Isn't that what we're doing, Griffin? You spend more time here during the week than you do in Paoli. And there're very few weekends we're not in Paoli. So, I don't know what it is you want."

Griffin took a deep breath. "I want you, me and the girls to live together under one roof."

For a moment, Belinda let herself believe she was mistaken when she tried analyzing the complex man sitting beside her. "You want us to shack up together?"

"Live together."

"Live. Shack. Same difference."

"What do you think?"

"I think you're crazy. What message would we send to our nieces if we shack up together?"

"It doesn't have to be 'shacking up,' as you put it."

"Pray tell, Rice, what would it be?"

"We could get married."

Belinda stared at Griffin Rice as if he'd taken leave of his senses. He'd mentioned marriage as if he were negotiating a deal. Give me this and I'll concede that. And, she wondered, what provoked his spur-of-the-moment proposal?

The sex was great—no, it was better than great. It was incredible. And what about love? Did he actually believe she would marry him when not once had he said or indicated that he loved her?

A hint of a smile ghosted across her face as realization dawned, just as the sky cleared with the sun rising each morning. "This is about Raymond, isn't it?"

"Who?" Griffin asked, feigning ignorance.

"Sunshine. This is about him, isn't it? You still don't believe that we have a platonic relationship and if I became your wife then you'd make certain he'd be out of my life—permanently. Thanks, but no thanks, Griffin. I don't want to marry you."

"This is not about Sunshine."

"Who is it about, Griffin, because it's definitely not about *us.*" Pushing to her feet, she stood up and went into the house, leaving him staring into space.

The soft slam of the door caught his attention and Griffin thought Belinda had come back because she'd changed her mind. He schooled his features so not to reveal his disappointment when Sabrina and Layla came out of the house.

Sabrina stared at her sister. "Uncle Griff, can you please drive us to the mall?"

He frowned. "Didn't we have this conversation yesterday?"

"Yes," Layla said quickly. "But we forgot to buy something for Aunt Lindy's birthday."

Griffin stood up. "When's her birthday?"

"May twenty-eighth," the girls said in unison.

He wanted to tell his nieces that he didn't want to go back to a mall two days in a row because he hated fighting the parking-lot traffic. He also detested the crowds. If they'd spent the weekend in Paoli then he would've driven them to a smaller mall that featured specialty shops instead of the large department stores.

Mother's Day had come and gone and the day hadn't gone well with the teenagers. They spent the day in their rooms, refusing to go to their grandparents' house for Sunday dinner.

It ended when he sat down with them to let both girls know how much Belinda had been hurt by their behavior, but that she understood they missed their mother, that although she would never replace their mother she loved them as if she'd given birth to them. The day ended with the four of them crawling into Belinda's bed and falling asleep.

He woke hours later and carried the girls to their bed, then drove back to Paoli. Griffin didn't know how Belinda did it. She made parenting look so easy when in reality it was the hardest job in the world.

Reaching into the pocket of his jeans, he took out his car keys.

"Let's go."

"We have to get our money," Layla said excitedly.

"I'll cover you this time," Griffin offered.

The two girls exchanged a glance. Sabrina smiled at her uncle. "We have to get our purses."

"Hurry up." His voice was fraught with resignation. He didn't know what it was with women and handbags. It was as if they couldn't go anywhere without a purse attached to their wrist or shoulder.

Griffin found himself sitting on a tufted chair in a jewelry shop while a saleswoman showed Sabrina and Layla gold lockets.

Layla beckoned to him. "Come, Uncle Griff, and look at this one. Do you think Aunt Lindy would like it?"

He stood and came over to the counter. His nieces had selected a variety of heart-shaped lockets. "Which ones do you like?" They pointed to two lockets. "I like this one," he said, pointing to one with a diamond on the front.

"We don't have enough money for that one," Sabrina said.

He pulled her ponytail. "Don't worry about the price. Pick out whatever you want."

Griffin wandered over to the showcase with diamond engagement rings and wedding bands. He spied one that would look perfect on Belinda's hand. Motioning to a salesman, he pointed in the case. "I want to see that one."

Light from hanging lamps caught the brilliance of the diamond solitaire. He didn't know if it would fit Belinda, but he didn't care. "I'll take it," he said softly. "I don't want my daughters to know I'm buying this for their mother, so let's not make a big show of it." Reaching into his pocket, he took out a case with his credit cards. He pushed one across the counter, winking when the elderly man smiled at him.

"What did you buy, Uncle Griff?" Sabrina asked when she saw him with the small shopping bag.

"It's just a little something for your aunt's birthday. Are you finished shopping?" he asked, smoothly changing the topic.

"We're going downstairs to the bookstore while you pay for the necklace. We'll meet you in front of the store."

Not waiting for their uncle to agree or disagree, the two girls raced out of the jewelry store. They needed to buy some magazines to get an idea of what they wanted to wear to their aunt and uncle's wedding.

Belinda's palms tingled from applauding as the entire cast of the school production of *Grease* came back for a third curtain call. She was startled when Griffin put two fingers in his mouth and whistled loud enough to shatter her eardrums. The spring concert was a rousing success.

Belinda had found herself singing along with Sandy and the Pink Ladies, and she was surprised when Griffin knew the lyrics to "Greased Lightning."

Both sets of grandparents had come to see the production, but Dwight and Roberta declined Lucas and Gloria's invitation to come with them to take their granddaughters out to an ice-cream parlor because they'd committed to a dinner-dance and they would already be late, but they hadn't wanted to miss seeing their grandchildren's dramatic debut.

Belinda kissed her mother and father, resplendent in evening attire, and watched as they rushed out of the auditorium. "Let's wait out in the lobby for the girls," she shouted to be overheard.

Slowly, they inched their way down the aisle and out of the auditorium to the lobby of the elite, private school. Sabrina and Layla would enter the ninth grade the next school year, and then she and Griffin would have to select a high school commensurate with their academic standards.

They'd attended a public school from the first to the third grade, accelerating to the fifth grade when they showed advanced aptitude. But at their present school, every student was gifted.

They didn't have to wait long as Sabrina and Layla appeared—both in stage makeup. Layla wore a cardigan sweater, buttoned in the back, poodle skirt, bobby socks and black-and-white saddle shoes. She'd tied a scarf around her neck and another around her ponytail.

Both girls squealed in excitement when Lucas and Gloria handed them bouquets of flowers. Lucas hunkered down and made a big show of kissing each girl on the cheek. "The flowers are from both your grandma and grandpa. They had to leave. What's in the shopping bags is something else Grandma and I brought back for you." They'd bought so many souvenirs for the girls they'd decided not to give them everything at the same time.

Layla smiled and leaned closer to Lucas. "Can we look now?"

"No, baby girl. Open it when you get home."

Sabrina squinted at Lucas. "Grandpa, we're much too old to be baby girls."

Lucas tugged on the end of her ponytail. "I don't care if you're thirty, you'll always be a baby girl to me."

Griffin patted his father's shoulder. "Dad, it's time we leave before we won't be able to get a seat."

Nodding, Lucas rose to his feet. "The girls can ride with me and Glo."

Griffin winked at his mother. "We'll meet you there."

"Your father has really mellowed," Belinda said as Griffin headed in the direction of the ice-cream parlor.

"Yeah. That's what Mom says. She claims going away together was the best thing for him."

"For him, or for them, Griffin?"

"I think it was good for both of them. They needed time away to deal with whatever they needed to deal with."

Chapter 15

Griffin sat in the shiny lipstick-red booth with his mother and Layla, while Sabrina, Belinda and Lucas sat opposite them. They'd ordered floats and sundaes smothered with endless toppings.

"This is decadent and fattening," Gloria said, spooning ice cream, whipped cream and chopped nuts into her mouth.

Layla picked colorful candies off her sundae. "My favorite is Gummi Bears."

Griffin smiled at his mother. "Didn't you join a gym?"

"I did, but the question should be, do I go."

Lucas stared at his ex-wife. "I'll go with you when I'm not working."

Sabrina patted her grandfather's arm. "Do you still work at the hospital, Grandpa?"

"No, sweetheart. I retired from the hospital pharmacy and now work part-time."

"Is that good?"

He nodded. "It's very good. I have a lot more time to do all the things I've always wanted to do."

Layla took a sip of water. "Grandpa, can you take Breena and me with you when you go to Europe again?"

"That depends on your aunt and uncle. We can't take you anywhere unless they say it's okay."

"Is it okay?" the girls asked in unison.

Belinda looked directly at Griffin. "We have to talk about it."

"And it all depends," Griffin added.

"On what?" they chorused.

"On your grades *and* how well you do your chores."

Layla rolled her eyes. "Now you sound like Aunt Lindy."

Griffin lowered his eyebrows. "You didn't know your Aunt Lindy and I are a team?"

Sabrina sucked her teeth. "I knew that. I heard you talking to Grandma and you told her that you love Aunt Lindy."

A silence descended on the table so thick it was palpable as the six people in the booth exchanged glances. "Did I say something I wasn't supposed to say?" Sabrina whispered, as if telling a secret.

Gloria glared across the table at her granddaughter. "You're not supposed to listen in on other people's conversations. And if you do, then you're not supposed to repeat it."

"I wasn't listening in, Grandma. I just happened to walk in the kitchen while he was talking to you. Besides, he was talking loud. If it was a secret, then he should've been whispering."

Belinda's heart beat rapidly against her ribs with Sabrina's revelation. Griffin had told his mother that he loved her and he hadn't told her.

The nerve of him! The absolute nerve of him!

Gloria touched a napkin to her mouth. "I don't know about anyone else, but I'm ready to turn in. Belinda, would you mind if the girls stayed with me tonight? After all, there's no school tomorrow."

"Yes, Mom, they can stay." Griffin had answered for Belinda. He knew she wanted answers, answers only he could give her. And, if she went off on him he didn't want the girls around to hear them arguing. He didn't want to subject them to what he and Grant had gone through as children.

"I asked Belinda, Griffin," Gloria admonished softly.

"I'm sorry, Mom."

Belinda blinked as if shocked back to reality. "Yes, Mrs. Rice, they can stay over."

Gloria gave her a saccharine smile. "I think it's time you either call me Mom or Gloria. It's up to you."

Belinda returned her smile. "Thank you—Mom."

Sliding out of the booth, Griffin reached into his pocket and tossed a bill on the table. Extending his hand, he gently helped Gloria out of the booth. "We'll bring over a change of clothes when we come to pick them up tomorrow."

"Don't rush, son. I'll give them something to wear. It may not be their style, but it'll keep them clothed." Tiptoeing to reach him, Gloria kissed Griffin's cheek. "Good luck with Lindy."

"Thank you."

Griffin had thought he was alone when he'd told his mother that he was in love with Belinda and wanted to marry her. He was waiting for the end of the school year to tell her, but his niece had let the cat out of the bag. He had to deal with it now—not later.

Not a word passed between them during the drive from the ice-cream parlor to Griffin's house in Paoli. He had wanted to tell Belinda that he loved her—loved anything and everything about her. It wasn't just her passion, that she held nothing back when offering herself, but it was also her strength, intelligence, determination, dedication and devotion to her students and to their daughters. There was also the playfulness and wit, the way she shed her inhibitions when she was rolling on the floor with Cecil and Nigel. He loved her even when they didn't agree on child rearing, because they were totally committed to the twins' well-being.

Griffin closed his eyes rather than watch Belinda pace the length of the patio in Paoli. It wasn't that long ago that she'd ordered him to meet her on the porch at Donna and Grant's house so they could talk. That time it'd been about his buying gifts for their nieces, and now it was about *them*.

He opened his eyes at the same time a frown furrowed his smooth brow. "Lindy, please sit down and talk to me."

"Why, Griffin, did you have to tell your mother before you told me?"

"I planned to tell you, but I wanted to wait."

She stopped long enough to give him a hostile stare. "When? Eleven years from now?"

"No, darling. First, I wanted to wait until the school year was over. I didn't want any distractions when we sat down to plan our future. Then, I changed my mind and wanted to tell you on your birthday."

"You can't plan a future with me if you don't tell me how you feel about me, Griffin Rice. You told your mother that you loved me. Don't you think it's time you tell me to my face?"

Griffin went to Belinda, pulling her gently into his embrace. "I love you, Belinda Jacqueline Eaton. I've loved you for a very long time, but you wouldn't let me get close to you. It took a tragedy—when I realized I'd lost my only sibling—to shake me to the core. But I will fight like hell to hold on to the only woman I've ever loved."

Belinda couldn't stop the tears that were welling up in her eyes from flowing. Her lower lip trembled. "I should kick your behind, Griffin Rice, for waiting all these years to tell me this. What happened to the big-shot, hard-nosed lawyer who will go to the mat for his clients, but can't tell a woman that he likes her?"

Cradling her face in his palms, Griffin wiped away her tears with his thumbs.

"I don't *like* you, Belinda. You like *me*. I *love* you!"

"No, Griffin. I don't like you."

"What!"

A trembling smile found its way over her face. "I love you, Griffin Rice. I love you," she repeated it over and over as he picked her up and swung her around.

Griffin stopped, lowering her feet to the patio floor. "I'm going to ask you to do something for me, not to-night, but soon."

Easing back, Belinda stared up into the eyes of the

man she'd loved for so long that she couldn't remember when she didn't love him. "What is it?"

"Call Sunshine, and tell him that if he ever comes within ten feet of my fiancée again I'm going to hurt him real bad," he said, emphasizing the last four words.

Belinda smiled through the tears that were turning her eyes into pools of smoky quartz. "I told Raymond about you, and he says that exchanging Christmas cards will be the extent of our friendship. He didn't think he would be as understanding if you were my friend, and I was sleeping with him."

"I've changed my mind about Sunshine. I think I like him. And I'm sorry that I called him a chump and a con man."

Moving closer, Belinda kissed the cleft in his sexy chin. "You were jealous, when you had no need to be. It was you I was sleeping with, not Raymond."

"Lucky me. I'm the one who gets the nasty girl."

"You turned me into a nasty girl, Griffin Rice."

"Guilty as charged." Bending slightly, he swept her up in his arms. "Let's go inside and test the nasty meter again. But, before we do that we should talk about a few other things."

"What other things?"

"When do you want to get married? Do you want to live closer to Philly or here in Paoli? Do you want to increase our family—"

Belinda placed her hand over his mouth. "Stop talking, counselor. I can answer all those questions for you right now. I'd like to get married sometime this summer, preferably before the end of July. I'd prefer living in Paoli, but of course that means our daughters will have to change school districts. And yes, I'd like to begin increasing our family as soon as possible. Are there any other questions?"

He shook his head. "That's enough for now."

Griffin locked the door and carried Belinda up the staircase to what would become their bedroom. There was only the sound of measured breathing as she and the man holding her to his heart placed her on the bed. Leaning over, he brushed a kiss over her parted lips.

"Don't move. I know your birthday is a couple of days away, but I'd like to give you your gift now." Belinda leaned over on her elbows, her chin resting on her hands as she watched Griffin walk to the triple dresser and open a drawer.

He returned to the bed and sat down next to Belinda. Reaching for her left hand, he slipped the ring on her third finger, exhaling audibly. It was a perfect fit.

Belinda couldn't stop shaking. The brilliant emerald-cut diamond ring surrounded by baguette diamonds was magnificent. For the second time in a matter of minutes her eyes filled with tears. "I… I don't…"

"If you don't like it, then I'll take it back and you can pick out one that—"

"I love it, Griffin. I love you," she said, interrupting him. Putting her arms around his neck, she pressed her face to his warm throat. "When did you buy the ring?"

"I don't remember."

Belinda gave him a skeptical look. "I don't believe you."

"I bought it almost two weeks ago."

"You were that certain I'd marry you that you bought me a ring?"

"No. I bought it, hoping and praying that one day you'd accept it."

"Before you told me that you loved me?"

"I was going to do that—eventually."

"What am I going to do with you, Griffin Rice?"

Leaning back against the headboard, Griffin stared directly at Belinda. "You're going to marry me and give Sabrina and Layla a few brothers and sisters—technically they'll be cousins. And we'll grow more in love with each other as we grow old together."

"I'm never growing old, darling, and I don't want to stop being a nasty girl."

He trailed a series of kisses down the column of her neck, while unbuttoning her blouse. "Even when you're ninety-two and I'm ninety-seven you'll still be my beautiful, precious, nasty girl."

Belinda's breathing quickened as if she were panting, while Griffin stripped her of each article of clothing. She wanted him to go faster, but he seemed determined to take his time.

Her blouse, slacks and bra lay in a pool at the foot of the large bed. Once he'd taken off her panties, she lay completely naked and vulnerable to his ravenous gaze.

Going to her knees, she undressed her fiancé as slowly as he'd undressed her. And, when he lay on his back, all of his masculine magnificence was on display for her hungry gaze. A look of heated passion passed between them. This coming together would be different from all the others. The ring on her finger symbolized a shared commitment, a continuous bond of love that had no beginning or end. This night wasn't hers or Griffin's, but theirs.

Supporting herself with her hands, she lowered her body until her breasts were molded to his broad chest. "Do you want it nasty, or do you want it nice?"

Smiling, Griffin closed his eyes. "I'll take it any way and any how you choose to give it to me."

It was Belinda's turn to smile. "Like Tina Turner sang in 'Proud Mary,' I'm going to give it to you nice before it gets rough."

Griffin opened his eyes as an expression of unabashed carnal instinct spread across his face. "Serve it, Eaton." His rich, deep voice had dropped an octave. "Oh!" he bellowed within seconds of issuing the challenge when Belinda's mouth branded him her possession, swallowing back the expletive.

Her tongue took him to a place where he'd never been, and he surrendered all he was, had been and ever hoped to be. Her hot breath seared his loins and he went still, unable to protest or think of anything except the exquisite pleasure Belinda offered him. Clamping both hands over his mouth to muffle the groans crowding his throat, Griffin arched his pelvis off the bed. His passions were building quickly and he knew it was just a matter of time before he wouldn't be able to control where they'd be spent.

He sat up quickly, reaching for Belinda's hair. She emitted a small cry of surprise when he forced her to release his erection. Not giving her the opportunity to protest, he flipped her over and entered her in one, sure motion that buried his sex so deeply inside her that their bodies ceased to exist as separate entities.

Belinda's arms went around Griffin's waist as rivulets of sweat bathed his back and dotted her hands. She couldn't think of anything except the hard body atop hers as together they found a rhythm where they were in perfect harmony. The contractions began as flutters then increased in intensity until the hottest of fires swept over her, leaving tiny embers of ecstasy that lingered long after she'd returned from her free fall.

Reaching down, Griffin cupped her hips in his hands, lifting her higher and allowing for deeper penetration, then quickening his movements and bellowing out her name as he spilled his passion inside her hot, wet body. There was only the sound of their labored breathing in the stillness of the bedroom as they lay motionless, savoring the aftermath of a shared, sweet fulfillment.

As they lay in bed, their sexual passions momentarily sated, Belinda thought of her sister. She wished her sister could have been there to see her exchange vows with Griffin. But she knew Donna was smiling.

"Darling?"

Griffin smiled. "What is it, baby?"

"If we have a girl I want to name her Donna. But, if it's a boy then it'll be Grant."

Griffin felt a rush of tears behind his eyelids. He'd cried when told of his brother's death, and there was no doubt he would cry again—at the birth of his and Belinda's child. It didn't matter whether it was a boy or a girl. It would be loved, cherished and, of course, spoiled. He would make certain of that.

Turning his head, he fastened his mouth to the side of her neck. "Those are wonderful names."

Belinda smiled. "I didn't think you had it in you, but I think I'm going to give you a passing grade in the daddy category."

Griffin chuckled. "Does this mean I'm going to get an A?"

"Don't push it, Rice," she teased.

"What grade will you give me?"

She wrinkled her nose. "B-plus. If I give you an A then you'll end up with a swelled head."

"You keep cranking up that nasty meter and another head will remain swollen."

Belinda landed a soft punch on his shoulder. "You are so nasty, Griffin Rice."

Lifting his head, he flashed a wide grin. "I know, and you like it, don't you?"

"Hell, yeah!"

"That's my girl!" Griffin withdrew from Belinda and pulled her against his chest. "Did I tell you that I loved you?"

She wrinkled her nose again. "I don't remember. But you can tell me, just to refresh my memory."

And Griffin knew he would tell Belinda that he loved her—every day for the rest of their lives together.

* * * * *

SWEET DECEPTION

Blessed are the meek: for they shall inherit the earth.
—*Matthew* 5:5

Chapter 1

The buzz of the intercom echoed throughout the spacious co-op. "I'll get it," Myles Eaton announced loudly from the bedroom. Pressing the button on the intercom, he spoke into the speaker. "Yes?"

"Mr. Eaton, there's a take-out delivery in the lobby for you."

"Please send it up."

Zabrina Mixon stepped inside the apartment from the terrace, closing the sliding-glass door behind her. She liked seeing her fiancé dressed casually in T-shirts, shorts and sandals rather than a business suit. Suits always made him appear staid, standoffish. Her gaze lingered on his muscular calves before moving up to his broad chest and finally his ruggedly handsome face. His face was symmetrical with a dark brown complexion, deep-set eyes and a lean, angular jaw that became more pronounced whenever he smiled. His gorgeous smile drew attention to his perfectly aligned white teeth.

She couldn't remember when she hadn't been in love with Myles Eaton. He'd taught her to ride a bike, and whenever she fell he'd brushed off the dirt from her scraped knees and elbows, then helped her to get back on. Her infatuation began in childhood when Myles became her prince.

"I've finished setting the table," said Zabrina.

Myles smiled at his fiancée. He hadn't believed his luck when he'd finally opened his eyes to his sister's best friend. He'd thought of her as a younger sister until her eighteenth birthday. It was the first time that *he* had kissed her. A few years before that *she* had kissed him before he left Philadelphia to attend Penn State. Her excuse was that she hadn't wanted him to miss her.

Zabrina kissing Myles had left him feeling unsettled, because at eighteen he was an adult—a sexually active adult, and he had not wanted to take advantage of a teenage girl. However, several years later, they both had changed. Zabrina left home to attend Vanderbilt University School of Nursing in Tennessee while he was headed to Pittsburgh to enroll in Duquesne University School of Law.

By the time she was in college, there was nothing prepubescent about Zabrina Mixon. She was no longer tall and gangly, her body had filled out with womanly curves and her voice had deepened to a low, sexy tone that never failed to send shivers up and down his body. The sound of her voice was only matched by the luminous hazel eyes that pulled him in and refused to let him go.

Zabrina had a way of seducing him without saying a word. All she had to do was look at him and he forgot any woman he'd ever known. They reconnected whenever they returned home during semester breaks, but it wasn't until she'd graduated from college that he'd proposed marriage and she'd accepted. They'd talked about having a June wedding, but the establishment where they wanted to have the reception was booked solid until October. They'd reserved the last Saturday in October, because neither wanted a winter wedding given the unpredictable weather.

Myles winked at Zabrina. "Go back outside and relax, baby. The food is on its way up and I'll bring everything out to the terrace."

She returned the wink, then retraced her steps. Settling into an oversize pillow on the terrace of Myles's fourteenth-floor co-op, Zabrina waited for him to join her.

After her twelve-hour shift at a busy Philadelphia municipal hospital, she'd checked her cell phone for messages earlier that day. There were two: one from her father to let her know he was having dinner with an up-and-coming local politician who wanted Isaac Mixon to run his campaign for reelection to the state assembly, and the second from Myles.

After listening to Myles's message asking her to meet him for dinner at his apartment, she'd gone home to shower and change her clothes, then walked the short distance from the condominium where she lived with her father to Myles's high-rise. The doorman at the luxury building had greeted her by name. Within days of Myles slipping the diamond engagement ring onto her finger, he'd given her a key to his co-op and had officially notified the building management to grant her complete access.

The sun slipped lower, taking with it the intense summer heat as a cool breeze swept over her face and body. Lighted votives that she'd positioned around the terrace flickered like fireflies with the encroaching darkness. Philadelphia had experienced the most brutal heat wave it'd had in years. A steady two-day rain had finally broken the ninety-plus-degree heat and the streets in the City of Brotherly Love once again teemed with residents and tourists taking advantage of the more comfortable summer temperatures.

Turning her gaze away from the panoramic view of the twin glass spires of Liberty Place soaring above the Philadelphia skyline, Zabrina saw Myles holding a shopping bag from which emanated the most mouth-watering aroma.

"Something smells wonderful."

Myles leaned over and kissed the hair she'd brushed off her face and secured in a single braid. "That must be my linguine with garlic and olive oil."

"Phew," Zabrina said, pinching her nostrils. "Remind me not to kiss you."

"What if I brush my teeth and use mouthwash?"

She wrinkled her nose. "I'll think about it," she teased.

Myles sat opposite Zabrina, reached into the bag and took out a small container of Caesar salad, then two larger containers with his entrée and Zabrina's Caesar salad with grilled chicken. "Wait, darling, we're missing something."

Zabrina examined the place settings. "What's missing?"

"Wine and music."

"What are we celebrating, Myles?"

He stood and leaned over the table. "My love for you, darling."

Zabrina rose to brush her mouth over his, her eyes filling with tears. She never tired of hearing him say that he loved her. "And I love you, too, Myles Adam Eaton."

Myles returned with a bottle of wine, glasses and a small portable radio that he'd tuned to an all-music station. He filled the wineglasses with a light rosé, raising his goblet in a toast. "Here's to the sexiest and most beautiful woman in the world. I'm counting down the days until I can make you my wife."

Zabrina paused, trying to keep her fragile emotions under control. She touched her glass to his. "Here's to the man who makes me feel alive, look forward to tomorrow and to all my tomorrows as his wife."

A wave of sadness came over her like a rushing wave. She didn't know why, but she felt like crying. In exactly three months she would exchange vows with the man she loved beyond words. How many women, she wondered, were fortunate enough to marry the first man they'd fallen in love with? Not too many, so she'd counted herself blessed.

"Hear, hear," Myles intoned before taking a sip of wine.

"I hope your client is toasting you for keeping his butt out of prison."

A scowl settled across his features. He'd made it a

practice not to discuss his work with Zabrina, but the name of his high-profile client was on the tongue of most Philadelphians after the aide to the mayor had been charged with a sex crime.

"Jack Tolliver was innocent and apparently the prosecutor agreed with me when he threw out the charges for lack of evidence."

"But didn't he admit to sleeping with the woman?"

Myles rolled his eyes upward. "Yes, baby."

"So, who's to say it was consensual?"

"He said he didn't rape her."

Zabrina gave him a quizzical look. "And you believed him?"

"Yes."

"Just because he said he didn't do it?" She gestured with her fork. "Darling, Jack Tolliver is a lying, cheating politician who wouldn't recognize the truth if it jumped up and bit him on the ass."

Myles angled his head. "Are you angry with Jack because he cheated on his wife with another woman, or are you angry because he's a politician?"

"It's because he's a politician, Myles. I know he's human, but when he stands up in front of millions of voters asking for their trust, the least he could do is not betray their trust—and his wife's—by creeping with a married woman."

"You're too young to be so jaded when it comes to politicians, baby. Perhaps you should stay away from your father's friends."

He'd gotten the judge to dismiss the case because the plaintiff's rape kit had turned up evidence that she'd slept with his client *and* with another man. If Myles was going to toast anything it was that DNA forensics had helped to exonerate or convict suspects in some of the most violent crimes.

"My father's friends are just that—his friends. The only interaction I have with them is when I stand in as his hostess. Other than that, I loathe their fake smiles, weak handshakes, lecherous stares and the rare occasion when they brush against me pretending that it was an accident."

Myles went completely still, his frown deepening. "Is someone bothering you?"

She waved a hand. "No, darling. Most of them are around the same age as my father, so I ignore them."

Zabrina stared at her fiancé across the small space. Lately, she and Myles saw less and less of each other. Her eight-hour shift rotated every three months, and then there was overtime. Myles had passed the bar and clerked for a judge before becoming a trial lawyer for a Philadelphia firm handling high-profile cases. His ultimate goal was to make partner within ten years.

Swallowing a mouthful of pasta, Myles met Zabrina's eyes. They appeared catlike in the candlelight. "Can you take a couple of days off?"

"Why?"

"I'd like for us to go away together so we can spend some quality time together."

Reaching over the table, Myles grasped her hands. "I saw more of you before we were engaged than I do now."

Zabrina sobered. He'd read her mind. "That's because *you've* become a workaholic."

"I want to make partner, Brina."

She wanted to tell Myles there were no guarantees that he would make partner even if he worked ninety hours a week, while winning every case for the firm. But she held her tongue because she didn't want him to think she wasn't supportive.

"Where do you want to go?" she asked.

His grip tightened on her fingers. "I'll leave that up to you."

It took only seconds for her to make a decision. "I want to go to Buenos Aires."

"Buenos Aires, Argentina?" She nodded. "What's in Buenos Aires?"

"Tango lessons," Zabrina replied. "I want our first dance as husband and wife to be a tango, and what better place to learn the dance of love and passion than in Argentina?"

Rising, Myles walked around the circular table and gently pulled Zabrina to her feet. He dipped his head and pressed his mouth to the column of her scented neck. "I happen to believe we dance very well together."

She giggled like a child. "Are you talking about the horizontal mambo?"

"Yes, I am."

Moving into his embrace, Zabrina wrapped her arms around Myles's waist. He felt so good, smelled so incredibly delicious. His cologne was specially blended to complement his body's natural pheromones. She closed her eyes and smiled. "I seem to have forgotten the steps."

Pulling her closer, Myles reveled in the soft crush of firm breasts against his chest. "How long has it been, baby?" he whispered.

Zabrina thought back to the last time they'd made love. "It's been at least three weeks."

"I promise to make love to…"

She placed her fingertips over his mouth, stopping his words. "Don't promise. Just do it."

Bending slightly, Myles swept his fiancée up into his arms and carried her off the terrace to the bedroom. He hadn't wanted to believe he hadn't made love to Zabrina in weeks. When, he thought, had his work taken precedence over the woman he loved and planned to marry? She'd become the most important thing in his life, yet he'd let something else replace her.

Their candlelit terrace dinner was forgotten when he placed Zabrina on the bed, his body following hers. It took less than a minute for Myles to remove her sandals, sundress and panties. The light from the bedside-table lamp, dimmed to its lowest setting, spilled over her nude body, making it appear like a statue of gold.

He undressed and then moved over her. "I can't believe I've neglected you for so long. I want you to remind me when I get so caught up straightening out other people's lives that I forget what I have right in front of me."

Zabrina buried her face between Myles's neck and shoulder at the same time her arms went around his waist. "How often do you want me to remind you?"

"Every night," he said in her ear.

She opened her eyes and smiled. "If that's the case, then I'll be certain to do it."

Myles breathed a kiss under her ear, along the column of her neck and to her throat. His rapacious tongue charted a path down her body as he suckled one breast, then the other. Zabrina's breathing came faster and faster. His tongue swept over her like a wildcat savoring its kill. He tasted her belly. Effortlessly he turned her over to taste her back, nipping the skin covering her hips. Pressing a kiss to the small of her back, he moved lower to the area between her legs. Myles anchored his hands under her thighs and pulled her up into a kneeling position.

Zabrina was on fire! It was as if Myles had struck a match and set her ablaze. The increasing heat between her legs escalated as her hips undulated in a natural rhythm that communicated a long-denied need.

Myles felt and inhaled the rising desire from the slender body pushing back against his belly. He hardened quickly, so quickly he feared spilling his passion on the sheets. Guiding his erection, he eased it between Zabrina's thighs. The two of them sighed as flesh closed around flesh, making them one.

Grasping her waist with both hands, he held her captive as she pushed back to meet his strong thrusts. He closed his eyes and bit down on his lip to keep the groans building in his throat from escaping, but the rising passion was too much and he moaned as if in pain. But it was the most pleasurable pain he'd ever experienced.

He didn't know what it was about Zabrina Mixon, but once she had offered him her virginal body, every woman in his past had ceased to exist. And what he couldn't understand was how had he gone nearly a month without making love with her. Had his quest to make partner taken precedence over the woman he loved? Zabrina didn't want him to make promises, but he promised himself that tonight would signal change. He would put his fiancée first and his career second.

Heat began in Zabrina's core and spread outward like spokes on a wheel. Reaching for the top of the headboard, she held on to the carved mahogany as if it were a lifeline. And at that moment it was. Unfamiliar sensations raced through her body, cutting a swath of pleasure that lifted her beyond ecstasy. She was caught up in a maelstrom of passion that bordered on hysteria. Her throat was burning from the screams that emanated from somewhere she hadn't known existed, then, without warning, the orgasms came, one after the other, overlapping until she felt herself succumbing to the deepest desire she'd ever experienced.

Myles held Zabrina's waist in a punishing grip as he rested his head on her back. He clenched his teeth so tightly his jaw ached, and try as he could he couldn't hold back the passion threatening to erupt at any moment. Sucking in a lungful of breath, he surrendered to the raging fire in his loins, his body shaking like a stalwart tree in a storm.

In a moment of madness they'd surrendered all they were and would ever be to each other.

Chapter 2

The reason you've been feeling so tired is that you're pregnant.

The doctor's diagnosis played over and over in Zabrina Mixon's head until she felt as if it were a mantra. Warm tears spilled down her face, blurring her vision, but she could still see the indicator wand that came with the home pregnancy test. She *was* pregnant. She, a registered nurse, who hadn't believed her ob-gyn, had stopped at a local drugstore and bought a kit to conduct her own test.

Her gynecologist had changed her contraceptive three times, the third being a lower-dose pill. The other two had adverse side effects: headaches, nausea and tender breasts. Apparently the lowest dose was too low, because she was now among the one percent of women who'd gotten pregnant on the pill. She and Myles Eaton had talked about starting a family, but at twenty-three Zabrina had wanted to wait at least two years. Two years would give her time to adjust to married life.

She'd been counting the days before she would exchange vows with the man she'd fallen in love with after they'd only dated a month. He'd waited a year to propose marriage and she'd accepted. It was now two weeks before her wedding and she would walk down the aisle with a new life growing inside her. It wasn't how she'd planned to start married life.

Discarding the pregnancy kit in the wastebasket, Zabrina washed her hands. She walked out of the bathroom, stopping when she heard voices coming from the living room. She recognized her father's voice and another that was vaguely familiar. A third voice, this one deeper than the others stopped her mid-stride. This voice she knew. It belonged to Thomas Cooper, her father's protégé. Alarmed, she made her way into the living room.

"What's going on here?"

Isaac Mixon turned when he heard his daughter's voice. "When did you get home?"

Zabrina's gaze shifted from her father to the other two men. It was obvious they'd thought they were alone. "I got here about twenty minutes ago." She glared at City Council President Thomas Cooper, who, it was widely rumored, had aspirations to become Philadelphia's next mayor. "Were you threatening my father?"

Thomas Cooper flashed a smile, the one he'd perfected for the media and his constituents. "Zabrina, please come and sit down."

Zabrina's eyebrows lifted. "You're inviting me to sit down in *my* own home?"

The practiced smile vanished quickly. "Mixon, I think you'd better convince your daughter to listen to what we have to tell her, or she'll read about your arrest in tomorrow's Philly *Inquirer.*"

Isaac crossed the room and cradled his daughter to his chest. "Please, Brina, let me handle this."

Light brown eyes flecked with hints of green studied the face of the man who'd protected her since her mother had died the year Zabrina had celebrated her seventh birthday. Isaac Mixon had become father *and* mother, refusing to remarry because he claimed he didn't want to subject her to a dreadful stepmother. She knew he dated women, but he'd never brought one home.

She nodded. "Okay, Daddy." Isaac pulled out a straight-back chair for Zabrina to sit in, and she watched as her father walked over to the floor-to-ceiling windows to peer out at the Philadelphia skyline.

It was the third man in the room who spoke first. "Miss Mixon, your father has been misappropriating monies from Councilman Cooper's campaign contributions."

A heavy silence filled the room as four pairs of eyes exchanged glances, and Zabrina wondered how many more shocks she would have to endure in one day. First there was the news that she was carrying a child, and now the threat that her father was facing arrest for stealing money from the man whose political career he'd shepherded from political analyst to city council member and now city council president.

She didn't believe it, she couldn't possibly believe it.

Her father didn't have financial problems. In fact, she knew for certain that he was solvent. It was she who reconciled his bank statements because Isaac Mixon didn't want to have anything to do with money. He was an ideas person, not a numbers guy. In fact, he was a political genius when it came to political campaign strategies.

"I don't believe you," she told the well-dressed man with a sallow pockmarked complexion. It was almost impossible to discern the color of his eyes behind a pair of thick lenses perched on a short nose that gave him a porcine appearance.

"Perhaps Councilman Cooper and I should leave you alone with your father for a few moments so he can bare his soul. Perhaps then you'll believe me."

Thomas nodded to Zabrina. "Mr. Davidson and I will be in your father's study. Please, don't get up. I know where it is."

Zabrina felt her throat closing as a wave of rage held her captive, not permitting her to draw a normal breath. It was the second time the arrogant politician had usurped her in her home. Once she'd reached sixteen she'd thought of the three-bedroom condo as *hers.* It was then that she'd assumed the responsibility of mistress of the house when standing in as hostess for Isaac Mixon's many political confabs and soirées.

She drew in a breath and closed her eyes. When she opened them and stared at her father he seemed to have aged within a matter of seconds. "What's going on, Daddy?"

Isaac Mixon knew whatever he'd been instructed to tell his daughter was going to destroy her. But either he had to lie or go to jail for a crime he did not commit. And disclosing what he knew meant his chances of survival were slim to none. Thomas Cooper had too many connections in *and* out of prison.

He walked across the living room and sank down on a love seat. "I'm sorry, baby girl, I—"

"You're sorry, Daddy!" Zabrina hadn't realized she was screaming, and at her father no less. "You're sorry for what?"

"I did divert some of Tom's campaign funds."

"Divert or steal, Daddy?"

Isaac saw fire in his daughter's eyes, the same fire that had burned so brightly in her mother's eyes before a debilitating disease had stolen her spirit and will to live. Zabrina had inherited Jacinta's palomino-gold coloring, inky-black hair and hazel eyes that always reminded him of semi-precious jewels. He hadn't celebrated his tenth wedding anniversary when he lost his wife, but fate hadn't taken everything from him because Jacinta lived on in the image of their daughter.

"I took the money," he lied smoothly.

"But why did you do it? You have money."

Isaac lowered his salt-and-pepper head, focusing his attention on the thick pile of the carpet under his feet. He knew if he met his daughter's eyes he wouldn't be able to continue to lie to her. "I…I've been gambling—"

"But you never gamble!"

"But I do now!" he spat out in a nasty tone. "I bet on everything: cards, ponies and even illegal numbers."

Zabrina's eyelids fluttered as she tried processing what her father was telling her. "Why didn't you use your own money?"

He glared at her. "I didn't want you to know about my nasty little addiction."

"How much did you take?"

"Eighty-three," Isaac admitted.

"Eighty-three…eighty-three hundred," Zabrina repeated over and over. "I have more than that in my savings account. I'll go to the bank tomorrow and get a bank check payable to Thomas Cooper—"

"Stop, Brina! It's not eighty-three hundred but eighty-three thousand—money Tom gave me to pay off loan sharks who'd threatened to kill me." Tears filled Isaac Mixon's eyes as his face crumpled like an accordion. "I took twenty thousand from the campaign fund and borrowed the rest from a loan shark. "Right now I owe Thomas Cooper more than one hundred thousand dollars."

"What about the money in your 401K?" she asked.

"I'll have to pay it back," Isaac said.

"How about selling the condo?"

Isaac shook his head. "That would take too long."

Zabrina's eyes narrowed. "How much time has Thomas given you to repay him without pressing charges?"

"He wants my answer now."

"Answer to what, Daddy?"

Isaac's head came up and he met his daughter's eyes for the first time, seeing pain and unshed tears. "Thomas has threatened to have me arrested unless I can get you to agree to…" His words trailed off.

Zabrina leaned forward. "Get me to do what?"

"He wants you to marry him."

Her father's words hit her like a punch to the face,

and for a brief moment she believed he was joking, blurting out anything that came to mind to belie his fear. Her hands tightened on the arms of the chair.

"Thomas Cooper wants to marry me when he knows I'm going to marry another man in two weeks?" Isaac nodded. "I can't, Daddy!" She was screaming again.

Isaac pushed to his feet. The droop of his shoulders indicated defeat. His so-called protégé was blackmailing him because of what he'd witnessed when he'd walked into Thomas's private office: Councilman Cooper had accepted a cash payment from a local Philadelphia businessman whom law officials suspected had ties to organized crime.

It was a week later that a strange man was ushered into Isaac's office with a message from the businessman: *forget what you saw or your daughter will find herself placing flowers on her father's grave.*

Later that evening he'd met with Thomas who had made him an offer he couldn't refuse. The confirmed bachelor talked incessantly about enhancing his image before declaring his candidacy for the mayoralty race, and then had shocked Isaac when he told him that he wanted to marry his daughter. Nothing Isaac could say could dissuade Cooper even when he told Thomas that Zabrina was engaged to marry Myles Eaton. Thomas Cooper dismissed the pronouncement with a wave of his hand, claiming marrying Zabrina Mixon would serve as added insurance that her father would never turn on his son-in-law.

Zabrina didn't, couldn't, move. "I don't believe this. This is the twenty-first century, yet you're offering me up as if I were chattel you'd put up in a card game. I could possibly consider marrying Thomas if I wasn't engaged or pregnant. But, I'm sorry, Daddy. I can't."

Isaac turned slowly and stared down at his daughter's bowed head. "You're what?"

Her head came up. "I just found out this morning that I'm pregnant with Myles Eaton's baby."

"Does he know?" Isaac's voice was barely a whisper.

"Not yet. I plan to tell him later tonight."

"But you won't tell him, Zabrina. The child will carry my name," said Thomas confidently.

Zabrina hadn't realized Thomas and the other man he'd called Davidson had reentered the living room. "Go to hell!"

The elected official's expression did not change. "Mr. Davidson, perhaps you can convince Miss Mixon of the seriousness of her father's dilemma."

The bespectacled man reached under his suit jacket, pulled out a small caliber handgun with a silencer, aiming it at Isaac's head. "You have exactly five seconds, Miss Mixon, to give Councilman Cooper an answer."

Zabrina's heart was beating so hard she was certain it could be seen through her blouse. "Okay!" she screamed. "Okay," she repeated, this time her acquiescence softer. There was no mistaking defeat in the single word.

Thomas smiled for the first time. "Not only are you beautiful, but you're very, very smart. We'll marry next week in a private ceremony. And, you don't have to worry about me exercising my conjugal rights. Our marriage will be in name only."

A rage she'd never known burned through Zabrina. "Does that leave me free to take a lover or lovers?"

The councilman's smile faded. "In two years you'll be the wife of Philadelphia's next mayor, so I doubt that with the responsibility of raising a child and taking care of your social obligations, you'll find time to open your legs to another man."

She felt the overwhelming sick feeling that came with defeat, but she wasn't going to let the blackmailing SOB know that. "One of these days I'm going to kill you."

A slight arch in his eyebrows was the only indication that Thomas had registered her threat. "Take a number, Miss Mixon." He motioned to his gofer to put the gun away. "I suggest you call your *fiancé* and tell him you found a better prospect."

The footsteps of the two men were muffled in the carpet as they turned and walked to the door. The solid slam of the door shocked Zabrina into an awareness of just what had taken place within a matter of minutes. She'd agreed to marry a man she'd come to detest when the baby of another man she'd pledged to marry in two weeks was growing beneath her heart.

She registered another sound, and it took her several seconds to realize her father was crying. Even when they'd buried her mother she hadn't seen Isaac cry. She stood up and walked over to her father. Going to her knees, Zabrina pressed her face to his chest. It wasn't easy to comfort him when she was sobbing inconsolably.

It was later, much later when Zabrina retreated to her bedroom to call Myles Eaton to tell him that she couldn't marry him because she was in love with another man. There was only the sound of breathing coming through the earpiece until a distinctive click told her Myles had hung up.

She didn't cry only because she had no more tears. Her mind was a maelstrom of thoughts that ranged from premeditated murder to the need to survive to bring her unborn child to term. She may have lost Myles Eaton, but unknowingly he'd given her a precious gift—a gift she would love to her dying breath.

Chapter 3

Ten years later...

"I can't believe you're marrying your sister's brother-in-law."

"Believe it, because in another week I'll become Mrs. Griffin Rice."

A hint of a smile lifted the corners of Belinda Eaton's mouth as she stared at Zabrina Cooper. As she'd promised when she'd run into Zabrina at a fundraiser, she'd called to set up a dinner date with the woman who at one time had been engaged to her brother.

Her twin nieces, Layla and Sabrina, whom she and Griffin legally adopted after their parents died in a horrific head-on automobile accident, were spending the weekend with their paternal grandparents, giving Belinda the time she needed to meet with her childhood friend and finish packing her personal belongings before she moved into Griffin's house. They had gone from being godparents to parents, after Belinda's sister, who was married to Griffin's brother, died tragically in an auto accident, leaving the twins orphans.

The skin around Zabrina's large light brown eyes crinkled when she smiled, something she hadn't done often, or in a very long time. The only person who could get her to smile or laugh spontaneously was her son. Adam was not only the love of her life, he was her life. Her mother had died when she was young, and she'd buried her father four months before she'd become a widow. Aside from an aunt and a few distant cousins there was only Adam.

She sobered, staring at the woman who, if she'd married Myles Eaton, would have become her sister-in-law. To say the high-school history teacher was stunning was an understatement. The soft glow from the candle on the table flattered Belinda's flawless sable complexion. A little makeup accentuated the exotic slant of her dark eyes, high cheekbones, short straight nose and generously curved full mouth. A profusion of dark curly hair framed her attractive face.

Zabrina's gaze moved from Belinda's face to her hand, which flaunted a magnificent emerald-cut diamond ring surrounded with baguettes. She remembered the engagement ring Myles had slipped on her finger, a ring she had returned to him via a bonded messenger hours after she'd called him to let him know she couldn't marry him because she was in love with another man.

"I knew there was something going on between you

and Griffin when you two were maid of honor and best man at Donna and Grant's wedding." Belinda's older sister had married Griffin's older brother.

Belinda took a sip from her water goblet. "That's where you're wrong, Brina. Griffin and I barely tolerated each other. What I hadn't realized at the time was that I was in love with him. But instead of letting him know that, I acted like a junior-high schoolgirl who punches out the boy so everyone believes that she despises rather than likes him."

Zabrina stared at her bare hands resting on the tablecloth. "It was the same with me and Myles. He used to tease me mercilessly until I kissed him. I don't know who was more shocked—me or him."

"You kissed my brother first?"

Zabrina's face became flushed as she cast her eyes downward. "He was leaving for college, and I didn't want him to forget me."

"And apparently he didn't," Belinda said softly.

Zabrina looked up and her eyes met Belinda's. "I was thirteen when I kissed Myles for the first time, and I had to wait another five years before he kissed me back. Myles claimed he didn't want to take advantage of a minor, so he felt at eighteen I was old enough either to let him kiss me or punch his lights out." Her eyes brimmed with tears. "The happiest day in my life was when your brother asked me to marry him and one of the darkest was when I called to tell him I was in love with another man."

Reaching across the table, Belinda placed her hand over Zabrina's ice-cold fingers. "What happened,

Brina? I know you loved my brother, so why did you lie to him?"

The seconds ticked off as the two women stared at each other. They'd met in the first grade and become fast friends. Then tragedy had separated them for a year when Zabrina's mother was diagnosed with brain cancer.

Isaac Mixon moved his wife and daughter to Mexico for an experimental treatment not approved by oncologists in the United States. Zabrina had just celebrated her seventh birthday when Jacinta passed away. Her body was cremated and her ashes scattered in the ocean.

Zabrina returned to the States with her father, not to live in the stately white Colonial with black trim but in a three-bedroom condominium in an exclusive Philadelphia neighborhood. She and Belinda no longer attended the same school, yet they'd managed to get together every weekend. Belinda would either stay over at Zabrina's, or she would sleep over at Belinda's. Though Belinda had two other sisters, Zabrina Mixon had become her best friend *and* unofficial sister. But a lifetime of friendship had ended with a single telephone call to Myles Eaton.

Belinda stared at the beautiful woman with the gold-brown skin, gleaming black chin-length hair and brilliant hazel eyes. She remembered photographs of Jacinta Mixon, and Zabrina was her mother's twin.

"I had to, Belinda," Zabrina said in a soft voice. "I wasn't given a choice."

"Who didn't give you a choice, Brina?"

Zabrina averted her gaze, staring out the restaurant window at the patrons dining alfresco in the warm June temperatures. "It had to do with my father." Her gaze swung back to Belinda and she closed her eyes for several seconds. "I've already said too much."

"Are you saying you were forced to marry Thomas Cooper?"

"The only other thing I'm going to say is I didn't want to marry Thomas. Please, Belinda, don't ask me any more questions, because I can't answer them."

She'd promised her father she would never tell anyone what he'd done although she was tempted to do just that after burying Isaac Mixon. However, she'd changed her mind when she thought of how it would've affected Adam. Her son idolized his grandfather.

"You can't or you won't?"

"I can't."

Their waiter approached the table, bringing the difficult conversation to an end. The two women ordered, then settled back to discuss Belinda's upcoming wedding.

Belinda touched a napkin to the corners of her mouth. "I know you sent back your response card saying you're coming, but I want to warn you that Myles will also be there. He came in from Pittsburgh last night and plans to spend the summer here in Philly."

Zabrina nodded. She'd had more than ten years to prepare to meet Myles Eaton again. Marrying Thomas Cooper would've been akin to a death sentence if not for her son. Raising Adam had kept her sane, rational and out of prison.

"It's been a long time, but I've known eventually we would have to come face-to-face with each other one of these days." She couldn't predict what Myles's reaction would be to seeing her again, but she was certain he would find her a very different woman from the one who'd pledged to love him forever.

The two women talked about old friends, jokes they'd played on former classmates and the boys they'd had crushes on but who hadn't given them a single glance. They talked about everything except the loss of their loved ones—Belinda's sister and brother-in-law and Zabrina's parents.

Both declined dessert and coffee. "Who's your maid of honor?" Zabrina asked.

Belinda wanted to tell Zabrina *she* would've been her matron of honor if she had married Myles. "Chandra. She's scheduled to fly in Monday, because she has to be fitted for her dress." Belinda's sister had joined the Peace Corps and was currently teaching in Belize. "My cousin Denise will be my other attendant. Myles will stand in as Griffin's best man and Keith Ennis will be a groomsman."

With wide eyes, Zabrina whispered, "Baseball player Keith Ennis?"

Belinda smiled. "Yes. He's one of Griffin's clients." Her fiancé was the lawyer for half a dozen superstar athletes.

"It looks as if you're going to have quite the celebrity wedding."

"All I want is for it to be over, so that my life can return to normal."

"Are you going on a honeymoon?" Zabrina asked.

"Yes. We're going to spend two weeks at a private villa on St. Kitts. I plan to sleep late, take in the sun and eat and drink until I can't move."

Zabrina smiled again, then her smile vanished when she spied the man she hadn't expected to see until Belinda's wedding. Myles Adam Eaton had walked into the restaurant with a beautiful, petite dark-skinned woman with her hand draped possessively over the sleeve of his suit jacket. Myles immediately glanced in her direction. Their eyes met, recognition dawned and then the moment passed when he dipped his head to listen to something the woman was saying. To say time had been kind to Myles was an understatement. Quickly averting her gaze so Belinda wouldn't see what had gotten her attention, she signaled for the waiter.

"I'll take the check please."

Zabrina silently applauded herself for becoming quite the accomplished actress. It'd taken a decade of smiling when she hadn't wanted to smile, uttering the appropriate phrases and responses when attending political events, even though she'd wanted to spew expletives. She didn't know if the woman on Myles's arm was his wife, fiancée or date for the evening, but it didn't matter. Zabrina didn't ever expect to become Mrs. Myles Eaton. Having his son was her consolation for having to give him up.

"I told you I was treating tonight," Belinda said between clenched teeth.

Zabrina took the leather binder from the waiter. "You can treat the next time."

She didn't tell Belinda that with all of Thomas Cooper's so-called political and legal savvy he'd neglected to draw up a will, and she'd inherited a multimillion-dollar home, which she'd promptly sold, and investments of which she'd had no previous knowledge. She'd sold the shares before Wall Street bottomed out and deposited the proceeds into an account for her son's education. Becoming a wealthy woman was a huge price to pay for having to give up the man she loved while denying her son his birthright.

Zabrina settled the bill, pushed back her chair and walked out of the restaurant, Belinda following, without glancing over to where Myles sat with his dinner date. She waited with Belinda for the parking attendants to retrieve their cars from valet parking. Her car arrived first.

She hugged her childhood friend. "I'll see you next week."

"Next week," Belinda repeated.

Zabrina got into her late-model Lincoln sedan and maneuvered out of the restaurant parking lot. She hadn't realized her hands were shaking until she stopped for a red light. She closed her eyes, inhaling a lungful of cool air flowing from the automobile's air conditioner. When she opened her eyes the light had changed and she was back in control.

Myles Eaton pretended to be interested in the menu on the table in front of him to avoid staring at the table where Zabrina Mixon and his sister had been. A wry smile touched his mouth. He'd forgotten. She was no longer a Mixon. She was now Zabrina Cooper.

As an attorney and professor of constitutional law, he'd memorized countless Supreme Court decisions, yet he had not, could not, did not want to remember the dozen words that had turned his world upside down.

His fiancée, the woman to whom he'd pledged his

life and his future had waited until two weeks before they were to be married to call and tell him she couldn't marry him because she was in love with another man. And when he'd discovered the "other man" was none other than Thomas Cooper, his rage had escalated until he realized he had to leave Philadelphia or spend the rest of his life obsessing about the woman who'd broken his heart.

Thomas Cooper used every opportunity to parade and flaunt his much younger wife. Myles could still recall the photographs of a very pregnant Zabrina with the councilman's hand splayed over her swollen belly at a fundraiser. Then there was the official family photograph with the haunted look in Zabrina's eyes when she'd stared directly into the camera lens. There were rumors that she'd been afflicted with chronic postpartum depression, while others hinted that marital problems had beset the Coopers and they were seeing a marriage counselor.

All of the rumors ended for Myles when he requested and was granted a transfer to work out of the law firm's New York office. Adjusting to the faster pace of New York had been the balm he needed to start over. The cramped studio apartment was a far cry from his spacious condo. But that hadn't been important, because most nights when he came home after putting in a fourteen-hour day he'd shower and fall into bed, then get up and do it all over again.

He'd given New York City eight years of his life before he decided he didn't want to practice law, but teach it. He contacted a former professor who told him of an opening at his law-school alma mater. He applied for the position, went through the interview process and when he received the letter of appointment to teach constitutional law at Duquesne's law school in Pittsburgh, he finally found peace.

"What are you having, Myles?"

His head jerked up and he smiled at the woman who'd become his law-school mentor. Judge Stacey Greer-Monroe had graduated from high school at fifteen, college at eighteen and law school two months after her twenty-first birthday. Myles thought Stacey was one of the most brilliant legal minds he'd ever encountered, including his professors.

"I think I'm going to order the crab cakes."

"What's the matter, Professor Eaton? You can't get good crab cakes in Steel City?" Stacey joked.

His smile grew wider. "I get the best Maryland-style crab cakes west of the Alleghenies at a little restaurant owned by a woman who moved from Baltimore. Sadie G's has become my favorite eating place."

Stacey lowered her gaze rather than stare openly at the man she'd tried unsuccessfully to get to think of her as more than a friend. But their every encounter ended with a hug and a kiss on the cheek. After he was jilted by his fiancée Myles continued to regard Stacey as friend and peer. Their relationship remained the same after he'd moved to New York and then Pittsburgh when they communicated with each other online.

Stacey's hopes of becoming Mrs. Myles Eaton ended when her biological clock began winding down and she married a neurosurgeon she'd dated off and on for years. She was now the mother of a two-year-old daughter.

"So, you're really serious about putting down roots in Pittsburgh?"

Myles's dark eyebrows framed his eyes in a lean mahogany-brown angular face that once seen wasn't easily forgotten. "I've been house-hunting," he admitted. The one-year lease on his rental would expire at the end of August. "And I've seen a few places I happen to like."

Stacey angled her head. "I thought you'd prefer a condo or co-op."

"I'd thought so, too. But after living in apartments the past nine years I'm looking to spread out. I don't like entertaining only a few feet from where I have to sleep."

"You could buy a duplex."

Myles studied Stacey's face, one of the youngest jurists elected to Philadelphia's Supreme Court. Stacey Greer-Monroe had always reminded him of a fragile doll. But under the soft, delicate exterior was a tough but fair judge. Her grandfather was a judge, as was her father. And Stacey had continued the tradition when she was elected to the bench.

"I miss waking up to the smell of freshly cut grass and firing up the grill during the warm weather."

Stacey smiled. "It sounds as if you're ready to settle down and become a family man."

Myles wanted to tell her he'd been ready to settle down ten years before. Then he'd looked forward to marrying Zabrina and raising a family, but that changed when she'd married Thomas Cooper and gave him the son that should've been theirs.

"Excuse me, Judge Monroe, but are you ready to order a cocktail?"

Frowning slightly, Stacey shifted her attention from

Myles to their waiter. Talk about bad timing. She was just about to ask him whether he was seeing a woman, and, if he was, was it serious? "Yes." She smiled at Myles. "Do you mind if I order a bottle of champagne to celebrate your return to Philly?"

"Not at all, Judge."

He'd come back to Philadelphia to spend the summer and reconnect with his family. He'd checked into a hotel downtown for the week. After the wedding he would move into Belinda's house for the summer. His sister hadn't decided whether she wanted to sell or rent her house. It was to be the first time in a decade that he'd spend more than a few days with his parents, siblings and nieces.

Waiting until the man walked away, Stacey said to Myles, "I told you never to call me that!"

"Aren't you a judge, Stacey?"

"Yes, but only in the courtroom."

"I've never known you to be self-deprecating. When we met for the first time all you talked about was becoming a judge."

"I was all of twenty-six and I wanted to impress my very bright protégé. You had to know that I liked you."

"And I told you I was in love with someone else," Myles countered.

A beat passed. "Are you still in love with her, Myles?"

His eyebrows flickered before settling back into place. "Yes," he admitted truthfully. "A part of me will always love her."

Stacey curbed the urge to reach across the table to

grasp Myles's hand. "I'm glad I married when I did, because I'd still be waiting for you to notice me."

He angled his head and stared directly at his dining partner. "I noticed you, Stacey, only because you were trying too hard. The flirtatious looks, the indiscriminate touching and the occasional kiss on the lips instead of the cheek were obvious."

Stacey's lashes fluttered as she tried to bring her emotions under control. She'd always thought she'd been subtle in her attempts to seduce Myles Eaton, but evidently she had been anything but. "You knew?"

He nodded. "I knew, and I promise I won't tell your husband."

"You must have thought me a real idiot."

Reaching across the table, Myles covered her hand with his. "No, Stacey. We weren't that different. We both wanted someone we couldn't have."

He'd wanted Zabrina at eighteen, and at thirty-eight he still wanted her.

Chapter 4

It was a picture-perfect day in late June when two ushers opened the French doors and Dr. Dwight Eaton escorted his daughter over a pink runner monogrammed in green with the couple's initials. Light and dark pink rose petals littering the runner had been placed there by the bride's nieces wearing pink-and-green dresses and headbands with green button mums and pink nerines, the colors representing Belinda's sorority, Alpha Kappa Alpha.

The one hundred and twenty guests, welcomed with champagne and caviar into a Bucks County château built on a rise that overlooked the Delaware River, stood as the intro to the *Wedding March* filled the room where the ceremony was to take place. The restored castle and all of the estate's thirty-two rooms were filled with out-of-town guests and those who didn't want to make the hour-long drive back to Philadelphia after a night of frivolity.

Zabrina felt her heart lurch when she saw Belinda. Her childhood friend and sorority sister was ravishing in an ivory Chantilly lace empire gown with a floral appliqué-and-satin bodice. Embroidered petals flowed around the sweeping hem and train of the ethereal garment. She'd forgone a veil in lieu of tiny white rosebuds pinned into the elegant chignon on the nape of her long, graceful neck.

At that moment Zabrina was reliving her past—she should have walked down the aisle on her father's arm as Myles waited to make her his wife. Blinking back tears, she stared at his distinctive profile as he stood on Griffin Rice's right.

She noticed changes she hadn't been able to discern the week before. His face was thinner, there were flecks of gray in his close-cropped hair and there was a stubborn set to his lean jaw that made him appear as if he'd been carved from a piece of smooth, dark mahogany. Her gaze dropped to his left hand. She smiled. He wasn't wearing a ring.

Zabrina had searched her memory for days until she matched the face of the woman clinging to Myles's arm with a name. The woman was Judge Stacey Greer-Monroe.

She smiled when the rich, deep voice of the black-robed judge punctuated the silence. Griffin Rice, devastatingly handsome in formal attire, stared directly into the eyes of his bride as he repeated his vows. There was a twitter of laughter when the judge pronounced them husband and wife and Griffin pumped his fist in the air. It was over. Belinda was now Mrs. Belinda Rice.

The wedding party proceeded along the carpet to the reception. Zabrina didn't notice Belinda, Griffin, Keith Ennis, Chandra or Denise Eaton. Her gaze was fixed on Myles as he came closer and closer, and then their eyes met and fused. His eyes grew wider as a wry smile parted his firm lips.

The smile, Myles and his powerful presence were there. Then they vanished as he moved past her. Emerging from her trance, she followed the crowd as the hotel staff ushered everyone down a wide tunnel that led outside where an enormous tent had been erected. Belinda and Griffin stood in a receiving line, greeting family members and friends who'd come to witness and celebrate their special day.

Belinda's eyebrows shot up when she saw her friend. Zabrina had cut her hair in a style that drew one's attention to her luminous eyes. Raven-black waves were brushed off her face. The style would've been too severe for some with less delicate features. She was stunning in a silk chiffon off-the-shoulder black dress that hugged her upper body, nipping her slender waist with a wide silk sash before flaring around her knees. Stilettos added several inches to her impressive five-foot-seven-inch height.

"You look incredible," Belinda gushed.

"Thank you. And you're an amazing bride, Lindy."

Zabrina stole a glance at Griffin Rice as he leaned down to whisper something in the ear of an elderly woman who giggled like a teenage girl. She'd thought him breathtakingly handsome when she was a teenager, and her opinion hadn't changed. His deep-set dark eyes and cleft chin had most women lusting after him. But Griffin had always seemed totally oblivious to their attention. It was apparent he'd been waiting for his brother's sister-in-law.

Griffin turned his attention to Zabrina. She looked nothing like the young woman he remembered. "Thank you for coming." Leaning forward, he pressed a light kiss to her cheek.

"Thank you for inviting me." Zabrina knew she couldn't hold up the receiving line. "I'll be in touch with you guys after you come back from your honeymoon." When she'd married Thomas Cooper he'd made certain to isolate her from everyone in her past.

"Your name, miss?" asked a hotel staffer as she stood in front of a table stacked with butler boxes.

"Zabrina Cooper."

He handed her a box. "Your table number and menu are in the box, Ms. Cooper."

In lieu of a guest card, each guest was given a personalized butler box with a leaf-colored letterpressed menu and table number. The pink-and-green color scheme was repeated in the pastel-toned chiffon on the ceiling of the tent, table linens and carpet. The lights from strategically placed chandeliers provided a soft glow as the afternoon sun cast shadows over the elegantly dressed guests as they found their way to their respective tables.

Waiters were positioned at each table to pull out chairs and assist everyone as they sat on pink-cushioned bamboo-gilded chairs. And because Zabrina had returned her response card for one, she was seated at a table with other single guests. She offered a smile to the two men flanking her. The one on her right extended his hand.

"Bailey Mercer."

She stared at the young man with flaming red hair and blue-green eyes, then took his hand. It was soft and moist. As discreetly as she could without offending him, she withdrew her hand. "It's nice meeting you, Bailey. I'm Zabrina."

He draped an arm over the back of her chair. "Are you a guest of the bride or the groom?"

"The bride," she said.

"Are you a teacher?"

"No. I'm a nurse." Zabrina realized he just wanted to make polite conversation. "Are you a guest of the bride or groom?" she asked.

"Griffin and I were college roommates."

"Are you also an attorney?"

Bailey leaned closer. "I'm a forensic criminologist."

Suddenly her curiosity was piqued. "Who do you work for?"

"I'm stationed in Quantico."

"You work for the Bureau?" she asked. The FBI was the only law-enforcement agency that she knew of in Quantico, Virginia.

Bailey nodded. "I'm going to the bar to get something to drink. Would you like me to bring you something?"

Zabrina smiled. He'd segued from one topic to another without pausing to take a breath. "Yes, please."

"What would you like?"

"I'll have a cosmopolitan."

Music from speakers mounted overhead filled the tent as guests filed in and sat at their assigned tables. Bailey returned with Zabrina's cocktail and a glass filled with an amber liquid. Smiling, they touched glasses.

Myles returned from posing for photographs with the wedding party to find Zabrina smiling and talking to a man with strawberry-blond hair. Sitting at the bridal table afforded him an unobscured view of everything and everyone in the large tent.

There was something in the way she angled her head while staring up at the man through her lashes that reminded him of how she'd look at him just before he'd make love to her. It was a come-hither look that he hadn't been able to resist.

What Myles hadn't been able to understand was how he and Zabrina were able to communicate without words. It could be a single glance, a slight lifting of an eyebrow, a shrug of a shoulder or a smile. It was as if they were able to communicate telepathically, reading each other's thoughts. Right now he knew she would be shocked if she saw the lust in his eyes. The spell was broken when a waiter took his dinner and beverage request.

"I almost didn't recognize Zabrina," said Griffin Rice.

Myles gave his brother-in-law a sidelong glance. "She *has* changed." And he wanted to tell Griffin the change was for the better. When he'd caught a glimpse of Zabrina the week before he'd thought her lovely, but tonight she was breathtakingly stunning.

Griffin's gaze met and fused with Myles's. "She'd dropped out of sight for years. Rumors were circulating that she and Cooper had divorced. But when reporters asked him about his wife he claimed she preferred keeping a low profile."

Myles's eyes narrowed slightly. "Who's the guy with her?"

"Bailey Mercer. We were college roomies."

The smile that softened Myles's mouth crept up to his eyes. It was apparent Zabrina had come to the wedding unescorted. He'd planned to ask her to dance with him and nothing more, since he hadn't wanted to act inappropriately *if* she had come with a date. Now that he knew she was alone things had changed. Myles had waited ten years for an explanation for Zabrina's deception *and* he intended to get an answer before the night ended.

The waiter brought drinks for those at the bridal party table, followed by other waitstaff carrying trays laden with platters of curried scallop canapés, walnut and endive salad and mushroom rolls. Dozens of lighted votives in green glasses flickered like stars when the chandeliers were dimmed, creating a soft, soothingly romantic atmosphere.

Myles ate without actually tasting the food on his plate. He was too engrossed in the woman sitting close enough for him to see her expressions, but not close enough to hear her smoky voice. He wondered if Griffin's former college roommate was as enthralled with her as he'd been. What he did do was drink more than he normally would at a social function. It didn't matter, because he wasn't driving back to Philadelphia. He'd reserved a suite at the hotel.

And, he refused to fantasize that his sister's wedding was his and Zabrina's. He and Zabrina had planned their wedding, honeymoon and life together, but all the plans had come to naught two weeks before the ceremony when his fiancée called to tell him she was in love with another man and she couldn't marry him.

Myles still remembered her passion whenever they shared a bed, and wondered whether she'd screamed Thomas Cooper's name in the throes of passion. Zabrina had always had an intense distaste for politicians. Yet she'd married one. And what about her claim that she'd wanted to wait two years before starting a family? She'd wasted no time in giving Cooper a child.

The music playing throughout the dinner ended when a live band took over, playing softly as toasts to the bride and groom were made.

Dwight Eaton wiped away tears as he smiled at his daughter. There was no doubt he was thinking of his eldest daughter whom he'd buried eight months earlier. Myles toasted the newlyweds, providing a lighter moment when he reminded everyone that Griffin Rice was so intent on joining the family that he'd become his brother-in-law for the second time.

A hush descended over the assembly as they watched Griffin ease Belinda to her feet, escort her to the dance floor and dance with her to the Berlin classic "Take My Breath Away." It was their first dance as husband and wife.

Myles finally got to twirl his sister around the dance

floor after she'd shared a dance with their father. "Does Griffin know he is a lucky man?" he asked, executing a fancy dance step.

Belinda lifted the skirt of her gown to avoid stepping on the hem. She gave Myles a demure smile. "I'd like to believe that I'm lucky that Griffin didn't marry some other woman, leaving me pining for him for the rest of my life."

Myles recalled the conversation he'd had with Stacey. She'd waited for him to come around and think of her as more than a friend, and when it hadn't happened she'd opted to marry someone else. He was certain his sister would've done the same.

"You're too much of a realist to spend your life dreaming of the impossible."

Belinda smiled at Myles. "What about you and Brina?"

A slight frown furrowed his forehead. "What about us?"

"You still have feelings for her, don't you?"

"Of course I have feelings for her, Lindy. After all, I did promise to marry the woman."

"What about now, Myles?"

"What about it?" he said, answering her question with one of his own.

Belinda gasped softly when Myles swung her around and around. Her brother had always been a very good dancer, and it appeared that he hadn't lost his skill. She wasn't certain whether his dancing prowess came from years of martial arts training or from a natural grace and style that turned heads whenever he entered a room.

Although he'd earned a black belt in tae kwon do, he intensely disliked competition.

Belinda leaned closer, pressing her mouth to his ear. "You haven't taken your eyes off her all night."

Myles's expression did not change. "Is that why you invited her, Lindy? Did you decide to become a matchmaker after I'd agreed to be Griffin's best man? Don't you think she hurt our family enough when she waited until two weeks before we were to be married to tell me that she was in love with someone else? Then, a week later she marries Thomas Cooper."

"I didn't invite her to spite you, Myles. It was only a couple of months ago that I ran into Brina for the first time in almost ten years. When she confessed that she hated Thomas Cooper as much as she loved you, I knew something wasn't quite right."

A sardonic smile spread across his face. "So, she lied twice. Once when she told me that she was in love with another man, and again when she tells you that she hated her husband."

Belinda shook her head. "It's all too confusing. When I asked her why she'd married Thomas, she said she couldn't tell me. She mentioned something about swearing that she'd never tell anyone."

"Swore to whom?"

"That I don't know, Myles."

The song ended and Myles led Belinda back to her seat beside her husband. He'd heard enough. He needed answers. He wanted answers and he intended to get them.

His gaze searched the crowded dance floor for Zabrina, but she was nowhere in sight. She was missing and so was Griffin's college roommate. There was no doubt they were together. Wending his way across the tent, Myles stepped out into the warm night air.

Chairs and love seats were set up on the verdant lawn for those wishing to get away from the frivolity to sit, talk quietly and/or relax. Dozens of lanterns were suspended from stanchions surrounding the magnificent estate. He saw Zabrina with her red-haired dining partner sitting together on a love seat. She'd rested her head on his shoulder while he massaged her back.

Taking long strides, Myles approached the couple. "Is she all right?"

Bailey Mercer glanced up to find the groom's best man looming over him like an avenging angel. "Zabrina said she needed some air."

Myles hunkered down and placed the back of his hand against her moist cheek. "Brina, darling, are you all right?" The endearment had slipped out as if ten years had morphed into a nanosecond.

Zabrina heard the familiar voice from her past, and she tried smiling but the pounding in her temples intensified. "I don't know."

"What did she eat or drink?" Myles asked Bailey.

"She didn't eat much, but she did have three cocktails."

Effortlessly, Myles lifted Zabrina off the love seat, while coming to a standing position. "She can't drink."

Bailey stood up. "What the hell are you talking about?"

"She usually can't have more than one drink or she'll wind up with a headache."

"I'll take care of her," Bailey offered.

Myles glared at the man. "Walk away."

A flush suffused Bailey's face, the color increasing to match his hairline. He moved closer. "I said I'll take care of her."

Myles angled his head. "Don't get in my face," he warned through clenched teeth. "Look, man," he said, his tone softer, calmer. "Just walk away while you can." That said, he turned on his heels and carried Zabrina past the tent and into the hotel. He slipped in through a side entrance and took a staircase to the third floor. When he set Zabrina on her feet to search for his room's cardkey, she dropped her evening purse, spilling its contents.

"Muh—my things," Zabrina slurred.

"Don't worry about them, Brina. I'll pick them up after I get you inside."

Zabrina swallowed back a rush of bile. She felt sick, sicker than she had in a very long time. Her first experience with drinking alcohol had become a lasting one. But it was apparent she'd forgotten. She hadn't known what possessed her to have a third cosmopolitan. What she should've done was stop after the first one. But she'd wanted to forget that the past ten years hadn't existed. She wanted to blot them out by drinking until she passed out. She hadn't passed out, but she did have an excruciating headache.

Myles had always teased her, calling her a very cheap date. Her colleagues couldn't understand why she opted to drink club soda with a twist during their employee gatherings. Some had asked whether she was a recovering alcoholic, but she reassured them that she did drink, just always sparingly.

She closed her eyes as her dulled senses took over. Being cradled against Myles's broad chest brought back a rush of memories that made Zabrina want to weep. He'd always been there for her, had promised to love, protect and take care of her. He no longer loved her, yet he was still looking after her.

Myles walked through the entry, the living/dining area and into the bedroom. He placed Zabrina on the king-size bed, removed her shoes and covered her with a lightweight blanket. "I'll be right back."

He returned to the hall to gather up the jeweled compact, the tube of lipstick and a set of car keys that had fallen out of her bag. He pocketed the keys. Zabrina was in no shape to get behind the wheel of a car, even if just to drive it out of the parking lot. A cold chill swept over him when he thought of her trying to drive back to Philly under the circumstances. Either she would kill herself or someone else.

Closing the door, he slipped the security lock into place and returned to the bedroom. Zabrina hadn't moved. She lay on her back, eyes closed and her chest rising and falling in a slow, even rhythm. He smiled. She'd fallen asleep.

Myles reached up and undid his silk tie. Undressing, he placed his clothes on the padded bench at the foot of the bed. Clad in only a pair of boxer briefs, he retreated to the bathroom to shower and brush his teeth.

Zabrina was still asleep when Myles reentered the bedroom. She lay on her right side, her head resting on her hands and her legs pulled up into a fetal position. A smile tilted the corners of his mouth when he stared down at her. She was so incredibly beautiful and so very cunning. When he'd asked Zabrina to marry him he never would've thought she would deceive him, especially not with another man.

Reaching over, he turned off the bedside lamp. The light from the sconce outside the bathroom provided enough illumination to make out the slight figure on the bed. Sitting on the mattress, Myles studied the woman whom he'd never forgotten. He'd once admitted to Belinda that he had two passions—Zabrina Mixon and the law. Despite her deception, his feelings hadn't changed. Nothing had changed. Zabrina was still his passion.

Slowly, methodically, he undressed her. She stirred briefly before settling back to sleep. Waiting for her breathing to resume a measured cadence, he anchored a hand under her hips, easing her dress down her bare legs. Myles didn't know why, but he felt like a voyeur when he stared at Zabrina's half-naked body. She hadn't worn a bra under the dress. He recalled her preference for sleeping nude, but decided not to remove her bikini panties.

She moaned softly when he eased her between the sheets. He waited a full minute, then shrugged off his robe and slipped into bed beside her. It was as if nothing had changed. Pressing his chest to her back, he rested an arm over her waist, pulling her closer. The angry words Myles had rehearsed so many times he could recite them backward he'd erased from memory. He buried his face in her hair and inhaled the lingering floral fragrance of her shampoo.

"Myles?"

He froze when Zabrina whispered his name. "Yes, baby?"

"I…I…I'm sorry," she slurred.

There came a beat. "So am I," Myles whispered. "So am I, Brina," he repeated.

Myles wasn't certain what she was apologizing for, but he knew why he was sorry. He was sorry they hadn't gone through with their plan to marry, sorry that her son wasn't his and sorry it had taken almost a decade for him to get the opportunity to confront her about her deception.

Chapter 5

Zabrina knew something was different when she opened her eyes. She wasn't in her bed, *and* she wasn't alone. She sat up quickly, chiding herself for the sudden action. Her head felt as if it was in a vise, and her mouth was dry as sandpaper. She closed her eyes and sank back to the pillow.

"Are you all right?" asked a deep voice in the dimly lit space.

She didn't know if she was dreaming or hallucinating, because she couldn't believe she was in bed with Myles Eaton. "Is that you, Myles?"

The seconds ticked. "Yes, it is. Who were you expecting? Bailey Mercer?"

Turning over and pressing her face to the pillow, Zabrina muffled a moan. "That's not funny."

"What's not funny, Brina, is you drinking until you nearly passed out."

"I didn't pass out."

"No, but you were asleep before I got you into bed. You're lucky it was me and not your redheaded admirer. There was the possibility that he could've taken advantage of you."

Zabrina ignored the reference to the man who'd become her dinner partner. She sat up again, pulling the sheet up to her chin. "Where am I?"

"You're in my hotel room." Rolling over, Myles turned on the lamp on his side of the bed. The glowing numbers on the clock-radio read 1:22 a.m. "What time do you have to pick up your son?"

"Adam's in Virginia with my aunt's grandchildren."

Myles froze for a beat. He glanced over his shoulder to see the haunted golden eyes staring back at him. "You named Cooper's son Adam?"

A pregnant silence filled the space as Zabrina tried to form her thoughts. If she hadn't been under the influence she would've been able to spar verbally with Myles, but not now. She knew how persuasive he could be once he set his mind to something. That was what had made him an incredible trial attorney. He'd ask the same question ten different ways in an attempt to agitate and confuse a witness, and if she wasn't careful he would trip her up and uncover the truth about her son's paternity.

What frightened her most was Myles finding out that she'd had his child and passed it off as Thomas Cooper's. Although Adam's birth certificate listed Thomas

Cooper as his father, Myles still had the law on his side if or when he decided to sue her for custody.

"I named *my* son Adam."

Myles ran a hand over his face. Zabrina had admitted to him that Adam was her favorite boy's name even before he'd told her it was his middle name. "Wasn't he also Cooper's son?"

"He was never Thomas's son. He was always too busy pressing the flesh and seeing to the needs of his constituents to play daddy even though Adam practically worshipped the ground Thomas walked on." She emitted a soft sigh. "I suppose not every man who's a father is father material."

"What about you, Brina?"

"What about me?"

"How are you coping with the loss of your husband?"

Zabrina's fingers tightened on the sheet clutched to her chest at the same time she affected a wry smile. "You see how I'm coping, Myles. I've become the merry widow. I know I can't handle more than one drink, but that didn't stop me from having three. That's how I'm coping," she spat out.

"Do you drink in front of your son?"

"You think I've become an alcoholic, don't you?"

Myles shook his head. "I didn't say that, Zabrina."

"But isn't that what you're implying, Myles?"

"No, it's not." Gathering the sheet, Zabrina tried getting out of bed, but Myles thwarted her attempt to escape him when his hand went around her upper arm. "Where do you think you're going?"

"I'm going home!"

One second she was sitting half on and half off the

bed and within the next she found herself sprawled on her back, Myles straddling her. "I don't think so. Your son just lost his father. Do you want him to lose his mother, too?" He'd bared his teeth like a snarling canine. "If you try to walk out of here in the condition that you're in, then I'll call the police and have you locked up."

He hadn't wanted to remind Zabrina that less than a year ago the Eatons and Rices had buried their daughter and son after they'd died in a head-on collision with a drunk driver. The loss of his sister and brother-in-law was devastating to both families. Whenever he returned to Philadelphia, Myles always expected to see Donna's inviting smile and infectious laughter.

Zabrina's eyes filled with tears and overflowed, tears she hadn't been able to shed after the police had arrived at her home to tell her that her husband had drowned in a boating accident off the Chesapeake. The media was respectful of her grief when told by the Coopers' housekeeper that the reclusive widow of Pennsylvania's junior senator was too distraught to conduct an interview. She'd gone into hiding again, resurfacing six months later at a fundraising event for mayoral candidate Patrick Garson.

She'd given Thomas Cooper nearly ten years of her life and six months was long enough for her to pretend to be the grieving widow. She didn't cry for Thomas because she didn't want to be a hypocrite. She hadn't lied to Belinda at the fundraiser when she'd told her that she hated Thomas as much as she loved her brother.

Cradling her face between his palms, Myles lowered his head and brushed his mouth over Zabrina's in an attempt to comfort her. "It's okay, baby. Let it out."

Zabrina had lost her father and husband, her son had lost his father and he knew her drinking too much was a feeble attempt to mask the pain. She wasn't weeping, but sobbing. Deep, gut-wrenching sobs that knifed through Myles like a rapier. Gathering her closer, he held her until the sobs faded into a soft hiccupping. He counted off the minutes until he heard the soft snores. Zabrina had fallen asleep.

As much as he loathed releasing her, Myles knew he couldn't spend the night straddling her body. Reluctantly, he lay beside Zabrina, holding her protectively as he joined her in sleep.

When Zabrina woke again she found herself in bed alone. The scent from Myles's cologne lingered but the heat from his body was missing. Sitting up and pulling the sheet to her breasts, she glanced around the room. Sunlight came through the lacy panels at a trio of tall windows.

The suite in the restored château hotel preserved a sense of family and intimacy. Furnished in French country decor with a four-poster bed, massive ornate armoire, triple dresser and mirror, and chairs with carved arms and petit-point cushions, it was a scene from *Dangerous Liaisons.*

Reaching for the black silk robe at the foot of the bed, she slipped into it and moved off the bed. Zabrina still didn't want to believe that she'd shared a bed with Myles Eaton. What she found laughable was that he was the only man she'd ever slept with. As promised, her marriage to Thomas had been in name only. They'd had adjoining bedroom suites, but Thomas had never exercised his conjugal rights, and that had become the best feature of their peculiar marriage.

At first she'd believed Thomas hadn't wanted to touch her because she was carrying another man's baby, but even after she'd given birth to her son, Thomas hadn't approached her. Zabrina didn't know what to make of her husband's sexual proclivity. She'd thought he preferred same-sex liaisons until she inadvertently discovered he'd been sleeping with his cousin's wife, and that her two sons weren't her husband's, but Thomas's. Zabrina didn't care who he slept with as long as he didn't try to consummate their sham of a marriage.

She walked into the bathroom, closing the door behind her. A low table held a supply of feminine grooming products along with a comb, toothbrush, toothpaste and mouthwash. She brushed her teeth and then stepped into the shower. Standing under the spray of a hot shower Zabrina swore never to overindulge again.

The smell of coffee met her when she emerged from the bathroom, her hair covered with a towel and her body swathed in black silk. She'd turned back the cuffs on the robe and looped the belt twice around her waist. However, there was little she could do with the lapels that kept slipping to reveal the tops of her breasts.

Myles walked into the bedroom at the same time she reached for her dress. "Breakfast is here. Come and eat."

Zabrina felt her pulse kick into a higher gear when she stared at the man who she couldn't remember ever *not* loving. Instead of the tuxedo from the night before, he wore a pair of faded jeans, running shoes and a golf shirt that revealed solid pectorals and biceps.

"I'd like to put on some clothes."

Myles extended his hand. "You have clothes on, Brina. Come and eat before the food gets cold."

It was apparent he wasn't giving her much of a choice. And it wasn't that she *wasn't* hungry. The night before she'd elected to drink rather than eat, and Zabrina was certain that the lack of food had contributed to her feeling hungover. She approached Myles, placing her hand on his outstretched palm. He'd showered, but hadn't shaved and the stubble on his dark face enhanced his blatant masculinity.

Cradling the small hand in the crook of his elbow, Myles felt the fragility of the slender fingers. Although she'd had a child, her body was much slimmer than he'd remembered.

He pulled out her chair at the table in the dining area and then sat beside her. "How do you feel this morning?"

Zabrina gave him a sidelong glance. "A lot better than I did last night."

Myles gave her a warm smile. "Good." He gestured to her covered plate. "Eat, Brina."

She removed the cover and was tempted to salute him for telling her to eat. Myles had ordered a spinach omelet, bacon and a slice of buttered wheat toast for her. "You remembered my favorites." Her voice was barely a whisper.

Myles filled a glass with orange juice from a carafe, placing it in front of her plate. "I took a chance when I ordered it. People's tastes sometimes change."

Zabrina wanted to tell him she hadn't changed that much. Aside from having his son, her feelings for him hadn't changed. "Have you changed, Myles?"

Myles poured orange juice for himself. "Yes, I have. What has changed most are my priorities. Remember when all I talked about was making partner?"

She smiled. "Yes."

"After five years of working in New York, I finally made partner. After the announcement was made everyone at the firm got together at a restaurant to celebrate. But then when I woke up the next morning it was if nothing had changed. My name was added to the firm's plaque and letterhead and I moved into a large corner office. But I realized all of it was nothing more than vanity."

"That's the same with titles and awards," Zabrina said in a quiet voice as she speared a small portion of omelet. "When all is said and done it's only vanity. It won't make you healthy, keep you out of jail or avoid death."

"My, my, my," Myles drawled. "You're really cynical, aren't you?"

"Cynical or truthful, Myles?" she said.

"You've done well for yourself, Brina," he countered. "Your husband may have lost his bid to become mayor of Philadelphia, but he made out even better when the governor appointed him to fill a vacant U.S. senate seat."

She swallowed a portion of the spinach and feta cheese omelet. "That was Thomas's ambition, not mine."

Myles took a sip of orange juice. "Please answer one question for me, Brina?"

"What is it?"

"If you disliked politics so much, then why did you marry a politician?"

Zabrina sighed audibly as she recalled her carefully rehearsed script as to why she'd broken their engagement to marry Thomas Cooper. "I was in awe of Thomas Cooper, and I suppose him being twenty years my senior made him even more intriguing. He asked Daddy if he could marry me just weeks before you proposed."

"Were you sleeping with him?"

"No, Myles. I've never been one to sleep with more than one man."

How virtuous of you, Myles mused. "What did your father tell him?"

"He told Thomas he couldn't tell me who to marry."

Myles glared at her. "You accepted my proposal, while you were thinking of marrying another man."

Zabrina felt the heat of his gaze as she stared at her plate. She couldn't look at Myles or she would be forced to blurt out the truth. "When I spoke to my father he told me to follow my conscience."

"And what did your conscience tell you?"

"It told me to marry Thomas."

"It told you to marry Thomas," Myles mimicked. He sobered quickly. "Thomas Cooper took the woman who was to become *my* wife and claimed the son that should've been ours because you followed your conscience. If I'd followed my conscience, then I would hate you for your deception. But I don't hate you, Zabrina, because then I wouldn't have been able to move on with my life."

"Have you moved on, Myles?"

"Yes. I'm seriously considering buying a house."

Her eyebrows lifted. "You're buying a house in Philly?"

"No, Brina. I'm looking for one in Pittsburgh."

He'd moved on with his life, while Zabrina didn't know what she wanted to do with hers. And it hadn't dawned on her until now that Myles could possibly have a woman in Pittsburgh waiting for him to return at the end of the summer.

There had been a time when Myles was considered one of Philadelphia's most eligible bachelors, and she'd been too enamored of him to notice that other women flirted shamelessly with him. And why shouldn't she when, as a teenager, she'd done exactly that—flirted shamelessly with him.

They ate their breakfast in silence, each lost in their personal thoughts. Zabrina wished it'd been different, that she could've been matron of honor and Myles best man for Belinda and Griffin's wedding, that her son was Adam Eaton not Cooper, that every night she would go to sleep and every morning wake up beside Myles. She wanted to give Adam the brother or sister he always talked about.

But it was not to be, because she'd played the sacrificial lamb for her father in order to keep him from going to prison. She didn't regret what she'd done and would do it again if faced with the same predicament.

Thomas Cooper's promise that their marriage was in name only and the fact that she'd had Myles Eaton's son made her sacrifice more than worthwhile. Her father was gone, Thomas was gone and Myles was no longer in her life. Unwittingly, he'd given her a gift she would cherish forever.

Myles followed closely behind Zabrina's car during the drive to Philadelphia. Although she'd said she was no longer feeling the effects of the alcohol she'd consumed the night before, he wanted to make certain she arrived home without a mishap.

He was surprised when she maneuvered into an enclave of recently constructed one-family homes less than a quarter of a mile from where Belinda had purchased her house. With him living in Belinda's house for the summer, he and Zabrina were within walking distance of each other.

She'd moved out of the mansion where generations of Coopers had lived for a more modest lifestyle with her son. An emotion came over him that he immediately recognized as a newfound respect for Zabrina. When she'd ended their engagement he'd conjured up dozens of reasons why she didn't want to marry him: he had been too demanding, he had convinced her to sleep with him when she hadn't been ready, he had put pressure on her to become a mother when she'd wanted to wait at least two years.

He'd blamed himself, until the news surfaced that Zabrina Mixon had married Thomas Cooper in a private ceremony. Then it had all made sense. Thomas had come from a long line of African-American politicians in Philadelphia dating back to the 1890s. Cooper was handsome, eloquent, wealthy and twenty years her senior. He was also a close friend of Isaac Mixon, and Zabrina marrying Cooper would cement the relationship between the consummate politician and the masterful political strategist.

Shifting into Park, Myles sat staring out the windshield as Zabrina got out of her car and came over to his driver's-side window. He smiled. Even with her bare face and her hair brushed off her forehead and behind her ears, she was still ravishing.

Reaching into the open window, Zabrina rested a hand on Myles's wrist. "Thank you, Myles."

His gaze lowered, lingering on her full, sultry mouth. "For what?"

"For taking care of me last night."

"Think nothing of it. That's what friends are supposed to do. Take care of each other."

Her eyebrows lifted slightly. "Are we friends, Myles?"

"Yes," Myles said after a long pause. "If we weren't friends, then I would've had sex with you. And, because it didn't happen, that makes us friends."

Zabrina closed her eyes for several seconds. Myles *had* changed. In the past, whenever she'd mentioned them having sex he'd corrected her to say it wasn't sex but making love, then had gone on to explain the differences.

"How else can I thank you aside from saying thank you?"

Myles reached for his cell phone resting in a console between the seats of the Range Rover. "Give me your numbers and I'll call you."

"Call me for what?" she asked as a thread of suspicion crept into her voice.

"Perhaps we can get together to take in a movie or go out to dinner before I go back to Pittsburgh."

Zabrina forced a smile. She didn't want to start up with Myles again only to have him leave at the end of the summer. Ten years before, she'd left him, and now he would be the one to leave her.

"Okay." She gave him the phone number to her house and her cell. Then, on impulse, she leaned into the window and pressed a kiss to his jaw. "Thank you again."

Myles nodded, mildly surprised at Zabrina's display of affection. He sat motionless, watching as she walked to the entrance of her home, opened the door and closed it behind her. He still could see the image of her long, shapely legs in the stilettos.

His gaze shifted to the tiny phone in his hand. Common sense told him to delete Zabrina's numbers, but he'd never been rational when it came to her. From the moment he'd kissed her for the first time, to when they'd shared a bed for the first time, nothing between them had ever been sensible.

He ran his free hand over his face as if to wipe away the frustration and pain of the past ten years. Myles couldn't fathom why despite her deceit he still wanted her. Just when he was certain he was over Zabrina, she was back in his life, reminding him of the searing passion they'd shared.

And despite her heart-wrenching deception, he still wanted her.

Chapter 6

Myles clocked the distance it took for him to drive from Zabrina's house to his sister's. It took exactly three minutes door to door.

He parked his sport-utility vehicle in the driveway rather than in the two-car garage. It was Sunday and he would've usually shared dinner with his parents, but after last night's wedding reception he knew the elder Eatons wanted to either sleep in late or relax.

He still had to settle into the house where he planned to spend his summer. Belinda had given him a quick walk-through of the two-story white house framed with dark blue molding and matching shutters. He'd teased his sister, saying that if she'd known she would be moving to Paoli less than six months after renovating the second floor to accommodate the needs of two teenage girls she could've saved a great deal of money.

He got out of the SUV, retrieved his overnight and garment bags from the rear seat and made his way up the porch. Myles unlocked the front door and deactivated the security system. Leaving the garment bag on a chair in the entryway, he walked to the rear of the house to the laundry room to empty the contents of the overnight bag into the hamper. Belinda had given him a crash course on operating the digital washer and dryer, which meant he didn't have to send out his laundry.

Not having a house with a porch and not waking up to trees and a green lawn weren't the only reasons why he'd grown tired of living in an apartment. Myles had also grown tired of shopping every week because he lacked storage in his apartment. He preferred going to a supermarket warehouse several times a year to buy in bulk. His teaching schedule had increased from two to three constitutional law classes, and his free time was now at a premium—he didn't want to get into his car and go shopping on a weekly basis. He liked big-city living, but as he grew older he realized he preferred a slower pace.

He'd grown up with his parents and three sisters in a six-bedroom, four-bath farmhouse in a Philadelphia suburb. His mother was a stay-at-home mom, negotiating the many squabbles between her four rambunctious children, while their physician father treated his many patients in the office connected to the main house. He knew Dwight Eaton was disappointed that none of his children had elected to pursue a career in medicine, but he had supported them in whatever career paths they'd chosen.

Myles hadn't realized he wanted to become a lawyer

until he joined his high school's debate team. His verbal skills and quick thinking made him a standout whenever they competed with other high schools. Once he entered college he was able to hone his skills in mock court trials.

Walking out of the laundry room, he checked the pantry, then the refrigerator. When he'd called to tell Belinda that he planned to spend the summer in Philadelphia she'd offered him her house. The furniture in his nieces' bedrooms had been moved to Griffin's house in Paoli, but Belinda hadn't taken any of the other furniture. His sister had restocked the refrigerator and pantry before his arrival, making moving in smooth and stress-free.

When Belinda had informed him that she was going to marry Griffin Rice, Myles hadn't wanted to believe that two of his sisters had fallen in love with brothers. But, when he rethought the relationships in his family, he realized his sister Donna had named one of her daughters for his girlfriend. When Donna and Grant's fraternal twin girls were born, Donna had named one Sabrina, using the traditional *S* instead of *Z*.

He'd just turned on the under-the-counter television when the doorbell rang. Myles walked out of the kitchen to the front door. When he opened it he found his youngest sister Chandra and his twin nieces grinning at him.

"Surprise!" they chorused.

Chandra held up a large white shopping bag. "I brought breakfast."

Myles opened the door wider, smiling. "Come in. I hate to ruin your surprise, but I already ate breakfast."

Sabrina went on tiptoe to kiss her uncle. "Gram and

Gramps put a Do Not Disturb sign on their doorknob, so Aunt Chandra decided on a take-out breakfast."

Sabrina was the mirror image of Belinda at her age. Myles had always thought her a little too mature and serious for her age. Layla, on the other hand, was more laid-back, funky. Both wore braces to correct an overbite, but it was Layla who opted for colorful bands rather than the clear ones worn by her twin. The girls would celebrate their thirteenth birthday in the fall, and every time he saw them they appeared to have grown several inches.

"Who's watching the puppies?" he asked the girls.

Belinda had called him earlier that spring to tell him that Griffin had purchased two Yorkshire terriers for their nieces with the hope that it would make them more responsible. He was introduced to the two puppies for the first time when he drove to Paoli to reunite with his brother-in-law.

Layla shared a look with her sister. "Nigel and Cecil are with the lady who owns their mother."

Sabrina sniffled. "Aunt Lindy and Uncle Griff said we can't have them until they get back from their honeymoon."

Chandra registered her brother's what's-going-on look? "Mom and Dad's subdivision has a no-dogs rule and Griffin's mother and father are leaving for Martha's Vineyard tomorrow."

Myles stared at his youngest sister. Although she'd recently celebrated her thirtieth birthday she looked much younger. Chandra's normally gold-brown complexion was several shades darker from the hot tropical sun. She'd spent more than two years in Central America as a Peace Corps volunteer. Chandra had taken a leave from her teaching position at a private elementary school to teach in Belize. She was also much thinner than she'd been in years. Either she wasn't eating enough or she was working much too hard.

"They can stay here with me," Myles volunteered, "that way you can come over and play with them." Ear-piercing shrieks filled the air as Layla and Sabrina jumped up and down, hugging each other.

"Thank you, Uncle Myles," they said in unison.

He tugged gently on the hair Layla had secured with an elastic band. "You're very welcome. After you guys eat breakfast, we'll drive over to Paoli to pick up your puppies."

Chandra handed Sabrina the bag. "Please take this into the kitchen. I need to speak to your uncle for a few minutes."

"Are you going to talk about grown folks business?" Layla asked.

"Yes, Miss Know-It-All," Chandra teased.

"Do we have to wait for you before we can eat, Aunt Chandra?" Sabrina asked.

Chandra shook her head. "No. You can eat without me." They sprinted toward the rear of the house. She realized it had to cost Griffin and Belinda a small fortune to feed growing teenagers.

Reaching for his sister's hand, Myles led her out to the porch. "What's up?"

Leaning against a thick column on the porch, Chandra folded her arms under her breasts. "Where did you disappear to last night?"

He narrowed his gaze. "It's been a very long time

since I've had to account for my whereabouts, *little sister.*"

Chandra stared at her bare toes in a pair of leather sandals. "That came out all wrong."

"I'd say it did," Myles drawled.

A slight frown furrowed her smooth forehead. "I'm only asking because you disappeared at the same time Zabrina did, and I thought maybe the two of you were together."

"And what if we were, Chandra?"

"Were you?"

There came a beat of silence as brother and sister stared at each other. "Yes. She had too much to drink, and I took her to my room so she could sleep it off."

Chandra closed her eyes while shaking her head. "Myles, you do realize what you're doing?"

"What are you talking about?"

"Why are you starting up with her again? If she left you once, then there's always the possibility that she'll leave you again."

"Who said I was starting up with her, Chandra? What did you expect me to do? There was no way I was going to let her get behind the wheel of a car when she was under the influence. Her son recently lost his father and grandfather. Did you expect me to stand by and let him lose his mother, too?"

"I can understand your concern, Myles. But Zabrina is not your responsibility."

"She was last night."

"What about this morning? What about tomorrow and the next day and the day after that?" Chandra stopped her rant long enough to study her brother's impassive expression. "You're still not over her, are you?"

Myles, swallowing the biting words poised on the tip of his tongue, struggled not to lose his temper. When Zabrina had ended their engagement all of the Eatons were upset with the news. But twenty-year-old Chandra had appeared almost indifferent to the calamity as everyone scrambled to call out-of-town friends and relatives to inform them the wedding had been canceled. Apparently it'd taken a decade for Chandra's resentment of Zabrina to fester before coming to the surface.

"Let it go, Chandra." His voice, although soft, was cutting and lethal.

"But, how can you—"

"I said to let it go," he repeated. "What goes on between Brina and I has nothing to do with you."

She rolled her eyes. "If that's the way you want it."

Myles shot her a warning glare. "That's exactly how I want it." Turning on his heel, he opened the door and went inside the house, leaving his sister staring in his wake.

Chandra exhaled a breath. She didn't want to fight with her brother. As it was they rarely saw each other since she'd joined the Peace Corps, and she couldn't remember the last time Myles had spoken so harshly to her.

Myles was the perfect older brother, because he'd always protected his younger sisters. Once Myles reached adolescence his father had told him that it'd become his responsibility to take care of the women in the house, and that included his mother. She'd believed it had something to do with their father juggling his schedule when he was on call at the hospital while running his medical practice. Dr. Eaton had become an anomaly as one of a few general practitioners to still make house calls.

Unfortunately there was no one to protect Myles from Zabrina Mixon's treachery. Donna and Belinda were more vociferous in expressing their rage. But Chandra hadn't said anything because it'd been the only time in her life when she'd seriously considered giving someone a serious beat-down. By the time she'd returned home from New York, where she'd been enrolled at Columbia University, her anger had subsided.

Myles wanted her to let it go, and she would. She only had another three days before she returned to Belize, and she didn't want to spend the time she had left in the States arguing with her brother.

Leaning away from the column, she walked off the porch and into the house.

Zabrina sat on a cushioned rocker on her porch, watching as dusk descended over the landscape like someone slowly pulling down a shade. She'd prepared a light dinner, watched the evening news, then settled down to read. But restlessness, akin to an itch she couldn't scratch, assailed her and she gave up trying to read to sit on the porch.

She hadn't wanted to admit it, but she missed her son. She'd agreed to let Adam spend a month with his great-aunt and younger cousins. Zabrina had wrestled with her conscience when her cousin had asked Adam to spend time with her young children, and in the end had relented.

Her son was bright, curious and amazingly artistic, and she'd found it a daily struggle not to become an overly protective mother. Permitting Adam to spend time with his cousins was the first step.

Resting her bare feet on a cushioned footstool, she closed her eyes and inhaled the scent of blooming night flowers. The gentle peace she hadn't felt in years swept over Zabrina. Her three-bedroom, two-bath house was much smaller than the twelve-bedroom mausoleum she'd lived in with Thomas, but it was hers and hers alone. Once she decided to sell the house that had been home to generations of Coopers she knew she'd taken the first step to empower herself.

Thomas's attorney had encouraged her to hold on to the house and property for investment purposes. What he didn't understand was that she hated living in a place that made her feel as if she were in a museum. She'd had someone from an auction house appraise the house's contents, and was shocked with the final accounting.

"What's up, Zabrina?"

She opened her eyes and sat up straighter, hearing her closest neighbor's greeting. The day she and Adam moved in, Rachel Copeland had come over with her eight-year-old daughter and eleven-year-old son to introduce her family and bring her a pan of lasagna. Rachel confided that she'd been praying for someone with a child to purchase the newly constructed home so her children would have someone to play with. Most of the homeowners in the two-or three-bedroom subdivision were either young childless couples or retired couples looking to downsize.

She and Rachel had one thing in common—both

were widows. Rachel had lost her military career-officer husband in Afghanistan. Although Zabrina told her that she'd lost her husband in a drowning accident, she'd neglected to tell her that her late husband had been Pennsylvania's junior senator. She'd managed to keep to herself while settling in. A bus came to pick up Adam to take him to a private school and brought him back in the afternoon.

Zabrina waved to her neighbor. "Not much, Rachel."

Rachel walked up the porch steps and folded her tall, slender body down into a dark green wicker chair with a green-and-white-striped cushion. "The weather is really nice tonight."

Zabrina smiled at her neighbor. Rachel's pale blond hair was pulled off her thin face into a ponytail. She would've been thought of as plain if not for her large eyes that were more violet than blue. Her nose was straight, thin and her lower lip full enough to make her appear petulant. Rachel revealed that she'd been a catalogue model before she married her late husband.

"It's perfect." A ceiling fan stirred the warm gentle breeze.

Rachel let out an audible sigh. "I don't know why I hadn't thought of putting in a ceiling fan on my porch."

"I almost regretted having it installed when I caught Adam poking at it with a tree branch. There were splinters everywhere. Once I made certain he was not injured, I grounded him for a week. And that meant no drawing."

"No drawing or no television?"

"For my son it's no drawing. He says he wants to be an animator when he grows up."

Rachel's pale eyebrows shot up. "He likes drawing that much?"

Zabrina nodded. "Yes. It's become an obsession with him. I've tried to get him involved in other things, but he quickly loses interest."

"My Maggie is a dance fanatic and Shane believes he's a kung fu master. I spend all of my free time chauffeuring them between dance and karate classes. My mother came over earlier and took them home with her. Now that they're on summer break I'll have a little more time for myself." Rachel sat up straighter. "What do you say we go out clubbing one night next week?"

Zabrina gave her an incredulous look. "You're kidding, aren't you?"

Rachel leaned forward. "Do I look like I'm kidding? My husband's been dead three years and he had long talks about what he wanted for me if he didn't come back alive. He told me that he didn't want me to spend the rest of my life mourning for him, and now I realize what he was trying to tell me. I'm thirty-four years old and I'm lonely *and* horny. Even if I don't sleep with a man I want one to hold me close and tell me things a woman wants and needs to hear."

Zabrina smiled. "Well, if you put it that way, then I'll go out with you."

She wanted to tell her neighbor that she hadn't been out clubbing but had gone to a wedding where she'd flirted with a man she had no intention of seeing again, and she'd drunk too much to forget another whom she'd never stopped loving.

Rachel's smile was dazzling. "Thanks." She pushed

to her feet. "I don't know about you, but I'd like to go for a walk."

Zabrina swung her legs over the footstool and stood up. "Let me get my shoes and I'll join you."

Zabrina was glad Rachel had suggested going for a walk. It was just what she needed to shake off a case of doldrums, and she'd quickly discovered they weren't the only ones who were out for a walk. Couples—young and some not so young—strolled along a lit path that bordered a bird sanctuary. There were joggers and others walking dogs.

She and Rachel talked about everything from recipes to the economy and their children. What they did not talk about were men, or the lack of men in their lives. Zabrina understood Rachel's need to meet a man. After all, she'd had more than three years to mourn the death of her husband and the father of her children, while her own arranged marriage had ended less than a year ago.

Reaching for Rachel's arm, Zabrina pulled her away from two frisky puppies heading for her. "Watch out."

Rachel shook off her hand, bending down to touch the tiny bundles of fur. "Aren't you two just too cute?"

Zabrina glanced up at the man pulling gently on the leashes of the yapping Yorkshire terriers. "Myles?"

Myles nodded. "Good evening, Brina."

"What...what are you doing around here?"

Myles's gaze swept over the woman who unknowingly still held a piece of his heart. "I'm staying at Belinda's house."

Her eyelids fluttering, Zabrina tried to process what Myles had just told her. "But, she told me she was moving to Paoli." A small town north of Philadelphia, Paoli was a friendly close-knit community of fifty-four hundred that was family-oriented.

"She did, but with the housing market the way it is she's decided to hold on to her house until the market improves."

Zabrina hadn't realized how fast her heart was beating until she felt the rapid pulse in her lip. Myles was going to spend the summer in a house within walking distance of her own. Each time she walked or drove along the road near the bird sanctuary she knew she would always look for a glimpse of Myles Eaton.

She pointed to the puppies that were now yapping at Rachel. "Do they belong to you?"

"No! Do I look like the lap-dog type?"

"Easy, Myles," Zabrina said, biting back a smile. She knew she'd hit a raw nerve because she was aware that he liked big dogs.

"They belong to my nieces."

She hunkered down, rubbing one of the pups behind the ears. "You are so cute. What's your name, baby?"

Myles stared at Zabrina kneeling on the ground in front of him, curbing the urge to run his fingers through her hair. He recalled the number of times he'd wakened to find her long hair spread over the pillow beside his. Those were days and nights he'd believed would never end.

"I think that one is Cecil, and the other is Nigel."

Zabrina came to her feet. "They are adorable. Please excuse me, but I'm forgetting my manners. Myles, this is my neighbor Rachel Copeland. Rachel, Myles Eaton."

Rachel offered Myles her hand. "It's very nice meeting you. How long have you and Zabrina known each other?"

Myles stared at Zabrina. "We grew up together."

"Zabrina and I are going clubbing in a few days. Would you like to come with us?" Rachel asked. She wasn't smiling, but grinning. "You can bring your wife or girlfriend along if you want."

"Rachel!"

Zabrina couldn't understand what had gotten into her neighbor. First she'd talked about being horny, and now she'd invited a stranger to go out with them, as well as Myles's wife or girlfriend, though Zabrina doubted he had one. If he'd had a wife there was no doubt she would've come with him to her sister-in-law's wedding, and if there was a serious girlfriend, then she, too, would've attended the wedding.

Rachel turned and glared at Zabrina in disbelief. It was apparent Myles and Zabrina hadn't seen each other in a while or else she would've known he lived within walking distance of their subdivision. And inviting him to go out with them, even if he was involved with someone, would be the perfect cover for them not to look like two desperate women trolling clubs to pick up men.

"It's obvious you and Myles haven't seen each other in a while, so I thought inviting him along would give you two the opportunity to reminisce."

Myles smiled when Zabrina stared at the ground. He knew she was uneasy about interacting with him, because what they'd shared the night before wasn't easily forgotten.

"Rachel's right," he said quietly. "Hanging out together will allow us to talk about old times. Where and when are you going?"

Rachel spoke first. "We're not certain. But it will be this week." She pulled a tiny cell phone from the pocket of her shorts. "Give me your number and I'll call and let you know."

Myles noticed the narrow gold band on the ring finger of the chatty blonde's right hand. His gaze shifted to Zabrina's bare fingers, then her wide-eyed stare. "I have Zabrina's numbers," he said, after a long pause.

Rachel clapped her hands. "That's great! You can call her and she'll let you know what's up after we decide on a place…unless you can recommend one."

"I'll let Brina know." Myles didn't want to commit until he spoke to a former high-school classmate. Hugh Ormond had changed careers, going from investment banker to chef and eventually opening an upscale restaurant that featured dining and dancing a block from Broad Street, affectionately known to Philadelphians as Avenue of the Arts.

Rachel extended her hand for the second time. "Again, it's a pleasure to meet you, Myles."

He smiled the sexy smile that never failed to make a woman take pause. "The pleasure is all mine, Rachel."

Zabrina's neighbor had provided him with the perfect excuse to see her again.

"I guess we'll see you soon," Rachel crooned.

Myles's smile grew wider. "That you will." He nodded to Zabrina. "Good night, Brina."

She returned a smile that failed to reach her eyes. "Good night, Myles." She bent over to pat the Yorkies.

They jumped up in an attempt to lick her face, but she pulled back in time.

Taking Rachel's arm, she forcibly pulled her to retrace their route. "I could kill you for inviting Myles to go out with us," she hissed between her teeth, although they were far enough away from Myles so that he wouldn't hear her rant. "You made it seem as if we're desperate, widows gone wild."

Rachel extricated her arm. "What are you talking about?"

"What if I didn't want him to go out with us?"

"Why wouldn't you, Zabrina? Didn't the two of you grow up together?"

"I was friends with one of his sisters."

"Is he married, Zabrina?"

"No."

"Does he have a special woman?"

"I don't know," Zabrina answered truthfully.

Rachel flashed a knowing smile. "We'll find out soon enough when we all go out together."

Zabrina stopped mid-stride. "Why your sudden interest in Myles Eaton?"

Resting her hands on her slim hips, Rachel pushed her face close to Zabrina's. "I'm not interested in him for myself, but for you. You were so busy playing with the puppies that you couldn't see the lust in Myles's eyes. And if I didn't know better I'd think you have something wrong with your eyes if you didn't notice that he's so hot he sizzles."

"If he's so hot, then why don't you go after him?"

"Maybe I will once I find out whether he's available. That is, *if* you don't want him."

Rachel's pronouncement rendered Zabrina speechless and motionless. She'd seen a photograph of her neighbor's late husband, and he was the complete opposite of Myles. But who was she to say what Rachel's type was? She didn't want to admit that she was jealous. For years she'd thought of Myles as hers even though she'd married another man. Every night when she went to bed—alone—she pretended Myles Eaton was in bed with her. And there were times when she prayed he wouldn't find another woman to love because that meant losing him forever. Myles had always said that when he married it would be for the rest of his life.

The sky had darkened and millions of stars twinkled in the heavens when Zabrina and Rachel returned home. She said good-night to Rachel, walked up the porch to her house and unlocked the door. Silence greeted her as she walked in. It wasn't often the house was silent because either a radio or the television provided background noise while she cooked or completed her household chores.

After Adam came home from school he went through the ritual of washing his hands and changing out of his school uniform before settling down at the kitchen table to do his homework. By the time he finished dinner was ready. It was their time together when Adam recounted what had gone on in his classes.

Although Adam looked nothing like Myles, his facial expressions and body language were almost identical to his biological father's. Zabrina dreaded the time when she would have to tell her son the truth about the man who'd fathered him.

She dreaded it almost as much as the revelation that the grandfather he'd loved and respected was a thief.

Chapter 7

Zabrina had just finished applying her makeup when the doorbell chimed. The contrast of the smoky shadow on her eyelids made her eyes appear lighter than they actually were.

As promised, Myles had called her Monday evening to inform her that he'd made dinner reservations for three at a popular restaurant in the heart of downtown Philadelphia that featured live music and dancing. His mention of reservations for three answered her question as to whether he would have a fourth person join them. If she hadn't lived a cloistered existence for the past decade, Zabrina would've invited a man to come along as her date in order to put some physical distance between herself and Myles, because it would take a miracle for her to exorcise him from her heart. He was the first man with whom she'd fallen in love, and she would love him forever.

Walking out of the en suite bathroom through the bedroom, she made her way down the carpeted hallway to the staircase in a pair of four-inch black crepe satin Christian Louboutin pumps with an asymmetric bow. She'd selected the designer footwear for Thomas's swearing-in ceremony, but hadn't attended because she'd come down with pneumonia and her doctor had advised against traveling to D.C.

What was ironic was that her closets were filled with designer clothes and shoes she'd never worn, shoes and clothes purchased for her by the young man whose responsibility it was to dress his boss and his boss's wife. Most times the designer garments remained on the padded hangers when she refused to attend a dinner party or fundraiser with Thomas. He had lost his temper several times, but when she threatened to divulge that he'd blackmailed her into marrying him he glared at her and stalked out of her bedroom suite. It was the last time he'd asked her to accompany him. However, her wardrobe continued to increase with Thomas's hope that she would eventually change her mind.

She never did.

When she'd taken the shoes out of the box, Zabrina glanced at the price tag for the first time. Spending nine hundred dollars for a pair of shoes was unconscionable, and there were at least four-dozen boxes containing shoes comparable to the pair she'd selected to go out with Myles and Rachel. Slim black stretch cuffed slacks and a white long-sleeved cotton wrapped-waist blouse completed her casual chic outfit.

Glancing through the side window in the door, she saw Myles's SUV parked in her driveway. She opened the door and went completely still as a sensual smile spread across Myles's face. The gesture made her feel something she'd almost forgotten existed. Even when she woke Sunday morning to discover that she was sharing the same bed as Myles Eaton, none of the sensations now coursing through her body had been evident. Maybe it was because her senses had been dulled by alcohol, but the tiny tremors between her legs made it difficult for her to maintain her balance in the high heels.

"You're early." He'd come half an hour before he was supposed to pick her up. She opened the door wider, and he walked into the expansive foyer that led to the living room. She closed the door, turned around pressing her back to the door.

Myles registered the husky quality of her voice. His smile slipped slowly away when he stared at Zabrina under the soft, flattering glow from a chandelier hanging overhead. Unconsciously Zabrina was seducing him with her smoky voice and sparkling eyes. His gaze lingered on her face. Her luminous eyes, the exotic slant of high cheekbones and her full lush mouth were sexually arousing. She was thinner than she'd been when they were engaged, but her size did not diminish her femininity. There was enough roundness in her hips to belie any notion of her being mistaken for a boy.

Leaning closer, he kissed her cheek. "How did you get so tall?"

Zabrina laughed softly. "It's the heels." Extending her foot, she displayed the stilettos.

His eyebrows lifted. The heels she wore were higher

than the ones she'd had on at Belinda's wedding. "Are you certain you'll be able to dance in those?"

Zabrina affected a sensual pout, drawing Myles's gaze to lips enhanced by a glossy magenta. The shade was perfect for her lightly tanned face. "I'll sit out the fast tunes." His eyelids lowered, reminding Zabrina of a predator watching and waiting for the exact moment to seize its intended prey. "Should I add your name to my dance card?"

If you think I'm taking you out so you can dance and flirt with other men, then you've truly lost your mind.

The thought had popped into and out of Myles's head in the blink of an eye. In that instant he had to admit that Chandra was right. Just when he'd believed he'd gotten over Zabrina, she'd come back into his life. Even if he'd been able to exorcise her from his thoughts, what he hadn't been able to forget was the searing heat and passion between them.

The first time he and Zabrina had shared a bed he'd known she was different—special. And it hadn't had anything to do with her being a virgin. There was a time when Myles thought he'd remained faithful to his sister's best friend because he'd taken her innocence. But, when he compared her to the other women he'd slept with, he knew her virginity did not figure into the equation. The reality was that he had fallen in love with Zabrina before they'd slept together.

She could always get him to laugh even when he hadn't felt like laughing. She wasn't as needy as some of the women he'd known. They were the ones who complained if he didn't call them every day, or tell them they were pretty. Not only was Zabrina beautiful, but she was also smart and independent—something he hadn't expected her to be since she'd grown up pampered by her father.

He hadn't remembered Zabrina's mother that well. He'd been twelve when she'd finally lost her mother to brain cancer. At that age he'd begun noticing girls and sports had become a priority. However, he wasn't completely oblivious to the gossip about Jacinta Mixon's shadowy background. Some said that the beautiful woman was the product of a short-lived marriage between an African-American soldier and a young woman he'd met in the Philippines. Others claimed that she'd come from Mexico with her migrant farming family and caught the eye of Isaac Mixon when he was stationed at Fort Sam Houston in Texas. Whatever her racial or ethnic background, Jacinta had given Isaac an incredible child.

Myles blinked as if coming out of a trance. "What do you think, Brina?" he asked after a long silence.

A slight frown appeared between Zabrina's eyes. Myles was looking at her as if she were a complete stranger. "I don't know what to think. That's why I asked, Myles."

"Of course I want to dance with you."

She smiled. "Good. I just have to comb my hair, then I'll be ready." She'd washed her hair, applied a small amount of gel and all she had to do was style it.

"Do you mind if I look around your house?"

Myles's question threw Zabrina for a few seconds. "No, I don't mind. Why don't you come upstairs with me, then you can work your way down."

"I'm trying to get an idea of what kind of house I want to buy."

Turning on her heels, Zabrina walked to the staircase. "Whatever you choose should complement its surroundings," she said over her shoulder as she climbed the stairs. Myles was right behind her.

"There are a few new developments going up in some of Pittsburgh's suburbs, but what I don't want is a cookie-cutter house."

"Why don't you have it built to your specifications?"

Myles stared at the gentle sway of hips as Zabrina made her way along the carpeted hallway. "I don't want to wait that long. I have a lease on an apartment that's due to expire at the end of August. I'd like to move into a house before Labor Day. I've been preapproved, so all I have to do is find the house I want."

Zabrina stopped at her bedroom. "I'm going to be in here. The bathroom is across the hall, my son's room is on the left and a guest bedroom is at the end of the hall on the right."

Myles stared at the woman whose head was only several inches below his. Zabrina stood close to six feet in her heels. "How many bathrooms do you have?"

"There are two full baths upstairs and one half bath off the kitchen."

"Your house looks bigger than Belinda's."

"It is. Her subdivision is ten years older than this one. The same developer designed both subdivisions. But when he decided to build here, putting up McMansions was all the rage. These homes are what I call mini-McMansions. The smaller ones range between twenty-five hundred and three thousand square feet. The larger ones go as high as five thousand square feet."

"I doubt if I'll need five thousand square feet. Three or four would be more than enough. What I really want is a wraparound porch, lots of trees and enough property that a couple of dogs can have the run of the place."

Zabrina patted his arm.

"It sounds as if you're nostalgic for your childhood home."

A beat passed as Myles thought about what Zabrina had said. She was right. He *was* nostalgic, longing for what was and would never be again. "Maybe I am," he admitted reluctantly. "What about you, Brina?"

"What about me?"

"You've spent the past decade living in a mansion with a staff to see to your every need, and you gave it all up to live here?"

Her delicate jaw hardened. "That house wasn't mine. It belonged to Thomas. As his widow I could do whatever I wanted with it, and I decided to sell it."

"What about your son, Brina? He's a Cooper. Shouldn't he live in his family's home? After all, the house was his birthright."

Thomas Cooper came from a prominent Philadelphia African-American family. Ephraim Cooper had been accused of being a front man for a group of unscrupulous businessmen when he sold worthless railroad stock to poor blacks who wanted to cash in on the American dream.

Ephraim, a self-taught attorney, successfully defended himself in court, suing the men he worked for. He won the case and earned a reputation as a champion of the underdog. The publicity made him one of the most sought-after attorneys in Philadelphia. He enlarged his practice, built what came to be known as Cooper Hall and eventually returned all of the monies to those who'd invested in the phony railroad stock scheme. Before Ephraim passed away he'd been referred to as the unofficial mayor of Philadelphia's Negro population.

Zabrina closed her eyes and swallowed hard in an attempt to suppress the rage threatening to erupt. When she opened her eyes all traces of gold were missing, leaving them a cold, frosty green.

"Do not talk to me about something you know nothing about. What I did was sell what you think was my son's so-called birthright and put the proceeds in an account for his future. His education and the man that he will become mean more to me than his living in a museum with servants waiting on him hand and foot."

Myles realized he'd pushed the wrong button when he'd mentioned her son. It was apparent discussing Adam Cooper was taboo. It was a mistake he would not repeat. "You're right. I'm sorry," he said, apologizing.

Zabrina nodded. "I'm sorry I went off on you, Myles. I suppose I'm a little protective when it comes to Adam."

He winked at her. "I guess being protective comes with parenthood. Now that I've taken my foot out of my mouth I'm going to see the rest of your house."

Myles walked to the end of the hall, peered into the guest bedroom and flipped the wall switch. The space was twice the size of his Pittsburgh bedroom. Zabrina had decorated it in a soft, calming taupe and seafoam green. The room held a queen-size bed, double dresser and nightstands, and a love seat covered in soft green was positioned under a trio of windows. Sheers were hung above the windows, a rug in a muted color, a stack of books and magazines on a low table beside the love seat and the ceiling fan overhead created a calm, relaxed feel to the room.

Turning off the light, he moved down the hall to the bathroom: recessed lights, white mosaic tile, a garden tub with a Jacuzzi, twin stainless-steel sinks, a freestanding shower and a dressing area with mirrored walls made the space appear twice as large.

Adam's room was the quintessential boy's bedroom with a trundle bed covered with a red, white and blue patchwork quilt. The colors were repeated in the rug and built-in shelves cradling books, a desktop computer, printer and television. The bedroom was spotless.

Myles's mouth twitched in amusement when he remembered Roberta Eaton's reaction whenever she opened the door to his third-story bedroom. Because he was the only boy, he'd been given the attic bedroom. She usually had to scour the room to find mismatched socks under the bed, underwear, T-shirts and occasionally dress slacks on the floor of the closets in order to put them in the wash or send them to the dry cleaner. It was only when he moved into his own condo that he took steps to keep his living quarters neat *and* clean. He hired a cleaning service. He walked over to Zabrina's bedroom, rapping lightly on the door.

"Come in," Zabrina called out from somewhere behind the door.

Myles entered the master bedroom, stopping when he saw the elaborately carved mahogany four-poster bed with all-white bed linens that was the room's focal point. The mahogany furniture and creamy white fabrics harkened back to a bygone era where women sipped tea on the veranda.

"Where are you, Brina?"

"I'm in the bathroom."

He turned in the direction of her voice and stood at the entrance to her bathroom. It wasn't a bathroom so much as it was a home spa. A cedar soaking tub, candles and incense, a built-in bench lined with pillows for lounging or meditating offered a comfortable spot to stretch out before or after soaking or sitting in the sauna. The windows were covered with shades that let light in while providing complete privacy.

Zabrina sat at a dressing table putting the finishing touches on her hair. Using her fingers, she'd lifted the damp strands at the crown and feathered wisps over her forehead.

Myles entered the bathroom. "Did all of this come with the house?"

Smiling at his reflection in the mirror, Zabrina shook her head. "Unfortunately, it didn't. I had to sleep in the guest bedroom for three weeks while the contractor completed the renovations. I was vacuuming up dust for at least a month."

He took another step, bringing him closer to where she sat. "It's incredible."

"If you ever want to come over and unwind in the sauna, just let me know. Spending half an hour in the steam shower, then soaking in the tub is the cure for whatever ails you."

Myles pushed his hands into the pockets of his suit

trousers. "As much as I'd like to take you up on your offer, I can't do that, Brina."

Gazing into his dark eyes in the mirror, Zabrina frowned slightly. "Why can't you?"

"What would your son think if he saw a strange man lounging in his mother's bathroom?"

Zabrina came to her feet, her gaze meeting and fusing with Myles's. "Do you think I would invite you to come over when my son is here?"

"You tell me, Brina."

"The answer is no, Myles. Adam has never seen me with any other man except for Thomas. And if he were to see one in my bedroom then it would be my husband."

Raising his right hand, Myles ran the back of it over her cheek. "Would you ever get married again?"

Zabrina closed her eyes rather than look at the tenderness in Myles's eyes. "I would if he were the right man."

He frowned. "What do you mean by the right man?"

She opened her eyes. "He would have to be a good father and role model for Adam."

"What about you, Brina? What would you want for yourself?" Myles asked.

Brina said the first thing that came to mind. "Sex."

Myles lowered his head, unable to believe what he'd just heard. "You're kidding, aren't you?"

"Do I look like I'm kidding?"

Zabrina hadn't lied to Myles. It had been more than a decade since she'd been made love to. Unlike Rachel, who admitted to being horny, she had been too ashamed to openly admit it until now. Ten years was a long time to deny her own needs or the strong yearnings that unexpectedly swept over her. Surprised by her admission, Myles stared at her in disbelief.

"Why are you looking at me like that? Would it be less shocking if the roles were reversed, and you were the one saying that you wanted to have sex with me?"

"Is that what you want from me?" he asked, recovering his composure.

"Sure, but only if you're up for it," she countered. "It would just be for the summer."

"What about Adam?"

"What about him, Myles?"

"You can't expect me to sleep with you while he's in the house."

Zabrina was hard-pressed not to laugh. For the first time in years she felt empowered, dictating what she wanted or didn't want to do with every phase of her life. Although she'd refused to pretend to be the dutiful wife when Thomas wanted her to accompany him, legally she'd been his wife. Even after her father had passed away, Zabrina still hadn't been willing to divorce Thomas. As long as he didn't try to exercise his conjugal rights or interfere with her relationship with Adam she'd continued to play out the charade.

"We can sleep together at your place whenever Adam stays with his relatives or has a sleepover with his friends."

"What happens at the end of the summer, Zabrina?"

Myles was still trying to grasp the enormity of her unusual suggestion. This was a Zabrina he truly didn't know. When it came to women he'd always been the one doing the propositioning and usually not the other way around. This was not to say that women hadn't let him know they were interested in more than a platonic liaison, but they'd never been as candid as Zabrina.

"We go our separate ways to live our separate lives."

Damn, he mused. When had she become so insensitive? "Why me, Brina?" he asked. "Why not choose some other man to be your sex toy?"

"Why not you, Myles?" she said, answering his question with another question. "We have a history. And if people see us together they'll think we're just old friends hanging out together for the summer."

"Friends who were once engaged," Myles reminded her.

"That, too," she countered. "There are a lot of couples who were either married or break up and are still friends."

Her initial bravado fading quickly, Zabrina chided herself for broaching the subject of sleeping with Myles. Her ego and vanity had surpassed common sense. She tilted her chin in a haughty gesture. "Forget I mentioned it."

Reaching out, Myles pulled Zabrina close to his chest. A mysterious glow fired the raven orbs staring back at her. "I can't forget it any more than I can forget what we had, or what we once meant to each other. If you want a sex partner for the summer, then I'll oblige you. And don't concern yourself with birth control, because I'll assume responsibility for using protection."

Pinpoints of heat flamed in her face. She'd just propositioned her former fiancé, and he'd accepted. At thirty-three she'd become not only reckless, but shameless. Sleeping with Myles meant she didn't have to troll the clubs or the Internet looking for a man.

"Thank you." It was apparent he'd remembered the number of times she'd had to change contraceptives because of the side effects.

"You're welcome," Myles whispered, seconds before he sealed their arrangement with a searing kiss that weakened her knees. Nothing had changed. It was as if a day rather than a decade had passed between them. Her arms came up, she pressing closer as she wound her arms around his neck, while reveling in the taste and feel of his mouth on hers.

Zabrina clung to Myles as if she depended on him for her next breath. She loved him. She missed him and the passion he elicited with a single glance. Her fingers grazed the nape of his neck. Zabrina wanted Myles, wanted to strip him naked and lie between his legs until he assuaged her pent-up sexual frustration.

The doorbell rang for the second time, and she went completely still. "That's Rachel," she whispered against Myles's parted lips.

Cradling her face between his hands, Myles winked at Zabrina. "Send her away."

With wide eyes, she said, "I can't. Rachel has been really looking forward to going out tonight."

His eyebrows lifted as he brushed his mouth over hers. "What about you, Brina? Are you looking forward to going out, too?"

"Yes, I am," she said truthfully.

"Okay. To be continued."

"To be continued," she repeated. Hand-in-hand, they walked out of the bedroom and down the staircase. Zabrina reached for her small leather purse while Myles opened the door.

Rachel Copeland had morphed from a suburban housewife into a seductive siren. Her blond hair was a mass of tiny curls, and a body-hugging tank dress and matching strappy black sandals had replaced her ubiquitous T-shirt and jeans. Despite having given birth to two children there was no doubt she still could get modeling assignments.

Zabrina gasped. Rachel was certain to turn heads with her revealing outfit. "You look incredible, Rachel."

Rachel tossed her head and her flaxen curls bounced as if they'd taken on a life of their own. She looked every inch the model with her expertly made-up face. "Thank you. And, you're one hot-looking widow!"

Zabrina winced. Rachel was the widow of a war hero, and she saw herself as a single mother. Glancing over her shoulder, she smiled at Myles. "We're ready whenever you are."

He waited for Zabrina to punch in the code for the security system and lock the door. He escorted both women to where he'd parked his SUV. Opening the passenger-side door, he scooped up Zabrina and placed her on the leather seat, then helped Rachel into her seat. He'd doubted whether either of them would've been able to get into the vehicle unassisted because of their footwear.

Try as he could, Myles didn't understand why women insisted on wearing such high heels. However, there was an upside to stilettos—they made a woman's legs look incredibly sexy.

After all, he was a leg man.

Chapter 8

Myles pocketed his valet stub, then escorted Rachel and Zabrina through the restaurant's parking lot to Whispers. The upscale supper club had a three-week wait for dinner reservations, but Myles had jumped to the head of the list because he and Hugh Ormond had played on the same high-school football team. They'd lost touch after graduating, but reconnected the year before at their twentieth high-school reunion.

A doorman opened the door for them, his gaze sweeping over the two women clinging to Myles's arm. "Welcome to Whispers. I hope you and *your ladies* have an enjoyable evening."

"*Are* we your ladies, Myles?" Zabrina teased, sotto voce. His response was to narrow his gaze.

"How on earth did you get a reservation to this place?" Rachel whispered to Myles.

"A friend owns it."

"I'm going to like hanging out with you and Zabrina." Rachel had read about the grand opening of the club in the entertainment section of the local newspaper. The food critic had given the cuisine, decor, ambience and live entertainment his highest rating.

Myles approached the hostess. "I have a reservation for three at seven."

The young woman smiled at Myles. "Your name, sir?"

"Eaton."

Her smile brightened when she signaled the maître d'. "Mr. Ormond wants you to let him know when the Eaton party arrives."

The dark-suited, slightly built, balding man bowed elegantly from the waist. "*Monsieur, mesdames*. Please follow me."

Zabrina shared a smile with Rachel. The establishment was intimate and aesthetically pleasing, confirming it was the ideal venue for a rendezvous. Tables with seating for two or four were positioned far enough away from other diners to insure privacy. If they'd been placed closer, the restaurant's seating capacity would have doubled.

Whoever had designed the restaurant had incorporated elements of feng shui. The interior had come alive with live plants, the soft sound of gurgling fountains and an enormous fish tank, filled with colorful exotic fish, that spanned the entire length of the wall.

They were shown to a table with seating for four near the band playing Latin music. Several couples were up on the dance floor, swaying to the seductive rhythm.

Myles pulled out a chair, seating Zabrina, while a waiter came over to seat Rachel. Myles glanced up when a shadow loomed over the table. Rising to his feet, he gave Hugh Ormond a rough embrace.

Hugh pounded his former schoolmate's back. "I'm glad you could make it." He took the empty chair as Myles made the introductions.

"Hugh, the lady to my left is Zabrina Cooper and the one on your right is Rachel Copeland. Ladies, Hugh Ormond, owner and executive chef of Whispers."

Zabrina and Rachel gave the obligatory greetings, both enthralled with the man who exuded charm effortlessly. Tall and solidly built with cropped sandy-brown hair and sparkling gray eyes, Hugh Ormond had a quick smile and a velvet voice. When he ordered a bottle of champagne for the table, Zabrina felt the heat from Myles's gaze on her face. She sat up straighter when his hand caressed the small of her back.

"Don't worry, baby. I promise not to take advantage of you if you have more than one glass," Myles whispered in her ear.

"I'm not worried, darling," she said softly. "I trust you."

The moment the endearment slipped from her lips Zabrina felt as if time stood still, as if the past ten years hadn't happened. A slow warming began in her chest and wove its way down her body and settled between her thighs.

She'd thought herself brazen when she'd told Myles that she wanted him to make love to her but realized she was being honest. It was the first time since before she'd called her fiancé to tell him that she was in love with another man that she was honest with him *and* with herself.

What Zabrina had tired of was: pretending she was a dutiful wife when she posed with Thomas and Adam for an official family photograph, pretending all was well whenever they were forced to share the same space, pretending to grieve the loss of her husband *and* pretending to be strong for her son when he had to deal with the loss of his grandfather and father within months of each other.

Adam loved Thomas, but adored his grandfather. Isaac was always there when Thomas hadn't been. And whenever his father was around, the young boy did everything possible to get Thomas's attention. Once Thomas was appointed to fill the vacant senate seat, spending more time in D.C. than he did in Philadelphia, Adam transferred his affection from his father to his grandfather.

In order to help her son cope with the loss of two important men in his life Zabrina had arranged for him to see a child psychologist, and what was revealed in those sessions had rocked Zabrina to her very core. Adam had said Thomas always made him feel like a dog as he patted his head whenever he told him he'd aced a test. It'd been Grandpa who took him to baseball and football games when his father was too busy. It'd been Grandpa who accompanied his mother to parent-teacher conferences and it'd been Grandpa who'd saved every one of his drawings and had them bound like the many books lining the mansion's bookshelves.

She was forthcoming when she accepted blame for the distance between father and son, because Thomas had never really wanted children. Zabrina didn't tell the psychologist that she'd been blackmailed into marrying Thomas Cooper, but knew eventually she would have to tell Adam the truth. She wanted to wait until he was old enough to understand the reason she had to protect his beloved grandfather.

"Are you all right, Brina?"

She blinked as if coming out of a trance. "Yes. Why?"

Myles gave Zabrina a long, penetrating stare. She appeared distracted, and he wondered if it was because they'd agreed to sleep together again. Cupping her elbow, he leaned closer. "Come dance with me."

"Now?"

"Yes, now."

Myles wanted to talk to Zabrina, but he didn't want Hugh or Rachel to overhear what he wanted to tell her. He stood up and then eased Zabrina to her feet. Wrapping an arm around her waist, he led her to the dance floor. Easing her into a close embrace, he molded her length to his.

"What's the matter, Brina?" He felt her stiffen with his query before she relaxed again.

"What makes you think something is the matter?"

"You're distracted, and I've never known you to daydream."

Zabrina closed her eyes. "That's because I've changed, Myles. I have a lot more responsibility now."

"That may be true, but it's more than that."

"What are you getting at, Myles?"

"Why did you really ask me to sleep with you?"

Zabrina knew she couldn't tell him that her husband

had never consummated their marriage, so she said the next best thing. "I'm lonely, Myles. I've been lonely for a very long time."

Myles missed a step with Zabrina's admission, but recovered quickly. It was apparent her marriage to Thomas Cooper was far from ideal. But then, what had she expected from a politician? It was apparent her late husband had neglected her and she wanted Myles to make up for the loss of affection.

"I can't be a substitute for your late husband, Brina."

"There's no way you would ever be a substitute for Thomas." Myles visibly recoiled as if she'd struck him. "We slept in separate bedrooms."

At first Myles thought Zabrina was comparing him to Thomas in bed, and now her revelation that she and her late husband did not share a bed was too much for him to grasp.

He pressed his mouth to her hair. "I really don't want to know what went on between you and Cooper, because what goes on between a man and his wife is sacrosanct. I'm not going to lie and say I don't have feelings for you because I do. I realized that the day I saw you in the restaurant with my sister, and the most difficult decision I've ever had to face in my life was not making love to you Saturday night. You were in my bed, naked and I still couldn't bring myself to touch you. I also have a confession to make."

"What's that?" Zabrina asked.

"I would've asked you to sleep with me even if you hadn't asked first. It doesn't have to be tonight or tomorrow night, but when it happens it will be the right time and we'll both know it."

Zabrina wound her arms around Myles's waist inside his jacket. Hot tears pricked the backs of her eyelids as she struggled to bring her fragile emotions under control. He'd just validated why she'd fallen in love with him so many years before. He'd never put any pressure on her to sleep with him, and when she had finally offered him her innocent body, the shared experience was one she would remember forever.

"Myles?"

"What, baby?"

"Why didn't you marry?" she asked softly.

"If I had found a woman like you, then I'm certain I would've married her."

Zabrina wanted to believe he'd waited for her, that he couldn't forget her just like she couldn't forget him, but she wasn't that vain. What she did believe was that there were people who were destined to be together. It'd been that way with her and Myles.

The song ended, and Myles escorted Zabrina back to their table where Hugh and Rachel were talking quietly to each other. There was something in the way the restaurateur was staring at the attractive blonde that made Myles pause. Hugh had married his high-school sweetheart, but the union had lasted less than three years. He'd admitted to several long-term relationships, but wasn't ready to commit to marrying again.

Hugh came to his feet with Zabrina's approach. "I'm off tonight, but I was just telling Rachel that if you want something that's not on the menu, then I'll prepare it for you."

Rachel shook her head as she ran her fingers through her hair as if fluffing up her curls. Zabrina caught her meaning immediately. "That's not necessary. I'm more than willing to order from the menu."

"I'll order from the menu," Myles said, agreeing with her.

The sommelier arrived with a bottled of chilled champagne and four flutes. Hugh sampled the wine, smiling. "It's very good." The wine steward filled the flutes, nodded, then walked away.

Hugh raised his flute, and the other three followed suit. "Here's to friendship—old and new."

"Old and new," chorused Myles, Rachel and Zabrina, who only took a sip of the champagne. Myles didn't have to concern himself with her overindulging tonight because she didn't like champagne.

Over the next two hours they were served a four-course dinner that was nothing short of a culinary feast. The lobster bisque, the mixed green salad with the restaurant's secret vinaigrette, the parmesan-roasted asparagus, prime rib, stuffed pork chops, almond-crusted salmon and the dessert of vanilla gelato topped with puréed cherries, grated lemon zest and ground cinnamon left everyone pushing away from the table.

Hugh, who admitted he didn't dance, sat talking quietly to Rachel while Zabrina and Myles joined other couples gliding across the dance floor. It was close to eleven when Zabrina said she was ready to leave. Her calves were aching from dancing nonstop in four-inch heels.

They said their goodbyes to Hugh, who insisted they not remain strangers. He kissed Zabrina's hand, then Rachel's. "You don't have to wait for Myles to bring you back. Both of you are welcome at any time."

Rachel gave him a demure smile. "It may be a while because I heard there's a three-week wait for a reservation."

Reaching into his jacket, Hugh took out a business card, jotted down a number and handed the card to Rachel. "That's the number to my cell. Call and let me know when you're coming, and I will make certain there will be a table for you."

A rush of color flooded Rachel's face. "Thank you, Hugh."

He leaned over and kissed her cheek. "You're welcome, Rachel."

Hugh walked them to the parking lot, then waited for the valet to bring Myles's SUV around, waving until the taillights disappeared from view.

Myles walked the short distance from Rachel's house to Zabrina's, finding her in the kitchen, barefoot, filling a glass with water from the dispenser on the refrigerator door. Slipping out of his suit jacket, he draped it over the back of a counter stool.

"We have to do it again."

Zabrina jumped and water sloshed out of the glass and onto the floor. She hadn't heard Myles come into the kitchen. She blew out a breath. "What are you trying to do? Give me a heart attack?"

"No. Next time I'll make some noise. Let me do that," he said when she reached for a paper towel to blot up the water. Easing the wad of paper from her fingers, Myles wiped the splatter. A mysterious smile parted his lips when Zabrina stared up at him. "After you drink your water I want you to go upstairs and pack a bag with a change of clothes and whatever else you'll need for a couple of days."

Her eyebrows flickered. "Where am I going?"

He took a step. "You're coming home with me."

"To do what, Myles?" Zabrina's husky voice had dropped an octave.

"I'll let you decide that."

"What if all I want to do is eat and sleep?"

"Then that's what we'll do."

Zabrina took a step, pressing her chest to his. "So, the choice is mine?"

"The choice has always been yours, Brina. If the choice had been mine we would've looked forward to celebrating our eleventh wedding anniversary and Adam would've been an Eaton, not a Cooper."

She decided not to respond to his baiting. "What about your nieces?"

"What about them, Brina?"

"Aren't they coming over to see their puppies?"

Lowering his head, Myles nuzzled the side of her neck. "My mother took them to Martha's Vineyard to spend some time with Griffin's parents. They're not expected back until Sunday. And that gives us at least three full days and nights to hang out together."

"That sounds like a plan."

"I thought you'd like it. When do you expect Adam to come home?"

Glancing up over her shoulder, Zabrina smiled at the man pressed against her back. Unconsciously, as if they'd rehearsed and choreographed a dance, they'd reverted to their familiar embrace of her settling easily against his body. It felt so good to have him touch her without the artifice of dancing together. She knew they couldn't relive the past, but she planned to enjoy whatever time was given to them. Even if it was only one night, then she would have the memory of that night to hold on to forever.

Just like life, there were no guarantees, no promises of tomorrow. If she and Myles were to have a second chance she would count it as an added blessing. If not, then she would continue to improve on the new life she'd made for herself and her son.

"He's not expected back until the end of July. But I told my aunt to call me and I'll drive down and pick him up if he starts complaining that he wants to come home."

Myles wrapped his arms around her waist. "Do you miss him?"

"I miss him a lot more than I'm willing to admit. I realize he's getting older and he can't remain a mama's boy for the rest of his life, so that's why I agreed to let him spend a month in Virginia."

She missed Adam and she'd missed Myles. Resting her head on his shoulder, Zabrina closed her eyes. Time stood still as she reveled in the moment where words were unnecessary. Although she didn't want to move she realized she wouldn't be able to avoid the inevitable. It was she who'd issued the challenge when she'd asked Myles to make love to her. Little had she known that he was contemplating the same if she hadn't been so impulsive. Whoever made the first move no longer mattered, because she and Myles wanted the same thing.

They were adults—very consenting adults who weren't looking for that elusive happy-ever-after ending. They would engage in a summer tryst and when it ended it would be without angst or expectations of something. Zabrina wasn't looking for more. She just wanted to relive a small part of her past when her cloistered world had been perfect for a young woman with stars in her eyes.

"Are you going to sleep on me, baby?"

She smiled. "No. You're a drug, Myles Eaton." *A very potent, habit-forming drug,* she mused.

He chuckled softly, the deep, warm sound caressing Zabrina's ear. "Will you please explain that very peculiar assessment of yours truly."

"With you I'm always relaxed. I can always be myself."

"Are you saying you couldn't be yourself as Mrs. Thomas Cooper?"

"What I'm saying is that I wasn't permitted to be me. After Thomas's accident I thought of reverting to my maiden name, but I didn't want it to cause a problem for Adam."

"Why would that pose a problem for him, Brina?"

"He told me that he was glad that he had the same last name as his mother. So many mothers of his classmates have different surnames because they've been married two and sometimes three times. Some of the kids were very confused about the whole multiple-marriage and blended-family dynamics."

"That's a heavy topic for a young boy to concern himself with."

"When you meet my son you'll know why he thinks the way he does."

Myles wanted to tell Zabrina that he didn't want to

meet her son, because it would reopen an emotional wound that had taken a long time to heal. "I'm looking forward to meeting him." It wasn't a complete lie. He wanted to meet the boy who was the light of Zabrina's life. "But, right now I'm contemplating doing unspeakable acts with his gorgeous, sexy mother. You'd better go upstairs and pack or we'll end up on the kitchen floor or countertop, and that will prove disastrous because I don't have any protection on me."

Zabrina wanted to tell Myles that it wouldn't be a bad thing. He'd gotten her pregnant once, and if she were to have another child, then she wanted it to be his. Perhaps this time it would be a girl, then Adam could have the sister he'd been asking for.

When he asked her for a sibling, it was always a sister, which stunned Zabrina because she'd thought he'd want a younger brother. But Adam wisely said he didn't want to have to share his computer games with his brother, while his sister would rather play with her dolls and other girly things.

Easing out of Myles's embrace, she stood on her tiptoes and brushed her mouth against his. "Don't run away."

"I can't..." Myles swallowed the other words poised on the tip of his tongue. He wanted to tell Zabrina he couldn't walk away from her even if his life was in jeopardy, that he planned to spend as much time with her as his or her schedule permitted until the end of summer.

Zabrina waited for him to finish his sentence, but when he didn't she walked out of the kitchen, leaving him staring at her back.

Myles knew he had to be careful, very, very careful

or he would find himself so deeply involved with his former fiancée that he wouldn't be able to easily distance himself when it came time to return to Pittsburgh. What he had to continually remind himself of was her deception, and despite not being able to forget Zabrina he knew for certain that he would never forgive her.

Chapter 9

Myles sat on the porch, waiting for Zabrina. Streetlamps that harkened back to nineteenth-century gaslights glowed eerily along the streets that made up the subdivision. A slight smile lifted the corners of his mouth. Someone had left bicycles and skateboards on the lawn of a house across the street without fear they wouldn't find them the next day.

Zabrina had chosen the perfect community in which to raise a child, unlike some neighborhoods where the sound of gunfire and the sight of crime-scene tape were all too familiar. He and his siblings were more than lucky to have had Dwight and Roberta Eaton as their parents—they were blessed.

Roberta, who had given up her career as a teacher to stay at home with her children, said she'd never regretted the decision because she'd utilized her skills when she taught them to read before they were enrolled in kindergarten. There was no trying to circumvent completing homework or a school project because Bertie Eaton was always there to offer her assistance.

And the worst thing about having a doctor and a teacher for parents was that he couldn't feign not feeling well to get out of going to school. A quick examination from Dr. Dwight Eaton verified whether he was well enough to attend classes, and if not, then Bertie would make arrangements to pick up homework assignments. He'd grown up with the constant reminder that he was an Eaton, and he must not do anything to disgrace the family name.

His great-grandfather came to Philadelphia as a young boy during the Great Migration from the South. Daniel Eaton worked two jobs all his life to give his children what had eluded him—a college education. Myles's grandfather earned a law degree from Howard University and three of his five sons followed in his footsteps when they became lawyers, while the other two earned medical degrees. The five brothers married women who were teachers, establishing the criteria for future generations to select a career in medicine, law or education.

He found it ironic that he'd come back to Philadelphia to spend the summer with his family for the first time in over a decade, but they'd all left town: Chandra had flown out of Philadelphia International earlier that morning for a return flight to Belize, his parents had taken their granddaughters to Cape Cod to join their paternal grandparents, and Belinda and her husband were in the Caribbean for a two-week honeymoon.

He'd teased his mother, saying he hoped his presence hadn't scared everyone away. Roberta Eaton's response was that she never planned anything for the summer because Dwight would always surprise her with impromptu mini vacations.

The soft click of the door closing garnered Myles's attention. Rising to his feet, he saw that Zabrina had cleansed her face of makeup and brushed her hair off her face. Tank top, cropped pants and a pair of mules had replaced her slacks, blouse and heels.

Zabrina handed Myles a large weekender travel bag. "I'm sorry I took so long. I had to shower and shampoo the gel from my hair."

He dropped a kiss on her damp hair. "That's all right, baby. I was just sitting here taking in the sights."

She inhaled the fragrance of blooming white flowers that opened at nightfall. The sound of an owl's hooting joined the cacophony of crickets serenading the countryside. "I love sitting out at night. One time I fell asleep on the chaise and probably wouldn't have gotten up if a bug hadn't crawled into my nose. Talk about snorting and slinging snot."

Throwing back his head, Myles laughed at the top of his lungs. "That's something I would've paid to see."

She swatted at him. "That's not right, Myles Eaton."

"It serves you right. Remember the time I begged you to go camping with me and you said you were a city girl? Well, that little bug was paying you back for dissing his folks."

Zabrina flashed an attractive moue. "I'm still a city girl."

Putting his arm around her waist, Myles pulled her closer. "Come on, city girl. It's way past my curfew."

"What's the matter, doll face, can't hang?"

"You're going to pay for that remark."

Zabrina wiggled her fingers. "Ooo-oo. I'm so scared."

"You should be." He led Zabrina off the porch to where he'd parked his vehicle. "Speaking of hanging, I'd like to go shopping tomorrow so I can buy you a housewarming gift."

"Thank you, but I don't need anything."

Myles held open the passenger-side door, waiting until Zabrina was seated before he rounded the Range Rover and got in beside her. "Yeah, you do."

"What do I need?"

"A hammock."

Averting her gaze, Zabrina stared out the side window as Myles backed out of the driveway. The Eatons had put up an enormous hammock on their back porch and she'd lost count of the number of times she'd fallen asleep in Myles's embrace after they'd read to each other. For Zabrina it was the novels of Jane Austen, and for Myles it was C. S. Forester. Forester's *The African Queen* was her favorite, along with the 1951 film adaptation starring Katharine Hepburn and Humphrey Bogart.

"A hammock would be nice."

"Don't sound so enthusiastic, Brina."

"I don't mean to sound ungrateful."

"Then what's the matter?"

She turned and stared at his distinctive profile. "It's about us, Myles."

"What about us, Zabrina?"

"We can't go back and redo the past, or right the wrongs."

The muscles in Myles's forearm hardened beneath the sleeve of his shirt as the fingers of his right hand tightened on the leather-wrapped steering wheel in a death grip. "When did you become so vain? My offer to give you the hammock has nothing to do with my attempt to relive the past. I just thought your son and his friends would enjoy it."

A blush crept into her cheeks, flaming with humiliation when Zabrina realized her faux pas. Had she read more into Myles's offer to give her a hammock because she was hoping he would forgive her and they would pick up where they'd left off before her damning telephone call?

How, she thought, had she been so silly, so out of touch with reality? Did she actually believe he would be able to trust her again after she'd not only humiliated him, but also his family?

She was angry and annoyed, angry with Myles because of his acerbic retort about her attempting to flatter herself. And she was annoyed at herself for being embarrassed. "I'm certain Adam will enjoy the hammock."

Myles gave Zabrina a quick glance before maneuvering into the driveway of his sister's house. He knew by the set of her jaw that she was upset. Well, she wasn't the only one. He didn't want to deceive Zabrina or himself into believing they could pick up where they'd left off. Not one to say never, Myles knew *if* he and Zabrina were to start over the impetus would have to be life-changing.

Zabrina stared out the windshield as Myles cut the engine. She hadn't moved when he got out and came around to assist her. Her body was rigid, stiff enough to break into a thousand tiny slivers if she'd been glass, and she chided herself for agreeing to spend the night with Myles. She stood off to the side when he unlocked the door, deactivated the security alarm, then extended his hand.

Myles saw Zabrina staring at his hand as if it were a venomous reptile. Her expression was one he remembered well. He and Zabrina rarely argued, only because she refused to argue. She said it was futile to debate someone whose profession it was to argue cases. Rather than concede defeat, she remained silent. And the silence was more effective than any spoken word.

"I'm sorry for saying what I said about you being vain, because I of all people should know there isn't a vain bone in your body."

Zabrina rolled her eyes at him. "Say it like you mean it, Myles."

A hint of a smile softened his mouth at the same time as he took a step. Myles angled his head and brushed a kiss over her parted lips. "I'm really sorry, baby. Will you forgive me?"

Zabrina bit back a smile. "I'll think about it."

He kissed her again. "Don't think too long. After all, you did promise to give me the next three days, and I'd hate to have to spend the time with you giving me the silent treatment."

Myles might have changed, but not so much that he could deal with Zabrina shutting him out. Whenever they disagreed on something she would stop talking, claiming his debating skills far exceeded hers. He'd tried to tell her that it wasn't about debating but about talking things out. He hadn't wanted her to agree with him on everything as much as he wanted her to see more than one side of a particular topic. As a trial attorney he was expected to sway a jury to believe his client's innocence, yet his powers of persuasion were lost on his fiancée.

Myles exhaled a breath. It'd been a very long time since he'd thought of Zabrina as his fiancée. Perhaps if he'd allowed himself to become more involved with some of the women he'd dated over the years, then he would've been able to completely get her out of his system.

Zabrina placed her palm on Myles's outstretched hand, smiling when his strong fingers closed over hers. The calluses from his martial arts training still hadn't faded completely. She'd loved seeing him compete as much as he'd disliked competing. Her breath would catch in her throat when he walked into the center of the arena, bow to his opponent, then, in lightning-quick fashion, take him off his feet. The day he received his black belt she celebrated with the Eatons when they all went out to dinner at a restaurant featuring Asian cuisine.

Myles pulled her gently into the circle of his embrace, resting his chin on the top of her head. "How you doo-in?" he asked in his best New York inflection.

Zabrina smiled. "It's all good."

"I have to take a shower, so you can either wait up for me or go straight to bed."

She let out an audible sigh. They were about to embark on something she couldn't have predicted the night she'd met Belinda Eaton at the fundraising dinner. Belinda hadn't mentioned Myles and she hadn't asked because she didn't want to hear that he'd married and fathered children, children that should've been theirs.

"I'm going to turn in. My legs feel as if someone pounded them with a mallet."

Lifting his head, Myles pulled back and stared into the pools of brown and gold. "I'll give you a full body massage."

"How much are you going to charge me?" Zabrina teased.

"I'll try and think of something comparable to what a masseur would charge for house calls."

"Can you give me a hint, because I may not have enough money with me?"

Myles's expression went from soft and open to sober within seconds. "I don't want or need your money. And if you ever forget that I'll make certain to remind you."

Zabrina was successful in not visibly flinching as his words hit her like stones hurled from a sling shot. Her eyes turned cold and frosty again. "What do you want from me other than the sex I'm willingly offering?"

"What about the truth, Zabrina?"

She was taken aback by his demand. "I've told you all I can tell you at this time."

Zabrina knew she hadn't been completely honest with Myles not because she didn't want to be but because she couldn't. The first time she'd lied to Myles it was to protect her father, and she continued to lie to protect her son. How much more pain would he have to experience before reaching adulthood? As a parent it was her responsibility to protect her child, and she would do so until Adam was an adult, even if it meant forfeiting her life.

Myles knew Zabrina was hiding something and he was certain it had something to do with Thomas Cooper. He wanted answers but not at the risk of alienating her. What he had was time—almost eight weeks—in which to wait and watch for her to let down her guard. "If that's the case, then I have to respect your decision."

"Thank you, Myles." Zabrina was relieved he'd decided not to push the issue.

"Why don't you go in and I'll bring in your bag."

Zabrina walked into her childhood friend's living room. The pale carpeting and fabric were a testament that Belinda hadn't decorated her home with children in mind. Walls painted a soothing powder blue were the perfect contrast to the off-white sofa and chairs. The color was repeated in the silk throw pillows and the trim on the off-white rug. Milk-glass vases in varying heights lined the fireplace mantel. White trim on the mantel and French doors emphasized the room's architectural details.

She and Belinda used to spend hours fantasizing about the homes they wanted when they married, and Zabrina never would've imagined that she would become mistress of Cooper Hall. She would've traded everything—the mansion, fancy clothes, priceless pieces of jewelry and the allowance Thomas deposited into an account for her to keep the household running smoothly—to live in a hovel with Myles Eaton.

"Brina?"

She turned to find Myles standing at the entrance to

the living room, cradling her quilted bag to his chest. "Yes."

"Come. I'll show you to the bedroom."

Her heart beating a staccato tattoo against her ribs, Zabrina closed the distance between her and Myles. She hadn't felt this anxious even when she'd decided to sleep with Myles for the first time.

"Let's do this," she whispered.

"Whoa. Wait a minute, Brina. Do you hear yourself?"

"What are you talking about?"

"Why are you making it sound as if this is a paid assignation? As if you're offering yourself up to me for a price?"

"Myles, don't. You have no idea what it took for me to ask you to go to bed with me."

Myles's expression was one of restraint and patience. "Stop beating up on yourself, Zabrina. Didn't I tell you that I would've asked you if you hadn't asked me? And if you hadn't had too much to drink Saturday night there is no doubt you would not have left the hotel room without my making love to you. When I saw you with that…that dude I wanted to beat the crap out of him."

With wide eyes, Zabrina searched Myles's face for a hint of guile. "Why? He didn't do anything to you, or to me."

"I was jealous, Brina. I was jealous as hell because he was touching you."

She shook her head in an attempt to bring her fragile emotions under control. She loved Myles, always had and always would, but if Myles was jealous of her and Bailey Mercer then his feelings for her went deeper than he'd admitted.

"You don't ever have to be jealous of me with another man."

Reaching out, Myles cradled her chin in his hand, raising her face to where it was inches from his. "What about Cooper, Brina? Shouldn't I have been jealous of him, too?"

Zabrina pulled her lip between her teeth, increasing the pressure until she felt it pulsing in pain. "No. Remember, I told you we had separate bedrooms."

Raven orbs narrowed under a sweep of inky-black eyebrows. "You never slept with him?"

"Yes, we did sleep together *very* early in the marriage," she answered truthfully. She and Thomas had shared a bed the night they were married. They'd occupied a luxury suite following the private ceremony and the reception dinner at the Sheraton Society Hill Hotel. The beauty and understated elegance of the hotel set on a cobblestone street in Society Hill had failed to offset her dark mood. They'd checked out the following morning and Zabrina had moved into her suite of rooms at Cooper Hall where she didn't have to share a bed with her husband.

It wasn't what Zabrina said, but what she didn't say that tugged at Myles's heart. Not only did she crave physical fulfillment but her loneliness was a result of lack of companionship. Senator Thomas Cooper had earned the reputation of looking out for the residents of the Commonwealth of Pennsylvania—everyone but his wife and son.

He smiled and the gesture was as intimate as a kiss. "Let's go to bed, darling."

Zabrina followed Myles to the rear of the house where walls of French doors covered with silk panels opened up to a bedroom. He touched a wall switch and the space was flooded with soft light from table lamps with pale blue pleated shades. Every piece of furniture and all the accessories were in varying shades of white. The absence of color in the bedroom was offset by the calming blues in the adjoining sitting/dressing room with blue-and-white-striped cushions on a white chaise. A blue-and-white-checked tablecloth on a small table with two pull-up chairs created the perfect spot for breakfast or afternoon tea.

"It's so beautiful." She couldn't disguise the excitement in her voice.

Myles set her bag on the carpeted floor next to a bedside table. "Belinda moved her bedroom downstairs when she gave Layla and Sabrina the run of upstairs. There are two half baths in each of what used to be their bedrooms and a full bath on the second floor. There's also a half bath off the kitchen with a shower stall that I've commandeered, so you can have any of the ones upstairs."

Zabrina's gaze widened when Myles slipped out of his tie and suit jacket, and she prayed he wouldn't undress in front of her. Although she was more than familiar with his body, she still didn't feel completely comfortable with him. Too much time had elapsed for her to pick up where they'd left off before.

"I'll try and wait up for you."

Myles winked at her. “Remember, I owe you a full-body massage.”

She returned the wink. “If that’s the case, then I’ll make certain to stay awake.”

Tossing his jacket and tie on the chair in the sitting area, he turned and walked out of the bedroom. Zabrina sprang into action when she opened her weekender, removing the nightgown she’d packed on top of the bag. She’d showered, shampooed her hair and brushed her teeth in the hope she would have less physical contact with Myles before sharing a bed.

She undressed, pulled the nightgown over her head and slipped between the sheets. Reaching over, she turned off the lamp on her side of the bed and waited for Myles.

Chapter 10

Zabrina hadn't realized she'd dozed off while waiting for Myles to join her in bed until the heat from his body warmed into hers. Stretching languidly like a cat, she smiled and snuggled against his length.

"What took you so long?"

With his arm around Zabrina's waist, Myles pulled her closer, fitting his groin to the roundness of her hips. "I was only gone about fifteen minutes."

"That was fourteen minutes too long."

He nuzzled her neck, inhaling the lingering scent of her perfume. The fragrance wasn't the same as the one she'd worn years before. It was more sophisticated, more woodsy than floral. Zabrina had matured and so had her perfume.

"You're demanding."

"Weren't you the one who said that if you want something, then demand it."

He smiled. "Yes, I did. How are your legs?"

"Better, now that I'm not standing on them."

"Do you still want that massage?"

"Yes please."

Myles shifted, rising to his knees and eased Zabrina to lie on her belly. "When did you start wearing nightgowns to bed?" The white cotton garment with narrow straps crisscrossing her back was sensual and virginal. And because it concealed the curves of her slender body he found it was more provocative than a sheer garment.

Resting her head on her folded arms, Zabrina sighed softly. "I started when I became pregnant. Walking around naked with a big belly wasn't a nice sight. I couldn't bring myself to look in the mirror until I was fully dressed."

Sliding to the foot of the bed, Myles began massaging her ankles. "That all depends on who's looking at the belly."

"What are you talking about?"

"I find pregnant women very sexy. They're like beautiful ripe fruit bursting with life."

Zabrina moaned softly when his strong fingers kneaded the tight muscles in her calves. "You wouldn't have said that about yours truly."

"I'm certain you were beautiful, Brina."

She moaned again. Myles's hands had moved from her calves to her thighs. "That feels so good."

Myles concentrated on the tight muscles in Zabrina's legs and thighs, his fingers working their healing magic. He remembered another time when he'd given her a full-body massage. It was the day after he'd taken her virginity.

Zabrina had complained that every muscle in her body ached, and after giving her a bath he'd dried her off and gently massaged muscles she'd never had to use and muscles she didn't know she had.

Instead of returning home during spring break, Myles had arranged for Zabrina to meet him in Virginia Beach. They'd checked into a hotel, ordered room service and spent the week making love. He knew even before she'd offered him the most precious gift a woman could give a man that he was inexorably and hopelessly in love with Zabrina Mixon.

Reaching up, he pulled her arms down to her sides to make it easier for him to slide the straps of the nightgown off her shoulders. The skin on her back was flawless. The glow from the lamp on his side of the bed had turned her into a statue of molten gold. Sliding a hand under her belly, Myles eased her off the mattress while effortlessly removing the nightgown. It was the second time in a week that she'd lain in his bed while he undressed her. He smiled. It was a habit he could very easily get used to.

Zabrina gasped when she felt the brush of Myles's penis over her buttocks. The hidden place between her legs grew warm, moist. She smothered a moan. It'd been so long, much too long since she'd felt the pleasurable sensations. Her libido had gone into overdrive during her confinement, but after she'd delivered Adam she felt absolutely nothing. Viewing an erotic film or reading erotic literature did nothing to arouse her and she was resigned to believing that she would never feel desire again. But Myles had proven her wrong. She felt desire, and being with him made her feel feminine, sexy.

"Am I hurting you?" Myles asked in her ear. He'd straddled her body while supporting his greater weight on his arms.

Zabrina moaned again, this time as a rush of moisture bathed her core. "No."

She bit her lip to keep from begging him to end the sensual torment that made her feel as if she were coming out of her skin.

Myles didn't know how long he could continue to touch Zabrina without being inside her, because it was becoming more difficult with each passing minute to keep from spilling his passion on the sheets. He'd become aroused the instant he'd walked into the bedroom to find her in his bed. It'd been a long time since he'd experienced an instantaneous erection. It hadn't happened since he was an adolescent.

Then he'd lost count of the number of times he'd embarrassed himself whenever he saw a girl he liked. Rather than approach or say anything to her he'd walk away before she noticed the bulge in his pants.

By the time he'd begun sleeping with Zabrina he was totally in control of his body. Even when other women brushed up against him or leaned over to permit him an eyeful of breasts, he did not react. He realized then that it was the brain that dictated sexual desire. No matter how provocatively a woman dressed or flirted, if he wasn't attracted to her then she couldn't arouse him.

He pressed a kiss on Zabrina's shoulder. "You've lost weight."

"Not that much," she mumbled.

Myles's thumbs moved over her spine. "You're thinner now than when we were together."

"I haven't lost my booty."

"It's still not as full as it used to be."

Zabrina raised her head, peering at Myles over her shoulder. "I thought you were a leg man."

He smiled, flashing straight white teeth. "I like legs, but I like tits and ass, too."

"Myles!"

"What's the matter, baby?"

"I have never known you to refer to a woman's breasts as tits."

His hands stilled, his eyebrows lifting. "I may never have said it around you, but if you're offended then I'll say *T* and *A*."

Her cheeks flamed. "I'm not a prude, Myles."

"Out of bed, yes. In bed, no."

The heat in her face increased. Zabrina never saw herself as prudish. She'd thought of herself as reserved. Perhaps her aloof persona came from being raised by her father and not her mother. Isaac Mixon presented himself as a gentleman in every sense of the word. He was elegant, erudite and had impeccable manners.

Being Isaac's daughter had its advantages and disadvantages. His political savvy permitted him entrée into social circles that someone with lesser clout would never have broached. She was introduced to the sons and nephews of the political elite and if she hadn't been so besotted with Myles there was no doubt she would've accepted the advances of some of the young men destined for careers in public service.

What she'd come to detest was performing as hostess for her father. Men, most old enough to be her father and grandfather whispered licentious comments to her in the hope she would take them up on their ribald suggestions. One man in particular pursued her relentlessly until she deliberately poured a drink in his lap. He called her a bitch, and unfortunately for him Isaac overheard the slur. Two other men had to restrain her father, while the lecherous cretin made his escape.

Myles lowered himself until he lay prone over Zabrina's slight frame. "You feel and smell so good, baby."

Zabrina welcomed his weight. "I've missed you so much."

There was so much emotion in her declaration that Myles felt his heart miss a beat before resuming. She missed him and he'd missed her. He closed his eyes. "I've missed you, too."

"Will you make love to me, Myles Eaton?"

A beat passed. "Yes, I will." Rising slightly, Myles turned Zabrina onto her back. A slight frown appeared between his eyes when he saw hers filling with tears. "No, baby. Please don't cry."

Tears were his Achilles' heel. If Zabrina had come to him instead of calling him with the news that she was ending their engagement, Myles knew he wouldn't have taken it so hard. Even if he hadn't been able to get her to change her mind at least he would've been given the opportunity to challenge her. And if she'd cried he would've forgiven her and wished her the best.

The call was impersonal, and her voice that of a stranger. There was little or no emotion in her voice when she recited what sounded like a rehearsed script. Stunned, he'd hung up, shutting out her monotone and closing the book on the sensual adventure he'd shared with the woman he'd wanted to spend the rest of his life with. And despite her sweet deception, Zabrina was back, back in his life and back in his bed.

Zabrina closed her eyes, hoping to stem the tears pricking the backs of her eyelids. "I'm not crying because I'm sad, Myles."

He pressed his mouth over one eye, then the other, tasting salt. "Then why are you crying?"

"I'm happy, darling. The last time I felt this way was when I saw my son for the first time."

Myles went still. "Did he abuse you?"

Zabrina opened her eyes. "What are you talking about?"

"Did Cooper abuse you?"

She dropped her gaze, staring at his bare chest. "Physically, no."

"So, he abused you emotionally." The question was a statement.

Zabrina shook her head. "I can't explain it, Myles. Our marriage was very strange, and that's all I'm going to say about it. Thomas is gone and I'm free, free to live my life on my own terms."

Burying his face between her neck and shoulder, Myles breathed a kiss there. He'd gone to bed with women where a third person was in bed with them because they hadn't been able to exorcise former husbands or boyfriends. Their inability to let go had doomed their relationships from the start. Zabrina's declaration that she was free to live her life on her terms meant there were no ghosts from her past to interfere with their summer liaison.

"We can't right the wrongs or turn back the clock," he said in a quiet voice, "but what we can do is heal."

Zabrina had begun to heal the day she'd become a widow. Any power Thomas Cooper had over her died with him. Surprisingly, she'd never wished him dead, but for him to fall from grace.

Smiling, she wrapped her arms around Myles's neck. "Sometimes, counselor, you talk much too much."

He winked at her. "What would you have me do instead?"

Pulling his head down, she pressed her mouth to his. "This. And this." Zabrina kissed him under an ear.

"That's nice."

She bit down on his lower lip, suckling it and simulating his making love to her and achieving the response she sought when Myles moved his hips against hers. "How was that?"

Myles leaned over, opening the drawer to the bedside table and removing a condom. If he didn't put on protection now he knew it wouldn't happen, and what he didn't want was to get Zabrina pregnant. He'd used protection when they'd begun sleeping together. However, once she went on the Pill their lovemaking had become more frequent, more spontaneous and more intense.

With the latex sheath in place, he began the journey to reacquaint himself with her body. Every muscle in his body screamed, vibrated. The scent of the perfume on her silken skin rose sharply in his nostrils, heating his blood as Myles fell headlong into the lust holding him captive. He kissed her forehead, her nose, her mouth, then moved lower to her throat where a pulse beat erratically as her breathing quickened.

Zabrina was hot, then cold and then hot again. The pleasure Myles wrung from her was pure and unrestrained. The sexual passion of her body after years of celibacy had been awakened and she wanted him, all of him inside her.

"Please, Myles."

"What, baby?"

"Don't make me wait."

"I thought you liked foreplay."

She was on fire. Feelings she'd thought dead were back, making her aware of the strong passion within her. All memories of being held in Myles's protective embrace, the pure, unrestrained ecstasy that took her beyond herself and the pleasurable aftermath of a shared lovemaking that made them cease to exist as separate entities came to mind. She liked and wanted foreplay, but not now, not after ten long, lonely years during which she'd had to deny being female.

Her fists pounded his back. "Ditch the foreplay, Myles! I need you! Now!"

Myles wanted foreplay, a long, leisurely exploration of the body he'd fantasized about whenever he took another woman to bed. Their faces had become Zabrina's, their bodies Zabrina's, and whenever he climaxed it was her name that resounded in his head. She'd been so indelibly imprinted in his heart that he found himself comparing every woman to her.

It'd gotten so bad that he'd consciously embarked on a quest to see how many women he could bed before exorcising Zabrina Mixon, but he'd scrapped it because he thought of his sisters and of some man taking advantage of them.

He'd lectured Donna, Belinda and Chandra, telling them he would commit capital murder if any man harmed them. It took a while, but he realized it'd been the wrong thing to say to them; whenever they ended a relationship they were reluctant to talk about it.

Grasping his erection, he pushed gently into her vagina, increasing the pressure until a small cry from Zabrina stopped him. She was tight, tighter than he'd remembered. He was only halfway inside her. "Easy, Brina. Try to relax."

"I am," she gasped in sweet agony and unable to believe the tumult of intense pleasure holding her captive, refusing to let her go.

Still joined, Myles cupped her hips, lifting her body off the mattress and in one, sure thrust of his hips her body accepted every inch of him, both of them sighing in unison. He felt her flesh pulsing around his, pulling him in farther.

Zabrina wrapping her legs around his waist had become Myles's undoing. It was his favorite position because it permitted deeper penetration. She'd missed him and he'd missed her. He missed the intimacy, the shared moment when they became one and the lingering pulsing aftermath of the shared ecstasy where no words were needed to communicate with each other.

Zabrina prayed she wasn't dreaming and that when she woke she wouldn't be alone in bed. After her first trimester she'd experienced a resurgence of sexual desire that was frightening. She went to bed crying for Myles to come and lie beside her, and when her crying jag ended the dreams took over. Erotic dreams where she relived making love with him and her body reacted.

She woke to intense orgasms, the walls of her vagina contracting and her body drenched in moisture. The dreams continued nightly until she woke one morning to intense pain in her lower back. When the pains continued unabated she knew she was in the early stages of labor.

The dreams stopped altogether after Adam's birth, and as much as she tried, she couldn't conjure up any erotic images to assuage her sexual frustration. After a while, she stopped trying and embraced celibacy as if it were her fate.

Myles wasn't a dream, the strength in the hands gripping her hips was real and the hard, engorged penis moving in and out of her in a measured cadence was beyond real.

Desire rose so quickly that Zabrina felt as if she was caught in a maelstrom of sexual hysteria bordering on insanity. She wanted to move, but Myles, holding her fast, wouldn't permit movement as he quickened his thrusts. The raspy sound of his labored breathing against her ear escalated. He began chanting and it took a full minute before she could understand what he was saying.

"Baby, oh, baby, baby, baby," Myles crooned over and over when he felt the buildup of pleasure at the base of his spine. He knew it was going to be over and he wanted it to go on until he was repaid tenfold for the years when he'd wanted to go to sleep and wake up in Zabrina's arms.

He'd lied to himself at Belinda and Griffin's wedding. He'd wanted their wedding to have been his and Zabrina's. And, although he hadn't met Adam, he wanted the boy to have been his and Zabrina's. All of the things Thomas Cooper shared with Zabrina should've been his. It was as if the man had stolen his life.

He released her hips to grasp her legs and settle her ankles over his shoulders. What he saw in Zabrina's golden gaze sent a wave of fear throughout his body. The expression on her face was one he'd seen countless times in the past. She was still in love with him. She loved him as much as he'd loved and continued to love her.

When she confessed that she hated Thomas Cooper as much as she loved you I knew something wasn't quite right. He hadn't believed Belinda when she'd told him what Zabrina told her.

He also hadn't believed Zabrina when she told him that she wanted him for sex. A woman asking him to sleep with her just for sex made him feel cheap. It was no different than a hooker asking him if he wanted her to show him a good time—for a price. And, Zabrina's price was sexual favors because she was sexually frustrated. After all, she did admit that she and her husband slept in separate bedrooms.

She wanted sex for the summer, whereas he wanted more. And the more was starting over. He wanted to move her and her son to Pittsburgh where people wouldn't recognize her as the widow of Pennsylvania's junior senator.

Myles closed his eyes against her intense stare, not seeing the rush of blood suffusing her face and chest, or the hardening of her nipples and pebbling of her breasts' areolas as an orgasm held her in its grip. It released her at the same time another one swept her up, holding her trapped in a pulsing, pleasurable passion before releasing her to another—this one more turbulent. Her body vibrated liquid fire and Zabrina finally surrendered to the passion as tremors seized her until she shook uncontrollably.

"M-y-l-e-sss!" His name, tumbling from quivering lips, came out in syllables.

Myles answered her entreaty when he ejaculated into the condom. The strong pulsing continued until he collapsed heavily on her body. He lay on Zabrina, helpless as a newborn, while he waited for his heart to stop slamming against his ribs.

He was uncertain how long they lay together, their bodies still joined, but Myles was loath to withdraw from her warmth. He wanted to lie between her scented thighs forever. But he did withdraw, leaving the bed to go into the bathroom to discard the condom, lingering long enough to wash away the evidence of their lovemaking. He took a quick peek at the puppies sleeping atop each other in their crate, then returned to the bedroom.

Zabrina had fallen asleep, her features angelic in repose. He loved her, she loved him and they'd agreed to sleep together for the summer. Where, he mused, would that leave them come summer's end? Would she be willing to give up her new home and friends to follow him across the state? Or would he be forced to sacrifice his teaching position to go back to practicing law?

Slipping into bed beside Zabrina, he pulled the sheet up over their naked bodies and extinguished the light.

Turning on his side, he pressed his chest to her back, rested his arm over her hip and joined her in the sleep reserved for sated lovers.

Chapter 11

Zabrina managed to slip out of bed without waking Myles. She used an upstairs bathroom to shower and dress. The puppies were awake, growling and nipping at each other when she went over to the crate in a corner of the laundry room. A baker's shelf held an assortment of doggie food and supplies. She wasn't certain whether the dogs were permitted the run of the house, so she closed the louvered doors before opening the door to the crate. The Yorkies came at her like fluffy bowling balls, jumping up while trying to lick her face.

"Sorry," she said softly, "but I don't kiss doggies." Without warning, the doors opened and the dogs shot past her.

"That's good to know," said a familiar baritone behind her, "because I'd hate to be charged with animal cruelty because two little fur balls are attempting to hit on my woman."

Zabrina took a quick glance at Myles, finding him incredibly delicious in a pair of gray paisley-print silk boxers. "I know you're not talking about hurting the babies."

Bending slightly, Myles cupped her elbow, easing her up to a standing position. "I will if you decide to bring them into the bed with us."

Seeing the skin crinkled around his eyes told her he was kidding. He was the one who'd grown up with a menagerie of animals in and around the Eaton house, while the building she lived in with her father had a no-pets rule. Myles had his dogs, Donna her rabbits, Belinda her cats and Chandra fish, but the youngest Eaton daughter also had to have baby chicks every Easter. The elder Eatons didn't mind the animals but the rule was the cats and dogs had to be neutered or spayed. Once the rabbits began multiplying they were given to a local pet store. When the baby chicks grew up to become hens and roosters they also found new homes at a farm.

"Do they sleep in the bed with your nieces?"

"No. Belinda was emphatic when she reminded the girls that the first time she found the dogs asleep in their beds will be the last time. Why did you let them out?"

"I was going to clean their crate," Zabrina said.

"I'll clean the crate, and after I take a shower I'll start breakfast."

"While you're doing that I'll take Nigel and Cecil for a walk."

Myles smiled at the woman who'd offered the most exquisite pleasure he'd had in years, resisting the urge to pick her up to take her back to the bedroom. He found her enchanting in the body-hugging jeans, fitted T-shirt and sandals. With her freshly scrubbed face and short hair in sensual disarray, she projected an air of innocence. His gaze lingered on her full lips; he didn't know how it was possible but he felt sexual magnetism radiating from her like sound waves.

Zabrina knew what Myles was thinking because it was the same with her. Making love last night had only served to whet her sexual appetite. After all, she had more than a decade to make up in less than eight weeks. Even if they made love every day for two months it wouldn't put a dent into the number of times they would've made love if they'd been married.

"Please hand me their leashes and harnesses. Now that you've opened the door I'm going to have to go and look for them."

Myles stopped her when he reached for her hand. "Watch."

Pursing his lips, he whistled, the piercing sound reverberating throughout the kitchen. Within seconds the two puppies came sliding across the tiled floor, sitting obediently at his feet while he slipped on the harnesses, attached the leads and handed them to Zabrina.

She flashed a dazzling smile. "I'm impressed."

His smile matched hers, slashes appearing in his lean jaw as he inclined his head. "Thank you, darling."

She kissed the stubble on his chin. "You're welcome, darling. How long do you usually walk them?"

"Half an hour to forty-five minutes."

"Please hand me a couple of poop bags and we'll be on our way."

Zabrina pushed the small plastic bags into a pocket of her jeans and her cell phone into another. The puppies were wiggling, making strange noises and pulling on their leads in their impatience to go outdoors. She led them out a side door and into the warm, sun-filled morning.

Nigel and Cecil stopped every few feet to sniff grass, fire hydrants and lampposts. They took off running when a squirrel raced across the road, but she managed to pull them back to walk beside her. She couldn't whistle between her teeth like Myles, but watching *Dog Whisperer* had come in handy. She'd become a pack leader. There were other people walking their dogs. Some of the canines stopped to sniff the Yorkies and others walked by as if they didn't exist.

I've become a true suburban housewife, she thought. She mentally corrected herself. If she'd married Myles, then she would've become the housewife. Going to bed with Myles, making love, walking dogs and sharing breakfast. That was what she would've had *if* her father hadn't had a gambling problem, if he hadn't stolen from Thomas Cooper and if he hadn't gone to loan sharks to pay off his gambling debts.

The *ifs* assaulted her until she felt like screaming at the top of her lungs. Whenever she recalled the scene with Thomas and his muscle pointing a gun at her father's head she chided herself for giving in too easily.

If the man Thomas called Davidson had killed her father there was no way he could've gotten away with it. If they'd shot her in order to eliminate a witness they still wouldn't have gotten away with it.

Zabrina walked as far as her subdivision before

retracing her steps. The puppies weren't as frisky as they'd been when they'd begun their walk. The rising humidity signaled another hazy, hot and humid summer day. Without warning, Cecil and Nigel started running and when she looked down the street she saw Myles sitting out on the porch. Scooping up a puppy under each arm, she approached the house. Myles stood up, came off the porch and took the dogs from her. He looked incredibly sexy in a black tank top and khaki-colored walking shorts. His head came down and she raised her face for his kiss.

"How was your walk?" he whispered against her lips.

"Good."

Myles kissed her again. "As soon as you wash up we can sit down to eat."

Zabrina went into the house, Myles following with Nigel and Cecil. She washed up in the half bath off the kitchen, while the puppies went back into their crate.

She sniffed the air. It smelled like apples. "Something smells delicious. What did you make?"

"Come out and see."

She dried her hands, then walked out of the bathroom and into the kitchen. Myles stood behind a chair in the dining nook, waiting to seat her at the table covered with a linen tablecloth with cross-stitch embroidery.

"Do you want me to set the table?"

Myles's hands circled Zabrina's waist, lifting her to sit on the table. Repositioning the chair, he sat down in front of her. "I just set the table, Brina. Now, I'm going to have my appetizer before we sit down to breakfast."

Zabrina stared at the flecks of gray in his cropped black hair. "What on earth are you talking about?"

Unsnapping the waistband of her jeans, Myles lowered the zipper. Placing his hand over her belly and the other under her head, he eased her back onto the table. Half rising, he loomed over the woman who made him do things he didn't want to do; she made him love her when he had every right to hate her.

"I'm going to do to you now what you wouldn't let me do last night."

Zabrina opened her mouth to protest. The words died on her lips when his mouth covered hers, swallowing her breath. "Myles! No-oo! Please don't."

Her pleas fell on deaf ears and her shame increased. Myles had her jeans and panties down around her knees, his face buried between her thighs, all the while holding her wrists in a strong grip. The first time he'd introduced her to a different form of lovemaking she'd refused to look at him for days, so great was her shame. It was the first and last time Myles had attempted to make love to her with his mouth and tongue. Now, she was at his mercy and the sensations washing over had her feeling as if she were losing touch with reality. Zabrina floated in and out, gasping and sobbing as she attempted to sit up, push his head away, but to no avail.

Like a man seated at a banquet table, Myles feasted on the swollen mounds of flesh at the apex of Zabrina's thighs. Not only did she smell delicious, but she tasted delicious. He caught the engorged bud between his teeth, increasing the pressure until Zabrina's hips came off the surface of the table. Her breath came in deep surrendering moans, her head thrashing from side to side. She arched, fell back and then arched again as moisture pooled into his mouth.

Myles was relentless. He didn't love her flesh, he worshipped her. Without warning it happened. The soft pulsing grew stronger, more intense. The measured contractions shook Zabrina, her legs trembling uncontrollably. But he was ready. Pulling her closer, her hips on the edge of the table, he lifted her until there was no space, no light between his mouth and the entrance to her vagina.

She screamed once. Then again. And again. Her final scream made the hair stand up on the back of his neck, yet he wouldn't give her ease. Myles wanted the memory of his mouth on her to become an indelible tattoo that no other man could eradicate.

Eyes closed, chest heaving, Zabrina lay spent, unable to move. The orgasms had come so quickly, were so intense that her heart had stopped for several seconds and for the first time in her life she had experienced *le petit mort.*

She was still in a prone position when Myles returned with a warm cloth to wash between her legs. "I'm going to pay you back for that stunt."

Myles leaned over her, smiling. "What are you going to do, baby girl?"

"You'll find out soon enough," she teased.

He wiggled his fingers. "I'm scared of you." Wrapping his arm around her waist, he eased her up. "I'm going to clean off the table, then we'll eat."

Zabrina wrinkled her nose. "I'll never look at this table the same way again."

Myles helped her off the table. "And I'll never think of appetizers the same way again."

She landed a soft punch on his shoulder. "When did you become a dirty old man?"

"I wasn't one until I accepted the position to become your sex toy."

Crossing her arms under her breasts, Zabrina angled her head. "Perhaps I should've checked your credentials before I hired you."

"My credentials are impeccable, beautiful."

The sweep hand on the clock over the kitchen sink made a full revolution before she said, "Yes, they are, Myles."

He winked at her. "I made cinnamon waffles with caramelized apples for breakfast."

He remembered, Zabrina thought. Myles had remembered her favorite breakfast food. She loved all types of waffles covered with every fruit imaginable. He'd introduced her to fried chicken and waffles with a tangy honey-strawberry topping, which had become her favorite.

A sad smile touched her mouth. They had the summer in which to recapture a modicum of happiness that promised forever. *I can do it,* she mused. *We can do it.*

Myles set up the oversize hammock between two large trees in the rear of Zabrina's house rather than on the front porch. He was surprised at the size of the lot on which her house had been erected. The subdivision had only ten homes, but if they'd been built on smaller lots the number of structures could've been twice that. It was apparent the developer wanted to give the residents the feel of estate living. If it had been a gated community, then it would've provided maximum security.

Stepping back, he surveyed his handiwork. "Do you want to try it out?"

Zabrina smiled at Myles. "Sure." Sitting on the hammock, she grasped it with her left hand and lifted her left leg, then her right leg and hand until she lay on the tightly slung cord.

Myles applauded softly. "Nice technique."

He remembered the first time Zabrina had attempted to get into the hammock—she'd fallen and hit her head on the floor of the porch. The impact of the fall left her motionless. Too frightened to move her, Myles ran to get his father who was seeing a patient in his home office. Dr. Eaton revived her and personally drove her to the hospital for an evaluation. Isaac Mixon arrived in time to hear the neurosurgeon tell him that his daughter had suffered a mild concussion. It would be another six months before Zabrina attempted to get on the hammock, this time with explicit instructions as to the proper technique.

Smiling, Zabrina beckoned to Myles. "Come, get in with me." She scooted over and he climbed in beside her. Snuggling against his chest, she looped her leg over his bare ones. "This thing is large enough for Adam *and* Rachel's two children."

"You're going to have to show them how to get in and out without falling and breaking something."

She winced. "I can't imagine either of them spending the summer with their arms or legs in a cast. Remember the summer you sat around with your arm in a cast?"

Myles grunted. "Please don't remind me." He'd broken several bones in his right wrist during a martial arts competition. The pain was excruciating yet he'd kept fighting. He won the competition, earned his brown belt and spent the summer sitting around the house watching grass grow. If it hadn't been for Zabrina he believed he would've gone completely mad. Her father dropped her off every morning, and after playing with Belinda she would join him in the hammock to read. Most times she'd end up falling asleep and he'd lie there staring at her.

She'd been so young, so innocent and so untouchable. It was the summer Zabrina Mixon had become more to him than his sister's friend. It was the first time he saw her as a young woman and a companion. Her straight body had developed womanly curves, her voice had changed to a low, smoky quality that caught one's attention the moment she opened her mouth. And, with her jet-black hair and jewellike eyes she had morphed into an incredibly beautiful adolescent.

Things had changed when one of his friends made a crude comment about Zabrina's mouth and what she could do to him. Myles had caught the much taller and heavier boy by the throat within seconds and would have nearly crushed his windpipe if the other boys on the football team hadn't pulled him off. It was the first and last time he touched someone outside the realm of competition. It was also the first time he realized his protective instincts went deeper than taking care of his sisters and Belinda's friend.

Torn by ambivalent feelings, Myles decided going away to college rather than commuting was best because it put some distance between him and a teenage girl. What frightened him more than facing charges of statutory rape was what it would do to his family's reputation and what Isaac Mixon's reaction would be to his taking advantage of his daughter. And he knew he'd made the right decision when Zabrina kissed him. There was nothing chaste or innocent in the kiss, and it was another five years before he sampled the sweetness of her sexy mouth again.

"Brina, baby. Are you falling asleep?"

She stirred. "I was before you called my name."

"Why don't we go inside and lie down?"

"I don't feel like moving."

"It's getting too hot out here." Midday temperatures were already in the high eighties and meteorologists were predicting the mercury was going as high as the mid-nineties.

Rolling over, Zabrina opened an eye and peered at the face close to hers. She always marveled at the length of Myles's eyelashes. Whenever he closed his eyes the tips of his lashes grazed his high cheekbones.

"What do you have planned for the rest of the day?" she asked.

"I'll leave that up to you," Myles countered.

"I've been craving crab cakes."

Myles lifted his expressive eyebrows. "Are you sure you're not pregnant?" he teased.

"Of course I'm sure. You're the only man I've slept with, and I'm expecting my period in a few days, so bite your tongue, Myles Eaton."

"Do you want more children?"

His question startled her. What did he expect her to say? If they'd been married there was no doubt she would've had at least another child, or maybe two more. "Yes."

A silence followed her answer as Myles wrestled with his conscience. He'd always wanted children, and he'd wanted Zabrina to be the mother of his children. "How does Adam feel about you having more children?"

"All he used to talk about was having a sister because the kids in his classes would come to school with the news that they had a new baby brother or baby sister. Now I think he's resigned to being an only child."

"You never liked being an only child."

Zabrina sighed audibly. "I hated it. Belinda was the closest thing to having a sister. After we moved to the city, I used to nag my father so much about spending time with Belinda that he finally gave in and let me come to your house or let her come to mine every weekend."

"Are you thinking of remarrying?"

"No."

"Then how are you going to give your son a brother or sister?"

"Either I'll have an affair and get pregnant, or adopt."

An angry frown settled into Myles's features. "Having an affair is wrong, Brina."

"Why is it wrong, Myles?"

"You would sleep with a man, get pregnant and not let him know you were having his baby?"

With wide eyes, she met his angry glare. *Why not,* she wanted to tell him. *I did it with you.* "That would be best if I didn't want to be bothered with him."

Myles's frown deepened. "What do you mean by not wanting to be bothered with him? Why deal with him in the first place if you don't want to be bothered?"

"Haven't you slept with women you didn't particularly like?"

"No. Every woman I've slept with I liked in one way or another."

"Well, I know men who don't care if they like a woman or not. It's just another warm body for them when they need someone to scratch their itch."

"You'd pick up a complete stranger, lie down with him just to get pregnant?"

"I didn't say that, Myles, so don't try and put words in my mouth."

Myles couldn't believe what he was hearing. This was a side of Zabrina he'd never seen. He couldn't imagine her dating a man, sleeping with him, then walking away when she found herself pregnant.

She was nothing like the young woman who'd parried the advances of other men to *save* herself for him. She'd been very popular in high school. What he'd found startling was that she was liked by boys and girls equally. There were occasions at high school when the more popular the girl was among the boys, the more the other girls lined up against her. Zabrina always had a smile for everyone, diffusing whatever problems she would've faced.

"I'm willing to become a sperm donor if you want another child." The instant the words were out Myles knew he couldn't retract them.

Zabrina stared at the man lying beside her as if he'd taken leave of his senses. "You're crazy!"

"No, Brina, you're the crazy one. Wouldn't it be better to know something about your child's father? I'm disease-free and to my knowledge there have been no crazies in the family tree for the past three generations."

Her eyes grew wider. "Yes, there is. *You're* crazy."

He smiled. "No, I'm not. Here I'm willing to help you out and you tell me I'm crazy. If anyone is crazy, then it's you if you're considering picking up some asshole you know nothing about."

Her temper flared. "The difference between you and some *asshole* is he won't insinuate himself into my life and my children's. And I know you well enough to know you would want to be involved in the lives of your children."

"You know me well, Zabrina," Myles drawled arrogantly. "There's no way I'd walk away from my child or children no matter what the situation between me and their mother."

"That's why you can't become a donor." She held up her hand when Myles opened his mouth to come back at her. "I know we've always gotten along, but I've changed. Things I wanted ten years ago I don't want now."

"Does that include marriage?"

"Yes, it does. Once was enough, thank you very much. And if I do agree to let you father my child there are risks."

"What risks?" he asked.

"That you would sue for custody."

"I'd like joint custody, but I'd never take a child away from his or her mother."

"You say that now, Myles. But, what if I do or say something to piss you off?"

"It still wouldn't happen."

"I can't take that risk," Zabrina said. "After all, you're an attorney and you still have a lot of friends and colleagues who are judges. The odds of me keeping my child are slim to none."

"When did you become so distrustful?" Myles asked with no expression on his face. "There was a time when you trusted me with your life."

She dropped her gaze. "I told you, I've changed."

Rather than agree with her Myles decided to drop the subject. He'd temporarily taken leave of his senses when he'd offered to get Zabrina pregnant. It was *he* who wanted to turn back the clock. What he'd forgotten was there were no do-overs when it came to life. One learned from one's mistakes, and hopefully would not repeat them.

It was apparent he was a slow learner.

Chapter 12

Leaning over the small round table, Zabrina peered at Myles through her lashes. The flickering light from a votive threw long and short shadows over his attractive male features. His large, deep-set dark eyes glowed like polished onyx.

"You didn't have to drive to Baltimore to eat crab cakes, darling."

A hint of a smile touched the corners of his mouth. "If you want authentic Maryland crab cakes, then you go to Maryland. It's just like Philly cheesesteaks or New York pizza. Why settle for an imitation when you can get the real deal."

"So, if I want deep-dish Chicago-style pizza you'll drive there for me?"

Myles angled his head, admiring the woman sitting across the table. When he'd told her they were going out for dinner she'd changed into a flattering rose-pink sleeveless dress that nipped her waist and flared around her knees. The hot summer sun had darkened her face to a rich chestnut brown that brought out a spray of freckles over her nose and cheeks. His gaze lingered on loose tendrils of hair falling over her forehead, then to the rose-pink gloss on her generously curved lips.

Once he thought about his offer to father a child for Zabrina he realized it wasn't as much for her as it was for Myles Adam Eaton. He would celebrate his thirty-ninth birthday in October and turn forty the following year. There was a time when he would've thought his life would be complete at forty and that he would be living the American dream with a wife, children, house and career. He hadn't thought that at his age he would've attained only two of the four.

"Yes, Brina. Have you forgotten that at one time I would've done anything for you?"

She speared a portion of crab, avocado and grapefruit salad with chive vinaigrette but didn't bring the fork to her mouth because she was afraid she would choke on the food. Zabrina closed her eyes, counted to three and then opened them. "No, Myles. I haven't forgotten."

"If that's the case, then why did you ask me?"

She set down her fork, her gaze never leaving Myles's face. It was their first full day together and she felt as if time had stood still, that they'd spent every day of the past ten years together. "I don't know," Zabrina said truthfully. "I keep forgetting that I'm the one that has changed. I'm now Zabrina Cooper and you're still Myles Eaton."

Myles wanted to tell her that she hadn't changed

that much, that she'd talked herself into believing that she was different. She may have been more wary, less trustful but their incredible chemistry hadn't changed.

"What's in a name, Brina? Names are changed every day for one reason or another."

Zabrina picked up her fork again and took a bite, savoring the sharpness of torn frisée and radicchio leaves and the semisweet tart taste of sections of pink grapefruit on her tongue.

"You're right," she agreed after swallowing a mouthful of salad.

His expression brightened. "So, finally we agree on something."

"We agree on a lot of things, Myles."

"Enumerate."

"We like each other."

Myles's expression changed, becoming stoic. "I think it's more than liking, Brina."

"What is it?"

"You tell me."

"It can't be love, Myles."

"And why not? There was a time when we were very much in love with each other."

Zabrina saw Myles looking at her as if he were photographing her with his eyes, and wondered if he could see what she'd tried vainly to hide. What she'd tired of was lying to him and to herself. She loved Myles, had always loved and would always love him.

"You're right," she repeated for the second time in a matter of minutes. "We did love each other, and not much has changed." A swollen silence followed her pronouncement. "I'm still in love with you."

Leaning forward, Myles rested an arm on the table. “You are still in love with me, or you never stopped loving me?”

A sense of strength came to Zabrina as she met his penetrating stare. She’d confessed to Belinda that she loved her brother, and what she hadn’t been able to tell him verbally she was able to do with her body. For more than ten long suffering years she’d yearned for Myles, cried herself to sleep, and if it hadn’t been for Adam she wasn’t certain that she’d have had the will to survive.

“I never stopped loving you, Myles. Is that what you want to hear?”

“No,” he replied softly, “it’s not so much what I want to hear but what I need to know.”

“Why?”

“I just need to know if we’re on the same page.”

“You don’t hate me for what I did to you?” There was no mistaking the astonishment in her voice.

“I didn’t hate you, but I did hate how you did it, Brina. If you’d come to me and told me you were interested in someone else I would’ve given you an out without the embarrassment you caused my family. What was so crazy was that I couldn’t even give them an explanation as to why.”

“You…you didn’t tell them I was in love with someone else?”

All of the warmth in Myles’s eyes disappeared, replaced with a cold loathing. “No. I didn’t tell them because I didn’t believe you. But, then when word leaked out that you’d married Thomas Cooper they had the answer.”

“I’m sorry, Myles. I’m so sorry for what I did to you

and what your family had to go through because of my deception." Unshed tears shimmered in her eyes.

Myles shook his head. He was confused. Zabrina admitted that she still loved him, yet she'd told Belinda that she hated Thomas Cooper. Which was it? Had she been in love with him *and* Cooper? Or had she loved Cooper more than she loved him? And he wondered what had happened between her and her husband to force them to occupy separate bedrooms.

"Were you ever in love with Cooper?" he asked. Myles chided himself for asking, but he had to know.

A sad smile trembled over Zabrina's lips. "No, Myles. I was never in love with Thomas Cooper."

He had his answer, but ironically it didn't make him feel any better. "Thank you for your honesty. I suppose you want to know..." Myles's words trailed off when his cell phone rang. Reaching into the breast pocket of his jacket, he stared at the display, then at Zabrina. The call was from a former law-school friend who'd set up an office in North Philly where most of his clients were indigent. Some were illegal immigrants seeking citizenship.

"Answer it, Myles," she urged softly.

"Thanks." He punched a button. "What's up, Willie?" Myles caught and held Zabrina's gaze as he listened to the drawling voice coming through the earpiece. "Look up Miller v. Albright, 1998. The facts are similar to your case. If the couple isn't married, and when the citizen parent is the mother, then the kid is a citizen if the mother meets minimum residency requirements. If the mom is a citizen, and in order for a foreign-born child to be a citizen, then she must have established residence here for a minimum period of time."

"What about the father, Eaton?"

"If the father is a citizen he must prove paternity by clear and convincing evidence, and show evidence of actual relationship with the kid during the period of the child's minority."

"Thanks, man, you just answered my question."

Myles smiled. "I'm glad I could help out."

"How much are you going to charge me, Eaton?"

"Now you know I offer friends the professional courtesy rate," he teased. "Send me seven thousand and we'll be even."

"Sheee-it," Willie drawled. "Even if you were for real, man, I wouldn't be able to pay you. It takes me about six months to pull down seven thousand in fees from clients who walk in off the street."

"How are you keeping the doors open?"

"I have a few private clients on the side."

"How *private,* Willie?"

"Now, Eaton, you should know I can't reveal names. Attorney-client privilege."

Slumping against the back of his chair, Myles stared out the window of the restaurant overlooking Baltimore Harbor. "Don't call me, Willie, when they come for you."

"What are you trying to say, Eaton?"

"You know what I'm trying to say, Willie. Because if your so-called private clients go down you're going with them. I'm glad I was able to help you, but I'm going to end this call because you interrupted my dinner." He tapped a button, ringing off. Exhaling, Myles returned the phone to his jacket. "I'm sorry you had to hear that," he apologized to Zabrina.

"That's okay," Zabrina replied.

He wanted to tell her that it wasn't okay. The call had interrupted what he'd wanted to say to Zabrina, something he knew would change them and his tenuous relationship with her.

"How do you remember all of those cases?" she asked, breaking into his thoughts.

Myles lifted a shoulder. "I don't know," he admitted. "I suppose it's like a song you've heard over and over. You find yourself singing along without actually thinking of the words."

Propping an elbow on the table, Zabrina rested her chin on the heel of her hand. "Don't be so modest, darling."

Assuming a similar position, he smiled at the incredibly lovely woman sharing the table with him. "You use that term rather loosely."

Her eyebrows lifted. "What term?"

"Darling."

"Does the word make you uncomfortable?"

Myles shook his head, his expression unreadable. His dark eyes caressed her face before his lids shuttered them from her gaze. "No, Brina. There aren't too many things that make me feel uncomfortable. I just need to know if you're calling me *darling* out of habit or if you actually think of me as your darling."

A frown appeared between Zabrina's eyes. "Why are you cross-examining me, Myles?"

"Just answer the question, Zabrina."

"Why?"

The corner of his mouth twisted in frustration. If Zabrina had a negative personality trait it was stubbornness. He'd lost track of how many times he'd walked away from her in exasperation rather than blurt out something that would've ended their relationship. If he pushed, then she pulled and vice versa. It was only in bed where they came together on equal footing.

"I need to know where we're going with our relationship."

"What relationship, Myles? I thought we agreed to sleep together for the summer, and when it ended we would go our separate ways."

"I didn't agree to anything."

"Yes, *you* did," she retorted.

"No, I didn't," Myles argued softly. "When I asked you what happens at the end of the summer, you were the one who said 'we go our separate ways to live our separate lives.' And when I asked why you'd selected me to be your sex toy, your claim was 'we have a history.' Now, that doesn't sound as if I agreed to anything."

"Do you remember everything I say?"

"If it's worth remembering, then the answer is yes. I'm going to ask you again. Where do you see our relationship going? Do you want to stop at the end of the summer?"

Zabrina's mind was a tumult of confusion. What did he expect her to say? *Yes, I want it to continue beyond the summer because I'm still in love with you.* But had he thought about the three-hundred-mile separation? She lived in Philadelphia while he wanted to put down roots in Pittsburgh. Then she thought about Adam. How would he react to seeing his mother with another man when he was still dealing with the loss of his father and grandfather? The family therapist said Adam was progressing well, and it was she who suggested he spend time away from his mother because Zabrina had begun to mollycoddle a boy who was naturally independent.

The therapy sessions were good for her, too, because Zabrina realized she had several unresolved issues going back to her loss of her own mother. She somehow blamed herself for Isaac not remarrying and her childhood fixation with Myles Eaton would've been very unhealthy if he'd opted to take advantage of her infatuation.

"No, Myles, I don't want it to stop at the end of the summer. But what—"

Myles held up a hand, stopping her words. "Let it be, Brina," he warned in a quiet tone. "We'll let everything unfold naturally."

"Request permission to ask one more question, Professor Eaton."

Shaking his head, Myles couldn't help smiling. "What is it, Nurse Mixon?"

It was Zabrina's turn to smile, remembering when she'd passed her nursing boards and Myles had teased her, calling her Nurse Mixon. The smile faded as she formed the question she knew would answer whether she could ever hope for or consider a future with the man who'd unknowingly given her a piece of himself she would love forever.

"Do you love me, Myles?"

The seconds ticked off as swollen silence wrapped around them like a shroud, shutting out anything and everything around them. The waiting sent Zabrina's pulse spinning, her mind a maelstrom of anticipation and dread. Myles's withering gaze pinned her to her seat like a specimen under glass that would remain preserved in its natural state for posterity. Even if she lived to be a hundred she would never forget the look in his eyes.

"Yes, I love you, Zabrina." The admission came from somewhere so alien to Myles he couldn't begin to fathom where. "I've loved you for so long that I can't remember when I didn't love you. Even when you became another man's wife I loved you. When you opened your legs for him I still loved you. When you gave him the son that should've been ours I continued to love you. And, despite your sweet deception, I don't want you ever to question my feelings for you." He paused. "Have I made myself clear?"

Blinking back tears of joy, Zabrina nodded. "Yes."

The stone that had weighed down her heart the day Thomas Cooper had walked into her home to blackmail her into marrying a man who held her father's fate in his hands was rolled away with Myles's declaration of love.

She was freed from the threats when Thomas had fallen overboard and drowned in the Chesapeake. But her feelings then paled in comparison to those now that she was being given a second chance at love.

Myles hadn't mentioned marriage, and at thirty-three that wasn't as important to Zabrina as it had been when she was younger. Her mantra of "enjoy what you have because when it ends you make certain you have no regrets" came to mind.

Pushing back his chair, Myles stood up, signaled the

waiter and dropped several large bills on the table. "The food and service were excellent."

The waiter inclined his head. "Thank you, sir. Please come again."

Zabrina looked at Myles as if he'd taken leave of his senses. They'd just sat down to eat and he was leaving. Waiting until they were in the restaurant's parking lot, she rounded on him.

"What was that all about back there? You drive all the way from Philadelphia to Baltimore to eat and then we leave before we finish our dinner."

Myles assisted Zabrina up into the sport-utility vehicle. "We can eat at home."

She caught his meaning immediately. "Oh, really."

He flashed a Cheshire-cat grin. "Yes, really. We can cook together."

"Before we go to bed, or in bed?"

Myles leaned closer. "Both." He shut the door with a solid slam, rounded the vehicle and slid behind the wheel.

Although he'd never been much of a gambler, this time he had gambled *and* won. He knew he couldn't continue to sleep with Zabrina and not know where their relationship was going. If she'd been any other woman Myles would've been more than willing to have a summer fling, then move on from there. But they'd shared too much, and there was too much history between them for him to relegate her to the faceless, nameless women with whom he'd shared forgetful minutes of passion.

Myles completed the hundred-mile drive between Baltimore and Philadelphia in record time, maneuvering into Zabrina's driveway. She wanted him to stop at her house first. He'd just cut off the engine when Rachel came racing across the lawn, arms waving excitedly.

Zabrina removed her seat belt. "Do you want to wait here, or come in with me?" she asked Myles.

He lowered the driver's-side window, opened the door and came around to assist her down. "I'll wait on the porch for you." Cradling her face between his hands, he kissed her forehead. "Don't rush. I know how you ladies love to chat."

Zabrina pursed her lips in a provocative way that stirred the flesh between his legs. He chided himself for telling her not to rush. If Rachel hadn't come over, Myles would've gone inside with Zabrina and made love to her without the benefit of protection. If she were to become pregnant he would become her husband, not a baby daddy.

Too many women were raising children in households without fathers. His nieces, who had lost both parents in a horrific automobile accident, had been legally adopted by their aunt and uncle. They were luckier than some children who would've become a statistic in the foster-care system.

Zabrina's neighbor was a war widow, leaving her to grieve the loss of her husband and the father of her young children. Zabrina had lost her father and husband within months of each other, leaving her son to grieve the loss of his father and grandfather. There had been too many losses, too much grief, especially for young children.

"Hi, Myles," Rachel called out as she mounted the porch.

"Hi, Rachel," he mimicked. "Bye, Rachel," he teased as she opened the door and went inside.

Chuckling to himself, he sat on the rocker and waited for Zabrina.

Rachel followed Zabrina into her bathroom, watching as she opened a drawer under the vanity. "I have a date," she said in a breathless whisper.

Zabrina turned and stared at her neighbor. Rachel's face was flushed with high color, her eyes large and sparkling like amethysts. "Who is he?"

Rachel pressed her palms together in a prayerful gesture. "Hugh Ormond."

"The owner of Whispers?"

"The one and only."

Zabrina screamed while jumping up and down like a hysterical teenager. She hugged Rachel, both of them doing the happy dance. "Yes, yes, yes!" she chanted. "I'm so happy for you. When did all of this happen?"

Rachel flashed a toothy grin. "He called me yesterday."

"How did he get your number?"

"Remember when he gave me his business card with his cell number?" Zabrina nodded. "Well, I called to make a reservation for my parents. I want to treat them to a night out for looking after Shane and Maggie, but the call went directly to voice mail. I left a message, asking him to return the call. When he finally called me back we ended up talking for an hour. He said he wanted to talk more, but he had to prepare for a private party. That's when he asked if I'd be willing to go out with him, and, of course, I said yes, but only after

I played a little hard to get. I can't have him think I'm desperate, which I am."

Zabrina felt her neighbor's excitement. "When are you going out?"

"Tomorrow night. Please don't say anything to Myles that I'm seeing his friend."

"Why would I say anything to him?"

"I just don't want to jinx myself, Zabrina. This is not the first time a man has asked to go out with me, but it is the first time I've accepted. There was something about the others that gave me the willies." Rachel paused to take a breath. "Hugh is different because I feel so comfortable talking to him—about anything. I know my reluctance to date is because of my kids. I don't want Shane or Maggie to think I'm trying to replace their father with another man."

Zabrina offered Rachel a comforting smile. "You're a young woman and you're entitled to adult male companionship. And by that I don't necessarily mean sex."

Rachel blushed again. "But I want *and* need the sex, Zabrina. My husband and I used to screw like rabbits."

"Whoa, Rachel, that's entirely too much information."

The blonde rolled her eyes. "When you've been without a man for as long as I have you're ready to post a sign on your back reading Man Wanted." She wrinkled her nose. "The only thing I've never been able to get into is online dating. Now that's some scary mess."

"I hear you," Zabrina agreed, not telling Rachel that it'd been longer for her, before she starting sleeping with Myles again, since she'd been made love to.

Other than trolling clubs, she wouldn't know where

to begin looking for a man. Fortunately, the only man she'd always loved had come back into her life when she least expected it.

She and Myles had put their past behind them in an attempt to move forward. However, one hurdle remained: their son. Zabrina knew Myles would eventually meet Adam when he returned from Virginia, but her uneasiness came from whether Adam would be willing to share his mother with a stranger.

"How are things going between you and Myles?"

Rachel's unexpected query pulled Zabrina from her reverie. She wanted to pretend she didn't know what her friend was talking about but knew it was futile. After all, she hadn't slept under her own roof in a couple of nights and her car hadn't been moved in days.

Resting a hip against the vanity she gave Rachel a long, penetrating stare. "Things are good."

Nervously, Rachel moistened her lips. "I know who you are," she said cryptically. "I know you're Senator Cooper's widow and that you were once engaged to Myles Eaton."

Zabrina's expression revealed none of what she was feeling at that moment: panic. She'd moved into her new home in mid-March and it was now the first week in July and not once in three months had Rachel given any indication that she knew who she was.

"How did you find out about me?"

"When you introduced me to Myles Eaton, I tried to recall where I'd heard his name. I searched the internet and came up with quite a bit of information," she rambled on. "And I know you ended your engagement to Myles and then married Thomas Cooper. Look, Zabrina, I know if you wanted me to know you would've told me. I would've asked but I was afraid you would've told me to mind my own business."

"How can I tell you to mind your business when my business is out there for everyone to read?" Zabrina asked. "I don't advertise who I am because I need to protect Adam. I've always tried to keep him out of the public eye, and so far I've succeeded."

Rachel pushed a smile through an expression of uncertainty. "Will you forgive me being nosy?"

"There's nothing to forgive." If anyone wanted to know about her, all they had to do was what Rachel had done—type her name into a search engine.

Flipping her ponytail over her shoulder, Rachel straightened to her full five-foot-nine-inch height. "I'm going to leave now, because I don't want your man mad at me for keeping you from him."

Zabrina exhaled a breath. She didn't want to be rude and tell her neighbor to go home, but Rachel tended to be Chatty Cathy. Wind her up and she'd talk for hours. And it was apparent Hugh Ormond liked her effervescent personality.

"I'll see you later," she said to Rachel.

"Later," Rachel repeated.

Waiting until her neighbor left, Zabrina gathered a supply of feminine products. Minutes later, she left the house to find Myles lounging on the rocker. He stood up as she closed and locked the door.

Myles wrapped an arm around Zabrina's waist as he led her off the porch. The day had begun with him waking up beside her and would end with her beside him. He didn't want to think of the day when he would have to return to Pittsburgh and not take her with him.

He'd lost her once because it was beyond his control. However, if it was within his control he did not intend to lose her a second time.

Chapter 13

Zabrina felt her heart rate kick into a higher gear as Myles maneuvered down the tree-lined street to the house where Belinda and Griffin Rice lived with their nieces. The newlyweds had returned from their honeymoon the week before and were now hosting their first get-together as husband and wife. In a matter of minutes she would come face-to-face with his parents, and interacting directly with Myles's parents wasn't something she was looking forward to.

She'd been surprised when Belinda called to invite her to Paoli for a time-honored Eaton Sunday dinner. Belinda said she'd already spoken to Myles, who'd offered to drive her. She'd declined previous invitations from Myles for her to share Sunday dinner with his mother and father, but Zabrina hadn't been able to form an appropriate excuse to get out of going to her childhood friend's house.

Since Adam was away, she'd changed her regular Sunday routine. In the past she would prepare an elaborate dinner for the two of them, followed by driving to their favorite ice cream parlor for outrageous frozen concoctions. Now, after attending church services she drove over to Chinatown where she ate at a restaurant featuring Chinese and Thai cuisine. It was early evening when Myles came over and crawled into the hammock with her.

The past three weeks with Myles had been near-perfect, offering her a glimpse into what her life would've been like if they'd married. They went to bed, woke up, prepared meals and took long walks together. Afterward they spent hours in the hammock either sleeping or reading aloud to each other. It was as if time had stood still before Thomas Cooper had revealed her father's clandestine gambling addiction and theft of campaign funds, or as if she hadn't been blackmailed into breaking her engagement to Myles to marry her blackmailer.

Myles, slowing and downshifting, took a quick glance at Zabrina's delicate profile. He knew she'd clamped her teeth together by the throbbing muscle in her jaw. Belinda had called to inform him that she'd invited Zabrina to come to Paoli for a cookout and asked that he bring her. None of the Eatons knew he was sleeping with Zabrina and he wasn't going to volunteer the information because he didn't want a repeat of the exchange he'd had with Chandra.

He'd never interfered in his sisters' relationships and refused to tolerate any intrusion into his own. Myles had to admit he was somewhat surprised when Belinda informed him that she'd invited Zabrina to her wedding. It was something his sister said that made him rethink his attitude toward the woman to whom he'd given his heart: *Even after a criminal has served and completed his or her ten-year sentence society offers them a second chance.* Zabrina Mixon-Cooper wasn't a criminal, she hadn't broken any law. The only thing she was guilty of was breaking his heart.

Reaching over, he placed his hand over hers. Her fingers were ice-cold. "Are you all right?"

Zabrina managed a tight smile. "I'm good."

Myles shot her another quick glance. "Your hands are freezing."

"Cold hands, warm heart," she quipped, smiling.

Executing a smooth left turn, he maneuvered into a wide driveway behind a gleaming black Volvo. "My folks are here."

Zabrina swallowed to relieve the dryness in her suddenly constricted throat. She didn't know what to expect from Dwight and Roberta Eaton, but she doubted whether they'd greet her as if she were a long-lost relative.

Symbolically, Roberta had become her surrogate mother before and after Zabrina's mother passed away. Whenever she slept over at the Eaton's large farmhouse-style home she was treated the same as the other Eaton siblings. Miss Bertie checked her hands for cleanliness before she sat down to eat and Miss Bertie braided her hair, always making certain the center part was straight. Bertie used to say that whenever she saw a little girl with a crooked part she felt compelled to pull the child aside and redo her hair.

She waited for Myles to come around and help her down. "Don't forget the flowers and gelato." Zabrina had urged him to stop so she could purchase a bouquet of flowers for the Rices' table and half pints of pistachio, chocolate-hazelnut, peach and caffe latte gelato, packed in a special container to keep them from melting. The day before he'd had a case of assorted wine and a box of sliced rib-eye steaks delivered to Paoli after Belinda mentioned they were going to break with tradition and dine alfresco.

Griffin and Belinda's house reminded Zabrina of the one her friend had grown up in. Stately maple and oak trees provided shade for the white vinyl-sided three-story house with black shutters. The smell of grilling meat wafted in the air.

Cradling the foam crate of ice cream and the flowers in one hand, Myles cupped Zabrina's elbow with the other. "They're probably out back."

Zabrina hadn't realized she was holding her breath until she experienced tightness in her chest and was forced to exhale. A pair of sunglasses shielded her gaze as she stared at Layla and Sabrina Rice splashing in the inground pool under the watchful gaze of Belinda's parents.

Griffin stood at the stove in an outdoor kitchen, grilling franks. His wife, wearing an apron with The Real Cook stamped on the bib, filled tall glasses from a pitcher filled with lemon and lime slices floating in a pale yellow liquid.

Layla, floating on her back, spotted her uncle first. "Uncle Myles is here!"

Belinda turned, frowning at her niece. "Layla, there's no need to shout," she admonished softly.

Zabrina saw everyone's gaze directed at her and Myles. When she realized he was still holding her arm, she eased it surreptitiously from his loose grip. No one, nothing moved. It was as if a frame of film was frozen in place.

It was Belinda who broke the spell when she wiped her hands on a towel. Arms outstretched, she walked over to her brother and kissed his cheek, then Zabrina's. "I'm glad you could make it, Brina."

Zabrina felt her anxiousness fading. "Thank you for inviting me. You look absolutely beautiful, Mrs. Rice." She pressed her cheek to Belinda's.

Married life agreed with Belinda Rice. The Caribbean sun had darkened her face to a rich milk-chocolate hue and her promise to eat and relax was evident because the hollows in her slender face were gone. With her relaxed hair pulled back in a ponytail, shorts, tank top, sandals and bare face she looked as young as her high-school students.

Belinda's smile was shy, demure. "Thank you. Once everyone has eaten, I'll take you on a tour of the house."

Myles handed his sister the bouquet of flowers. "Brina brought these for the table, and there's gelato in the cooler."

"Please give them to Mama. She's the expert when it comes to arranging flowers." Belinda handed off the cooler to Griffin. "Please put this in the freezer." The outdoor kitchen was fully functional with a stainless-steel stove, grill, refrigerator/freezer, built-in bar and sinks.

Myles walked over to his parents, leaned over to kiss his mother's cheek, handed her the cellophane-wrapped bouquet, then patted his father's shoulder in an affectionate gesture. "Brina came with me," he said, sotto voce. Extending a hand, he eased Roberta up from her chair.

Zabrina removed her glasses at Roberta and Dwight Eaton's approach. She'd exchanged nods of acknowledgment with the two at Belinda's wedding, but they hadn't spoken to one another. She extended her hand to Roberta. "It's so nice seeing you again."

Roberta ignored her hand to hug her, surprising Zabrina with the unexpected display of affection. "How are you feeling, child?"

Zabrina went still, then relaxed as she returned the hug. Had news gotten around that she'd had too much to drink at Belinda's wedding? "I'm well, Miss Bertie."

Roberta pulled back, staring up at the woman who'd made her only son's life a living hell. She'd wanted to hate the young woman who had deceived Myles, but couldn't. Zabrina was the daughter of a woman who'd died much too young, the best friend of her middle daughter, and someone whom she'd come to think of as her own daughter and the young woman who'd gotten Myles to fall in love with her when other women had tried and failed.

"You look very nice with short hair."

Zabrina, smiling, angled her head. "Thank you." She knew Roberta was looking for a crooked part, but she'd brushed her hair and kept it off her face and forehead with a candy-striped headband.

Roberta hadn't changed much. Her stylishly coiffed hair claimed more salt than pepper, and, although she'd added a few inches to her hips, she was still a very attractive middle-aged woman who'd been married to the same man for forty-two years.

Dr. Dwight Eaton came over to join them, his eyes warm, friendly behind a pair of rimless glasses. He, too, hugged Zabrina. It wasn't often that she saw the family doctor without his white shirt, tie and lab coat. Today he wore a golf shirt, khakis and slip-ons. A pager and two cell phones, devices that were essential to his profession, were attached to his belt.

"I didn't get a chance to talk to you at Lindy's wedding, but I wanted to tell you that I'm sorry for your loss. Isaac was truly a wonderful human being."

You wouldn't say that if you'd known he was a thief. Despite Thomas's accusations, Zabrina had never stopped loving her father. In fact, she loved him more because of his weakness. Fortunately, he'd stopped gambling, claiming he'd gone cold turkey once he became aware that he was going to become a grandfather. He said he didn't want his grandson or granddaughter growing up with the stigma that their grandfather had spent time in prison.

She hadn't wanted to believe Isaac, because Zabrina was aware that a gambling addiction was one of the most difficult to break. But Isaac was being truthful. She continued to monitor his bank accounts and Thomas had transferred the responsibility of handling his financial affairs from Isaac to another aide.

"Thank you, Dr. Dwight."

In keeping with her father's wishes, there had been a private ceremony, followed by cremation, and his ashes had been scattered in the ocean. Surviving family members included Isaac's sister, her daughter, three grandchildren, Zabrina and Adam. Thomas was saved the pretense of mourning his father-in-law. He was in Asia with several members of Congress on a fact-finding mission.

Roberta rested a hand on Zabrina. "I wish Dwight and I could've been there for you and your son when you lost Thomas Cooper so soon after losing your father. By the way, where is your son?"

"Adam is spending the month in Virginia with my cousin's children."

"I know you must really miss him," Roberta crooned.

"I do," Zabrina admitted.

She missed Adam, but not as much as she had the first week. It took three days of her calling her cousin twice a day to find out if Adam was having a good time, or giving her a problem before her Aunt Holly offered a stern lecture about the risks of being an overprotective mother. Holly sounded so much like Adam's therapist that she told the retired schoolteacher to have Adam call her whenever he felt like talking. He called home every third day before tapering off to once a week. Her son was expected to return to Philadelphia next Sunday. He'd begun whining that he wanted to stay longer, but Zabrina reminded him that his cousins were scheduled to go to a sleepaway camp for the first two weeks of August to give their parents a break from children.

She did promise Adam he could return to Virginia the following summer *and* go to camp with his cousins.

"Dad, the game is on!" Myles called across the patio.

Dwight pressed a kiss to his wife's cheek. "Excuse me, ladies." Turning on his heel, he rushed over to where Griffin had set a flat-screen television on a stand under the retractable awning shading the patio from the hot summer sun.

"Make certain you keep your eyes on your granddaughters, too, Dwight Eaton."

"I will, Bertie." Dwight shifted his chair where he could view the ball game and Sabrina and Layla.

"Come help me arrange your flowers, Brina. I don't understand these men and their obsession with a ball," she mumbled under her breath. "If it's not a golf ball, then it's baseball, basketball or football." Roberta's angry gaze met Zabrina's amused one. "What's up with the balls?"

Zabrina bit back a smile. "I don't know, Miss Bertie."

She remembered when Griffin, his brother Grant, Myles and Dwight would gather in the Eatons' family room to watch sporting events ranging from auto racing and bowling to soccer. If a ball was involved, then the men were armchair spectators.

The last time Zabrina had seen Layla and Sabrina Rice they'd been toddlers, so it was a bit unsettling to see them as young adults. It reminded her how much time had passed and that Myles's nieces and Adam were cousins. She followed Roberta into an enclosed back porch to a large updated gourmet kitchen, watching as the older woman retrieved a vase and filled it with water.

Roberta opened the cellophane wrapping and picked up stems of lily of the valley, snow-white roses and hydrangea, sweet pea, peonies and baby's breath. "I hope you and Myles get it right this time." She glanced up from her task to find Zabrina staring at her. "You think I don't know what's going on between you and my son?"

"I suppose you don't approve?"

"It has nothing to do with whether I do or don't approve, Brina. You and Myles are grown, and once my children were adults I learned to bite my tongue and keep my opinions to myself."

"I'm sorry—"

Roberta held up a hand. "Don't go there, Zabrina. Whatever happened between you and Myles is in the past. What's more important is the future. I know you love him, and that he loves you. That was very apparent when he couldn't stop staring at you at Lindy's wedding. You're luckier than most women, young lady, because you've been offered a second chance with a man you love."

"You…you believe Myles still loves me?" Zabrina had asked Roberta the question despite knowing the answer. He'd been forthcoming when he'd told her he loved her—in and out of bed.

"Myles never stopped loving you, Brina. No, he didn't tell me but I know my children a lot better than they believe I do. The back and forth between Griffin and Belinda was nothing more than 'I like you but I'm not going to let you know it.' Unfortunately it took a family tragedy for them to come together for the sake of my grandchildren. Griffin has shown that he can be a great father and Belinda is a wonderful mother." Roberta flashed a wide smile. "They've promised me that they're doing their best to give Dwight and me more grandchildren. Dwight wants a grandson, but I'm open to either a girl or boy."

Zabrina wanted to tell Roberta that she and Dwight had a grandson. Adam Cooper was their grandson. She'd mentally rehearsed how she would eventually tell Myles that Adam was his. She owed it to him and to Adam to let them know their biological connection. She'd sworn that she would never divulge the circumstances of her marriage to Thomas, but she hadn't sworn or promised anyone that she wouldn't tell Myles that he'd fathered her child. She knew she couldn't go back and right the wrongs, but she wanted to make certain to make sure things were right.

Adam had a right to know why Thomas had been so distant, why he wasn't or couldn't be the traditional father and why Isaac Mixon did all the things with him Thomas should've done.

And Myles had a right to know that he was a father and that he could share all the things with Adam he'd talked about when they were engaged. Myles, at twenty-eight, had wanted to start a family right away, while she'd wanted to wait, not because she'd wanted an extended honeymoon but because of a repressed fear that her life would duplicate her mother's, that she wouldn't live to see her child reach his or her majority.

"I love Myles, Miss Bertie. Even when I was another man's wife I still loved him. Some people would say I was an adulterer, but I really don't care. I never wished Thomas Cooper ill and I'm not ashamed to say I never shed a tear when the police told me he'd drowned, nor at his funeral."

Lines of concern furrowed Roberta's forehead. "What did he do to you, Brina?"

Without warning, her maternal instincts had surfaced. She'd come to love Zabrina Mixon as if she were a daughter after she'd lost her mother. Although she was raising four rambunctious children who insisted on bringing animals into her house, she'd welcomed Zabrina with open arms, because her rationale was, what was one more child at her table?

"He didn't do anything to me, Miss Bertie, that I hadn't permitted him to do."

"Had he harmed or posed a threat to your son?"

Zabrina's expression changed, her face suddenly grim. "No. And if he had I wouldn't have stayed with him. I don't know what's going to happen with me and Myles beyond the summer, but we'll probably remain friends."

Roberta gave her son's girlfriend a skeptical glance as she sucked her teeth. "Friends? Don't delude yourself, Brina. You and Myles haven't been friends in a very long time."

She knew she'd shocked Zabrina when her mouth opened but no words came out. Only someone visually impaired didn't see the tenderness in Myles's eyes whenever he looked at Zabrina. When they'd walked onto the patio Roberta hadn't missed how protectively Myles held on to Zabrina's arm. It was as if he had to hold on to her to make certain she wouldn't get away from him.

She also noticed something very different about

Myles that hadn't been apparent when he'd returned to Philadelphia years ago, trips that were too short and infrequent. She knew he was aware that Zabrina was now a widow, and once Belinda told him that she'd invited Zabrina to her wedding Myles spoke of a possible extended stay in Philly. This revelation shocked everyone—everyone except his mother. She knew if anyone could get Myles Eaton to spend more than a week in Philly it was Zabrina Cooper.

"You're right, Miss Bertie. Myles and I are sleeping together."

"Good." She placed the bouquet in the vase, and stood back to admire her handiwork. "Now, maybe you'll give me a grandchild, too."

"Who's going to give you a grandchild?"

Roberta and Zabrina turned to find Myles leaning against the entrance to the kitchen, muscular arms crossed over his broad chest. "Well, ladies? What's up?"

Roberta spoke first. "Why are you eavesdropping on a private conversation?"

Taking long strides, Myles walked into the kitchen. "I wasn't eavesdropping. I got here in time to hear the word *grandchild*."

"Your mother said she wants more grandchildren," Zabrina volunteered.

Myles lifted an eyebrow. "Bertie Eaton can speak for herself, Brina."

Pinpoints of heat dotted Zabrina's cheeks at his retort. Her eyes narrowed, reminding him of a cat about to pounce. "I'm more than aware of that, Myles Eaton."

Roberta recognized the tension between her son and Zabrina. It was palpable. Normally she wouldn't interfere in the scraps between her children and their partners, but she wasn't going to stand by and let Myles intimidate the woman who'd suffered too many losses in her young life.

"And you need to watch your tone, Myles Adam Eaton."

Myles gave his mother an incredulous look before his eyes narrowed. "What did I say?"

Roberta rested her hands on her hips, a gesture her children easily recognized. It meant she'd had enough and it was better that they walk away than stand and debate with her. "It's not what you say, but how you said what you said."

Myles threw up his hands. "How did I say it!?"

"What's going on in here, Mama?" Belinda had walked into the kitchen. "And, Myles, why are you raising your voice?"

Knowing when he was bested, Myles threw up his hands again, this time in defeat. "Women," he whispered under his breath.

Roberta cupped a hand to her ear. "You got a problem with the so-called weaker sex?"

Mumbling an expletive, Myles walked out of the kitchen to the sound of hysterical female laughter. Belinda had sent him to get Zabrina, and he'd reached the kitchen in time to hear his mother mention a grandchild. Roberta had talked about having more grandchildren after he'd proposed to Zabrina because Donna and Grant Rice had decided beforehand that they wanted two children, but hadn't counted on getting two at the same time.

Reaching for a napkin, Belinda blotted the tears filling her eyes. "That wasn't nice, Mama."

Roberta waved a hand. "It serves him right. There are times when Myles is full of himself. I've told him that with his attitude he should be sitting on the bench instead of teaching law."

"Judge Eaton," Belinda crooned. "I kinda like the sound of that. What do you think, Brina?"

Zabrina smiled. "It sounds good to me, too."

Picking up the vase of flowers, Belinda cradled it to her chest. "If Myles is appointed judge and you marry him, Brina, then I'll have to address your mail to the Honorable Judge Myles and Zabrina Eaton."

"I'm not marrying Myles." The protest was out of Zabrina's mouth before she could censor herself.

Wincing, Belinda bit her lip. "I'm sorry, Brina. I didn't—"

"Please don't apologize, Lindy. Myles and I are just hanging out together for the summer." For Zabrina, sleeping together didn't necessary lead to a marriage proposal, or a promise of happy ever after.

Belinda blew out a breath. "Now that I've taken my foot out of my mouth I'll take these outside. By the way, I sent Myles in to get you because he's offered to make Philly cheesesteaks."

Zabrina's eyes lit up. "Is he using Cheez Whiz or provolone?"

"Please," Belinda drawled. "It's a sacrilege not to go with the Whiz."

"Even though Dwight told me I should watch my cholesterol, I'm going to have a bite of his," Roberta said.

Belinda shot her mother a pointed look. "Now,

Mama, you know that Daddy's not going to let you take a bite of his Philly cheese with Whiz," she teased with the right amount of South Philly *atty-tood.* Regulars and tourists who lined up at Pat's or Gino's were familiar with the debate as to which sandwich was better: Cheez Whiz or provolone, *wit'* or *wit'out,* which translated into with or without onions. "We'll snack until the game is over," she continued, "then we'll sit down to eat dinner."

Zabrina wanted to tell Belinda she would eat dinner only *if* she wasn't too full. Somehow she'd forgotten the amount of food the Eatons consumed on Sunday afternoons. What she found surprising was that none of them had a weight problem.

She followed mother and daughter out of the kitchen to the rear of the house where the aroma of steak filled the air. Myles had taken over the grilling duties, chopping the thinly sliced steak as though he performed the task every day. A pot of Cheez Whiz sat on a back burner over a low flame. Griffin and Dwight, sitting on chairs while holding bottles of cold beer, groaned in unison when the Phillies pitcher gave up another run.

Accepting a glass of lemonade from Belinda, Zabrina put on her sunglasses, lay down on a cushioned lounger and closed her eyes. She'd applied a layer of the highest number sunblock to her face and arms. Reuniting with the Eatons had gone more smoothly than she'd anticipated. But, then again, ten years was a very long time to hold on to a grudge.

She knew firsthand how hate festered until it eventually destroyed its host. It was only when she'd unconsciously forgiven Thomas Cooper that she'd begun to experience a modicum of peace.

Life was good. She'd rediscovered love and passion with Myles Eaton, and she would reunite with her son in exactly one week. Her only concern was how Adam would react when she introduced him to his biological father for the first time.

Chapter 14

Zabrina kept pace with Myles and the real estate agent as the silver-haired, fashionably dressed woman gave them a tour of a house that had just come on the market.

The call had come in on Myles's cell phone before seven that morning. He'd joined her in the shower, announcing he had to return to Pittsburgh before noon and he wanted her to come along. It wasn't until they were an hour into the drive that he revealed his Realtor wanted to show him a house that met his specifications. The Realtor had downloaded pictures of the house to Myles's BlackBerry, and he was anxious to see it in person.

The house, all fifty-five hundred square feet of it, was magnificent. The sixty-year-old structure was erected on three acres overlooking a valley ten miles outside Pittsburgh. It had everything Myles wanted:

wraparound porch, fireplaces in each of the four bedrooms, four full baths, two half baths, entry hall, great room, living and formal dining rooms, three-car garage and screened back porch. The former owners had put the house up for sale and moved into a retirement community when it became impossible for them to maintain, and their children preferred condo living to mowing lawns and shoveling snow.

Mrs. Eck smiled at Myles. "I have documentation verifying the plumbing and electricity were updated two years ago."

Reaching for Zabrina's hand, Myles cradled it in the crook of his arm. "If I decide to purchase the house, then I'll hire my own engineer to check out everything."

"Mrs. Eaton, you also might want to update the kitchen appliances. That is, if you and your husband agree you want the house. Do you have children, Mrs. Eaton?"

Zabrina hesitated, while at the same time staring at Myles. He nodded. "Yes. We have a son." The admission had slipped out unbidden, but Myles didn't appear to notice her damning faux pas.

The petite woman with sapphire-blue eyes clapped her hands. "Wonderful. Come out back with me and I'll show you what the former owners erected for their grandsons."

Myles covered the hand tucked into his elbow as he followed Mrs. Eck across the kitchen and out a set of French doors to the backyard. He wanted the house. He'd wanted it even before seeing inside.

The smile that began with his mouth tilting at the corners spread to his eyes. Someone had built a miniature log cabin that doubled as a playhouse. The other surprise was a ladder attached to the trunk of a massive maple tree that led up to a large tree house. He hadn't met Zabrina's son, but he had no doubt the young boy would love spending time in the tree house or hanging out in the cabin.

"Do you think Adam would like it?"

Zabrina could hear her heart echoing in her ears. Myles was answering a question to which he knew the answer. *Their* son would love the tree house. She knew if she couldn't find Adam in the house then he would be either in the tree house or the log cabin daydreaming about the alternate universes he created in his fertile imagination that eventually came to life on paper.

"He would love it."

"How about Adam's mother? Does she like the house?"

Zabrina felt as if she'd been frozen for more than a decade and had begun to thaw. She couldn't remember when she hadn't been in love with Myles Eaton, and if she'd doubted her feelings, she knew now for certain that she was hopelessly and inexorably in love with him.

"Adam's mother loves the house."

A sense of strength and peace came to Zabrina with the pronouncement. She'd made her feelings for Myles known to him, his mother, his sister, and the only person that remained was *their* son.

Myles met the Realtor's hopeful expression with a warm smile. "If you'll allow me a few minutes, I'd like to talk to *Mrs. Eaton.*"

"Take all the time you need, Professor Eaton."

After waiting until Mrs. Eck returned to the house,

Myles cradled Zabrina's face in his hands. The rain blanketing the western part of the state had stopped, but one-hundred-percent humidity had frizzed her short hair.

"Do you like it, darling?"

Zabrina's eyelids fluttered wildly. "It shouldn't be whether I like it, Myles. The question is do *you* like it."

He nodded. "I love the house, I love you, and I want you and Adam to live here with me."

She stared at a tiny bird perched on the branch of a sapling. "I can't live with you, Myles."

"I thought you said you loved me."

Her gaze shifted to his mouth, bracketed with lines of tension. "I do love you."

"Then why won't you live with me?"

"If I didn't have Adam I would do it in a heartbeat. But what message would I send him if I shack up with a man who's not my husband? I thought sending him to a private school would shield him from kids whose mothers expose their children to a revolving door of men who come and go at will. One month there's Uncle Bobby, then six months later there's Uncle Jimmy. After a while the names and faces become a jumble. Some of them slept with the same men just to compare notes."

"How did you find out about his classmates' mothers' sexcapades?"

"Adam slept over at a friend's house and he heard someone call the mother a name. He came home and asked me what a ho meant."

"And you told him?"

"Of course I did, Myles."

Wrapping his arms around her waist, Myles molded

her to his length. “You think if you move here with me Adam will think badly of you?”

“Yes.”

“If you married me would you still be a ho?”

Zabrina could feel Myles’s heart thudding against her own. She realized he was as apprehensive about marrying as she was. “Are…are you proposing marriage?”

“No, Brina. I’m *asking* you to marry me.”

“Again?”

He smiled and attractive lines fanned out around his eyes. “Yes—again.”

She still hadn’t processed what she was hearing. “You want me to marry you because you want me to live in this house with you?”

Hard-pressed not to shake her until her teeth rattled, Myles clenched his own teeth to stop the curses poised on the tip of his tongue. “The house has nothing to do with it, Zabrina.” He angled his head and brushed a light kiss over her parted lips. “You said there were no do-overs in life, but you’re so wrong, Brina. Call it luck, fate, providence or destiny, but we’ve been given a second chance.

“I don’t know, nor do I care why you married Thomas Cooper. What matters is you’re free to marry whomever you want. If you don’t want to marry me, then I need to know now before I get in any deeper. And if you say no, then I’ll drive you back to Philly and I’ll never bother you again. That’s not a promise, Zabrina. That’s a vow.”

Zabrina saw the torture in the eyes of the man she’d once promised to marry. She’d deceived him once and he’d taken her back. Fate had given her a second chance and all she had to do was open her mouth and say yes.

Yes, I will marry you, Myles Eaton. Yes I will move to Pittsburgh and live in what will become our dream house. Yes I will share everything I have, and that includes your son.

"Yes," she whispered, the word coming from a place she hadn't known existed.

Myles's dark eyes riveted her to the spot. "Yes what, Zabrina?"

"Yes, Myles, I will marry you."

"Will you and Adam live here with me?"

This was the side of Myles that irked Zabrina. "What if I tell you that I want you to move in with me and Adam?"

"Then, I'd do it! I would move anywhere, Zabrina. Anywhere as long as it is with you."

She hesitated before giving him an answer. Zabrina knew Myles wanted the house, wanted it as much as he wanted to marry her, yet he'd give it up for her. She shook her head as tears pricked the backs of her lids. "If anyone's going to do any moving it will be me and Adam."

One moment she was standing and within the next Zabrina found herself swept off her feet as Myles swung her around and around, shouting at the top of his lungs. He was going to get everything he'd ever wanted: Zabrina, a son and their dream house.

"We'll get married as soon as we get back to Philly unless…"

"Unless what, Myles?"

He set her on her feet. "Unless we fly to Vegas, get married, then come back and have a little something for the family once you decorate the house however you want it."

"No. No," she repeated. "I can't do that to Adam."

"Do what?"

"Introduce you as my husband and his new dad the first time he meets you. I'm not saying I need his approval, but it's only fair that the two of you spend some time together before we all live under the same roof."

Myles ran a hand over his face. "You're right, baby. I'm sorry." His lips came down to meet hers in a dreamy intimacy that felt both trembling. "Let's go inside and tell Mrs. Eck that she can start counting her commission."

Zabrina wasn't certain whether she'd be able to sell her house, and if she couldn't then she'd rent it. She was sorry to leave Rachel and her children, but if her soon-to-be ex-neighbor wanted to come to Pittsburgh to visit, she and Myles had plenty of room to put them up.

"This is where I live, darling."

Zabrina walked around Myles's furnished apartment in what once had been a small hotel. He told her he'd turned down an offer for faculty housing because he valued his privacy. The accommodations were less than opulent, but serviceable and within walking distance of the law-school campus.

The apartment had a miniscule bedroom, a bathroom with a shower stall, basin and commode and a utility kitchen with a dining area. Everything was in its place, but somehow it still looked cramped to her. Myles stacked law books on the floor along one wall of the bedroom because he said there was no room for a bookcase.

"Do you mind if I open the windows, Myles?"

"Of course not." The windows hadn't been opened since he'd left a month ago.

Zabrina opened the windows overlooking the front of the two-story building. Now that she saw for herself the size of the apartment she realized why he'd wanted a lot more space. A futon doubled as a sofa in what passed for the living room.

They'd driven back to the real estate office with the agent, where Myles signed countless documents, then wrote a check for the down payment. Mrs. Eck told him that because he'd been preapproved he could expect to close on the property the third week in August. That would give him time to settle in before classes began.

The heat from Myles's body seeped into hers when he came to stand behind her. "What are you thinking about, Brina?"

"I'm thinking about going back to work."

"Why?"

"I miss nursing. I've managed to take some continuing education courses to stay current, but it's not the same."

Myles wrapped his arms around her waist. He pressed his face to her damp hair. "What about Adam?"

"What about him, Myles?"

"Who's going to watch him when you're working?"

Zabrina closed her eyes. "I'm going to go online and see if there are any school-nurse positions available. That way our hours will be the same."

Myles nuzzled the side of her neck. "We could hire a housekeeper who could also double as sitter."

"Let me check the employment possibilities first."

"Whatever you decide, Brina, I'll back you up."

How different her marriage to Myles would be from the one she'd had with Thomas Cooper. The time she'd broached the subject of going back to the hospital Thomas had reacted like a mad man. He claimed the wife of an important politician shouldn't be seen emptying bedpans, saying it was bad for his image. The following day her father had come to Cooper Hall to talk to her. When he'd told her that she shouldn't do or say anything to upset Thomas, she'd asked Isaac to leave. The look on her father's face was one she would remember all her days. Whenever Thomas couldn't get her to agree to something, he enlisted her father's assistance. And she knew if Isaac hadn't done his son-in-law's bidding, he would be reminded of the threat of going to jail.

Staring up at Myles over her shoulder, she blew him a kiss. "Thank you, darling."

"You're welcome. What do you think of my humble abode?" he whispered in her ear.

"It's very, very humble."

"Damn, baby, you didn't have to say it like that."

She giggled. "What did you expect me to say? That it's Buckingham Palace?"

"It's *my* palace—at least temporarily."

"True."

"Have you seen the royal bedchamber?"

Resting the back of her head on his shoulder, Zabrina closed her eyes. "I thought I caught a glimpse of it."

"Would you like to take a tour?"

Turning in his embrace, she stared up at Myles, stunned at what she saw in his dark eyes. Her whole body trembled from a need so great she felt as if she were coming out of her skin.

"I want you to make love to me."

The last word wasn't off her tongue when Myles swept Zabrina up in his arms and carried her into the bedroom. What happened next was a blur. Within minutes of him placing her on the bed, her clothes lay on the floor with his.

The blood had rushed to his penis so quickly he felt light-headed. Lowering himself he smothered her mouth with his, pushing into her body with one sure thrust of his hips. Her smell, her moist heat and the way her flesh fitted around his sent him over the edge. The rush of completion came so quickly that he pulled out and slid down the length of her body.

Bracing both hands on her inner thighs, he spread Zabrina's legs apart and feasted like a starving man. His rapacious tongue was unrelenting and uncompromising. He heard her screaming for him to stop, but he continued his sensual assault. It was when she arched off the mattress that he knew he'd brought her maximum pleasure.

Zabrina moaned softly when Myles moved over her languid body, gasping sharply when he entered her with a force that rekindled her waning passion all over again. At the moment his breathing quickened, she managed to slip out from under his bucking body. The sudden motion surprised Myles and he sat up, giving her the advantage she needed to take him into her mouth.

It was the first time she'd gone down on Myles and now she knew why he liked it. The position was one of power *and* control. Grasping his penis, she held it tightly as her tongue went up one side and then down the other as if she were licking a frothy confection.

A sense of strength came to her when he howled, flailed his arms and begged her to stop. Zabrina had no intention of stopping—not until he yielded to the pleasure he sought to withhold from her.

"Baby, baby, please baby, no," he chanted. It began as a litany that resounded in her head, and still she wouldn't relent.

Myles knew he had to extricate Zabrina's mouth before he ejaculated. He went completely still and when her head came up he moved quickly. Flipping her onto her back, he went to his knees, raised her legs in the air and entered her again. The turbulence of their passion knew no bounds when they shuddered simultaneously in a shared ecstasy that left both trembling.

Zabrina found herself crying and babbling incoherently as Myles lay down next to her. He held her as if she were a child until she quieted and drifted off to sleep.

Zabrina woke to find herself in bed—alone. Pinpoints of fading light came through the blinds at the single window. She sat up, swung her legs over the side of the mattress, then she felt the sticky residue on her thighs. She and Myles had made love without protection! A low moan slipped from her when she realized she was ovulating. How, she bemoaned, could she have been so careless? The door to the bedroom opened and the outline of Myles's body filled the doorway.

He touched the dimmer switch on the wall and the small space was filled with light from the table lamp. Zabrina stared at him as if he were a stranger.

"Where are my clothes?"

"I put them in the wash."

"In the wash?"

Myles walked into the room. He'd changed out of his slacks and into a pair of faded jeans. "I have a portable washer/dryer in a closet off the kitchen." He made his way to a chest of drawers and took out a T-shirt. He handed it to her. "You can put that on if you want. Personally I wouldn't mind if you run around in the buff."

She took the T-shirt, but didn't put it on. "I need to take a shower. I smell like sex."

"Wrong, Brina. You smell like a woman who has been made love to."

"Very funny, Myles."

"Before you take a shower I'd like to give you something."

Zabrina watched as he searched in the bottom of a narrow closet. He went to his knees, cursing under his breath. "What are you cursing about?"

"I'm looking for something" came his muffled reply. "Got it!"

Zabrina felt her knees give way slightly before she maintained her balance when she saw what Myles cradled on the palm of his hand. It was the ring she'd returned to him via a bonded messenger.

He beckoned her closer. "Come here, baby."

Zabrina held her breath, unable to move. It *was* a do-over. For the second time Myles Eaton would slip an engagement ring on her finger. She extended her left hand, unable to control its shaking. The ring was one she and Myles had designed together: an exceptional two-carat fancy yellow diamond in a square-cut modern shape set off by a carat of trapezoids and another carat of round diamonds in a platinum setting. The jeweler had said he was giving them a discount on the price of the ring when he charged them for the loose stones and not the setting. The final price tag was staggering, but Myles said she was more than worth it.

He went to his knees in front of her. "Brina Mixon, will you do me the honor of becoming my wife?"

She thought about telling him that legally she was Zabrina Cooper, but she didn't want to spoil the very special moment. Their gazes met, fused as they shared a smile. "Yes, Myles Adam Eaton, I will marry you."

He slipped the ring on her left hand. Her finger was smaller than it'd been years before. Myles stood up.

Zabrina held up her hand to the light. "Even though it's a little big, it is still spectacular."

Reaching for her hand, Myles dropped a kiss on her knuckle. "This is where it belongs, and no matter what passes between us I don't ever want you to take it off again." Turning her hand over, he pressed a kiss on her palm. "I'm going to have to fatten you up some," he teased.

"If you continue to make love to me without protection you won't have to worry about fattening me up. In nine months I'll look as if I've swallowed a watermelon."

"I'm sorry, Brina. I don't know what happened."

Looping her arms under his shoulders, Zabrina pressed her bare breasts to his chest. "I'll know in another week or two whether you're going to give your mother that grandchild she wants."

"My mother has been harping about having more grandchildren for years now. I think it started when Donna and Grant said they were stopping after the twins were born."

"She's blessed, Myles. Layla and Sabrina are incredible granddaughters."

Zabrina found the girls shy around strangers, but once they had warmed to her it was as if she'd known them all their lives. When she'd told them that she had a son they offered to babysit, until she revealed that Adam was a ten-year-old.

The girls had been bright and engaging when Zabrina had joined them when they took Nigel and Cecil for a walk. They'd showed her their new school before they retraced their steps and joined the rest of the family for dinner on the patio. Zabrina marveled at how well-adjusted her son's cousins were, because it hadn't been a year since they'd lost both parents in a drunk-driving accident.

Belinda had revealed that the girls had been in counseling to work through their issues of death and loss. She would've continued with the sessions if the twins hadn't decided they didn't want to keep talking about their mother and father.

Zabrina knew there would come a time when Adam would want to stop seeing his counselor. He hadn't gone in four weeks and she was anxious to see if missing his sessions had impacted his emotional growth.

Tilting her chin, she smiled at Myles. "I think I'm going to take a shower now."

He lifted his eyebrows questioningly. "Do you want company?"

"No, Myles. The shower stall is too small for two people."

"No, it's not."

Her smile slipped away. The three words spoke volumes. While she'd been pining away for Myles Eaton she realized he hadn't been pining for her. How many women had he slept with since their breakup? And how many had he made love to on the same bed where he might possibly have gotten her pregnant for the second time?

"I have to take a shower." She tried walking around him, but he blocked her way. "Please let me go, Myles."

"Look at me, Brina. I said, look at me," he repeated when she stared at the floor. Her head came up. "Yes, I've slept with other women, and I'm not going to apologize for it. But I want you to know that I never cheated on you when we were together."

"And I've never cheated on you, Myles. Not ever!"

A frown appeared between his eyes when he realized what she'd said. "What are you talking about?"

"Adam. He's your son, not Thomas Cooper's. I was pregnant when I married Thomas."

Zabrina clenched her jaw to muffle the sobs building in the back of her throat when she saw the tortured look in Myles's eyes. She'd planned to tell him that he was Adam's father, but she hadn't wanted it to come out like it did. She'd known however she told him it would be shocking *and* painful, however, the way Myles was glaring at her had chills pebbling her flesh.

"You're lying!" Myles said, after he recovered his

voice. He wanted to believe Zabrina was lying, lashing out to wound him because she was jealous he'd admitted to sleeping with other women.

"No, Myles, I'm not lying."

"You couldn't have been pregnant because you were on the Pill."

"Yes, I was on the Pill. I was taking the lowest dose, and I was one of a small percentage of women who get pregnant while taking the pill."

Zabrina's explanation grated on Myles's nerves. His hands snaked around her upper arms, holding her captive. "Why didn't you tell me, Zabrina? Why did you allow another man to claim *my* son, give him *his* name instead of mine?"

"It's too complicated to explain."

Myles shook his head as if to clear it. He couldn't believe what Zabrina had just told him. She had to be lying, just like she'd lied when she'd told him that she was in love with another man. Who was she? Had he fallen in love with a pathological liar?

He dropped his hands as if he feared contamination and she lost her balance, falling backward. Reacting quickly, Myles caught Zabrina before she fell. She was shaking uncontrollably. Sweeping her up into his arms, he placed her on the bed, his body following hers down.

Myles wanted answers, but more importantly he wanted the truth, and if he had to hold Zabrina prisoner in the small furnished apartment to get it he would do just that.

Chapter 15

"I was blackmailed into marrying Thomas Cooper."

The words burned the back of Zabrina's throat as they spilled off her tongue like bile. She'd sworn that she would never tell anyone how she'd come to marry Thomas, but she was tired, tired of lying and even more tired of hiding.

It was no longer about her or her father. Isaac Mixon was gone, impervious to the threats of a man obsessed with power. Thomas was gone and could no longer hurt her *or* her son.

She told Myles everything—leaving nothing out. She confessed to sharing a bed with Thomas on their wedding night without consummating their marriage. It was as if the floodgates were opened when she talked about the political photo-ops, how, after she gave birth, she withdrew from her social engagements and whenever she tried to exert her independence Thomas used Isaac as his enforcer *to keep her in her place.*

"He used fear and intimidation to control my father, and he knew I'd do anything to keep Daddy from going to jail."

Myles felt tightness in his chest before realizing he'd been holding his breath. He hadn't wanted to believe Zabrina, but there was no way she could make up a story so incredible and bizarre.

"Why didn't you tell me, Brina?"

"I couldn't," she whispered. "Thomas would've had someone kill my father." She told him about the man holding a gun to Isaac's head.

"No, he wouldn't. Your father was his trump and get-out-of-jail card and if he had Isaac murdered then it would've derailed his carefully orchestrated political career. Thomas couldn't marry his cousin's wife, so you became the pawn for a fortysomething bachelor who needed a wife to enhance his image, and Isaac delivered you like a trussed-up holiday bird. Adam was an added bonus he hadn't counted on."

"Adam carries his name, but Thomas hardly ever gave our son a passing glance."

Myles smiled for the first time since being told he'd fathered a child. Zabrina had said *our son.* He wanted to tell her Thomas ignoring the child wasn't a bad thing, because he planned to share things with Adam they should've shared years ago. It would also make it easier for him to step into the role of father because Adam wouldn't have to deal with guilt when he replaced one father figure with another.

"I'm sorry you had to sacrifice your happiness for

your father's misdeeds and I'm sorry Adam had to spend the first ten years of his life with a monster who didn't have the decency to pretend to be a father."

Zabrina grasped the front of Myles's T-shirt. "You can't tell Adam about his grandfather. It would crush him if he found out that Isaac stole money."

"Don't worry, baby. I won't say anything.

"If you hadn't waited ten years to tell me this I know I could've gotten your father off," he said after a comfortable silence.

"What are you talking about?"

"I would've taken on your father's case and because it was his first offense I would've asked the DA to give him probation. Then again, there could've been the possibility that the charges might have been thrown out."

Closing her eyes, Zabrina pressed her face to the side of Myles's neck. "I hadn't thought of that. How could I have been so stupid and gullible?"

"There wasn't much you could do with a gun pointed at your father's head."

"Yeah, but—"

"But nothing," he interrupted. "You couldn't risk trying to negotiate with a megalomaniac. There was still the possibility Cooper would've had someone hurt your father."

"But I should've trusted you, Myles, because you'd promised to protect me."

"Yes, I did promise. But you did what you did because you believed at that time it was best for your father and unborn child."

A beat passed. "Are you ready to meet your son? He's coming home Sunday."

"If I'm not ready, then I'll have to get ready."

"I'd like for us to wait a while before we tell Adam you're his biological father."

Myles kissed her hair. "I don't have a problem with that. It may be too much for him to take in right now."

"What about your family, Myles?"

"What about them, baby?"

"Are we going to tell them that Adam is an Eaton?"

Myles smiled down at the woman who'd sacrificed herself for her father. He didn't want to think of what she would do for their son. "We'll tell them after we legally change his name from Cooper to Eaton."

"Will he have to undergo a paternity test?"

"I doubt it, Brina. Cooper's dead so he can't contest it. I'm marrying Adam's mother, so it wouldn't be out of the ordinary that I'd adopt her child. Adam's actual paternity will remain an Eaton secret."

Zabrina reached up and traced the outline of Myles's expressive eyebrows with her forefinger. "When do you want to get married?"

"I'll leave that up to you. The last time we planned a wedding together I thought I was going to lose my mind. For this one I'm going to opt out of the planning. Let me know the date, time and place and I'll show up."

She gave him a soft punch to the shoulder, encountering solid muscle. "We don't have to rush and marry unless I find out I'm carrying another Eaton after that last stunt you pulled."

Myles held up his pinky. "No more unprotected lovemaking."

Zabrina looped her pinky with his. "No more unprotected lovemaking," she repeated.

"I'd like to make a few renovations to the house."

"What do you want?"

"I'd like to put in a home spa in the master bath. I also would like to redo the floors in the entry, kitchen and all of the bathrooms. Of course, the kitchen has to be remodeled and—"

"Whoa, hold up, baby girl. How much of the interior do you want to change?"

Zabrina wrinkled her nose. "I'll have to go through each room with a decorator, and then I'll make my decision. And don't worry about the cost. I'll pay for it."

"No, Zabrina. I'll pay for the renovations."

"You will not, Myles Eaton. I made out quite well for the ten years I had to spend in captivity. When Thomas Cooper died, he left me very well off, and I would like nothing better than to spend the money decorating my new home where I'll live with my husband and children."

"Let's make a deal, baby. You take care of what goes on inside the house and I'll take care of what goes on outside."

"Like riding lawnmowers and snowblowers?"

"There you go. I think you're getting the hang of it."

"How about the tree and playhouse?"

"That, too."

"Hammocks?"

"Hot damn, baby girl. You're a quick learner."

"You forgot something, Myles."

"What's that?"

"The grill. Who's going to do the grilling?"

Shifting on the bed, Myles straddled Zabrina, his face inches from hers. He couldn't believe they'd spent ten years apart, shared a child, when they could've been together as a family. If he hadn't hung up on her, if he'd demanded they meet in person, he knew he could've convinced her to tell him the truth.

"You grill inside and Adam and I will grill outside, because it's a man thing."

"Are riding mowers and snowblowers man machines?"

"Hell, yeah," he drawled. "Now, if you're ready to take that shower I'll show you that it's big enough for two people. I'll pick you up and if you loop your legs around my waist it'll work."

"You know right well what happens when I put my legs around your waist."

"And—so?"

Zabrina gave her fiancé a long, penetrating stare, wondering what was going on behind his impassive gaze. "You *want* another baby, don't you?"

He blinked. "Yes, I want a child, but I also want time to get to know my son."

"How long do you want to wait after we're married to begin trying?"

"No more than six months, Brina."

"Okay, darling. You'll have your six months, but if I get the baby blues, then it may be sooner."

"What-eva," he drawled, laughing softly.

Zabrina was sitting on the porch when her aunt's hybrid car maneuvered into the driveway. She stood up, waiting for her son to get out, not wanting to react like overly excited mothers who rushed to their children coming home from camp or vacation. A smile softened her mouth when she saw him. His face was several shades darker, his curly hair was too long and he looked as if he'd grown at least half an inch. He saw her and bounded up the porch steps.

"Hey, Mom. I missed you."

Zabrina hugged him, burying her face in his hair. He seemed so much more mature. Her son was growing up. Pulling back, she examined his face. There was no doubt he was her child, but she also saw traces of Myles that she hadn't realized were there before. Adam had inherited her hair, her coloring and her eyes. But the expressive eyebrows and mouth were Myles's.

"I've missed you, too, Adam. You look wonderful. There must be something in the water in Virginia, because you've really grown."

The solid slam of the car door caught her attention. It wasn't her aunt who had brought Adam home, but her cousin. "Hey, Tanya. I thought Aunt Holly was bringing Adam home." Zabrina came off the porch and hugged her flight-attendant cousin, who changed her hairstyle every year. She'd cut her hair and styled it into twists. It was perfect for her small, round brown face.

"She had a migraine this morning, so I volunteered to bring him back."

"Why didn't you call me, Tanya? I would've driven down to get him."

"No biggie, Zee. I'd love to hang out with you, but I must get back. I have an early flight tomorrow morning. Let me get his bags out of the trunk, then I'm on my way."

"Don't you want to stay a couple of minutes and have something to drink?"

"Thanks, but I have everything I need in the car. Mom washed all of Adam's clothes, so he didn't bring back any laundry."

"Tell your mother to call when she feels better."

"I will." Tanya opened the trunk, removing a duffel and backpack. She kissed Zabrina and hugged Adam, then she was gone. It took her less than ten minutes before she was back on the road.

Zabrina stood with her arm around her son's shoulders, waving until the hybrid's taillights disappeared. "How does it feel to be home?"

Adam smiled. "Good. I finished a lot of drawings. Do you want to see them?"

"Of course I do, but I need to talk to you."

Adam rolled his eyes. "Is it about going back to see Dr. Gordon?"

"No. Why?"

"I don't want to go back to counseling, Mom. I hate having to talk about Grandpa and my father."

"Are you sure, Adam?"

"I'm very sure, Mom."

"Promise me you'll let me know when you're feeling sad again."

"Aw, Mom!"

"Promise me, Adam."

He closed his eyes, his narrow chest rising and falling under a T-shirt with an image of President Barack Obama. "Okay, I promise. What do you want to talk about?"

"We'll talk inside." Picking up the duffel and leaving Adam to take the backpack, Zabrina led the way into the house and locked the door.

* * *

Zabrina sat across the table from Adam in the kitchen's breakfast nook, searching his face for a reaction to what she'd told him. She told him about Myles, how she'd fallen in love with him a long time ago, that they'd planned to marry before she married Thomas Cooper and that they'd found each other again, and this time they would marry and become a family.

"When are you getting married, Mom?"

Her chin trembled noticeably. Her son's voice was a monotone. It was obvious he wasn't happy that she had a man in her life. "We haven't set a date."

"Why?"

"We're buying a house." She made certain to say *we* rather than *I* or *Myles*. Zabrina had to impress upon her son that they were to be a family unit.

"Where?"

"It's near Pittsburgh."

"Why do we have to move there? What's wrong with Philadelphia?"

"There's nothing wrong with Philadelphia. Myles works in Pittsburgh. He teaches at a law school."

"He's a lawyer?"

"Yes, Adam. He's a lawyer."

Adam chewed his lip. "When am I going to meet him?"

"When would you like to meet him?"

"Now."

"Okay."

Zabrina got up and went over to the wall phone. It took less than a minute to relay Adam's request. She walked out of the house to wait on the porch. It was about to begin. It'd taken a decade for a father-and-son reunion.

Myles felt his heart stop then start up again when he saw his son for the first time. Adam looked like Zabrina, but there were subtle similarities that indicated the boy was his. The most startling resemblance was the hands. All of the Eaton men had the same hands. The first joint on the right pinky was a little crooked.

He held out his right hand. "Hello, Adam. I'm Myles."

Adam stared at the proffered hand, then shook it. "Hello."

Myles knew he had to take the initiative or they would continue to stare at each other. "There's a hammock in the back where we can talk." It was as close as he could get to his flesh and blood without making him feel uncomfortable.

Adam nodded. "Okay."

Myles led his son around to the back of the house. He heard the soft gasp from Adam when he saw the hammock. He showed him the technique for getting in, then stood back to allow him to execute it. The young boy got in on the first try, Myles followed, lying at the opposite end.

They swung back and forth for a full five minutes before Adam asked, "Are you nice to my mom?"

The question was not one Myles would've predicted from the boy. "Yes, I am, Adam. I'm very, very nice to your mother."

"Mr. Cooper wasn't nice to her."

"You called him Mr. Cooper?"

"That's what he wanted me to call him because everyone called him that."

Myles wished that Thomas Cooper were still alive so he could beat the hell out of him. "I'm nice to your mother because I love her. I've loved her for a very long time."

"Mom told me that you're going to get married."

"That's true, Adam."

"Will that make me your son?"

Struggling not to break down in front of his son, Myles took a deep breath. "Yes. It will make you my son. And if you want, your mother and I can change your name so you will be Adam Eaton instead of Adam Cooper."

Adam sat up. "Can you do that?"

"Yes, I can."

"When?"

"After your mother and I marry."

"Can you marry now?"

Myles also sat up. He'd thought Adam would resent him marrying his mother. "I guess we can. But I have to ask your mother if that's what she wants."

"She said she wants to marry you."

"I know that, and I want to marry her."

"But why can't you do it now?"

Myles didn't want to be manipulated by a ten-year-old even if he was his son. He gave him a level stare. "Your mother and I will talk about it. Okay?"

Adam nodded. "Okay."

"What do you like to do?"

"Draw."

"What do you draw?" Myles asked.

"Comics."

"Do you want to show me your drawings?"

"My mom doesn't like me to draw because she says she wants me to grow up to be a doctor or a lawyer."

You can grow up to be anything you want to be. Myles knew he was in for a fight with Zabrina, but he wanted their son to choose his own path. His father had wanted him to become a doctor, and he'd chosen law. If Adam wanted to be an artist, then, as his father, he would try to make it happen.

"Go get your drawings, Adam."

He waited in the hammock while the lanky kid with the mop of curly hair ran into the house. He returned with a sketch pad and a tin filled with colored pencils. Reaching over, Myles pulled Adam into the hammock and sat, stunned, as he stared at the colored images filling up the pages.

Adam was more than a good artist. He was exceptional. In fact, he was better than Myles had been at his age. "I used to draw, too."

"You did?"

"Yes," Myles said proudly. "But I never showed my work to anyone."

Excitement fired the gold in Adam's eyes. "What did you draw?"

"I liked drawing the Justice League of America."

"I draw the JLA, too," Adam said excitedly. The fictional DC Comics superhero team was a favorite of his. Turning the pad to a clean page, he handed Myles a pencil. "Who's your favorite in the team?"

Supporting the pad on his knees, Myles began making light strokes on the blank sheet of paper. "I like Black Canary and Flash."

Scooting over until he was seated next to Myles, Adam stared at the strokes taking shape. "I like Green Lantern, Batman and Captain Marvel. That's so cool. You're drawing Flash."

"It may be cool, but your drawings are much better. What grade are you in?"

Adam leaned closer, resting his head on Myles's shoulder to get a better view of the sketch. "I'm going into the seventh grade."

Myles stopped sketching and gave him a sidelong glance. "Do you mean the sixth grade?"

"It's the seventh. I went from the third grade to the fifth because fourth-grade work was too easy for me."

Hot damn! Not only was his son talented, but he was gifted. Myles lost track of time as he and Adam sketched the characters of the JLA. The sun had shifted lower in the summer sky when Zabrina came out of the house.

"Look, Mom! Myles and I are drawing together."

Moving closer to the hammock, she stared, stunned at the many characters on the sketch pad. She recognized Batman, Superman and Wonder Woman. "I didn't know you could draw," she said to Myles.

"That's because I was a closet sketcher. Adam's drawings are phenomenal."

"I know he's good."

Leaning over, Adam smiled at his mother. "Can I take lessons, Mom? Please."

"I'll have to think about it."

"What's there to think about, Brina?" Myles asked. "The kid is exceptional."

"Yeah, Mom. I'm exceptional. And Myles said he was going to take me to Pittsburgh tomorrow to see our new house. Do you want to come?"

Zabrina couldn't believe how quickly father and son had bonded. "I don't think so, darling. I have a few things I have to do around the house. You and Myles can go without me."

She would give father and son their time alone to get to know each other better. After all, she'd had her son for ten years and now it was time for her to share him with his father. Myles had come into Adam's life at the right time, because a boy approaching manhood needed a positive male role model in his life.

Adam was in bed when Myles and Zabrina crawled into the hammock together. They lay together without talking. It was a time when words weren't necessary.

It was Myles who broke the silence. "Adam asked why we couldn't get married now."

Zabrina's body stiffened before relaxing. "Why?"

She listened as Myles repeated what their son had said about Thomas Cooper. Her eyes filled with tears and rolled down her face when she realized what she'd done to her son by staying married to Thomas. It was apparent the child had seen and heard things she'd sought to shield from him.

"What have I done to my baby, Myles? I thought I was protecting him—"

"Stop it, Brina. You can't beat up on yourself for something over which you had no control. You did what you thought was best for yourself and your father."

"But I almost ruined our son."

"You didn't ruin him. Living with someone like Cooper taught him how *not* to treat a woman. Our son needs a normal life with a mother and father who love him and one another. What do you say, baby girl? Do I make an honest woman out of you, or are you going to turn into a low-class ho?"

"I'll low-class ho you, Myles Adam Eaton, when I make you go cold turkey."

"If you do that then we can't give Adam a brother or sister."

The seconds ticked. "You're right."

"I can make it happen in a couple of days."

"How?" Zabrina asked.

"We can apply for a license and I'll ask Judge Stacey Greer-Monroe to marry us."

"Where do you want to hold the ceremony?"

"I'll ask Belinda and Griffin if we can use their place. If the weather holds, then we can have it outdoors."

"When are we going to do this, Myles?"

"Next Saturday."

Zabrina closed her eyes. She didn't want to wait too long because she didn't want anything to come up that would prevent her from becoming Mrs. Myles Eaton. "Call Belinda."

Chapter 16

"Who wants more?" Zabrina lifted the corner of the French toast with the spatula, testing it for doneness before flipping it over on the stovetop grill.

"I do," Myles answered.

"Me, too." Adam garbled. His mouth was filled with food.

"Don't talk with food in your mouth," Myles and Zabrina said in unison.

"Okay," he mumbled.

Zabrina glared at her son. "Adam, you're still talking with food in your mouth."

"Sorry," he apologized after swallowing. "Can I have another sausage, too, Mom?"

"How many does that make?"

"I only had two. And, they were small."

Zabrina didn't want to call attention to Adam's sudden increase in appetite, because for years he'd been a picky eater. Spending a month with his cousins had definitely changed his attitude when it came to eating. Tanya's eleven- and thirteen-year-old sons were programmed to eat any and everything on their plates, including vegetables, or forfeit television and video-game privileges.

She'd gotten up early to prepare breakfast for Myles and Adam before they set out for Pittsburgh. Myles had promised to show the boy the house and have a late lunch at his favorite Steel City restaurant before driving back to Philly where they would go out for dinner as a family unit for the first time.

"What about you, Myles? Do you want more sausage?"

Myles shook his head. "No thanks. I'm good here."

He glanced at his watch. It was close to seven-thirty and he wanted to be on the road by eight. With a little more than three hundred miles between Philly and Pittsburgh he hoped to reach his destination before one. Usually when he drove alone he tended to speed, but with Adam in the car he knew he would have to keep to the speed limit.

The doorbell rang and everyone went completely still. "Are you expecting anyone?" he asked Zabrina.

She lifted her shoulder. "It's probably Rachel." It wasn't often Zabrina had early morning visitors. The exception was her neighbor.

Rachel's children were home after an extended stay with their grandparents, who'd indulged their every whim. It'd taken Rachel two weeks to get them back on a mealtime and bedtime schedule. She'd always had problems getting Shane and Maggie up in the morning so they would catch their respective school buses. Maggie and Shane's return had curtailed their mother's social life because her first date with Hugh had escalated to a minimum of two times a week.

Myles stood up. "I'll get the door."

Taking long strides, he walked out of the kitchen. He reached the door and peered through a sidelight. It wasn't Rachel. Opening the door, he nodded to a diminutive man. His eyes, in a dark weathered face, were smiling and he looked as if he'd slept in his seersucker suit.

"Good morning. May I help you?"

"Does Zabrina Cooper live here?"

"Who's asking?"

The man straightened as if the gesture would add an additional inch or two to his slight frame. "My name is Russell Newton. I am…was Isaac Mixon's attorney. I'm retiring and my secretary was packing up my files when she found this." Reaching into the inside of his rumpled jacket, he pulled out a white envelope. "Unfortunately, it was misfiled. It should've been delivered to Mr. Mixon's daughter within six months of his passing." He smiled, displaying a set of yellowing teeth. "But I always say, better late than never."

Myles extended his hand. "I'm Ms. Mixon's fiancé. I'll give it to her."

"No, no, no. I was instructed to give it to her personally."

He wanted to tell the man that he was more than six months too late. Isaac Mixon had died in his sleep last June, and pursuant to his instructions it should've been delivered to Zabrina on or before December. It was now early August, eight months later than the deadline.

"Who is it, Myles?"

He turned at Zabrina's approach. "Mr. Newton is here to give you something." Resting a hand at the small of her back, he dropped a kiss on her hair and then left her to deal with the odd little man.

"Would you like to come in, Mr. Newton?"

"No, no, no. I can't stay. My granddaughter is waiting in the car for me. I just came to give you this." He handed her the envelope. "It's from your father."

Zabrina's eyelids fluttered wildly. "What do you mean it's from my father? Isaac Mixon died almost a year ago."

Russell Newton ran a gnarled hand over a pate with sparse patches of white hair. "Mr. Mixon came to me and asked me to help him draw up a statement. It's not a last will and testament but more like a final confession. I witnessed it and so did my secretary."

"Why did you wait this long to give it to me?"

"I told your fiancé that it was misfiled. I just retired and I'm transferring my client files to another attorney. I know your father wanted you to see this, so I decided to deliver it personally."

Zabrina managed a tight smile. "Thank you, Mr. Newton."

He gave her a shaky bow. "You're welcome, Mrs. Cooper."

She watched the elderly man as he carefully navigated the porch steps and shuffled to the car parked behind Myles's Range Rover. Waiting until the driver backed out of the driveway and maneuvered down the street, she sat on the rocker and opened the sealed envelope. There was a single sheet of paper with a small key taped to the back.

Her eyes scanned the type, her eyes filling and making it impossible to see the words. Pressing a fist to her mouth, she bit down hard to keep from screaming. She didn't believe it. She couldn't believe it. She'd married and spent a decade with a depraved monster all for nothing.

Zabrina was still sitting on the rocker, her fist against her mouth when Myles returned to the porch. He saw the letter and hunkered down next to her. "What's the matter, baby?"

She shoved the paper at him. "Read it, Myles. Aloud, so I can hear what I've just read, because I still don't believe it."

Sitting on the footstool, Myles cleared his throat. "'My dearest daughter. I've instructed Russell Newton to deliver this to you—call it my confession—within six months of my passing. I am sorry you had to sacrifice the love of your life because of me—all because I was too much of a coward to stand up to Thomas Cooper and his hired muscle.

"'Thomas set me up to take a fall because of what I saw. I walked in on him taking a bribe from John Gallagher, a small-time hood the Philadelphia Police Department and the feds have on their organized crime radar. I left, thinking it was over, but a week later I got a visit from a stranger with a message from Gallagher's boss: *Forget what you saw or your daughter will find herself placing flowers on her father's grave.* Thomas came to see me later that evening, talking about how he needed to improve his image with a wife before he officially announced he was a candidate for mayor. That's when he mentioned your name. When I told him that you were engaged to marry Myles Eaton, he said that was of no consequence to him.

"'The sonofabitch concocted the story about me stealing from him, and then him having to pay off my gambling debts so I wouldn't inform on him. I've never bet on anything in my life. I've never even bought a lottery ticket. I hate that you had to become a pawn in something so heinous and depraved and that my grandson was deprived of the love and protection of his biological father.

"'And if you ever had a question as to whether Emory Davidson would've shot me, then the answer is yes. Would he have killed me? No. But I doubt whether I would've been able to walk again. His trademark is leaving his victims crippled or permanently maimed. I wasn't afraid for myself, precious daughter. I was afraid for you and the child you were carrying.

"'I've also told you that I believe in payback and you know what they say about payback: it's a bitch. The key taped on the reverse side opens the jewelry box that belonged to your mother. I took photos of Thomas's clandestine meetings that will shock a lot of people who've made Senator Thomas Cooper a demigod. Take the photos and this letter to the DA. I wish I could be there to see Thomas Cooper's fall from grace, but if he goes before me, you'll be free. And, if he goes after me, you still will be free to live your life as you should have. I have one other request: please let Myles Eaton know that Adam is his son. Love always, Dad.'"

Arms wrapped around her middle, Zabrina rocked back and forth as if in a catatonic state. She hadn't read wrong. Her father had sacrificed himself not to save his life, but to save hers. Hers and Adam's.

"Myles is my real father."

Adam had come out onto the porch without making a sound. Zabrina stopped rocking and Myles stood, meeting the wide-eyed gaze of the boy who'd probably overheard what he'd read aloud.

"Are you really my dad?" The last word was a sob.

Myles nodded, because his constricted throat wouldn't allow him to speak. The seconds ticked until he finally found the ability to speak the words. "Yes, Adam, I am your dad."

Adam took a step, his gaze shifting from his father to his mother. "When did you find out you were my father?"

Resisting the urge to reach out and cradle his son to his chest, to tell him he would protect him as he'd promised to protect his mother, he said, "Your mother told me two days ago."

"Why didn't she tell you before? That way you could've come and got me from Mr. Cooper."

Myles pushed his hands into the back pockets of his jeans. He wanted to comfort his son, reassure him the horror he'd experienced was over and would never be repeated. "If I'd known, Adam, I would've come to get you *and* your mother. No one or anything could've stopped me."

Adam pointed at Zabrina. "It's her fault."

"No, it's not her fault."

"Yes, it is. She should've called you."

Myles took a step and grasped his son's hand. "Come into the house with me."

Zabrina shot up as if impaled by a sharp object. "No, Myles!"

He gave her a chilling stare. Did she actually believe he would harm the boy? He hadn't had to play daddy but knew he would be much better in the role than Thomas Cooper. "Stay out of this, Brina. My son and I have to talk."

The tension seemed to leave Zabrina as she sank back to the rocker. She blew out a breath. She had to trust Myles and she had to prepare herself to share her son with him. "I'll be here," she said in resignation.

Myles winked at her as he opened the door and let Adam precede him into the house and back to the kitchen. Sitting at the breakfast nook, he sat opposite the boy who looked as if he were close to tears.

"Adam, son, you can't blame your mother over something she couldn't control. She married and stayed with Thomas Cooper not only to protect you but also your grandfather."

Adam's chin trembled. "But...but why didn't she call you?"

"Even if she'd called me I probably wouldn't have taken her call. I was very, very angry with your mother at that time."

"Are you angry now?"

"No, Adam. I'm not angry now."

"Do you love my mom?"

An expression of tenderness softened Myles's masculine features. "Yes, I do. I've always loved your mother. Even when I was angry with her I still loved her."

"Why did she lie, Dad?"

Dad rolled off the child's tongue as if he'd acknowledged Myles as his father for years instead of minutes. "She didn't lie, son. Your mother couldn't say anything because she believed your grandfather would've been arrested and sent to prison."

"Grandpa wasn't bad."

Myles smiled. "No, he wasn't. Your grandfather was one of the best men I've ever known."

Adam's expressive eyebrows lifted. "You knew Grandpa?"

"Yes. I knew your mother when she was just a little girl. She and my sister Belinda became best friends. Speaking of my sister, I want you to know that you have a couple of aunts, an uncle and twin cousins whom I'm certain will be glad to meet you. And then there are my parents, who are your grandparents. I'm going to have to warn you in advance that your Gram is going to act a little silly when she discovers she has a grandson."

"Does she have another grandson?"

"No. She only has granddaughters."

"When am I going to meet them?"

Adam's query gave Myles pause. He'd emailed the Realtor, telling her he wanted to see the house that afternoon, and she'd juggled her busy schedule to accommodate him. "Most likely it'll be tomorrow, because we have to go to Pittsburgh today."

A hint of a smile played at the corners of Adam's mouth. "When am I going to meet my cousins?"

"I'll call their aunt and uncle once we get on the road."

"When are you and Mom getting married?"

"Why?"

Adam's eyebrows nearly met when he frowned. "I don't want the kids in school to call her names."

Myles, leaning over the table, gave his son a withering stare. "I don't ever want to hear you call your mother a bad name. In fact I don't want you to call any female a bad name. Do you understand me?"

"Yes, Myles—I mean, Dad. But all the boys at my school do."

"I don't care what they say. No son of mine will ever disrespect a woman." He put out his fist, smiling when Adam touched it with his. "To answer your question as to when your mother and I are getting married, I still don't know. I called a friend who is a judge, but I have to wait for her to call me back. Right now I'm living in my sister's house not far from here. I'm going to ask your mother if you can spend a few nights with me so we can do guy things."

Adam's eyes narrowed. "What guy things, Dad?"

Myles lifted his shoulders. "I don't know. We'll think of something."

"What about a burping contest?" Adam suggested. "I can burp real loud. But, don't tell Mom because she gets real mad when I do it."

"It'll be our secret," Myles whispered. He laughed when Adam put out his fist for another bump. "Do you like dogs?" he asked his son as they walked out of the kitchen to return to the porch.

"I love them. I wanted one, but Mr. Cooper was allergic to dogs."

"When we move to Pittsburgh I'll let you pick out

the one you want. Your cousins Sabrina and Layla each have a Yorkshire terrier."

"Those are girl dogs, Dad. Boys have big dogs."

Dropping an arm over his son's shoulders, Myles pulled him close. "That's *my* boy."

Zabrina's long wait to become Mrs. Myles Eaton was going to end within minutes. Dr. Dwight Eaton led her over the red carpet at the rear of Griffin and Belinda Rice's house to where Myles stood with their son as his best man. She'd chosen a simple silk slip-dress gown with a seed-pearl bodice and a hem that flowed into a train. In lieu of a veil she wore a small pillbox hat covered with pearls.

Judge Stacey Greer-Monroe, in a black robe, stood ready to begin the ceremony that would bind Myles and Zabrina together as husband and wife. She'd been vacationing at her Puerto Rico condo when Myles had called to ask her to officiate at his wedding. Leaving her daughter with her husband, she'd booked a flight back to do the honors.

She was just as surprised as most Philadelphians when the news of the late Senator Thomas Cooper's association with known and suspected criminals appeared in the headlines. She was grateful that Myles was moving his wife and son across the state to live in Pittsburgh where they wouldn't be hounded by reporters and photographers.

Stacey smiled at Dr. Dwight Eaton when he placed Zabrina's hand in Myles's outstretched one. She wanted to tell Zabrina that she was one of the luckiest women in the City of Brotherly Love, having captured the heart of a man destined to one day sit on the bench. What she hadn't told Myles was that there was talk of appointing him to replace one of several judges who were rumored to be retiring in the very near future.

Zabrina smiled at Belinda, who was her matron of honor. It had been a long time coming, but both had managed to marry the men they'd loved for more years than they could remember.

Zabrina's Aunt Holly, Tanya and her husband and sons had driven from Falls Church the night before to meet the Eatons during the rehearsal dinner. Rachel and her children were warmly greeted by the Eatons. Myles's college and law-school friends came despite the short notice, and Hugh Ormond had volunteered to prepare the food for the reception.

She and Myles would enjoy a four-day honeymoon in Bermuda before returning to Philadelphia. They had another two weeks before they would close on the house, and the following week the fall semester at Duquesne was scheduled to begin.

Their original plan—for her and Adam to remain in Philly until renovations to the house were completed—was scrapped, because Adam complained that he didn't want to be separated from his father. Zabrina suspected the tree house, the promise of a dog and the hours he spent drawing with Myles were the catalyst for an almost instantaneous bond between father and son. They would live in one section of the house during the renovations and Adam would be enrolled in a private school less than a mile away.

She smiled at Myles when he gave her fingers a gentle squeeze. Her voice was clear, carrying easily in the garden as she repeated her vows. "I take thee, Myles Adam Eaton, to be my lawful wedded husband, to have and to hold from this day forward." She slipped a wide platinum band on his left hand.

Myles's baritone echoed as he repeated his vows, slipping a matching band on Zabrina's finger. A shaft of sunlight reflected off the stones in her engagement ring.

Judge Monroe winked at Myles. "By the power vested in me by the Commonwealth of Pennsylvania, I now pronounce you husband and wife. Myles, you may kiss your bride."

Wrapping his arms around Zabrina's waist, he lifted her off her feet and devoured her mouth as the assembled family and friends applauded and whistled. Passion and love were definitely sweeter and sexier the second time around.

* * * * *